A Witch's Ascension

A Witch's Ascension

A. T. NAPOLI

Cover design by Vi-An Nguyen

ISBN: 978-1-0394-6930-3

Published in 2025 by Podium Publishing
www.podiumentertainment.com

To the grandmothers,
the fiery women who came before.
Your love lives on every page.

CONTENTS

A Witch's Ascension

"At every moment of our lives, we all have one foot in a fairy tale and the other in the abyss."

—PAULO COELHO

PROLOGUE

Witches Are Real

Witches are real.

This is not a fairy tale.

This is not a joke.

I didn't realize it until I was in deep. And now, if you're reading this, it's probably too late for me.

The young man's smile faded. He muttered under his breath, "What the hhh . . . ?" and held the torn-out diary page closer.

If you're like me, then you've read about witches or seen them on TV. These witches are worse because this is real life.

Witches don't wave magic wands.

They don't have green skin or warts.

They don't live in candy houses and eat children . . . as far as I know.

Witches hide in plain sight. Bad things happen to the people around them. I would know.

They do make deals. I've seen their clients.

Witches have money. Town cars. Assistants. And covens.

And they do like to wear black. A lot of it.

You won't know they're the villains because they wear couture.

They are very rich and very powerful. They are amongst us. You can always tell a witch by their eyes. In some way, they always reveal themselves. They're not trying to hide. At least, not the ones I know.

The young man glanced over his shoulder. His eyes flicked to the door before returning to the note.

Charisma Saintly is their queen, although a saint she is not. It's all a ruse.

Only, before I realized, I had no idea that big business around witchcraft could even exist, let alone a queen of all witches. She's the most powerful of them all. And if she or hers find this, I'm as good as dead. If you're reading this, I probably am dead already.

I did something not nice, and it fired back. Someone got hurt. I saw Charisma kill one of her assistants and cover the whole thing up like an accident. Charisma is the match and the fire, and she will make it look like an accident when she disappears me too.

If anyone finds this, if I don't survive, please tell Joey that I love him, I really do. Tell Patricia I'm sorry. Tell my family too, even though I haven't talked to them in ages.

Brow furrowed, his bottom lip thoroughly chewed, he traced his thumb across it slow and absent. The flowery loops, the hurried scrawl—each word tugged at something knotted and unnamable inside him. Hurt . . . and something else. The final sentence echoed in his mind:

I'm going to stop her, if it's the last thing I do.

He shook his head with a sigh. Then he did a double-take and froze.

At the window, a shadow ducked. How long had it been there? Had it been watching him the whole time?

But what was most troubling was the laugh.

Or what *sounded* like one: a scuttling clang down the fire escape, a stutter of a car horn far below, the echoing thump of a pothole just right, the rattle of a trash can lid caught in the wind. The sounds layered—distorted, greasy, wrong . . . a laugh disguised as coincidence.

The young man held his breath.

Behind him, footsteps sounded up the stairs, echoing down the hall.

His hands moved fast. The note was folded in on itself along its creased edges, pressed into the spine of the diary it had been torn from, and had no doubt fallen out for him to find. Then it was tucked into the pocket of his jeans.

For another time . . . the young man thought.

With deliberate care, he stashed the diary back in its box and shut the lid, as if sealing it away could contain the stories already weaving through his mind. As he lifted the box into his arms, the shadow and greasy laugh slipped from his thoughts, but the scrawled words stayed with him, quiet yet unshakeable.

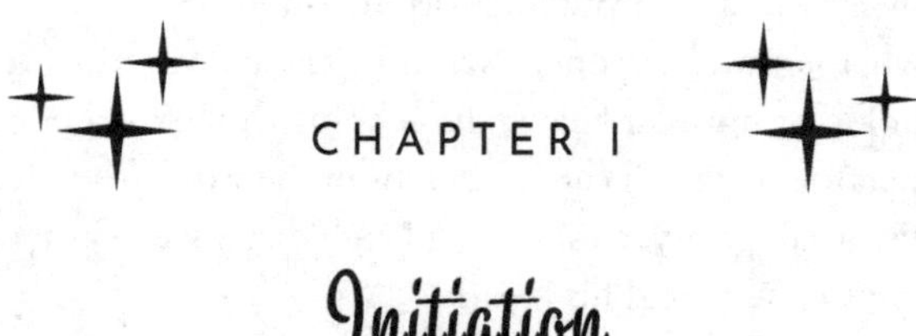

CHAPTER 1

Initiation

By the time Clark realized he had fallen for a trap and was lifted from bed, still asleep, he was too late.

The lid slammed down. His eyes snapped open. The latches clicked shut, and suffocating darkness swallowed him whole. Clark fought against the restraints, but the bindings around his wrists and ankles only tightened, the fibers mercilessly biting into his skin the harder he pulled. Panic struck like ice water to the face.

A scream ripped from his throat, guttural and raw, but the gag wedged deep in his mouth reduced it to a muffled, pitiful croak. His breath came in shallow, frantic gasps, echoing in a space too tight to breathe, too small to fight.

His container jolted, pitching him hard to the left. His head cracked against the lining, sending a constellation of stars shooting through the dark. Outside, laughter erupted, high and shrill, mocking and cruel. Their words slithered through the walls. Instantly, Clark knew those voices, their snide inflections, their English accents, their syrupy malice: they belonged to the coven of witches he worked for.

"Did you *see* his superhero underwear?" It was the coven's booker, Lorena Henceley, speaking. Erratic, Clark's heart pounded as humiliation mixed with fear.

"Ha!" another snickered. Her laughter curled at the edges—cold, sharp. "Pathetic." That was Lorena's haughty daughter and first assistant, Alicia Henceley.

"Bloody empaths," he heard yet another voice sneer, dripping with deep disdain. "Neither use nor ornament, if you ask me." This could only belong to the egomaniacal and smug third assistant Monica Chase-Whiteley, who seemed to despise Clark for no reason of his own and whom he loathed just as bitterly in return.

"A load of bollocks, really," Lorena added. "I just don't know what Charisma sees in him."

"Talk about main character syndrome with a loser's résumé," Monica sneered. To Clark, the relish in her voice was unmistakable. How gleeful they were. How hateful.

Lorena sighed. "This is what happens when the help forgets it's the help."

Alicia chimed in, "He thinks he could be an actual witch to rival the likes of us? *As if.*"

"Witch, my arse!" Monica exclaimed. "When I interviewed him, he said he 'assisted *lots*.' Liar. More like an obsessive-fan *psycho*."

Lorena howled, "Well, ladies—can't take the coven out of the gay, but you can take the gay out of the coven!" The three erupted into a cacophony of shrill, heinous cackling that clawed at his ears, his nerves, and his sanity, like nails on wood.

"This isn't funny! Stop! Let me out!" Clark tried to scream into the gag. "Why are you doing this?!" But it was no use. Only moments ago, he had been warm in bed in one of his boss's guest rooms, lulled to sleep by Emily's spiked hot cocoa. A few hours of rest lay ahead before their early morning flight to LA when—

Like a rock to the head, it hit him. One voice was missing. *Emily . . . !* he thought, the face of his blonde-haired bestie and Charisma's second assistant appearing in his mind's eye. Surely, she would know something was wrong when he failed to show up downstairs for their flight. But would she just assume he'd slept through his alarm? Shrug it off until it was too late?

Or worse: what would Lorena, Monica, and Alicia tell her? That he'd gotten cold feet and quit? Bailed at the last second and gone home? That she'd never have to worry about him again?

If he went missing, would she even know where to begin looking? By the time he was found, would he still be alive?

Where is Emily? Emily, where are you . . . ?! HELP!

Clark banged his fists and kicked his bare feet. Four corners. A fabric lining. He flailed against his confines as hard as he could—but the box was jostled, tilting him violently back and forth, a plaything in their cruel prank. The top of his head collided with the upper wall, and a sharp pain blossomed at the crown of his skull. A spray of stars burst across his eyes. The witches' laughter swelled again, sharp and mocking.

Clark squeezed his eyes shut, hoping, praying, begging to wake up from this nightmare.

Fragments of their conversation continued to filter through. Lorena spoke as brightly and casually as though she were ordering coffee when she said, "The help call the employees' quarters *Hell's Entrance.* Isn't that charming?" Clark could feel his body in motion, rocking side to side. Then, the container bucked upward, suspending him briefly in midair before slamming him down with a deafening clang: it was the metal floor of the freight elevator to Charisma's penthouse he knew oh so well. Lorena crowed with laughter. "Easy does it, boys!" Over the shrill cackles of the witches, he swore he heard male voices join in, their deep chuckles blending with the shrill mirth.

Clark's eyes darted wild and frantic in the pitch-black dark. He struggled against the bonds on his wrists and ankles and screamed again, this time as loud as he could, muffled and meager. Every cry tore at his throat. The humiliation of it all raged in his chest, but it was the fear—the sickening, bottomless, gnawing fear—that made his hands tremble against his restraints. They dug deeper and deeper into his skin, but he couldn't stop thrashing, screaming, begging for this to end.

With his bound hands and legs, he pushed and kicked, up and to the side, anywhere he could and as hard as possible.

"Simmer down, simmer down!" Lorena taunted, her voice punctuated by her sharp raps on the box. His container was jostled violently again, and their laughter cut through his cries. Clark screamed even harder. *Someone has to hear me. Anyone . . .* His aching throat strained into the gag.

The box tipped again. Clark lurched toward his feet, and this time for much longer. He was being moved in a sickening sway that stretched endlessly. One moment his body rocked to one side; the next, thrown another. Terror held his person rigid, making the shock of his impacts all the more painful. Then, without warning, a halt. He hit the ground with a smack to the back of his head again. There was an unsettling jostle: the container underneath him dragged, a loud grinding and scraping against a textured surface. Clark struck the northern wall once more before shuddering to a complete stop.

A pause outside. Clark held his breath and strained to listen. Then: "Problem solved," came Lorena's muffled voice—punctuated, he could swear, by the satisfied smack of her hands. "Thank you, boys! That will be all."

A metallic slam shuddered through the box, causing Clark to flinch. *That will be all?* What did that mean? What would they do to him now? Throw him off the roof? Into the river? Smash him in a compactor or saw him in half? Or was that the final slam of an incinerator door—his turn now to burn, like Charisma did to Melissa just months ago after he ratted her out to Monica? Each unknowable ending clawed at the edges of his frayed mind, more unbearable than the last.

But a fate worse than all the rest, than all he could imagine, had come to pass: *nothing*. Silence.

No voices. No heeled footsteps. No mocking laughter. Just stillness and silence. Just his labored breath and thundering heartbeat.

Help! he thought. *Anyone . . . Please . . .*

The gag pressed its stale, acrid taste to his tongue as he let out one last scream. His body sagged into his sweating restraints and the cold confines of the box; his hoarse cries thinned to ragged breaths that sank into stillness; and then, Clark gave up, the fight finally bleeding out of him.

He was all alone.

Time itself had unraveled. Seconds, minutes passed—Clark couldn't tell. The only constants were the cold sweat on his clothes, the unforgiving bite of the rope against his wrists and ankles, and the suffocating stillness pressing in on him from all around. It was so cold where he was, his body began to shiver, and he was beginning to lose the feeling in his toes.

Eventually, each breath grew shallower, harder to draw. Clark was fighting to stay awake when a cold panic began to grip him: the air had been growing thinner. *I'm suffocating . . .* This was how he would die, then and there. In the dark, trapped and all alone.

Why is this happening to me . . . ? Why are they doing this . . . ? How could I have been so stupid *. . . ?!*

Memories resurged uninvited, sharp and cruel in their clarity: the clandestine midnight meeting with his boss, Charisma Saintly the queen witch, her voice honeyed in chilling revelations—"I am the one all your beloved stories are written about"; the horrifying spectacle of former assistant Melissa Silvestri going up in flames, fired by murder and magic, and her screams lingering long after her body was gone; the heady rush of his first kiss with Joey that Labor Day in the grass, under the fireflies and cotton candy sky; and that innocent eyelash wish that summer—to do whatever it would take to make it, no matter the cost or sacrifice—that had set everything into motion and had led him here . . . It was all so bittersweet and distant now, like another lifetime, or someone else's life. All of it felt cruelly, heartbreakingly far away.

Would someone, anyone come looking for him? Would Joey? Could Clark even be found? Would the witches hurt Joey too for trying? A sharp pang stabbed through his heart, as if his chest were cracked and split open. Clark realized, with crushing certainty, that he would never see Joey or anyone else again. No final words. No goodbyes. Not even to Emily.

Emily . . . The name choked up his throat. *Emily, where are you . . . ?* His mind clawed for her, the one person who might have seen this coming. Hadn't she, Charisma's Death Oracle, capable of foretelling her clients' deaths, foreseen this? Had she known this would be his end all along? *Did she lie to me . . . ? I feel so stupid, and now . . .* Her face flickered behind his eyelids: her sad smile, her soulful eyes. *Were we even friends . . . ?*

The tears he had been fighting back finally broke free, ragged and heaving. He tried to swallow the sobs, to stifle the ache, but there was no stopping them now. His body trembled as the weight of his fate pressed down on him, crushing him in a torrent of endless sorrow.

Somewhere between awake and asleep, light and pitch-dark, there was release. Stars began to twinkle over him, as if he were drifting through the sky. His racing heart began to slow. His tears dried to his cheeks. His shaking eased. And a wave of sadness rolled over him, warm and numbing, like a gentle tide quietly pulling him under.

He was no longer trapped. Clark was a child again, lying beneath the elm tree in his parents' Astoria backyard. It was the night of his grandmother's funeral and he was still in his dress shoes. His tie, discarded in the grass. The smell of earth filled his lungs. Overhead, a twilight summer sky stretched endlessly, descending into night. The fireflies blinked back at him, and in the void, the faint stars above him began to shift. They swirled into a luminous spiral of light, a radiant coil that seemed to rise from within him simultaneously, unfurling along his spine and up to his crown like a serpent reaching for the heavens.

This memory wasn't just a recollection—it was an innate knowing that had always been. Clark felt the oneness of everything and the All, the same shared consciousness of existence: the celestial bodies above him, the ground beneath him, the tree, his small, mortal body. He knew it now as he did then. They were not separate. They never had been.

This must be what it feels like to die . . . he thought, the realization as gentle as the wind rustling the leaves above him.

At first, it was a flicker, faint and distant. Like a breath of dawn breaking through endless night, the golden light unfurled at the periphery of his mind. It wasn't just a light at the end of the tunnel—it was warmth, blooming across the void and smiling over him like a sunrise, pulling him gently forward by the place where the butterflies lived. Brighter and stronger, it grew until it wrapped him entirely, its touch weightless and tender, sinking deep into his very being.

A boundless calm filled him, vast and limitless, stretching beyond anything he could ever imagine. There was no box no darkness. No yearning, or emptiness. No pain. No judgment, no ego, and no self. There was no name even, no form, no past, no future, no time. Just peace. Just the certainty that settled over him: the life he had known had come to an end.

A faint sweetness shimmered in the air, a memory spun in a scent. He caught it, on the edge of his awareness: vanilla cupcakes from the coffee shop he'd worked in and known his entire life. And something else beneath it, subtle but potent, something rich. Something familiar.

Gardenias.

His grandmother's perfume mixed with the Parliaments she smoked, fiery and enduring, weaving through his consciousness, beckoning him home.

A voice called out, soft and familiar. She spoke his name.

Grandma Wanda . . . ? he asked. Clark was floating. Higher and higher he rose into the horizon, carried up by the warmth. It cradled him, pulling him closer and closer, until—

"Clark? *Clark!*"

Slap-slap went two firm pats to his cheek.

Clark stirred. Both eyes fluttered open, his vision swimming. Above him hovered Emily. Her blonde hair spilled forward like sunlight, lit by the fluorescents overhead. She watched him with that familiar, sad smile.

Emily sat back and Clark winced, squinting against the harsh light. Still, her warm hand lingered against his cheek.

"You okay, babes?" she asked. Clark's chest rose and fell in shallow gasps. Slowly the rhythm deepened, and he drew in the cold, damp air around him. He groaned.

Next to Emily sat a stout man in thick tortoiseshell glasses who Clark didn't recognize. The man wiped his gleaming, wet balding head with the back of his hand. He said in a gruff voice, "The kid's in shock, Em. Look at 'im. He's staring at me like I told him purgatory is in New Jersey and he just arrived."

Clark flinched as the man brought a box cutter close and crouched low beside him. He began sawing through the rope around Clark's arms and legs, which prickled in the dull burn of returning blood flow. The man glanced at Emily when he asked, "You want me to call an ambulance?"

Emily's eyes narrowed. "Oh sure, Morty. Call 911 and tell them what? 'We've got my coworker fresh out of a live burial, courtesy of a psychopathic coven of witches.' I'm sure they'll be *right on it.*"

Morty grunted. "Right . . . Good point."

Clark's shaky hands fumbled to pull the gag from his mouth. He winced, massaging his aching jaw. The fabric he had been clenching down on left a bitter, chemical taste of factory cotton on his tongue. His voice cracked, hoarse and raw, as he croaked, "Where am I?"

"The basement," Emily replied. "C'mon. Sit up. We'll miss our flight."

With their help, Clark sat upright. His eyes scanned the room, his breath catching as the scene came into focus. They seemed to be in an empty caged storage unit, its wire-mesh walls stretching high into the gangrene glow of the overhead lighting. Behind him, a heavy steel door hung ajar. His gaze lingered on a broken padlock lying discarded on the floor beneath it, its snapped metal shackle glinting up at him from against the concrete. Next to it, bolt cutters leaned against the wall like silent witnesses, confusion giving way to panic.

Then he saw it: the hollowed-out cavity in the wall behind the door, just large enough to fit a . . . —Clark looked down: his stomach churned as his eyes lowered on the bare wood coffin he was sitting in. The inside of the lid was marred with deep claw marks—marks he could not remember making. His eyes grew wide as he brought his raw fingernails trembling to his face. The room violently lurched: the spinning walls, the oppressive air. Clark pitched over and retched onto the concrete floor. The smell of bile and the spiked hot chocolate Emily had given him before bed permeated the air.

"It's okay, kid," said Morty, his gruff voice carrying an edge of kindness.

"No one was going to find me here," Clark muttered, his glossy eyes fixed on the coffin lid as he wiped his mouth with his gag. "They would've just . . . buried me away."

Emily nodded, her tone matter-of-fact, as she was so apt to speak. "Most likely."

"They were going to sacrifice me."

Morty and Emily said in unison, "Looks like it."

Anger surged through Clark, hot and wild. His legs shook as they helped him to his feet. He croaked, "That is so mean . . . !"

"You're right, babe," Emily replied, her dry wit barely softening the truth. "It so is."

How childish he must have sounded, standing there on his Bambi legs, dressed in his superhero underwear and sleep-time shirt clinging to his damp skin. His chest felt tight, his heart screaming against his ribs. "They can't get away with this!"

Morty looked at him, one skeptical eyebrow raised. "Yeah? And what are you gonna do about it, kid? These are career witches. Nepo hires. They've been at this their whole lives."

Emily's voice broke the silence. "C'mon, we've got a flight to catch."

Clark's voice quivered with barely unrestrained rage. "I . . . How . . . How can I go back?" His fists clenched. "They're evil and *insane*!"

Above them, the fluorescent light buzzed, building in an electric hum and shattering with a thunderous pop. They were showered in an explosion of sparks and glass. They ducked instinctively, shielding their heads. All three exchanged wide-eyed glances.

"You don't have to do anything you don't want to," Emily said, straightening up and leading them out of the caged unit. "You can turn around. You can walk away forever, and let them think that they've won. Or . . ." She paused, holding out her open hand. "You can come with me and show them who they're messing with."

Clark hesitated. His eyes darted between Emily's unwavering calm and Morty's stony expression, searching for answers that neither could give. Running away and never coming back wasn't an option—he knew too much. No one just quits Charisma, seeing as how that ended for Melissa . . . On one hand, he could go home. That would mean giving them exactly what they wanted: scaring him into submission, just as he was promoted and things were looking up. It would give them a rise there would be no coming back from. He could already feel their hollow eyes on him, smirking, satisfied. Plus, who knew what other calamities would befall him by their hand, what other traps they'd set for him. Would they ever let him rest? He would be looking over his shoulder, maybe for the rest of his life.

And, on the other hand . . . He turned to the storage unit behind him. Clark wondered how long they had planned this entrapment. How long the tunnel in the wall had been there waiting to eat him alive. Was he really going to turn away now? Leave what he'd started unfinished?

Emily's voice cut through the haze. "Up to you."

Clark's hand paused and the universe held its breath with him. Then, slowly, deliberately, he placed his hand in hers. Emily smiled.

"Time to go to work," Emily said. "We gotta get to the airport or the plane will leave without us."

Morty cleared his throat. "Don't worry about me," he grumbled as they turned on foot. "I'll just be here to clean up youz guys' messes—as usual!"

Emily paced back and wrapped her arms around him. "Thanks, Morty. I owe you one."

Morty patted her off with a grunt, but his stoic demeanor had cracked just enough to betray a flicker of warmth. "Don't mention it, sweetheart."

Clark, unsure of how to express his gratitude, managed a quiet, simple, "Thank you," and extended his hand for a shake.

Morty gave him a firm shake back and nodded in return. His eyes narrowed as he said, "You two take care of each other." Then he looked directly into Emily's eyes and said, "Keep him out of trouble, Em."

Emily pulled Clark down the long row of storage units and out into the basement hall. He recognized it instantly as they approached the freight elevator Clark had long been accustomed to taking, up the 131 stories to "Hell's Entrance" and Charisma's air-mansion. She pushed the button for "up."

"What do you say we skip the stairs?" she asked with a faint smile. "Work shoes," she added. They looked down at her black high heels, then at Clark's bare feet and legs. A shiver ran through him; he was suddenly acutely aware of how cold he was. Emily stepped closer and rubbed his shoulders, offering what warmth she could.

Clark turned to look at her and asked, "Who was that?"

"Who, Morty? He's Charisma's financial advisor. He lives in the building so he can be at her beck and call."

"Wow, she would do that? Put him up in her building?"

"I don't think he has much say in the matter . . ."

Clark let out a few coughs. He nodded, processing her words before curiosity bubbled up again. "How did you know where to find me?"

Emily hesitated, her eyes flicking to the floor for a brief second before meeting his. "Well . . ." She paused, as though searching for the right words. "You showed me . . . I think."

Clark's eyebrows shot up in surprise. "What do you mean?"

"I was asleep and suddenly you were in my dreams—or, at least, I thought they were dreams at first. But I wasn't asleep anymore, not really. It was like I was caught somewhere in between. I couldn't see you or where you were, but I could hear you say my name and I could hear you . . . crying. I knew you were lost in the dark, and confused . . . and scared. I jumped out of bed and got ready in a hurry. And suddenly it was like there was a light anchored to my mind's eye, an orb—like a lighthouse, only I couldn't see the destination. It was like a lantern in a fog pulling me forward, step by step. Downstairs. To the storage unit.

"The feeling of you was so strong when I got there it was like a siren. The fluorescent over the storage unit was flickering, almost like it was trying to speak to me. That's when, behind the door in the wall, I saw it. A light, dim and indigo. I just knew it was you. Like you refused to be extinguished."

The elevator dinged on arrival.

"I could hear you saying my name—and the words 'I'm so stupid' over and over again. You've really gotta stop putting yourself down, babes . . . Anyways, I called Morty right away." They stepped on and pressed *1*. She said in his thick, gravelly New York accent, "'*Good thing I'm up at three every morning!*' I don't think he was being sarcastic."

Clark frowned as they stepped in. "Did you know they were going to do this?"

Emily hesitated again before speaking. "Well, yeah," she admitted, "I had some idea."

The elevator dinged again.

Clark froze. The betrayal hit him like ice in his veins. "You *knew*?" Clark pulled his shoulder away from her arm and stood back. He regretted it instantly: the chill of the early-morning January air flooded the elevator as it let them into the service corridor and onto the street. "You knew and you didn't tell me?!"

Emily's lips parted as she searched for the words. Gently, she said, "I didn't know what, or when, or how. I just knew they were up to something. Do you really think they'd clue me in, when they know we're besties? I told them whatever they were up to, they'd better play nice. Like they would ever listen to me."

Clark stared at his feet while mulling over her words. Did she really have a choice after all?

"At least I thought . . ." She hesitated, a faint pinkness creeping up on her cheeks. "Maybe boozy hot chocolate would at least help you, you know . . . not panic."

Clark looked up at her. Emily met his gaze.

"*Not panic?*" Clark exclaimed. "As if!"

Emily smacked his shoulder. "Oh, don't be mad at me." She stepped closer and opened her arms. "Come here." She pulled him in and rubbed the warmth back into his shoulders. "I'm the only one here who's got your back. Don't forget."

In a way, he knew she was right. How could he stay mad at the person who had just saved his life?

Outside the building on Sixth Avenue a black town car idled, its exhaust curling into the frigid morning air. Clark paused as he opened the car door. "But, what about my things? My clothes?"

"Please. You think I wouldn't handle it?" She gave his back a pat as he climbed in.

On the seat was a neat stack of clothes for Clark: his black button-down one size too big, thrift-store slacks, well-worn high-top Chucks, and an outdated cell phone. He could only assume his luggage bag was stowed away in the trunk. Emily winked back as she slid beside him. The driver began their journey to the airport.

As he pulled his coat on, Clark asked, "So what was yours? Your *initiation*."

"Well," she began, "one way to test a witch is to put her in crisis. You know, tie her to a chair, throw her in a river, and see if she floats like during the Trials. A witch reveals herself in times of adversity—or *himself*. Sorry!"

"Oh no," Clark said, eyes wide. "What did they do to you?"

"They did just that," Emily said matter-of-factly. "Tied me to a chair and threw me off Charisma's yacht."

Clark gasped. "No!"

"Yes."

"How did you survive?" Clark's mouth hung open.

"I floated."

Clark nearly giggled. Her smirk was subtle but wry, and her eyes sparkled with amusement. "Honestly? I'm still not sure! Maybe I can hold my breath for longer than I know . . . Sometimes I dream about that . . . *incident*—something sharp freeing my wrists and feet—but all I know is I woke up on the swim platform at the back of the boat. You should have seen their faces when I turned up, wet and furious."

Clark shook his head, incredulous. "Sounds like a hazing to me."

"Yeah. But don't worry; I got them back."

"You did?"

"Oh, yeah."

"*Please!* Tell me everything!"

Emily glanced out the window, then looked at him with a conspiratorial grin, leaning back in her seat. "Oh, just a simple return-to-sender spell! All their little efforts backfired spectacularly. For the belladonna Melissa slipped into my drink that rendered me unconscious, Melissa fell into narcolepsy. For months she'd randomly fall over at the absolute worst times, like with clients—*so* funny! For tying me up, Monica's arms went mostly paralyzed—totally useless from the shoulders down! She still drops her phone from numb fingers from time to time. For throwing me over, Alicia's Gift of Gab made her sound like she had two helium tanks for lungs. She had chipmunk voice so bad she barely spoke for a month."

"Hilarious! And Señora *Lorraine*?"

Emily spoke with mock gravity as she said, "Oh, Lorena. She got the best of them. For masterminding the whole charade, her glamour glitched out so bad, she looked like a drowned rat no matter what she did. Dripping hair, sopping clothes, and run mascara—the works. Charisma would look at her and laugh right to her face. She called her 'Budget' for weeks."

Clark did a spit-take, doubling over as he burst into laughter. The smile seemed to break the spell, easing something inside of him. He wasn't so sure he understood the mechanics completely, but nevertheless he said, "You're my hero."

Their giggling tapered off into a calm, companionable quiet. A chance to catch their breath. Clark glanced sideways and broke the silence. "Do you tell anyone about this? Your boyfriends? Your family?"

Emily looked long and hard at him, her blonde hair glinting in the flickering streetlamps. "No," she finally said. "I don't."

"Why not?" he pressed gently.

Her voice was as calm and detached as ever, her matter-of-fact, unaffected way smoothing over the gravity of her words. "The less anyone knows the better. It's safer that way. That's just how it's got to be . . ." There was always a wry, world-weary way of how she spoke about even the most macabre of things. Clark got the sense that to Emily, whose witch's "Gift" was foreseeing death and the inevitable end, all that was left was a distance she kept between herself and the world. After telling Clark of discovering her late mother, maybe it was all she had left.

Something shifted then, something Clark didn't know he could do too. Emily's voice entered his mind, clear and unmistakable: *I knew where you were,* Emily said mind to mind, *because we're friends . . . You know that right . . . ?*

The words came as naturally as the thought itself. *I know . . .* he thought back. She reached for his hand and Clark squeezed it in return, an unspoken gratitude filling the seat between them.

"Here, take this," Emily said aloud, breaking the quiet. "It'll protect you when it's given by someone who cares." As the Lincoln Tunnel lights flashed in bursts across the car interior, Clark watched her produce a tiny blue-eyed evil eye charm from her purse.

"When it's filled up and done its job," she said, "it will break off—"

No sooner had the charm been dropped into Clark's open palm did it split clean in two and roll away, bouncing off the car floor and disappearing out of sight. Their eyes met in mirrored disbelief.

"Luckily," Emily said, recovering quickly, "I always keep a spare." With one hand on the other, she pulled a ring off her finger and slipped it onto Clark's pinky. Clark held it close to the window: a blue eye on a thin gold band with many tiny serrated lashes winked up at him in the light.

"I can't accept," he said to her softly.

"Keep it," she insisted. "It might come in handy." She grabbed Clark's hand and didn't let go. As the car emerged from the Hudson and rose from the tunnel into the New Jersey morning, the world out the windows seemed more gentle, less sharp. Clark looked toward the island of Manhattan glittering in the distance. Then his eyes met hers. As the streetlights flickered past, their rhythmic glow catching in Emily's limitless blues, all the world and all his worries—his ordeal, his fear, his doubts—seemed to fade away, and he knew that Emily felt the same too.

The driver took them down a quiet I-95. *What's LA like . . . ?* Clark had asked at some point. The two laid their heads on the leather headrests, occasionally stealing a glance and a smile as they soundlessly conversed about yoga, smoothies, and Charisma's star client, Felicity—the pop icon at the center of a spiraling scandal. She was holed up in her bungalow, refusing to finish filming her movie. It was why Charisma and the coven were flying in—to make sure she did.

Eventually, they rolled into Teterboro Airport and up to security. The driver leaned out the window and handed over a sleek leather folder containing the necessary identification and flight clearances. The guard flipped through it, nodding briskly before waving them through. One guard peered through the tinted windows and briefly caught Clark's eye, who turned to glance at Emily. She sat back with an air of practiced indifference, another work commute like any other. The ordinary to the extraordinary, Clark mused. He wondered if this would ever be his normal, too.

The car glided onto the smooth tarmac and stopped just short of Charisma's private jet. It was larger than Clark anticipated—he could swear it was almost the size of a commercial plane. As he exited the car, his eyes trailed up the tarmac to its all-black fuselage gleaming under the floodlights like polished obsidian (*of course it's black,* Clark thought wryly). Stamped near the nose in gold lettering was its designation: *G650ER—Tempest.* The clock on the dashboard read 4:42 a.m.

An attendant stood in waiting by the stairs. Clark instinctively headed for the trunk to do the heavy lifting but was shooed away. Flustered, he hurried to catch up to Emily, who had already climbed the first few steps of the boarding stairs. She paused, turned back to him, and held out her hand. Clark anchored his hand in hers. With her lead, he stepped through the threshold and into a world he had only ever dreamed of—one that he might never fully understand.

CHAPTER 11

NDA

When Emily entered with Clark in tow, nose held high, the shift in the cabin's air was instant and electric.

"Felicity's job is to finish the movie," Lorena was saying, sharp and smug, "and she's not getting out of it ali—" She stopped. Her words faltered as she, Alicia, and Monica turned, sitting up straighter in their plush leather seats. Their disbelief quickly gave way to knowing smiles as they exchanged sly glances.

"Well, well, well," Lorena drawled. She popped the lid back on her lipstick and snapped her black compact shut with a sharp click. "Look what Emily fished out of the ground and dragged to work."

Alicia taunted, "Back from the dead already?"

Monica's perfect white smile was all teeth, sharp and insincere, as she said, "Back from the dead already? How utterly unnecessary of you." Alicia barely stifled a laugh. "Guess you *can't* take the trash out without it trying to crawl back in."

"It's like I always say, ladies," Lorena chimed, her voice oozing with glee: "Bury your gays!"

"Gag the fag!" Monica jeered.

"You hag!" Lorena shrieked. Emily shot them all a glare that could cut through steel.

"Funny joke, guys," she said flatly as she pushed through to her seat.

Clark trailed a step behind her, a beat too slow, his steps unsure. The cabin felt cavernous, their every wild, hollow eye raking him over from head to toe as he passed. The scrutiny prickled like needles. Suddenly, he was painfully aware of his shoulders up to his ears, thrift-store clothes, sweat-plastered hair, and the red marks burning on his wrists beneath sleeves that felt far too long.

"Oh, lighten up, Em," Monica chimed. "We would've gotten him out . . . eventually." Her hollow gray eyes glittered with amusement as she returned to scrolling on her phone. Clark felt the corner of his mouth quiver and his jaw clench as he filed past, caught again between anger and humiliation. Was this really happening? Minutes ago, he was clawing out of a coffin—now here they were, on their phones and laptops. Business as usual. His fists were tight at his sides while he willed himself to keep it together, even as the memory of their cruel laughter played on a loop in his mind.

"Yeah, don't be such a wet mop," Alicia said, peering over the top of her laptop and her seat. She added with a smirk to Clark, "You look like shit." Alicia's smile faded in an instant. "At this hour?" Her phone was pressed up to her ear. "Thank goddess for technology, I guess . . ." Her voice shifted, serious and high-flown: "Alicia Henceley-Saintly, first assistant to Charisma Saintly . . . No, she is not available then . . ."

Footsteps approached, sharp and unmistakable even against midsize-jet carpeting. The cabin's commotion came to such a deafening silence that their ears popped.

"That's right, bitches—playtime's over. Big Red says shut the fuck up!" Charisma herself swept into the cabin like a storm wearing a smile, her copper hair a fiery crown. "We just received clearance to leave. Hortencia! Fire it up!" she shouted over her shoulder. "Now that you children are quite finished playing with your food . . . We are right on time."

Clark's throat tightened as her sharp yellow-green eyes scanned the room. From the seat next to his he could feel Emily shift closer to him mind to mind, a quiet anchor amid the chaos.

"Ladies," Charisma said, her voice dripping with sarcasm. "I trust you've all been productive in my absence?"

"Always, darling," said Lorena with a syrupy grin. She crossed her legs and tossed her hair over her shoulder as she pulled her laptop from her bag. "You know us, me lord. Work first, play later."

"Ha! We all know how you live to serve!"

"Wench!"

"Trollop!" The two cracked up, their cackles bouncing off the cabin walls. This time, Clark bit his lip, forcing himself not to laugh along. What evil jokers they all were. He hated that he liked the sound of Charisma's voice—hated that her laugh, to him, rang like bells.

The jet engines began to hum. The cabin buckled up. The jet taxied across the tarmac, and in no time, sped off its wheels and launched into the morning.

Some minutes later, the cabin leveled. The seatbelt sign dinged off and the coven dispersed like crows from a wire. Clark scanned the cabin, taking in the witches at work.

Monica was sprawled across two seats juggling her personal and work phones and her laptop. Alicia was focused intently on her laptop and clucking away on her call. "We are not going to that," she said, her tone aghast. "Their last party was absolutely dreadful. Not even the goodie bags were useful . . ." How the coven had tried to disappear him just hours prior and could carry on with their lives, seemingly unbothered, made Clark's chest tighten.

At the front of the cabin, Charisma and Lorena sat on the couch locked in conversation. The words "invited" and "investigation" drifted to Clark's ears, weightless as air. Had he tuned into their voices from afar, or had the words been drawn to him like iron to a magnet? Either way, Clark listened in.

"Will they follow the trail?" Lorena asked Charisma. "His parties, the freak-offs. The cooked books?"

Charisma said with vigor, "No. My protections are strong—stronger than their, stronger than their technology." She leaned back in her seat. "He'll take the fall. That much is certain. It was either me and the kids or him—and we both know he was never going to survive that."

"Then all is going to plan . . ."

"Indeed," Charisma agreed.

"And the Order?" Lorena asked, her voice lower still.

Charisma's yellow-green eyes narrowed. "Blinded by their own arrogance. They'll have no choice but to look to me once he's gone. The queen on her throne, as it should be. It's poetic, really. Men are so utterly pathetic."

The stewardess approached, bending down to serve Charisma's coffee order: two sugars and a splash of cream, he remembered well.

"And what about . . . *her*?" Lorena asked, her words so low they were swallowed up by the hum of the jet. Clark caught the question only by reading her painted lips: "Will she interfere?"

Charisma took a sip before speaking. Her voice was calm, deliberate. "Let her try. She and the Order may be nudging humanity toward ruin, but that ruin won't happen while I have a say, mark my words. This hellhole of a planet belongs to me and me alone."

"Oh, just imagine, sissy!" Lorena said, her hollow eyes glittering. "A world of our own."

"I can." Charisma sat up. "And when that time comes—and it will be sooner than you think—the Powers will have no choice but to bend to my will. By Witch's New Year, it'll be a new dawn, for us . . . and for me."

"Ingenious," Lorena purred. "How happy I am for you, Charisma."

Clark glanced at Emily, who was busy typing something hurriedly on her cell phone. What were Charisma and Lorena talking about? "Ruin," "a world of our own," "a new dawn"? And there they were again—the Powers That Be—just like in the note he'd intercepted weeks ago. An order of beings not on this plane of existence, Emily had explained the night before.

Then, from across the cabin, Charisma's sharp feline eyes locked onto his. A jolt of dread shot through his body, sudden and electric—like a thief caught in the act.

Lorena barked, "Shouldn't you be *busy with something?*"

Monica interjected without even looking up from her laptop. "Yeah," she said, "make yourself useful. Fetch us our coffees like you do—peasant!" The way her smile failed to reach her eyes . . . Clark's grip tightened on his armrest. Lorena and Monica exchanged slow, satisfied smirks.

Just ignore them . . . Emily thought to him. *They just want to get a rise out of you . . .* Instantly, he wished he had said something. Why was he such a pushover? And Charisma, just sitting there watching. Does she even care about me at all . . . ?

"Where was I?" Lorena asked, returning to their conversation. Charisma set her phone down. As if by the turn of a dial, her words slowly faded to mute, and the two slipped into an inaudible nothing.

Clark's mouth fell open. He had done the same during his first interview with Monica—tuning out the world in anxious silence, feeling so unprepared and out of place. He had assumed it was Monica's doing, but that midnight meeting, when he had stolen into Charisma's home, had changed everything. She had guided him to see the truth for himself, his own potential, what he himself had failed to perceive. That it had been him all along. She had shown him that.

There she was, the woman he so wanted to detest, but if he were being honest with himself . . . so fascinated him. What could it mean for Charisma, who surrounded herself with women like Lorena and Monica? Was she the worst of them all? How he could still admire her, even after she'd fired Melissa by death, stirred something he couldn't quite untangle inside him. Was it awe? Or shame? How could he take umbrage by her life, her choices, how she oozed of falsehood—everything about her—and at the same time feel . . . gratitude for the opportunities she had bestowed upon him?

What did that say about him?

"Sparkling or still, miss?" the stewardess asked Monica, polite but wary and breaking Clark's trance. She stood at a distance from Monica, whose gaze came to rest on her, cold and cutting. Clark watched as the attendant's smile faltered.

"I'm . . . I'm sorry, miss," she stammered. Slowly, she backed away before inexplicably bursting into tears and hurrying away. Clark's jaw braced.

The attendant returned not a moment later with a trembling tray bearing sparkling mountain water and a large cup of coffee with milk and sugar on the side. The glasses clinked as she set the glasses down, avoiding meeting Monica's eyes. "Here you are, miss," she murmured before quickly retreating.

That harpy . . . he thought bitterly. *She'll get hers . . .*

Suddenly, Monica's eyes snapped onto Clark's. Her glowering stare burned into his: he could feel the hatred radiating off of her, see it burn in the air around her like a fiery halo. Clark grew instantly dizzy. The air seemed to thicken, squeezing him from all around. His breath hitched. His vision blurred and his eyelids grew heavy. His head began to slump. He could feel the walls closing in, his energy being siphoned. Clark was back in the coffin, his ears ringing, his heart racing, pounding in his chest louder and louder, the air thinning and suffocating him all over again and the air around Monica growing searing and red-hot when—

STOP! Clark thought. Like a rubber band snapping back, the weight around him burst off and away. The cabin lights flickered. The plane shuddered and jolted up into the air, an unexpected turbulence. Instantly, Monica's water and coffee tipped off the table and onto her lap, spilling over her laptop, which hissed and sparked. She gave a startled yelp. In unison, the witches stopped to look up at Monica, then at Clark, puzzled.

Emily placed her hand on his arm, drawing his attention back to her. "Hey, Clark," Emily said softly. *Take a moment, yeah . . . ? Go wash up . . . ?*

The stewardess scurried to retrieve Monica's phone, but Monica clicked her tongue and waved her away. "Oh, for fuck's sake, gimme that!" she snapped as she snatched her phone and the linen napkin from the flight attendant's hand. She muttered something under her breath about not staffing the plane like a mall food court, her focus solely on the dark, unresponsive screen of her laptop. Her French-manicured finger furiously jammed its power button. "My laptop! My work . . . !"

Clark was wide-eyed. The coven had returned to their respective tasks seemingly unperturbed—but Monica's icy glare found him again. For a moment, her lips curled into a dark, thin, knowing smile as she shot him the most menacing of looks—a snake ready to strike. He knew without hesitation that he would feel her wrath again, but this time, Clark didn't flinch. Something in him had fought back—something that didn't cower, didn't submit. Something Charisma had once seen in him, that he was only just beginning to grasp.

Clark broke their eye contact with the snap of his seatbelt. *Yeah . . . Okay . . .* he thought back. Clark met Emily's grounding gaze before he stood and clambered to the restroom behind their seats at the back of the cabin.

Sliding the door shut behind him, Clark locked it with an uneasy sigh. It was just him and the hum of the jet engines now against his racing thoughts. Why was his heart pounding? Could it be finding himself in a small, confined space alone again? He leaned heavily against the cool marble countertop. Then he looked up.

The Clark in the mirror staring back left him breathless. His under-eyes were purple, his face gray, languid, and dry. Sweaty hair, downturned, bloodshot eyes, a crestfallen smile: his Christmas holiday sparkle had most certainly been lost. *How could I let them do this to me . . . ? I feel so stupid . . .* The person in the mirror was every version of himself he had tried to leave behind: the loner who buried himself in books; the dreamer who desperately yearned for a life worth more just out of reach; the errand boy who burned himself out for the desperate approval of people who would rather see him disappeared and gone. Staring back was every him that he was not: confident, unshakeable, and free.

Clark closed his eyes and drew a shaky breath. He had spent so long trying to prove himself, to show that he belonged in their world, but now . . . Did he even want to belong? Did he want to be like them—cruel, detached, and unfeeling? His heart ached at the thought.

Clark splashed his face with cold water and smoothed back his hair. He gave himself a weak half smile before running his hands over his shirt and stepping out the door—to almost run into the flight attendant who caught him outside. Wordlessly, she handed him a small pouch. Clark opened it, eyebrows raised: inside were toiletries, including a disposable toothbrush.

"Thank you," he said softly. She gave him a quick smile and wink before disappearing into the cabin, an opal-blue uniformed blur with a tray of coffee in hand—and one latte he knew was meant for him.

Clark busied himself helping Emily reorganize her client list and itinerary for her week in LA. Clark couldn't hide his excitement at the thought of managing his own clients someday, juggling his own deadlines and tasks.

"You'll be busy in no time and missing the days you weren't. Promise," Emily had reassured him.

Her words lingered as exhaustion crept over him, and he drifted off into a short nap. The touchdown of the jet's wheels jolted him awake. He was thankful no one seemed to notice—or if they did, they didn't care to say a word.

It was seven a.m. in hazy LA when they stepped out into the crisp morning air. *It's so dry here . . .* Clark mused. The sun had just risen over the horizon, casting long shadows across Santa Monica Airport. Deplaning was easy: the coven had filed behind Charisma and her crown of copper hair that gleamed in the sunshine into a sleek black Cadillac Escalade waiting on the tarmac. At the same time, their kits were loaded up into another—about twenty black trunks and luggage bags Clark knew all too well, having restocked them himself countless times: bags containing spell ingredients, tools, artifacts. The other bags, he figured, were the coven's opulent wardrobe.

Clark asked Emily mind to mind as he stepped into the backseat with her, *Who are* they . . . ? He nodded to the two broad, bearded men accompanying the coven, both in black leather jackets and boots. *They look just like . . .* Clark was about to say Monica's fling from last August, the one he had gossiped to Melissa about, leading them both to their exacting punishments and Melissa's firing by death. He could remember Monica writhing in agony on the glass floor of the Tower as if by electrocution, and the sight of Melissa, up in flames, her screams cutting through the night . . .

Charisma's bodyguards . . . Emily replied. *I'll explain later* . . .

Charisma and Lorena sat in the front, chatting the entire way there. It seemed that Felicity's ordeal was, to them, a joke.

"Her life *is* in tatters, poor thing," Charisma said cheekily. "Have you seen the tabloids? 'Inside sources' reveal she is behaving rather erratically. Dreadful innit?"

"Ah, yes, absolutely *dreadful*," Lorena said with a smirk. "And by 'inside sources,' don't they mean, well, you?"

"Indeed."

"Clever girl, you are," Lorena said. The two dissolved into a fit of giggles.

"Thank you, darling! Tip off the paps, doctor the evidence, pay off the judge, a court-sealed care plan—it was almost too easy."

"Provoking her into a tailspin was like taking candy from a baby. Honestly, a bit dull!"

"And now the public has turned against her and her parents, we will go by unscathed. A stroke of genius if I don't say so myself."

"Very much that, darling!"

"I told her sex sells. Americans *love* to tear down their heroes. She put it on herself."

"Ex-actly!" Lorena chimed. "Why must she dress like a slag? Do you know what I mean, babes?" She held up her phone for Charisma to see.

Charisma returned, "She does have nice tits, though, I'll give her that." She gave Lorena's chest a playful pat, who squealed, "Oi!" and gave a hoarse, open-mouthed cackle back.

Clark bit the inside of his cheek, barely suppressing a grin. He turned to Emily, but she was yet again locked onto her phone, too engrossed in whatever she was typing to pay attention.

"Felicity still has the kid, you know," Charisma added.

"Holed up in her room with her? No . . . !"

"Yes."

"I thought they'd have taken him from her by now."

"She had visitation and really ran with it, it seems. Not to mention, he's playing her son in the film alongside our tragic heroine," Charisma replied, her voice dripping in irony.

Lorena's expression softened, unnervingly so as she mused, "Oh, but I do love children! I so wish I could have had another." She reached out and pet Alicia's hair. The girl, who had been looking at her phone balked and whined, *"Mother!"* Lorena's sudden whimsy gave Clark an icky feeling. He had never heard her sound so mawkish.

So she does have a soul . . . Clark thought to himself wryly.

Shhhh . . . Emily's voice cut through his mind. *Thoughts can be loud, and we never know who's listening . . .*

Clark put down his book. While the car *oo*'d and *ah*'d as they passed Rodeo Drive, already plotting their shopping trip after lunch, Clark looked up 'Felicity news' on his phone. Headlines blazed across the screen:

"America's Falling Star: Felicity's Tragic Descent into Drugs, Debt, and Despair."

"Felicity Spirals: A Star's Final Days?" another tabloid claimed.

"Felicity's Freefall: America's Sweetheart Hits Rock Bottom."

"Paranoid," "unstable," and even a "danger to herself and her child," they read. The soundbites were all the same: the articles painted Felicity's promising career from her days as a child star, to her breakout debut as a worldwide #1 singer-dancer, to her promising, straight-to-the-top career as a Hollywood actress. Now, there were rumors of her refusing her work schedules, firing her team of handlers, recklessly spending, and even nasty, salacious rumors of long nights out and drug use. There were clips of her public outbursts, yelling and fleeing swarms of photographers and their mobs of flashing cameras, who vied for compromising and embarrassing shots to sell to the highest bidders. In one, her voice cracked as she yelled at them. Clark froze on a single frame—a close-up of her eyes. Something in them struck him as so familiar. In every video thereafter, she wore sunglasses at night.

The conservatorship trials during filming were publicized, of course ("From Red Carpet to Courtroom: Felicity's Legal Woes") with former key members of her team, including her own family, testifying against her. They claimed Felicity was "incapable of managing her life and career" and that they were in "fear for her life," and the life of her son. Article after article quoted an "inside source" close to Felicity and her team, which lingered with Clark long after they exited the SUVs into the LA sunshine, so harsh and false, and up the red-carpeted steps of the Beverly Hills Hotel.

Inside, the receptionist barely had time to whisper low to a coworker before the manager appeared, offering polished smiles and rushing to escort the coven personally. Clark watched with fascination as Charisma leaned back with regal ease and extended her hand to him, which he bent forward and kissed with the reverence due a queen bestowing favor upon a humble subject. In no time, they were back outside and packed onto golf carts, Charisma, Lorena, and Alicia in the first, and Monica, Emily, and Clark on the second, a procession of black heels.

The gardens of the hotel whipped past Clark, the only one paying attention. He blinked, shaking off his thoughts as the air carried the scent of blooming jasmine and freshly cut grass; the occasional bird called from the trees. Clark caught flashes of the hotel's sprawling amenities: a glistening infinity pool, a bustling outdoor café, and sunlit terraces where weekend guests lounged in plush luxury. He wondered when it would be his turn to indulge.

The carts came to a halt in front of a secluded bungalow, its pristine facade tucked at the end of a winding path. A group of whisperers loitered outside. Their conversations died quickly the moment Charisma stepped down, shrinking back like shadows retreating from the sun.

"Oh, thank gawd you're here!"

A rail-thin woman broke through the cluster of whisperers, her heels clicking hard against the sidewalk as she made a beeline for Charisma. She flung herself into her arms, a dramatic gasp escaping her lips, fingers clutching at Charisma's back as though they were the last solid thing in a collapsing world.

"This is just awful—just *awful*," she cried in a slight Southern drawl, her voice quivering on just the right note of devastation. Theatrical. Rehearsed. *Well-played*, Clark thought.

"It's okay, Hope, darling," Charisma said, smoothing a hand over

Hope's back. "I'm here now." Her embrace was slower, smooth, and measured. Certainly, Clark wasn't the only one who saw through the act.

But what struck Clark most wasn't the performance, it was the woman's hair—a bright, burnished copper. The same shade as Charisma's.

A woman dressed in designer black, balancing three cell phones, broke away from the group and strode toward them with exaggerated grace. She removed her sunglasses and greeted Charisma with theatrical air kisses, one cheek at a time. Her eyes, Clark clocked, were as empty as the witches he worked with.

"Darling," she cooed, one cheek at a time. "You look radiant as always."

"Oh, please," Charisma replied, cordial enough but barely sparing her a glance. Instead, her sharp gaze was fixed on the bungalow's door. "How long has she been in there?"

"Three days," Hope said, her voice cracking in all the right ways.

"Tsk tsk," Charisma replied. "That just won't do. If she won't come out, we'll have to go in."

"You know what she's like, darling," the other cut in, her accent as British as Charisma's. She fell in step beside Hope and Charisma as they moved toward the bungalow, the coven trailing behind her copper mane, sharp stiletto strides, and floral perfume. "She's refusing to negotiate with anyone."

She paused, switching to a mocking American accent with a slight Southern lilt—"*especially not Charisma and her gaggle of black-clad,* uh . . . leeches, I believe she said." She rolled her eyes for emphasis, eliciting a stifled laugh from Lorena. Hope shook her head and buried her face in her hands.

"Please," she said, "get my baby boy out safe and sound."

Charisma gave her a patronizing pat on the back before turning to the woman in black. "Does the press know yet? Who is she in contact with outside our orbit?"

The woman hesitated, shifting uneasily. "I'm . . . not sure."

Charisma's lips pressed into a thin line as she turned away.

"But!" she quickly added, her tone brightening. "We've been

keeping tabs on the outlets and socials in case this gets out. And, as you are well aware, her flip phone is heavily monitored and restricted per the conservatorship."

Charisma exhaled slowly, coolly. "This might be good publicity yet, but we need to be the ones to tell the story."

The woman in black gestured to another woman lingering at the edge of the group, also dressed head to toe in black. "We've got Dana Masters from *The LA Eye* in waiting and under NDA. She's ready to spin the story if she talks, but she won't come out."

"Not even for me," Hope interjected.

Charisma pulled a cigarette from her purse, lit it, and took a slow, deliberate drag. Smoke curled from her glossed lips as she fixed the woman in black with an unimpressed stare and blew the smoke in her face.

"That said," the woman in black replied, stifling a cough, "if she plays ball, we can control the narrative from here to New York, nay—Kalamazoo!"

Charisma rolled her eyes, her exasperation thinly veiled. "What is it you have been doing these three days? Because it most certainly hasn't been your job." She sighed, and the sound was heavy with irritation.

"Can you get her to come out?" Hope asked. "Can you really do it?"

"Hope, darling," Charisma said, taking her hand with a reassuring smile. "We'll handle this." She turned to the woman in black. "She'll have no choice but to cooperate. She is contracted to finish this project, and she knows it."

"That may be, but she's refusing to see you," she pointed out. "Or Lorena, or Alicia. You're too . . . familiar. She doesn't trust you."

At this, Monica smugly lifted her head, as if at the ready.

"And Emily?" Charisma asked, turning to the man. Clark was delighted to see a flicker of jealousy cross Monica's face.

"The uh, um, one who deals in . . . d-death?" Clark was amazed at how quickly her confidence had faltered in Charisma's presence. "No," she stammered. "The girl's paranoid enough! That might push her even further."

Emily remained pleasantly still and stoic as ever. Silence befell the coven, the weight of the impasse pressing down on them. Charisma turned her gaze once more to the bungalow. Her fingers tightened slightly on her cigarette.

"I've tried everyone and everything I can think of," the woman admitted. Was Clark imagining it, or were her knees shaking?

"I see," Charisma said tersely. "Regardless, the outcome will be the same."

Clark shifted his weight, his mind racing. *They need someone Felicity won't see as threatening . . .* he thought. *Someone who can approach her without sending her into a spiral . . .*

Monica cleared her throat, drawing in a breath to speak. But before he fully realized what he was doing, Clark rather softly said aloud, "I can go."

The words were barely audible over the buzz of whispered conversation, but they sliced through the group like a blade. Clark felt the familiar weight of all eyes snapping at once to him.

"What," Lorena hissed, stepping forward, her eyes narrowing dangerously, "did you just say?"

Louder this time, voice firmer, he repeated, "I can go." He added, "She doesn't know me. I'm a nobody to her. She might talk to me if she thinks I'm just here to help."

Monica and Lorena whirled on him at once. "You—"

All present fell dead quiet. All eyes turned to Charisma, who had raised her hand to silence them mid-sentence—and whose gaze fixed on Clark, long and probing. The whole world practically stopped under the spell of her feline yellow-green eyes. Clark could feel eyes dissecting him, peeling him back layer by layer. To have the woman's attention was always the oddest of feelings he could hardly describe. The thing he wanted most—for her to acknowledge his existence—and here he was, fighting the urge to look down at his shoes. He surrendered to her gaze, barely daring to breathe, refusing even to blink.

Lorena broke ranks and slowly advanced toward him, heels clicking one by one against stone. "Who on earth," she growled, "gave you permission to speak, let alone look Charisma in the eyes?"

Clark's body erupted into a sweat.

"The unmitigated gall!" she said. "Men and their egos, I swear. Why, the disrespect is—"

"Send the boy," said Charisma suddenly, cutting her off.

Lorena's face dropped in disbelief. "Sissy," she pleaded, almost turning her back on Clark, "you can't be serious."

"*Boy,*" . . . Clark thought.

Charisma waved her away. Her voice was firm as she said, "You think you can handle this?"

Clark nodded as he said, "Yes." His voice was steady but his palms were damp. *What the hell am I doing . . . ?!*

"Sissy," she hissed, pulling her and Clark to the side as the others watched with curiosity. Lorena whispered, "We have no way of knowing what he's like with clients. You want to send"—she sized him up and down and waved her arm—"*him?!* To one of our most important clients? Look." She turned to Clark and spoke slowly, as if to a child. "Where is it that you worked before?"

Clark said softly, "A coffee shop in Astoria." Didn't she remember his résumé?

"Of course I don't bloody remember your résumé!" Lorena snapped. Clark's forehead prickled and his stomach practically dropped into his pants. "What did you do at *the coffee shop*?" she mocked. "What were your responsibilities? Quick, answer me! Did you *talk* to people?"

"To customers?" Clark asked. "Yeah, I was a barista."

"I find that hard to believe." Lorena pressed her fingers to her temples. "Dear god-*dess*, the boy is out of touch!"

"I'm . . . personable! I'm good with people, as much as I can be . . ." Clark's words felt useless, even if he wasn't lying. Was he the chattiest barista? He wouldn't say that. Sure, he completed as many tasks as he could so that when a lull came, he could sneak a page of his current novel or enter a page into his homework. But didn't he remember the names of his regulars? Their orders, and the goings-on in their lives, the dramas of Astoria? Hadn't he tried his best?

Charisma and Lorena exchanged looks. Charisma turned to Clark, whose body stiffened up in the wake of her laser focus. Her words were direct: "You are to go in. You are to convince her to come out with the child. That's all."

Lorena pounced once again. This time she spoke dangerously low. "Listen to me: No gushing. No asking for photos with clients. No autographs. No selfies. Nothing. Nada. Do *not* make her uncomfortable! Do not embarrass us or ruin this for us. Your job depends on it."

By "job" Clark wondered if she meant his *life*.

Lorena added above a whisper, "If you fail, if you falter for even a second . . . I'll make you wish you'd stayed in that coffin. Got it?"

Clark nodded, his palms damp but his resolve strong. This was his chance—his moment to prove himself as an assistant. He just hoped he was ready.

"Okay," Charisma said firmly, turning back to the loiterers. "Send him in." Her words cut through the air, its weight undeniable.

"Honey? Sweetie darling," the woman in black said in a voice note as he walked Clark up the short steps to the white door, all eyes on him. "I have a handsome young man here, one of Charisma's newest, uh . . ."—she sized Clark up and down, from his scuffed Chuck Taylors to his discount button-down—". . . helpers. He's very sweet. He's offered to come inside and support you right now. We just want to help you, okay?"

A minute passed. Then another. The silence stretched, tense and taut. Clark wiped his palms on his pants. He turned: every pair of eyes was on him. Had he been chosen . . . or just sacrificed? He gulped.

Finally, from behind the door, there was the faint sound of scraping chairs and the clanging of something metal, and then—*click.* A slim crack opened in the doorway.

"Off you go," the woman whispered, giving Clark a shove.

The moment he stepped in, the door was slammed shut and bolted again. His eyes adjusted to the dim light of the foyer, and the sight before him left him momentarily stunned: Felicity had turned the room into a fortress. The door was crisscrossed with coat hangers interlocking the handle, while armchairs and end tables had been shoved into place as an improvised barricade. Clark took a few steps back. When she was done, she turned to face him. In her white crop top and pink pajama bottoms, her blonde hair loosely tied back,

Felicity was the most beautiful woman Clark had ever seen. He knew this from photos, in movies, and on TV, but here, the raw reality of it left him in disbelief.

After a long silence, Clark carefully uttered the word, "Hi!"

Felicity stared at him for a beat, as he was so used to, from his scuffed shoes to his bloodshot eyes—and then, to his complete shock, she burst into tears.

"Of course," she choked out, her voice cracking. "They sent a *kid*!"

"I'm not a . . ." Clark started, then froze. What could he even say?

She sniffed, wiping her eyes with the back of her hand. She said flatly, "You look like shit."

"I . . . Yeah, I know," Clark muttered, shuffling awkwardly. *Perfect. First impression: nailed it . . .*

"What did they do to you?"

What did they do to me . . . Clark parroted in his head. *Should I tell her . . . ?* Cautiously, he replied, "You really wanna know?"

She shrugged, and Clark hesitated before answering. "They stole me out of bed, buried me alive, and left me for dead."

Felicity clasped her hands to her face. "That is so *mean*!"

Clark couldn't help but chuckle. "I know, right?"

She returned a small laugh. "Sorry," she murmured, brushing her bangs from her face and wiping her pink eyes.

Clark returned a smile. "It's okay."

But Felicity was already heading out the foyer and down the hall. Clark trailed after her, not far behind.

They entered a dim living-dining room, the sun bleeding through the edges of the gold satin curtains drawn tight. Felicity collapsed onto the emerald velvet sectional and sank into a nest of bed pillows and throw blankets. Clark's eyes drifted to the coffee table—a clutter of Diet Pepsi cans, chocolate truffles, and glossy tabloids. Her face was splashed on every cover: *"Party Princess Felicity's Wild Nights Exposed,"* one read; *"Caught in the Act: Felicity's Secret Life Revealed"*; *"America's Star Collapses: Felicity's Public Meltdown."*

Her eyes flicked to him, then to the tabloids. She snapped, "It's not true! None of it!"

He sat in the armchair across from her. "I know," he said. "I believe you."

Her eyes narrowed. A long pause hung between them before she finally asked, "What's your name?"

"Clark."

"How old are you?"

"Twenty-four."

Her gaze traveled over him again, softer this time. "We're the same age." Then almost to herself, she added, "You look younger."

Compared to him, Felicity looked so much more mature—not in years, but in presence alone. Like her knees she tucked in close, her gravity seemed to pull the room and all its contents toward her, as though the air itself bent in her favor. Her heart-shaped face spoke of womanhood, but her bare baby skin, her soft cheeks, and her big, hazel-brown eyes sang of strength and sweetness. She was just a girl—already a mother and a star—no older than him. But those eyes, he understood, betrayed the wisdom of a soul who had lived many lives already . . . and paid the price for every one of them.

Clark spoke gently when he said, "Late bloomer, I guess."

Felicity replied, "You're so young to work for her." By *her,* Clark knew instantly who she meant.

"I think I'm the youngest wi—assistant she's ever had."

"Assistant. Sure," she said, giving him a side-eye and then looking off toward the closed window. After a moment, she added, "Why are you even here?"

Clark bit his lip and shrugged. "I wanna help."

She shook her head. "You can't help me. No one can." An edge crept into her voice, tears streamed down her cheeks, and she barely croaked, "You know I'm as good as dead."

Clark's brow crinkled. "What do you mean?"

"You know what I mean," she said, shaking her head.

"I don't," he insisted. "I swear."

She gestured to a thick tome with multicolored sticky notes all over, sitting under the magazines he had failed to notice. "Do you know what this movie is about, the one I'm filming? *The Cost of Magic*?"

"No . . ." Clark replied, his eyes widening as they flicked to the script.

She narrowed her eyes. "They didn't tell you?"

"No," Clark said, shaking his head for emphasis.

Felicity's gaze hardened. "Are you telling the truth?"

"Promise!" Clark said, holding her stare. "I don't know a thing about it, or why we're here besides that you've been cooped up for days and refuse to finish filming."

She paused. Softly she said, "You're not like the others, are you."

Clark said quietly, "Not at all."

Felicity sniffed, wiping her face with the back of her hand. "It's about a Golden Age Hollywood starlet who sells her soul for fame to a queen witch."

Clark's stomach tightened. Coolly, he echoed, "A queen witch?"

"Yeah. She gets everything she ever wanted—fame, fortune, love . . . the life of her dreams . . . but there's a price. There's always a price . . ."

Clark hesitated, his voice cautious. "What kind of a price?"

"The witch says, 'A life for a life, or . . . a new life for a new life.' In the end, the witch comes to collect her nut, and according to their contract, it's either her or her firstborn. Guess who she chooses?"

Clark's mouth flickered into a half smile. "So cliché," he replied, his tone wry.

"Tell me about it," Felicity muttered.

"But what could the witch want with your child? I mean—the actress's child."

"I dunno," she said darkly. "What do you think witches do with children in every fairytale? In every story?"

Clark gulped as he thought on it, his throat suddenly dry. "How does it end?"

"You know how it ends." For a moment, the two sat in silence. All was so quiet in the bungalow, they could hear the hum of the central air conditioning turn off. "I begged them to rewrite it. 'Give me a fairytale ending!' I pleaded. 'A prince to save the day, anything!' But it was no use . . . My agent's like, 'It's Oscar bait!' She's so fucking useless, that simp! My mother—ugh!—my mother said I 'have to' do it. 'Whatever Charisma says goes.' She's an executive producer."

"Your mother said that?"

"Yeah," Felicity continued, her voice tightening. "The two of them are good 'friends'"—this she put in air quotes—"whatever *that* means. Some mother she is! Charisma preyed on my mother, and my mother literally sold me out—me, her own daughter! She literally sold me out, and I went along with it thinking this was the best thing that could have ever happened to me. This was the best thing I could do, like Charisma is some kinda fucking fairy godmother or something . . ."

Felicity buried her face in her hands. Her shoulders bobbed up and down. Clark wanted to reach his hand out to her, but she was sitting so far away.

When she came up for air, she said, "It's like . . . I'm having to pay again and again for letting the wrong people in."

"I don't understand," Clark said gently. "Why don't you want to finish filming? You couldn't get out of it?"

She shook her head. "I can't."

"Why not . . . ?"

"Because . . . it's part of my contract with Charisma."

"Oh no . . ." Clark said.

Tears began to slip down Felicity's cheeks as she darkly replied, "Yes." A heavy stillness hung in the air in that dim bungalow living room. She buried her head in her hands again, her shoulders trembling slightly. Clark was reminded of Miss Honey, the ghost who had warned him on his first day: "Never sign a witch's contract, baby . . . Get the hell out now while you still can." He remembered all too well how she showed him her untimely end in flames—fired just like Melissa—her fate sealed by the very same woman.

"I'm not sure how to tell you this," Clark said slowly, "but Charisma is a witch."

Felicity abruptly stopped sobbing, dropped her hands, and stared at him. "Well, duh!" she said. "Everybody knows that!"

"Wait, what?" Clark asked. He furrowed his eyebrows again. "What do you mean, 'Everybody knows'?"

With a sniff, Felicity bent down and grabbed a box of tissues on the floor. Then, she launched off the sectional and walked around to the dining room table behind them. Clark watched her pick something up. Turning back, he was surprised to see her holding up a hexagonal alchemy bottle with a tasseled atomizer that Clark knew all too well: Charisma's signature fragrance, which had launched the previous year. *Charisma Eau de Parfum.*

"The last time I wore this," she said bitterly, swirling its chartreuse juice, "I had to run for my life to keep a mob of men off me—even the cops and my own security!" She set the bottle down with a clang on the glass coffee table. "And don't get me started on her cream. I refuse to let that anywhere near me."

"Cream? What cream?" Clark asked. "And, hey, you couldn't possibly have known though. Known what she is."

Felicity blew her nose and wiped it clean, as she walked back to her spot on the sectional. "Of course I knew," she said flatly. "She's not really hiding it, even if I didn't believe her at first. Did you?"

"Did I what?" Clark asked.

"Believe her," Felicity finished, her hazel-brown eyes searching his face.

Clark froze, reflecting on the months that led him here. Monica had told him outright she was an assistant witch for Queen Charisma, even mistaken him for a witch himself, but he hadn't really understood what she meant. He had spent weeks—no, months—wondering what kind of witches they really were, dismissing his growing worries . . . until it was too late. "Good point," he muttered, his head feeling suddenly faint. He pointed to one of the soda boxes near his feet. "Can I have one?"

"Help yourself," she said.

"Thank you."

Felicity threw him a bag of truffles too, then tore into another herself. With a weary sigh, she said, "Sweets are all that make me feel alive right now."

"I've got a sweet tooth, too," Clark admitted. Clark peeled the foil off a truffle and popped it into his mouth, suddenly realizing how much he had been running on empty since the night before. The tang of raspberry in dark chocolate burst onto his tongue. If this was her idea for a last meal, he couldn't imagine a better one.

"I signed a contract with a witch to make all my dreams come true—and I got exactly what I wished for. Everything and more! Now, either I give her what she wants, or she takes it herself. The ritual at the end of the movie? It's real. They're going to kill me. That's the deal. Life imitates art, right? I signed the contract, and now I have to pay."

"I still don't understand though," Clark said. "Why would she want you or your son *to die*?"

"Money," she said flatly. "And oh, I dunno, the same reason any witch would want a human sacrifice: power, maybe. Not to mention, they put all this posthumous stuff in my contracts about using my image after I die. Imagine the sales knowing I died while filming the *final scene*? And the insurance payout? Massive. I was warned to retire early: I'm worth more to them dead. Royalties and the keys to my estate on a silver platter, all thanks to the conservatorship!"

Clark shook his head, bewildered. "They can't get away with this. Have you told anyone?" He felt stupid as soon as the words left his mouth.

"Have you?" she shot back. "Did they believe you?"

Clark grimaced. He had confessed almost everything to Joey, who . . . might or might not believe him. Then there was Patricia, his mother's best friend, who had referred him to the interview in the first place. He shifted in his seat. "I tried," Clark admitted, "but it didn't make a difference."

"Right. What did you say, 'my boss is a murderous witch'?"

He thought about Patricia, how she told him to drop it. "I told my boyfriend about, well, most of it, but . . ." The word hung in the air. *Boyfriend* . . . Had he said that aloud before? The room went suddenly warm.

At this, Felicity's lips ticked up at the corners for just a second. "The people who are in the loop either work for her or know someone who does. It's Charisma's world," she said. "We're all just living in it, remember?"

The pieces in Clark's head start clicking into place. "He works at her restaurant."

"See? He's in her orbit."

The understanding dawned on Clark's face, the pieces clicking into place. "So you can't go to the press, and you can't talk about this to anyone. Especially not if the intent is to expose her or take her down in any way."

"I literally, physically can't. Every time I've tried to tell someone, *anything*, my phone goes staticky and dies, or my texts go undelivered, or I come down with laryngitis and lose my voice. Didn't *you* sign her NDA?"

Clark drew a sharp breath. He felt so stupid. Since he'd started working for Charisma, chronic tonsillitis had plagued his existence, his throat desperately aching with the unspoken—a hazard of the job for being an overworked intern, he had thought, or wanting to be seen and heard when the adults like Monica and Lorena told him he couldn't be, and having no one to confide in about what was going on. Quietly, he replied, "I know exactly what you're talking about."

"I can't talk about her or my contract with anyone outside her circle. Only to those *she* chooses to let in, to know what—who—she actually is. And, look," she said, reaching down. She produced a gold trash can from under the coffee table. From the bottom, she fished a heap of tangled wire and smashed electronic parts.

Clark frowned. "What is that?"

"They've been tapping me!" Felicity snapped, holding up the heap of wires. "I found these a few days ago. My internet access is restricted and monitored, I can't have my own phones—I literally can't talk to anyone about this outside of those who work for her, at least not with anyone who cares. My mother is useless, everyone hired works for her." Her voice cracked as she tossed the heap back in the can. "*Don't you get it?* They're going to take me away and punish me, and even if I could speak up about it, even if I managed to somehow come close," she said, smashing the trash can down, "I'd just look deranged! They've already painted me as out of my mind in the press. Who would believe me now?"

Clark was struck by her composure. After everything she'd just shared, he wasn't sure he would've managed even half as well in her place. Felicity didn't look like someone coming undone. Not to him. She looked more like a scared young woman in a gilded cage than an unraveling star.

"I just didn't . . ." She paused, trailing off. "I dunno . . . I thought things would be different on the other side of my wish. But they're not better. They're worse. So much worse. I haven't slept in . . . years! The work never stops—rehearsals, and studio time, and touring, and film sets, and on and on. They had me working all through my pregnancy and right after I gave birth. I need a break! I need rest! I'm losing my *mind!* And now . . . I thought I could have my baby and . . . disappear. That's all I've ever wanted. But they won't let me. Not my mother. Not Charisma. No one can help me."

She looked away again, her eyes as vacant as the drawn window. "Anyway," she said softly, "it's no use now. They're going to force me to finish filming. And then I die." Clark followed her line of sight to the window—heavy curtains drawn, a sliver of light escaping. The outside world passing her by.

Softly, he said, "We're going to stop her."

"It's done," Felicity said flatly. "There's no way out."

"There must be a way," Clark insisted. The doubt that gnawed at him couldn't be hidden, making Felicity look up to keep her eyes from streaming.

She took a deep breath. "I'd do anything to break the contract and take it all back. To take my life back. All this stuff—the fame, the money—it doesn't mean a thing. And when it disappears," she said, "you only have yourself to face. What did I have to gain actually? Was it worth it?" Clark looked away so she wouldn't see his own eyes were swimming.

"Mommy?"

The small voice startled them. Felicity and Clark turned. Her pajama-clad son stood in the hall behind the couch, rubbing sleep from his eyes. How quickly Felicity transformed—her tear-streaked face brightened; a radiance returned. It made Clark's chest ache.

"Good morning, sweetie," she sang, opening her arms. He toddled into her embrace. His head rested on her chest. "Did you sleep well?" she asked, stroking his golden hair. He nodded, looking curiously to Clark.

"Sebastian, this man is here to help me with my movie," she said. "Say 'Hi, Clark.'"

'Man' . . . Clark thought. *That's a first . . . !*

Sebastian gripped her tight as he mumbled, "Hi."

"Hi, Sebastian," Clark said, offering a smile and a wave.

Sebastian leaned in close and whispered in Felicity's ear, "Mommy, when can we go to the park like you promised?"

Felicity's eyes darted to Clark before she answered. "I'm sorry. I know I promised," she said. "Honey, Clark and I need to finish talking first. Why don't you go to my room and watch some TV for a bit, hmm? I'll try my best to take you later, okay?"

Sebastian's smile faltered for a second. His head dropped. "Okay," he murmured.

Felicity kissed his forehead and rubbed his back. "Thank you, sweetie. Love you," she said. He kissed her cheek and climbed off the sectional. Clark watched as his hand dragged along the wall while he padded to the bedroom, his tiny steps slow and reluctant.

Felicity turned to Clark. The room settled into quiet again. Finally, Clark said, "He's so smart."

Felicity's lips curled into a faint, wistful smile. "I know."

"How old is he?"

"He turns four in September," she replied. She placed her head in her hands and tucked her face into her knees, the tears welling up and spilling down her cheeks again.

"You're gonna have to come out eventually," Clark said softly. "You can't stay in here forever."

"I know," she whispered. "And they'll punish me for this when I do. They'll force me to finish this stupid movie, and then . . ." Her voice broke, but she pushed through. "They're going to kill me—and probably my baby too."

Felicity's shoulders sagged under her hitched breath. She reached back, pulled her ponytail loose, and shook her hair down, raking her fingers through her locks. Even like this, broken and defeated, she was beautiful in a way that reminded Clark of Emily and her sad smile.

Clark winced. He concentrated as hard as he could, swallowing the ache in his chest. The walls themselves seemed to lean in to watch as slowly, the distant hum of LA traffic, of birdsong and rustling palms, of distant voices and footsteps on pathways, the poolside sounds, and the tittle-tattle from the group waiting outside the white bungalow door, the sound of cartoons playing in the other room—all of it faded to silent. The world held its breath as Clark turned the noise of everything around them down to zero.

"We're gonna figure this out," Clark said. He crossed the living room carpet to kneel beside the emerald sectional. His hands hovered for a moment before reaching out. "I promise."

She placed her hands in his. Her fingers were small, cold, and delicate in his grasp.

"Take this," he said. He slipped the evil eye ring from his finger, the one that Emily had given him on their way to the airport that morning. He placed it in Felicity's hand. "It'll protect you when it's given by someone who cares."

For a moment, neither of them spoke. With one hand still on hers, Clark reached up and gently lifted a single, long eyelash from her cheek.

"Let's make a new wish," he said, holding the eyelash on the tip of his finger, careful not to let it slip away. He held it up. "One where you have your voice, where you and your baby live, where you're free."

She looked into his brown eyes. "Think it'll come true?"

Clark gave her a small, unwavering smile. "I know it will." She grabbed his hand and squeezed. Even with her eyes scrunched shut, Clark swore she was the most beautiful girl in the world. He asked, "What does that freedom feel like?"

Felicity's brow furrowed, a faint smile tugging at her lips. "Hmmm," she hummed, with her eyes still closed. "Like driving in my car with the top down, alone. No one knows where I am. It's just me, and the sun, and the open road." A single tear slipped down her cheek.

The world around them in that dim living room held its breath. Even the walls seemed to lean in, listening, until for a moment everything—the bungalow, LA, the whole world—fell away and disappeared. Clark and Felicity were the universe and themselves, all at once.

She blew. The eyelash floated away, caught on an invisible breeze.

And when she opened her eyes, Felicity was still in the same place.

CHAPTER III

Mother

Not long after Clark left her suite, Felicity was wheeled out on a gurney, stark against the pink-and-green hallways of the Beverly Hills Hotel. LAPD moved her in silence save for the crackle of their radios. A paramedic followed behind, carrying her son. Felicity did not resist.

Where are they taking her . . . ? Clark asked Emily, mind to mind.

Away . . . she replied. *On a 5150 . . .*

Behind them, Charisma followed closely with the coven in tow, *clack-clacking* against stone and tile. Her lips moved in hurried whispers with Felicity's frantic-eyed, black-clad agent, who walked very stiffly and clung on to her every word.

Then through the glass doors, Felicity was wheeled out and down the red carpeted steps.

Camera flashes detonated. Paparazzi swarmed, shouting her name, lunging over one another for their shot. Felicity was engulfed by the frenzy, her face drained of color under the harsh strobe of dozens of lenses.

When words could not be shared, Clark scrounged up all the love he could, and sent those feelings her way, like a hug on the wind. There was a tingle somewhere behind his eyes. For the briefest moment, Felicity's head turned as she was lifted into the ambulance, her gaze sweeping over the crowd before settling—was it on him?

The moment passed in a heartbeat, the ambulance door slammed shut, and the scene was swallowed up by swarming paps and their flashing lights, erasing her from view.

What happened in there . . . ? Emily asked him.

Well . . . Clark thought back. How could he possibly sum it all up?

Carefully, he scrounged up his feelings and pushed them gently toward Emily like a quiet tide. The realization unfurled across her face like a shadow creeping at dusk. Her eyes grew wet in the understanding, and she swallowed hard against the swell threatening to break.

In all the commotion, Clark had forgotten to check his messages:

(8:08 a.m. Joey DiMuccio): Hey babe, how was your flight? I had the strangest dream about you last night. You were trapped in a box somewhere underground. And Jessica would NOT let me sleep. So weird!

How's LA? Everything okay?

(9:31 a.m. Clark Crane): Hi babe! Weird!! Yeah, everything's great!!!

Joey replied almost immediately.

(9:32 a.m. Joey DiMuccio): We miss you 😊 !

Attached was a picture of him and Jessica, their runt of a stray black cat. Her head was pressed up against his, her large yellow-green eyes practically leaping through the screen.

(9:32 a.m. Clark Crane): I miss you too ♥!

One other message had come in.

(5:55 a.m. Maria): Hey pumpkin, just thinking of you. You were in my dream last night. How's work? Call me sometime. Love you

Joey had dreamt of him. So had his mother. Could he have unwittingly put out some kind of . . . distress signal?

The coven strode out the hotel doors and toward their waiting car, a caravan of black clothes on high heels, with Clark, their little duckling, following in their wake. The LA sun blaring down did nothing to clear the haze in his head. How could the world keep turning when people like Felicity were trapped by the hands of people like Charisma? And what could someone like him possibly do about it?

"Where to now?" he asked Emily.

"I've booked us in for lunch at the Chateau," Lorena announced, not breaking stride. "They have a table ready for us."

Clark's stomach grumbled, right on cue. "Oh great, I'm *starvles*!" he said.

Monica turned, her glacial eyes glaring at him. "Not you."

Lorena fell back to join her, while Charisma, Emily, and Alicia moved ahead without pause. "You," she said, stopping him short, "are going home."

Clark's stomach sank. Past Lorena, Clark looked to Emily, who had glanced over her shoulder but dared not break ranks. This time, he was on his own.

"Oh," he managed to say, swallowing his disappointment. "But I'm already here. Maybe I can offer an extra hand? Won't you need me to help with the kits?"

"That won't be necessary," Monica replied without looking up from her phone.

"Oh." Clark could hardly mask his hurt. "Okay."

"Sweetie darling." Lorena smirked, tilting her head. "You didn't actually think you'd be staying with us, did you?"

Monica added, nodding to his attire, "As if we would be caught dead seen with you at lunch." She lifted her hand, punctuating her words with a smug little flourish. "Some people want to go from here"—her hand rose—"to here, without paying their dues. We don't like those people here."

"Not at all. No clients of your own to call on," Lorena chimed, "no business to tend."

Monica said, "You are a dead weight as far as we're concerned."

Clark looked into their stone-set eyes, their perfectly manicured hair catching in the breeze around their alabaster faces. Surely this was some kind of cruel joke? Was he being punished for coaxing out Felicity? For doing as told and succeeding? What was the point of bringing him? *How will I get back . . . ?* Clark's mind raced, his thoughts darting to the private jet.

Lorena clicked her tongue as if reading his thoughts *(she probably is . . .* Clark thought). "Your flight was booked just moments ago." Her perma-frown lips perched into a mockery of a smile, all teeth. "Your car will arrive shortly. Toodeloo, darling!"

"Later, *Ass-toria*!"

One of the drivers produced his luggage bag without a word and unloaded it at his feet. "Charisma! Charisma!" two photographers exclaimed. Clark caught his disoriented reflection in the flash of the tinted windows as the coven's car pulled away, no chance for a good-bye. A soft alto voice brushed his mind.

Everything will be okay . . . Emily thought to him. *See you soon, babes . . .*

Yeah . . . Clark thought back, *see you soon . . .*

There was no bench in sight. Clark lowered himself onto the shaded curb, just to the left of the red carpet. He drew his knees close, trying to make himself smaller, as patrons glided by and cast him curious, judgmental glances. He tried to ignore them, instead focusing on his paperback copy of George Orwell's *1984,* the rhythm of cars coming and going, the glass doors sliding open and shut, and the paparazzi gradually disbanding, their fraternizing gradually fading as they took their leave. Laughter from the hotel's patio in the distance drifted faintly toward him. His black attire felt conspicuous, his baggage as heavy in mind as it was in hand.

Lorena hadn't booked him on the jet. Of course not. Instead, she'd banished him straight to coach on commercial—on a flight departing later that evening.

Clark was a loitering black cloud. When he was finally allowed to check-in, hours of restless waiting at LAX stretched before him, punctuated by burnt coffee, the monotony of boarding announcements, and the final pages of his book, *A Small Place* by Jamaica Kincaid. At 9:30 p.m., he found himself in seat 42C, wedged in the last row at the very back of the plane next to the bathrooms—no snacks, and no drinks.

Thanks a lot, Lorena . . . he thought bitterly. Clark didn't even have room to recline his chair.

Sleep was unthinkable. His ruminating mind refused to still, circling back to Felicity and her dire predicament. How had Charisma ensnared her so completely, while producing a movie that paralleled to boot? How was he—a witch's assistant—going to stop the most horrible person alive and save Felicity? And if Felicity could be saved . . . could he?

As exhaustion crept in, his well-loved copy of *A Streetcar Named Desire* slipped from his hand.

Suddenly Clark wasn't in the window seat at the back of the plane. He was back in his worst nightmare.

The coffin.

Lorena, Monica, and Alicia loomed above him, their hollow eyes gleaming, leering, laughing—with taunting, thunderous, cackling laughter that rang up and down his body. Their joy at his fear was almost worse than the fear itself. Monica's cold gray eyes burned the brightest—until they weren't gray at all.

They were green.

A sickly, menacing green. The Great Eye that had haunted him since first meeting her—a vortex that pinned him in its venomous glare.

The lid of the coffin slammed shut, plunging him into suffocating darkness again.

No air.

No escape.

"NO!"

Clark jolted awake. His chest heaved as he fought for air and clawed for reality, blinking at the cramped, stale space of the plane cabin. He fumbled for the time in the dim cabin lights: it was 3:00 a.m.

It was always 3:00 a.m. when the nightmares came.

Clark groaned. *I thought we were done with this, the nightmares, the eye . . .*

Guess not . . .

The gray-haired woman beside him cracked a disapproving eye open, shooting him the most irritated of looks. She huffed as she turned the other way, pulling her blanket tighter around her shoulders.

One red-eye to Chicago O'Hare and almost a day later, Clark finally came upon the ghostly, phosphorescent sky of the New York tristate outside the window of his connecting flight. The plane touched down at the concrete expanse of LaGuardia Airport on Sunday at 7:14 a.m.

Clark boarded the M60 bus to Astoria Boulevard. When he finally stepped off into the cold, the familiar streets seemed impossibly far from where he'd been, from how he had left them. By the time he climbed the five flights of stairs, walked down and to the left of the yellowing hall, and landed at the front of his grandma's studio apartment, it was 8:30 a.m.

Quietly, Clark turned the key and stepped inside. The familiar scent of old wood and dollar-store air freshener greeted him, the smell of home. Faint streaks of light seeped through the edges of the heavy drapes. Dust motes swirled lazily in the thin beams, while faint vestiges of silver January morning pooled on the wooden floor and wearily along the papier-mâché walls, thick with paint.

Jessica leapt from the bed, landing deftly and without noise on the floor before padding up to him. Clark bent down to scoop her up into his arms.

"Hi, sweet angel!" he whispered as she sniffed his face. He pressed a nuzzling kiss to the top of her head. She smelled faintly sweet, like the lingering fragrance of Joey's cologne on the sheets—a gentle homecoming he hadn't realized he so desperately needed.

The bed shifted, and Joey stirred. When he raised his head at Clark with his heavy teddy bear eyes, the gray world rushed back into color.

Joey softly said, "Hi," his voice thick with sleep.

Clark pulled off his shoes, peeled off his shirt, and stepped out of his pants, leaving them in a crumpled heap on the floor before sliding into the sheets beside him.

"You're home early," Joey noted, the hint of a question mark left on the pillow. Just a nod from Clark was all it took for his lip to quiver and the ache in his throat to swell—and for him to bury his face in Joey's chest. Joey shifted closer, his hand rubbing Clark's back in slow, steady circles.

Eventually, Clark's breathing eased. Its cadence synced to the rhythm of Joey's caresses and Jessica's humming purrs from her place at their feet, nestled in the warmth between them. In the cocoon of home, the weight of the day evanesced and Clark finally surrendered. His hurried thoughts slipped away into the quiet depths of slumber.

When he finally crawled out from under the blankets, Joey was gone. Clark pulled the sheets over his ears to drown out the hiss and clang of the silver radiator. But sleep wouldn't come, not with his mind beginning to race all over again, replaying the chaos of the past two days like a broken reel.

He turned to look at his phone.

"BRB," Joey had texted.

A moment to himself.

Next to the bed and off the shelf, Clark plucked his Froggie from his perch, a lovingly timeworn stuffed animal dressed in a witch's cloak and conical hat. He paused, looking down at the twinkly eyes, the sallow, olive-green skin like his own. A familiar return to softness—the texture of childhood, unchanged. A time when love didn't come with conditions . . . and magic didn't come at a cost. He kissed Froggie on the head.

With his other hand, Clark reached into his backpack and retrieved his diary, its spine soft and creased.

I'm home.

They tried to disappear me, but I survived . . .

I don't have nightmares when Jessica sleeps with me. No 3 a.m. terrors. No waking up drenched in sweat. She's my good luck charm.

Last night, she appeared in my dreams. At some point, she had climbed up right up beside me. I could feel her twitches before I drifted back off. Kittens are always so susceptible to stimuli:

sirens wailing,
the whistling wind through the crack in the window,
the screeching of the strays outside.

In this dream, we were running by the water through an empty Great Lawn at Astoria Park. Only, we weren't running to something—we were running from *something. I was following her lead, my legs moving with hers.*

What was she so afraid of?

The Shadow That Eats . . . *she told me with a single look of her eyes. Not in words, but more in feelings shaped into thoughts.* The Dream Stalker. The Scarer. The Devourer of Souls. The One That Makes the Strays Scream.

I had understood instantly that by "strays" she didn't mean just cats . . . Somehow I knew—shown by her eyes and at the same time Seen and Known by my own mind's eye—that as the sun dips below the Hell Gate Bridge and under the East River, the stray cats of Astoria scramble for their last forage and take their cover—fast. Because rising up from the dark water, It'll find you.

It hunts through the back alleys and under cars, scaling the fire escapes, and slips past the cracked, shuttered windows where the dreamers of Astoria sleep, like how Jessica had inevitably found me.

There was a howl, unlike any animal I've ever heard—chilling, maniacal, almost like laughter. It was the absence of warmth, the antithesis of love. I could hear it behind us, giddily lapping up the air, our scent on its tongue.

A twig snapped. I felt its breath. Just as I had turned back to look, Jessica leaped into my arms—and suddenly, we were back in our dark apartment, in bed.

What struck me about what Jessica had said—that this monster comes from under the Hell Gate Bridge—is that the East River is less a river and more a . . . turbulent estuary, one that has laid over a thousand souls to rest at its murky bottom.

It is so strange to me how my favorite time of day—when the sun tiptoes over the bridge and dives into the river, while the city sighs into evening—could be another's living horror.

"It's okay," Dream Jessica had told me, with a paw on my lap. Her gaze met mine, unblinking, vivid, steady. She said, "So long as we're together, I'll protect you."

Then I woke up.

I could still feel how the chill of winter air had clung to my skin, as if the dream had seeped into reality. When I opened my eyes, her smallness was still curled at my side. She yawned and tucked her paws over her little face, as if to say, finally, she was getting the sleep she deserved.

Clark paused, his pen hovering over the page. He reached out to pat Jessica, her soft fur warm beneath his hand. She mewed in lazy protest as he shuffled out of the sheets and stepped out of bed onto the cold floor.

Not far across the small studio apartment, he drew the curtains open. Outside the north-by-northwest-facing windows, an airplane lifted off from LaGuardia. A mourning dove perched on the fire escape peered in, and the red eyes of the RFK Bridge blinked back at him, as they always had since he could remember.

He glanced around that old-timey apartment, his eyes lingering on Joey's slow, inevitable integration (*read: his moving in . . .* Clark thought): his clothes squeezed into the dresser alongside Clark's. Candy, always candy, crammed in the cabinets and bedside table. And his toothbrush now permanently stationed on the holder of the wall-less bathroom next to the clawfoot tub. Everything was the same as he'd left it.

But he wasn't.

Clark returned to his diary.

Can I really be ready for more? More than this tiny apartment? More than poverty, more than living in the shadows? Wasn't that what I asked for on that eyelash wish last August, after my interview? The job. Joey. Growth. Maybe it's already coming true . . .

Maybe I'll have to be the assistant she can't fire . . .

Future Me, when I catch up to you . . .

I can't wait to catch up to you . . . What will become of me next?

I hope you're living everything I ever dreamt of in this moment and more. So much, much more.

A faint, almost imperceptible sound interrupted his daydreaming—a swish, followed by a whispered tap against the floor. Something had slipped from his diary.

Jessica lifted her head from where she lay, ears twitching. As Clark bent over the bed to fish it out from underneath, she padded closer, sniffing at the edge of the fallen paper.

It was a note.

Clark stilled. The paper was perfectly crisp, untouched—exactly how he had left it. He didn't need to read it to remember what it said. But against his better judgement, he did anyway.

It was his own hurried scrawl, looped and flowery.

Witches are real.

A whisper from the past. From the boy who that scrawled it more than a month ago—before LA, before the coffin, before becoming an assistant. Before he understood *just how real* witches could be. Before he thought he might be disappeared forever. His goodbye note. Meant to be found after he was gone.

Jessica mewed.

Clark exhaled and rubbed his temple. *Yeah. No kidding.*

Then he saw the other thing that had fallen with it.

A business card.

His eyes widened with recognition.

He flipped it over. Printed in precise, no-nonsense Garamond was a single phone number.

Mother.

The enigmatic crasher from last year's Halloween party and Charisma Saintly's alleged sworn enemy. The card's weight in his hand felt heavier than paper had any right to be.

At the jingle of keys and a click of the lock, Joey appeared at the door, his movie star smile wide and easy, firing up the butterflies. A brown paper bag of bagels was tucked under one arm, and two coffees balanced precariously in his hands.

Clark quickly wedged the business card into the inner lid of his diary and snapped it shut.

Joey kicked off his boots. He crossed the small apartment-bedroom, slow and steady, and cupped his hands on Clark's face, cool and certain.

The meeting of warm lips.

The breath of coffee between them.

The soft scrape of stubble on skin.

Everything else—the note, the card, the weight of all that had come to be, the uncertain future ahead—fell away for a spell. The walls leaned in, the universe folded around them, and they flew away on kisses that tasted like infinity.

By the time Sunday twilight wrapped them in Astoria Blue—the color of the bugleweed found in the park blocks away—Clark and Joey had become a tangled mound of blankets in bed. By the evening, the apartment smelled of pizza and soda dinner, powdered sugar zeppole dessert, and Dove soap shower—all in the lazy haze of their third companion for the night (or fourth, if you counted Jessica), Mary Jane.

Clark's thoughts drifted now and then, pulled from the TV by the faint chirp of crickets and the soft hum of cars on the overpass. All was mostly quiet. He counted the airplanes flying west and the number of windows in the building across the tree-filled alley-courtyard—yellow, low-hanging stars in his cloudy New York sky. The red eyes of RFK loomed in the distance, ever watchful.

Inevitably, Clark caught Joey's eyes starting to flutter. At the first snore, Clark escorted him up and to the sink where they brushed their teeth. Back in bed, with the television on low, they faced one another, rubbed each other's hands, then each other's arms.

Their nightly ritual complete. Familiar. Safe.

At bedtime, *Bewitched* bathed the apartment in black-and-white nostalgia—its 1960s witch and her mortal husband, the laugh track their lullaby. The title font reminded Clark of the Beverly Hills Hotel.

"I've seen every episode," Clark whispered across the pillow. "I used to stay up 'til three or four in the morning watching those old-timey shows."

Joey smiled. "Me too," he said softly. "My Nonna Margaret got me hooked."

"It was that or I'd fall asleep on the spines of my favorite hardcovers. Tragic," Clark said with a wry roll of his eyes. "My parents would get so mad at me when I wouldn't wake up for school. I had permanent dark circles the entire second grade. Those shows, those books, they were always like . . . places to come home to, you know? Predictable. Stable."

"I know what you mean," Joey said. Joey traveled across his pillow to Clark's, and planted a kiss on his forehead that made fireworks of his insides.

After some moments, Joey said, "Our chemistry is so good," and nuzzled into his neck.

"I feel the same," Clark whispered back, brushed his fingers through Joey's heartthrob hair.

Joey had a deep inhale at the nape of his neck, and trailed up his pulse to the back of his ear. His voice was low, almost a growl, as his hands slid Clark's side. "And you smell so good I can't resist you . . ."

Clark seized up, regretting instantly the spritz of gardenia-tobacco *Charisma* perfume he had sprayed after their bath. He gently pulled away. He didn't have the heart to tell Joey the truth—that *Charisma* was subliminally marketed as a kind of love potion.

Joey tilted his head, sensing the shift. "You wanna tell me what happened? Why you're back so early?"

Clark shook his head into the pillow. "I'm in now," he said. "I got the job. That's all that matters."

Joey's lips tensed. He gave a sidelong frown. A skeptical punctuation to the silence between them that stretched warm but laden with words unspoken. Then, after a moment, Clark said softly, "Hey, Joey?"

"Yeah?"

"Can I ask you something?"

Joey inched nearer. "Of course." His voice was barely above a whisper. Their faces were so close.

A pause.

"Why do you love me?"

There it was. The question had Clark teetering off the edge. It hadn't even been six months since they'd met, and already Joey had suggested at New Year's they talk about moving in. To another, bigger apartment.

To start a home.

Everything was moving so fast. Were they ready? *Am I . . . ?* Clark thought.

But Joey's face softened. "Why . . . ?" he asked. "Why not? You're different than the others. Special."

Clark erupted in a small sweat—and a small smile.

"I love how I feel when I'm with you," Joey said. "Like I'm the only person in the room. Like I'm the only person in the whole world that matters. Like the universe leans in just to hear us speak . . ."

At this, Clark's leg twitched.

"I knew from the first moment I first laid eyes on you," Joey said. "You're my person."

Clark had jumped into the void, and Joey had been there all along, waiting to catch him.

He'd survived.

Joey's eyes searched Clark's face. "Why do you love me?"

Clark said, "You're the Chrysler Building. The Mr. Big to my New York. Summer saxophones in the park and snow on a winter sidewalk. You're the city and the stars and everything in between."

Joey's face fell. He leaned in, his voice dropping to the softest of whispers. "I must be the Darren to your Samantha, too . . . because I think you've cast a spell on me."

Clark froze—his breath catching, heart thudding.

Then, even softer, Joey said those three words: "I love you."

"I love you, too," Clark breathed.

He cupped Joey's face and melted into a kiss that tasted like infinity all over again. Finally, unable to fight the heaviness of his teddy bear eyes, Joey yawned, "Goodnight, babe."

"Goodnight."

The ceremonious smell of coffee and cigarettes clinging to the yellowed halls of his building greeted Clark that Monday morning, 6:30 sharp. The smell, the peeling paint, and the scuffed floors had long since come to feel like home—his first real one since running away from his parents'.

Outside, the sky was still dark and overcast, a layer of low clouds reflecting the glow of streetlights. As he stepped out onto the train platform at 30th Avenue, Clark pulled out his phone.

"Inside Felicity's Breakdown: The Shocking Scene at Beverly Hills Hotel."

That was the first of many headlines Clark scrolled through on his way to work that Monday morning.

"American Royalty in Crisis: Felicity Taken Away by Authorities After Disturbing Standoff."

"Star Spirals Out: Felicity Barricades Herself with Son Before Police Intervention."

"From Red Carpet to Rock Bottom: Felicity's Public Struggles Take Tragic Turn with Emergency Psychiatric Hold."

Clark shifted in his seat, taking a deep inhale. On a whim, he typed "Felicity conservatorship" into the search bar. Dozens of articles and threads populated his screen, all dissecting the public court case that had taken place that fall.

One caught his eye: "Disbarred Attorney Earl D. Atwill Claims Felicity Is a Victim of Conservatorship Abuse."

According to the article, Atwill, a California lawyer, had tried to represent Felicity in her conservatorship battle. But because she was already represented, appointed by the probate court judge herself, the judge dismissed Atwill's filings as attention-seeking and unauthorized. Atwill's reputation tanked from there, culminating in his disbarment.

Yet, something about the article stuck with Clark: "There is no doubt your civil rights are being violated," Atwill had written to Felicity in a letter. "They will seize your child, your assets, and paint you as mentally unsound. They will not stop until they've denied you your freedom and depleted your finances. It begins with whispers about your stability, planted in the right ears, and snowballs into a public spectacle designed to convince the world of your incompetence.

"They will strip you of autonomy under the guise of protection. Your legacy will be theirs to control, your image repackaged and sold to the highest bidder. And you? You will be reduced to a name in their contracts, no longer a person, but a product."

"I am telling you this not as a scare tactic but as a warning. You are not the first, and you will not be the last. There is still time to act, but it won't be easy. This system—these people—know exactly how to keep you powerless. But know this—your voice is your weapon. Do not let them silence you. Fight like your life depends on it, because it does."

Clark reread the words as he boarded his train. He scanned the comments and threads beneath the article, trying to piece together the fragments of a lawyer dismissed as erratic and out of line. Maybe he was, but . . . maybe he wasn't entirely wrong.

There was one other news article buried under the Felicity scandal: "*Disgraced Billionaire Media Proprietor Edgar Dortier Faces Sexual Harassment and Child Trafficking Allegations.*

Here's Charisma's ex-husband . . . thought Clark. The details were harrowing—nearly a hundred accusations had surfaced, women and men coming forward with damning accounts of Dortier's predatory behavior and that of those in his circle. *Yikes* . . . he thought. What's more, reports linked him to trafficking networks operating in the shadows of his media empire. Some whispered of children. Investigations were underway, with more accusations coming to light each day, implicating not just him but those who had turned a blind eye to his actions. The allegations made Clark's stomach twist for the entire commute.

As the N train left Queensboro Plaza, a construction sign under the Queensboro Bridge flashed, *Expect work ahead*, just before plunging into the tunnel beneath the East River.

Clark's mind swam as the train dove beneath the river and back out.

Aboveground, a winter's wind danced through the steel canyons of Billionaire's Row, howling like a living thing. At Charisma's air mansion penthouse—aptly called "the Tower"—all was quiet in the absence of the coven and their queen.

Clark roamed the hallways, studying Charisma's photos on display of her with her celebrity "friends," and the portraits of women and their pet familiars, women of refinery amongst natural scenes of faraway places, holding red-eyed rabbits, wild-eyed jackals, frogs on leashes, and spotted cats like leopards.

Clark spent the morning stocking new shipments into the Closet, the coven's stockroom of witchery, where even the most quiet and unassuming of items hummed.

There on its pedestal, below the oculus in the ceiling that cast a beam of pale winter light into the room, was Charisma's tree terrarium—the inner eye of her Tower. Like a plasma ball of energy, its branches stretched outward, just shy of touching the edges of the glass dome that confined it.

Crown shyness . . . Clark thought, remembering the term for trees whose branches never quite meet, leaving a pattern of gaps in a forest canopy.

He inched closer still, transfixed: if one looked long enough, the tree's branches seemed to sway in an invisible wind within. It seemed to call to him in the words of its rustlings and the sway of its miniature red apples, its voice suffocated under its enclosure.

Clark's heart raced as he leaned closer to the glass. The ringing in his ears began to grow, soft at first, but rising to a shrill scream. Within the noise, words emerged, faint but unmistakable:

End me.

Clark's phone chimed, breaking the spell. He blinked and looked down at the screen.

(10:10 a.m. Lorena Saintly-Henceley): More shipments in the lobby. Stock those now.

Clark returned to his tasks like Cinderella resigned to her chores—but the terrarium's pleas remained buried in his mind for the rest of the day. All day, in fact, while he stocked and organized, the terrarium seemed to tug at the edges of his awareness, the soft hum of its consciousness invading his thoughts.

After lunch—a reheated bowl of Charisma's kids' lentil stew left behind in the fridge—Clark set to work dusting and cleaning parts of the library, a vast labyrinthine chamber hidden behind a false bookcase in Charisma's living room. To access it, one only had to crank back the porcelain hand on a shelf, a theatrical flourish Clark privately dubbed "witch's humor."

The library was less a repository solely for books and more reliquary, its shelves lined with powerful artifacts, weapons, trophies, and secrets. Some items were so powerful, in fact, they were off-limits behind glass, lock, and key, not to be touched, like a sword in a stone Clark had a barking suspicion about.

Before leaving for the day, Clark stole one last glance at the tree. From the door, its branches appeared still, the teeny, tiny red apples glinting in the oculus light. But he swore, right down to his soul, that he could feel it watching him back.

Clark was so preoccupied with thoughts of the terrarium that, as he was stepping onto the freight elevator to leave, his Chuck caught on the lip of Hell's Entrance. Clark stumbled forward, crashing into the corner of the elevator with a resounding *pang* against the metal freight elevator wall.

The sounds unearthed something in Clark. For a split second he wasn't in the elevator anymore—he was in the dark, face-up, trapped in a coffin.

"Careful!" Mai the maid exclaimed as she boarded with him. "You okay?"

"I'm okay!" Clark quickly replied with a forced smile. "Thank you."

Clark was thankful she was there to at least help him laugh it off, but the oddest feeling remained. He fought back the urge to run home. Instead, Clark did something so impulsive he surprised himself.

Perhaps it was instinct leading the way, but on his walk down 58th Street to the train, Clark pulled off to the side and unzipped his backpack. From inside, he produced Mother's business card from Halloween. Without thinking twice, he dialed the digits into his phone and lifted it to his ear.

The call rang three times, clicked, and ended.

Huh . . . Clark thought. *Should I try again . . . ?*

Before he could decide, his phone buzzed in his hand. A text appeared from "unknown": 111 Central Park North, PH.

A block west took Clark to the 2 express train from Columbus Circle, carrying Clark uptown in no time at all. By the time he had emerged from the subway, the sun had long since set. Clark's breath fogged in the crisp, dark air. Central Park stretched dark and sprawling ahead of him, its path devoid of its usual after-work bustlers.

When he got past security and arrived on the landing, the door was propped open, light spilling into the hall. He knocked.

"Come in," a voice beckoned, smooth and low. Clark opened the door and stepped into an open floor plan kitchen-dining room . . . of one of the biggest luxury spaces he had ever been in. Floor-to-ceiling windows framed the south-facing city skyline. At a round table under a pendant light sat an impossibly attractive woman dressed entirely in crisp white.

"Our doors are never locked," Mother said. Clark began to step forward as her voice sharpened. She barked, "Shoes off."

Clark froze.

She added, "This isn't a zoo." Then her face broke into a sheepish smile. He did as he was told, undoing his shoelaces and setting his Chucks to the side.

"The witch's assistant," Mother said cooly, rising to her feet as he entered. "We meet again." The eclectic group around her, on their phones and laptops, rose to their (shoeless) feet with her.

"Hi . . . everyone," he said. "I'm Clark."

Mother gestured languidly with a long, manicured fingernail, pointing to each person one by one: "Denise, Aurelius, Luiza, Dustin, Tristan, Míjiàn. And as for me," she said, turning to Clark and extending her hand, "you can call me Mother."

He approached her for a handshake. "No," she said, her voice velvet and iron. "Kiss it." Heat bloomed in to Clark's cheeks. He hesitated, giving a weak smile, then leaned in and pressed his lips lightly to the back of her hand.

The group's collective gaze bore down on him as he straightened up, his attention darting between the table, the assistants, and the apartment itself. Denise, Luiza, and Míjiàn were female-presenting, and Aurelius, Dustin, and Tristan—Clark couldn't help but feel a flicker of elation to see and relate—were male. No doubt this was the same group Clark had encountered at Charisma's nightclub So Below on Halloween, though now, out of costume, they appeared to be so . . . striking. Clark realized there was nary a thread of black on their persons, let alone the space—a mélange of colors like primary red, candy apple green, intoxicating violet, and deep jungle green. Charisma's, by contrast, was a white and gold marble palace, nary a color in sight. Looking down, he reflected on how he had taken advantage of the coven being out by wearing as much color as he could: his favorite baby-blue-button down and navy slacks. How drab and shadowy the coven's wardrobes were to him; how white-washed Charisma's world seemed to be.

Mother stepped behind him and placed her hands on his shoulders. "What do you notice?" she whispered, leaning into his ear. "It's nice, right?" She gave his shoulders a gentle squeeze. "*A real American coven.*"

Her words made Clark's skin buzz.

The apples of her high cheekbones gleamed in the light as her smooth skin broke into a beguiling smile.

"You're so beautiful," Clark said.

"Thank you, sweetie." He felt so at home in her honey-colored eyes . . .

Mother said, "Sit." Clark and the group did as commanded, her words like honey carrying the weight of undeniable authority, and in that moment, sweeter than all else. A prickle appeared on Clark's forehead, as it was apt to do.

"Well, don't just sit and stare," she barked. "Where are your manners? Fetch our guest a drink!" The assistants all braced against the table, but the nearest to the kitchen sprang from his chair first.

"Thank you, Tristan," she said. Mother turned to Clark, smiling again, and asked with a toss of her long, glossy dark hair, "What would you like, sweetie?"

"Oh, water is fine, please."

Tristan's voice was smooth—too smooth—as he offered, "Sparkling or still?" Clark noticed the careful way he moved, as if every gesture had been practiced. It reminded him of the flight attendant. Of Monica.

"Sparkling," Clark said, turning in his chair while managing a polite smile. "Thank you."

Mother's gaze didn't waver. She said slowly, "We've been wondering when you would show."

"Really?" Clark asked, his voice betraying a hint of curiosity. In a hurried shuffle of socks on tile, Tristan swiftly returned, placing a glass of ice with a lime wedge, and poured the drink himself. He even set a small charcuterie board neatly before Clark, with meats and cheeses and sliced apples.

"Oh yes," Mother said in her silken way. "We have been waiting for a soul like yours to come along. The potential I see in you is . . . well, extraordinary."

The praise made Clark uneasy, though he tried not to show it. "Thank you," Clark said again to Tristan, feeling the weight of the room's collective gaze as he reached for the glass and a grape.

Before he could take a bite, Mother tilted her head as she asked, "So, tell us, Clark: who are you?"

Clark hesitated, feeling the eyes of every gaze in the room pressing on him. *Quick: deflect . . .* he thought. "Um . . . My name is Clark Crane. I'm from Queens. I s-studied English lit; I love to read. And, um, I've never broken a bone."

Mother giggled. So did the others. "Sounds dreamy, Contestant Number One," she teased. Clark could feel the heat rising up to his cheeks and his pulse begin to rise in his ears. Clark smiled politely, looking at his hands on the white laminate table.

"But those are what you do," Mother continued, "and doing is not who you are. So I'll ask again. Who are you? Who is Clark? Look deeper."

"Um . . ." he began, looking to the others. "I care about how others feel. I'm really great with animals. And I might have a mild coffee addiction." He gave a dubious smile and a shrug, to the amusement of the table.

"That is doing. Who are you when you are *being?* Who is the real Clark? Do you know?"

Clark gulped.

"I dunno," he said. "I'm just me."

"You're right. The answer is you are *you*. You are your soul. And an incredibly powerful one at that. One that is at the right place at the right time."

"Oh," Clark replied.

"How long have you been practicing? Surely a long time, having graduated to assistant so fast."

Does the whole witching world know about that? Clark thought. Emily's voice sprang to mind: "You're the talk of the town," she had said to him in Charisma's guest room before their flight.

"Practicing witchcraft? Oh, not very long," he admitted aloud, rubbing the back of his neck.

Mother's smile widened, her teeth straight and white. "You must be a prodigy," Mother said. "In fact, I am certain you are. You are a very smart man, Clark . . . because you are here. Do *you* know why you're here? What made you decide to finally ring?"

"I'm . . . not sure." Clark said carefully, weighing each word. Every instinct told him to deflect—but instead, something urged him to lean in. He straightened his posture. "I wanted to meet you. To see what you . . . have to offer."

Mother leaned in, an amused smile playing on her lips. "Oh, baby, it is not just I who has something to offer you, but you who has something to offer us. You're here because you want to fight the good fight. You're here because this is *destiny*. Your soul knows this is where it begins. Where *you* begin. Allow me to explain:

"A little more than ten years ago, I was the queen of New York. This city was my queendom inherited, the most coveted in the world. It was the best of times. Everything passed through my hands: the clients, the culture, the power . . . until *she* arrived."

"Charisma Saintly," Clark said quietly.

"Yes, though a saint she is not." Darkly, Mother continued. "She claims to be the first witch, one who has gone by many names."

Hecate, Clark remembered her saying in their midnight meeting, *Medea, Lilith, Circe, Morgan le Fay*. "She told me, 'I am the one all your beloved stories are written about.'"

Mother nodded. "She would have you believe that she is the beginning and the end. That every tale of power, magic, and destruction belongs to her."

Her smile hardened. "But the truth is, Clark, she is a thief. A parasite feeding on the Gifts of others. She has taken more from us than given, our so-called sovereign queen reigning supreme. Only a handful of us who have descended from the Originals now survive. Those who have dared to challenge her? Silenced. Gone. Why do you think our numbers are so low? It was not witch hunters, no. The covens of the old world were scattered to the winds . . . by her."

A hush fell over the room. Mother's assistants sat very still.

"She doesn't care about anyone but herself, that narcissist. Every smile she flashes, every step she takes, it's all a calculated performance. She collects people like pawns on a chessboard to fulfill her every whim, only to burn them when it benefits her. She's divided us all and left her supporters to suffer and fall. You think she's leading you? Guiding you? No. She's using you, Clark. And when she's done, you'll be nothing but another discarded piece in her game."

Clark's stomach tightened. His eyes darted from assistant to assistant, their gazes tense on him.

Mother leaned back, and a warmth returned to the table. "Imagine, instead . . ." she continued, "working for me."

She motioned gracefully down the table. "Denise is Dominican-American. Luiza, next to her, is from Brazil. Both come from bruja families of immense influence and power, here and abroad."

Denise and Luiza exchanged a brief, knowing glance, their faces unreadable.

"Tristan and Dustin were homeless out west. I saved their lives. Isn't that right, boys?"

They nodded, answering in unison. "Yes, ma'am."

"Good, boys." Mother's body shifted to her left. "And Míjiàn, my first assistant, is a witch queen in her own right, hailing from China. Her influence spans oceans." Míjiàn's expression was as poised and unreadable as the others, a quiet but undeniable air of authority radiating from her.

"How my girls lead circles of their own back home but choose to stand by me speaks volumes, wouldn't you say?"

Clark nodded. He asked, "What about you? Where are you from?"

"I was born in New Orleans, baby," Mother said with a brimming smile and a slight twang curling her words. "I was raised on Chauncey Street, but I'm a southern girl at heart! And you, sweetie? Where did you say you are from again?"

"Astoria."

"Ooo-wee!" she exclaimed, her eyes lighting up as she looked to the table. "Did you hear that, y'all? We landed ourselves a native. Did you know," she said, turning back to Clark, "the largest exodus of witches after the Salem Witch Trials ended up here, in our great city?"

Clark's brows lifted in surprise. "I didn't know that!" he said.

"Indeed. New York City is the host to the most witches in the world. And this? This is a coven representative of America. Not just one of women who look and think like *her*." Mother paused. "Imagine: a place for all to belong—all races, all genders. You see, baby, under my wings, we build each other up. We thrive. I don't consider myself to be their boss, per se. I get my hands dirty just as much as they do. That is what makes a *leader*. That is why this is a round table. There is no head to sit at. Sure, I am the face of us, their parent. Sure, I hop to a fabulous party or dinner, or a fabulous destination now and again. I have properties in Nairobi, in Paris, in Beijing—where I found Míjiàn."

Clark turned to his right—Míjiàn only stared back.

"For all my children, I share my abundance, my gifts, and my clients too. Imagine, you under my tutelage. You would rise to your full witch's potential, to be one of the greats." Her eyes narrowed. "What is she teaching you now? How to abuse your assistants? *Hmph!*"

At this, Clark almost laughed. He bit his lip and grinned. How did she know?

"You deserve better, baby. You deserve respect. Appreciation. And power, baby. Power. All of this could be yours," Mother told him with her arms wide to encompass the room. "A place to belong, a community to land on, and . . . the mother in me you never had."

At this, Clark's eye twitched.

"What's the price?" Clark asked. He thought, *There is always a price . . .*

A slow, sly smile crept onto her face. "Straight to business. Clever man," she purred. Her wild eyes were alight with fervor and fire. She drew a long, measured breath, then spoke slowly, deliberately: "There is no price. Just destiny. I want you to take Charisma and her coven down . . ." Mother purred, "from the inside out."

Hanging in the air, a pause. Even the city's noise outside the windows seemed to hush. The growing wind, howling past the windows, was the only sound in the museum-quiet penthouse.

Clark blinked, stunned by the magnitude of what she was proposing. "But . . . how? How do you figure I do that?" He raised a brow, attempting to mask his unease. "I'm just a . . . um, well. I haven't even had my first client yet."

"Wait a minute," Mother said. "I thought you were the new assistant?"

"I am!" Clark admitted reluctantly.

"Well then?"

He hesitated. "But I don't even know how to work with clients yet." He watched her carefully to see how she'd react.

Mother let out an indulgent chuckle.

"Don't you worry about that, baby! That will come. Oh baby, that will come sooner than you think. Let me teach you. *I will be your guide.* And just think about it: with Charisma gone, you'll be working with me and mine—the artists, the entertainers, the tastemakers and culture creators. The greatest minds of our time." Her voice swelled with passion as she said, "With her out of the way, I can regain my foothold and take back this city. With you under my wings, I will lead us to impossible heights: a golden age, greater than we witches have ever known or could ever imagine. First New York, then the world."

Clark downed the last of his water. Her words echoed in his ears as he looked past her, out toward the cityscape. Charisma's tower reigned over the trees of the park—a dark crown above the city.

"What's the matter?" Mother tilted her head, her eyes boring into his. The familiar prickle stirred on Clark's forehead. "Not so convinced yet?"

Clark hesitated, choosing her words carefully again. "Why don't you do it?" he asked.

Mother's lips curled as she looked down and away. "We all have our place, baby," she said. "As for this witch, trust me: if I could, I would. Others have tried—and failed. There are protections—no, traps—magic and mundane: her team; her security; and her netherworldly bastions on guard, dispensing of even the most casual voyeur, let alone her sworn enemies . . ."

Clark stiffened as the memory came flooding back: the flapping of wings, the death roar somewhere between a lion and a bomb. He was instantly aware of the way his button-down grazed the long, faded scar down his back.

"Her fortress is . . . formidable. But you, you've already infiltrated her ranks. She will never suspect you, our little Trojan Horse."

Clark gave her a dubious half smile.

"Oh, baby," Mother said. "You have no idea how perfectly you fit the role. Don't you want to take her down?" She leaned in. "What are you gaining by being there, huh? Insult? Insanity? You wanna stay invisible? Live under her shadow forever? Let your potential rot . . . or worse?"

Her voice turned sharper.

"You gonna sit around and wait for *the copper-haired one* to decide your fate? You wanna end up unalived, another pawn in her game?"

Her words slithered into his mind, stirring fears he dared not acknowledge.

"Don't you want to take your fate into your own hands? Live life on your own terms? Get out from under her heel and take life by the you-know-what? What's your end goal then, anyway? Hmm? Why are you even there?"

"My end goal . . . ?" Clark began, twiddling his thumbs and searching for the words. Lorena's gray-green eyes flashed across his mind: *"Tell me,"* she had said to him last September, *"what is a boy—a man—like you hoping to gain by being here, in a place such as this?"*

Clark gulped.

"Well," he answered, "I dunno, it's the 'job every girl would kill for.'"

"But," Mother said leaning in closer and closer, "that is what other people want. What is it that *you* want—without all that noise?"

Her honey-colored eyes seemed to peel him back layer by layer. Clark felt a strange heaviness settle over him, as though the air itself pressed in, whispering questions he was lost on the answers to. The shadow of a September dream flickered past, dark and odd: there was a hum in the air, from unseen whispers of cloaked onlookers. From the shadows into the spotlight, the dark gold-brown eyes of an older Clark, his Ideal Self, stepped forward. That version of him, in his suit and his success, stared back at him with disdain for the long journey of becoming that lay ahead.

"I'm not sure," Clark answered with a wince, "but I know who I want to be at the end of it."

Unblinkingly, Mother stared into him. For a moment, he was trapped, mesmerized by her beauty and the magnetism of her presence. She bore into him deeper still, her voice carrying a weight that felt heavier than the words themselves, as she asked, "And who is he to you, the man at the end of this?"

A fierce prickle crept across Clark's forehead, unrelenting and intense. "Um, well . . ." The words seemed to come despite himself: "He's successful. Well-dressed. Well-respected. He has friends. Family. A partner. A community. He's . . . loaded. And handsome . . ." Clark blushed from hearing the words spoken aloud, surprised to give name to his most private thoughts and startled by the sound of his own longing.

"I see . . ." she said, slinking around him and wearing the most guileful of smiles. "The assistant wants to be the leading man of his own life."

Her intensity was unnerving. Her words snaked around him, teasing him bite by bite. Was Mother mocking him? Praising him? He couldn't tell.

"There's something else I want . . ." he said carefully.

"Oh?" Her eyebrows arched in intrigue.

"I want to help people," Clark said.

Delight broke across Mother's face. She gave a little laugh, and said, "You so will, baby!"

"No, well, I mean more than that." The words tumbled out in a rush. "I want to help *a person*. See," Clark said, "there's someone in Charisma's hold, someone I want to free. I'm not even sure I can talk about her."

Mother's expression didn't waver. "You mean Felicity?"

Clark's eyes darted around him, then back to hers. "Yeah, how'd you know?"

"Everybody knows," Mother said, shaking her head. The others sighed and nodded with her. "Do you realize the power of worship? Millions of people thinking your name, hanging on to your every word, your every move, wishing for you, dreaming of you . . . That girl is beloved by millions upon millions around the world. A goddess of beauty incarnate. Imagine for a second what her death—a light snuffed out by the hands of a witch like *her*—could do. The void left in its place to be filled by a witch's will is, well . . . It's a powerful sacrifice."

A pang stretched across Clark's stomach, that he could have had any hand in Felicity's ordeal.

"What's happened to her is, well," she continued, "let's just say it's one of the most evil things I've ever seen done to another woman. Stripped of her agency, her dignity, her power—all for profit and control. It's monstrous."

His shoulders sagged. The weight of the room came crashing all over him. Clark knew, more than ever, that he had to do something. "She's going to die when they film the last scene. I'm not sure how long they'll hold her for, but they're set to finish filming any day now. I want to help her. How can I help her?"

"Join me," Mother said, eyes gleaming, "and take Charisma down."

"If I do . . ." Clark said, his voice wavering. He looked away, shifting in his seat. "Well, I don't want to end up like the last assistant."

"You're already here, aren't you? Surely you've already chosen to risk it all by coming."

Clark opened his mouth, then closed it again.

"Besides," Mother said, "one should be so lucky to die for as noble a cause. To take down the most heartless, most pitiless witch the world has ever seen? A legacy worth everything," Mother said darkly. "But that won't be your journey. No, not while I'm protecting you. And when all is said and done, when we've brought Charisma to her knees, you'll have a place here with me. A home. A family."

Clark swallowed hard, her words pulling him deeper into their gravity. Could he really trust her? Could he risk everything for a chance to save Felicity—and maybe himself?

"Baby, don't you overthink it. Cut out all that doubt, all that negative self-talk. It dulls your shine and weakens your magic. With me to guide you, it will be *easy*. I will help you every step of the way. First, you will become invaluable. Make them need you, not the other way around. Be the best witch's assistant she's ever had by being the best *you* you ever were. Then, prey on their weaknesses. Appeal to their egos. Capitalize on their desires . . . I know you've done it before."

Clark furrowed his brows. "What do you mean?"

"Don't play coy," she teased. "Mother knows all. How did you manage to get rid of her? The last assistant. Silvestri."

Clark's clenched and his mouth went dry. He looked to the others, studying and still. "I-I dunno what you're talking about," he stammered. "I-I didn't get rid of . . . anyone."

But it was over as soon as it started. The thought had already taken hold, unbidden: Melissa, gone up in flames. His pulse quickened as he tried to shake it away, but the panic in his eyes betrayed him. Clark's forehead prickled so hard, he reached up to scratch it.

Mother leaned back. "Ah," she purred, her smile curling like smoke and her teeth flashing from across the table. "There it is."

Clark sat straighter. The room felt too still. The air too thick. But Clark found his voice again, steady, and edged now with something darker. "How? How would we do it?" His voice was steady but tinged with curiosity—and something darker.

Mother's expression turned sly, her fingers tapping lightly on the table. "First, her husband is on his way down. When he goes, so will her privilege, resources, networks, status, and connections. Slowly, we will open holes in her reputation, and stand aside as she hangs herself on public opinion. All the while . . ." She smiled menacingly. "We'll pluck her hive. Petal. By. Petal . . ."

She eyed him curiously. "You've heard it before, haven't you? Her tree. It's spoken to you."

For a moment, Clark's jaw slackened, but no words came. Quickly, he regained himself and said, "Yeah, it has, I think . . . Has it . . . with you?"

Mother's smirk deepened. "Let's just say a little birdie told me . . ." Her attitude was as coy as her grin. "I believe her ancient spirit is bound to that tree, and that the tree is stowed away somewhere safe, in a dimension attached to that terrarium. Without the tree, she can no longer reincarnate into this timeline. It's an unnatural thing, just like her. Removing it—and her—will restore balance to the world, for the highest good of all. You want to be on the right side of history, don't you, Clark?"

Clark blinked back. "Of course."

"Good." She leaned in closer, her honey eyes glinting with quiet, buzzing intensity. "That's when we take her out, once and for good."

A chill ran down Clark's back. The image of Charisma's ironclad tower struck by lightning flashed across his eyes. From a window, a body fell. Clark blinked. Mother noticed.

"That's right, baby," she purred. "Envision it. She will be so busy putting out fires she won't even realize what's happening to her, right under her nose. And when the moment is right, when her guard is down . . ." Mother's smile widened, more menacing yet. "We'll strike."

Clark's eyes widened.

"You don't have to be worried," she added smoothly, leaning back in her seat. "Leave that part up to me." Her certainty sent a chill skittering down his spine.

Clark raised an eyebrow. "Trophy husband, body incarnate, and army of skanks. Got it." *Like* that's *going to be easy* . . . Clark thought. A prickle darted across his forehead.

"Baby," Mother said, her voice smooth as honey, her gaze cutting straight through him. "It *will* be easy. I will guide you. But," she said with promise on her lips, "your new life is going to cost you." There was a wildness to that smile he so recognized as she declared, "To be the man you dream of becoming, you must sacrifice your old life for the new. One life for another. *A new life for a new life.* Do you understand what I am saying? Can you accept that?"

"I think so," said Clark. What other options did he have? "Okay."

From across the table, Mother stood and extended her hand. He rose, placed his hand in hers—and she pulled him in.

"Do we have a deal?" In the depths of her eyes, Clark saw a flicker of something: a storm gathering on the horizon, vast and inevitable.

"Yes," said Clark.

"Okay." Her honey-amber eyes twinkled. "Then it's done." The room was breathless. Without breaking eye contact, Mother turned her head slightly and commanded, "*Scram.* Clear out."

The assistants flinched. Clark watched carefully as they grabbed their coats off the backs of their chairs or off hooks at the door, filing out with their heads low. Not a word was spoken, only the sounds of the shuffle of footsteps, the whistling wind, and the soft click of the door behind them. The silence was electric. It was just him left with her.

"Class begins now," Mother declared. Her eyes seemed to look straight through Clark as she said, "You ever get the feeling like you're being watched? Ever feel your forehead prickle—" she asked, pointing to the center of her forehead with a single, long fingernail, "there?"

"Yeah, now that you mention it," he admitted. "All the time."

"Everything is permeable," said Mother, "even minds. That's your third eye being activated. A discerning witch can always feel the touch of another prying mind. If you're gonna be the great witch I know you to be—the one you already are—you need to learn how to protect yourself."

Clark nodded and gave a short, pained smile.

"Do you know what an aura is?"

"I think so," said Clark.

"We humans are beings of starlight, and you, sweet thing, are a *star.*"

"I am?"

"*Yes*. You're more than just flesh and bone. You're vibration. Pure energy. And that energy radiates from you in a halo of light called an aura. It's your signature. Your scent. Your shield and your sword. With it, we can emit frequencies that attract your desires, alert you to danger, and even strike your prey."

Clark thoughts drifted to Charisma's aura that night in the Tower when Melissa died: black, electric, and crackling with rage. A sense of dread racked his brain, as if he'd never be safe again knowing power like that could exist. But then, another memory came to mind: the witches in their circle just before, how their voices rose together, filling the room with a crescendo of light so radiant it felt like the universe had awoken to their will. That same consciousness had awakened something dormant within, and his halo-like aura, periwinkle and indigo, had mingled and danced with theirs under the Blood Moon. With clarity, he could recall an unshakable sense of safety that it had filled him with, a certainty of belonging to an eternal consciousness far greater than himself.

"They are also our best psychic defense," she continued, "shielding us from unwelcome minds, unwelcome magic, quieting the world around us—or sometimes rendering us temporarily imperceivable."

"Oh!" Clark said. "I think I can do some of those things! Sometimes when I'm stressed, I can turn the world to mute."

"Ex-actly! We are going to put you in the driver's seat of your destiny. You are going to create an aura so strong that no thoughts can escape and none can enter without your consent."

"Cool!" Clark blurted out.

"Come." She led them to the living room, a grand white-and-gold space filled with handcrafted pottery and a fireplace as fervent as Clark's piqued curiosity. The decor reminded him of Charisma's temple-like air mansion, though this room somehow felt less lofty and more . . . down to earth.

"The heartspace—the seat of the soul—emits frequencies more powerful than the mind ever could. It stars here," she said, touching her chest. "But it shines like a halo here." She touched the crown of her head, long fingernails on glossy hair. "A torus field that extends all around you." She squinted. "Can you see mine?"

Clark took a step back and eyed her carefully, scanning her perimeter. He squinted, even held his breath for a moment, but eventually shook his head.

"For magic to be real, first you have to believe it's real—*fully*. You are not your mind; you are not your thoughts. You are your soul, a big, bright soul, and your soul can see clearly what the mind refuses to. This is your Second Sight. Use it. Believe with unshakeable certainty that the Sight is already yours. That you were born to see beyond the veil of reality."

Clark furrowed his brows. His shoulders stiffened under the weight of her words. Mother burst out, "Suspend your disbelief, baby!" Her words had so much gusto that Clark practically flinched.

Suspend my disbelief . . . ? thought Clark. "Unshakeable certainty," Clark said, scratching his head. "Got it."

"Oh my god, you are too funny!" Mother chuckled. Her teeth were so perfectly white and straight, he felt a pang of jealousy. "Don't be so sarcastic. Surrender. Let go and *trust*!" Her voice softened to a maternal cadence as she said, "Your life up 'til now has been one big waking miracle. Why not let this moment be one too?"

"Um, okay," Clark said dryly. "I'll try." Clark sighed, a big, weary exhale. He let his eyes drift.

"Dial in, baby!" Her voice rang with a conviction so fierce it felt like the room trembled. "Live in the faith, not the believing—the knowing—that this is real. Magic is real. What do you see?"

There against the white of Mother's living room wall, something twinkled. The space between his eyebrows and along his crown had come online, prickling as if statically charged. For a moment it came into vision: Mother's aura glowed, a torus field of sage green at her crown cascading into teal shoulders and down.

"Oo! I think I see it!" Clark shouted.

"Good, baby!" Mother exclaimed. "Vulnerability becomes you. Now, close your eyes." Clark glanced at her in protest.

"Trust me." Step by high-heeled step, Mother circled him like a predator stalking its prey: "I want you to envision your happiest memory. The happiest you've ever been. Picture it in your mind's eye. Really see it. What are you wearing? What are you smelling, tasting, touching? Feel the *gratitude* for this moment. Let the joy of that gratitude fill up every corner of your being. What's the first thing that comes to mind? Think of this and only this."

Clark scrounged up his face.

"Don't think too hard now, my goodness!" she said with a tinkling laugh, amused at his struggle. Clark erupted in a small sweat. "Don't think, just . . . be. Be the memory, be the feeling."

With one eye cracked open, he asked, "I don't need a . . . a sacrifice?"

"A sacrifice?" She stopped, placing one hand on her hips. "For what?"

"For this."

"Not for this, baby. This one is built in. Innate." Her sly eyes narrowed on him. "Now, *close your eyes.* Just think of your most joyful memory and live in the gratitude of that moment. Quick, what's the first thing that comes to mind?"

Gratitude . . . he echoed internally. *The first thing to come to mind . . . ?* It wasn't far in the past, and it certainly wasn't about work: Clark's Coney Island date with Joey fell into his mind like a red November leaf. One unseasonably warm evening, Joey had picked him up after work to drive them downtown. It had been dark out early. Was it Daylight Saving Time? Clark recalled how happy he was just to be off work and on a date, to take his mind off things . . .

Clark could remember the nip in the air seeping through his jacket, brisk but not unwelcome . . . The savory taste of the chili over hotdogs, the sweetness of powdered sugar from a shared funnel cake, dusted on his lips . . . The pressure of Joey's hand, and the flutter of first love in his stomach . . . The night air whipping around their faces as they leaned in, the taste of anticipation on their tongues, the warmth of Joey's lips . . .

"Mmmm-mm! How *romantic*," said Mother on the seat across from them. Clark gasped. Mother laughed. There she was, winter-clad and materialized in his memory, her hands clasped under her chin and a ravenous glint in her eyes. "Don't let me interrupt, sweet thing, but do tell—where can I get me a fine-ass man to treat me like *this*?!"

Daydream Joey didn't seem to notice the intruder in Clark's mind, laughing to herself. Joey continued kissing Clark's neck, inhaling him deeply. Clark could feel himself blushing.

His voice cracked as he squealed, *"Mother!"*

"Stay with me, stay with me!" Daydream Mother said laughingly. "Okay, now, I want you to hold on to that joy and imagine it like sunshine, filling up your entire being. Let it shine out of you like the sun, from the top of your head out at about arm's length from your body."

Clark paid her a dubious look. Her knowing smile and the glint in her eyes gave him pause. He turned to Joey, held his head, and kissed him like he remembered, letting the memory take over.

Was he imagining it? From where the butterflies lived, a coiled energy began to emanate. He opened his eyes. It wasn't a torus field like Mother's, a bubble of cascading light all around her. No, Clark's was different—less a bubble and more so a modest halo around his head and shoulders, hanging maybe a few inches out all around. The air around his body seemed to shift, as though it too had come alive. And the Mother in his daydream flickered out of sight.

"Good, baby!" Mother in reality said.

But something else stirred beneath the joy, something that mixed and muddied the carnival colors of his memory. Clark remembered, too, that on the Ferris wheel, suspended so high above the world, with the city, the beach, and the treetops the color of waning fire, and the rest of their adulthoods laid out before them, Joey had looked into his eyes and told him, "I love you."

Daydream Clark was frozen into place, his heart soaring, and yet at the same time, left to wonder if it was all too soon. If he was enough.

A faint pop, like a lightbulb expired. His aura fizzled, dimming into a quiet dissolve. Mother stepped in front of him.

"Beware," she said. "Doubt and shame are powerful poisons. Either can kill your manifestations—or worse. They can weave unexpected and unavoidable consequences into any spell you cast."

Clark gulped.

"You don't want that, do you?"

"No," he said without hesitation.

"Didn't think so, honey. Let's try again."

Was that what I was really feeling, deep down all along? Doubt . . . ? Had the doubt of being with Joey kept him waiting for the other Ferris wheel cart to drop, with them tumbling down after it? Did he really feel mistrusting of their connection? Unworthy even? Why?

"Try a different memory."

Clark scrunched up his face. *Think, Clark, think . . . A happy memory . . . ?* A flickering candle just behind Mother caught his eye as he closed them, and, in his mind's eye, he saw himself blowing out his birthday candles at Northlight, Charisma's restaurant, this past October . . . The glittering of lights and cobwebs, city and stars, came back to him easily, vividly . . . He could feel the soft drape of his favorite baby-blue button-down, the shirt he'd worn that same day, its fabric light on his skin . . . The taste of his herb-roasted chicken under knife and fork on ceramic plate . . . How he salivated at the taste of his slice of Bruce Bogtrotter cake . . . The tart edge of the midnight margarita Joey had made him, periwinkle with a "spicy rim—salty and sweet"—"just how you like it," Joey might as well have said to the table . . .

From where the butterflies lived, a heat rose again, lifting him with it. Clark blushed into a radiant light, his aura flickering back to life—this time, a little brighter.

"You gonna finish that?'" It was Mother again, sitting across the table in his memory, wearing a glittering top, shadowy eyes, and her waist-length hair up in a high ponytail.

Clark slid his slice of cake to her.

"Rich," Mother said with a forkful of chocolate cake in her mouth. "That's the ticket. That's it, baby. That joy, love, and gratitude is the center from which your aura radiates. Stay there. Live in it, baby! Hold it for as long as you can—and don't mind me, I'll be right here!"

But the memory shifted. At the thought of the table, the large booth, the empty seats, the echoes of his friends' text messages came to dine, apologizing for not making it that night. The strained conversation about work, the forced cheer behind Joey's voice, Patricia's daughter, Nancy, and her husband, Paul, so empty and far away . . .

The warmth receded. His aura tinkered out, dimmed to a flicker and faded, gone as quickly as it had come, and leaving in its place a hollow chill in the air. Mother slid the clean plate to the center of the table.

"Hmmm," she said in reality, pulling up next to him. "Try again, baby."

Clark sighed. *How am I going to do this . . . ? Think . . . A happy memory, my happiest . . .*

He searched . . . And searched . . . So many had felt tainted now, soured by what had come.

There must be one . . .

He worked his way backward. Through the chaos, through the dark . . . And then—*Of course* . . . It was there all along. Labor Day Weekend. The playground in Long Island. His first date with Joey, just before diving into his junior assistant duties at Charisma's. He wore a graphic superhero tee and shorts, an unbuttoned henley, his hair slicked back, and just the right amount of chest hair peeking out from beneath his collarbone . . . There was the vivid green lawn and lush trees waving in the summer sun . . . The fresh, non-city air, the smell of Joey's cologne, and the dry cough of Clark's first puff of weed . . . He could still feel the grass on his skin as they sprawled under the wide summer sky, could see the fireflies come out as evening approached, could recall the feel of their first kiss that tasted of forever . . . A spontaneous, honest, electric outing.

"Young love," Mother said in his memory, perched on the swing set a few feet away. "So precious! So innocent!" This time she was in sneakers and jean shorts. She wiped her eye from beneath her baseball hat and sunglasses.

From the pit of his stomach where the butterflies lived, the warmth inside him coiled skywards, blossoming from his crown in a radiant crescendo of periwinkle and indigo blue. Finally, the light swirled around him, alive, vibrant, and uncontainable.

"Yes, baby! Look at you!" Mother said jubilantly. Her image vanished from his memory with a soft *pop* as Clark opened his eyes. In reality, she clapped her hands in delight and gave a hop up and down.

But there was something else in how the memory lingered. The sweet simplicity of the day soured as another thought crept in: how quickly childhood had come to a crashing end in Melissa burning up in hellfire, her screams giving way to stone gargoyles turned to a race to the flesh-eating death, to falling into the hands of a queen witch at midnight and the promotion he asked for that felt like selling his soul.

That first date was the last taste that he could remember of freedom.

His aura sputtered to a flickering gasp before extinguishing entirely, like a nova collapsing into silence. Clark exhaled in dismay, his shoulders sagging with it, leaving him wondering if it sucked a little happiness out of the room, too.

"That's okay, baby," Mother said with a step forward. "But my, my, my, what a pretty aura you have. Blue and indigo?" That prickle in his forehead appeared again, which he tried to ignore—Mother's inquisitive mind reading his own. "Your favorite color, like the bugleweed at Astoria Park—"

"—or the color of the sky at twilight, yeah," Clark finished.

Mother stood in front of him as she explained, "Magic is real because you are the universe made alive and whole. The power of thought, of awareness, of intention: it exists in you, because you are made of it. You are Source. You *are* magic. Anything you want, you can have. Never limit yourself," Mother said. She held him by the shoulders. "What is the level your *soul* is calling you up to? Listen to it. Live in it. Think bigger. Think limitless. Do you meditate?"

Clark parroted, "Do I . . . meditate?"

"Yes."

"Not really," he admitted.

"Meditate," she said simply, the word thick with promise. "You'll find that the source you draw from is already you, inside all of that runaway mind in that cute little head of yours," she said with a pop of her finger on his nose, "waiting to be remembered. Start meditating. Remember who you are, and in the meantime"—she said this with a nudge—"go get your money."

Clark managed a half smile back.

"Come here," she said, her voice low and steady.

Clark let her hands guide him to the corner of the room. "Face the mirror," she instructed, positioning herself behind him. She was as tall as Clark, but with a personality as big as hers, she seemed to loom well over his left shoulder. Her honey-brown eyes locked into his reflection, the cityscape in the windows sprawling out behind them.

"You know what one of my best friends and clients—the mother of drag queens—always says?"

Clark shook his head. "No. What?"

She smoothed the shoulders of his baby-blue button-down, her touch firm but deliberate, and gave them an approving squeeze. "If you like money," Mother said with a knowing grin, "wear a suit."

Clark scanned his reflection in that full-length mirror, olive on baby blue, just like he had a month before with Charisma standing behind him, her eyes assessing him like a project in progress. His eyes flickered up to meet Mother's with startling intensity. Mother, who saw him for everything he was and everything he could be. A flicker of recognition pranced across his eyes—his dreams last fall of meeting his Ideal Self, slick, sharp, and dashing . . . Wasn't his Ideal Self wearing a black suit in that dream?

"Hm . . ." he said, tilting his head slightly. "Thank you for . . . everything," he added, turning to look at her.

"Of course, baby," she warmly replied. The smile she offered was equal parts kind and calculating, an enigmatic blend of warmth and calculation. Something seemed so familiar about her . . ."Keep our little arrangement just between us, mm? And if you need anything, I'm just a text or phone call away."

Clark made his way to the door. His thoughts were swirling as he reached for the door handle when Mother's voice sounded from behind him again.

"Oh, and Clark?"

He paused mid-step and turned.

Mother's honey eyes shimmered with something Clark couldn't quite place. "Don't let a witch get you down."

A quick half smile tugged at his lips. Without another word, he nodded and stepped out onto the landing, shutting the door behind him with a click.

CHAPTER IV

House Call

Clark spent the rest of the week practicing what Mother had taught him.

Every evening after work, Clark would come home, drop his bag at the door, and meditate first thing. He would watch himself from the foot of his bed through the reflection of his TV screen until his focus blurred, his racing thoughts eased, his sense of self dissolved, and the air of his silhouette would flicker blue. Every evening, it was if the walls themselves leaned in, like the universe was watching him create. Eventually, exhaustion would pull him under, and leave him sprawled on the bed with the lights still on.

That's how Joey found him one night after his shift. Crawling into bed with him, he had gently kissed Clark's cheeks awake. "Hey, Sleeping Beauty," Joey had said. "Everything okay?"

"Just tired from work is all," Clark had replied. "Are you the handsome prince to wake me from my slumber with true love's kiss?"

"'Tis I," Joey had said, slipping under the blanket with him.

By the third day, Clark had achieved a torus field-aura of growing proportions, not just inches from his body, but almost a foot and counting. The color was so vivid, he could almost see it with his eyes closed. It didn't just hover in the air around him either. No: if he concentrated, he could make his aura pulsate and swirl like a living entity, resonating with a frequency that could even, on occasion, temporarily turn the world down to mute, as he was so apt to do.

Life that gray January had become lighter, more bright. Others took notice, even if, he reasoned, they couldn't see his aura. Strangers smiled at him on the subway. Tourists stopped to ask him for directions. Babies stared with wide, curious eyes, and passerby dogs wagged their tails as Clark would conjure up his dancing lights to their delight, perfunctory and joyous. Good fortune seemed to follow him, like the train arriving as he stepped onto the platform, and crosswalk signals lighting up at his approach as if the universe conspired in his favor.

Clark could see not just his own aura, but other peoples' too. Enraged reds of impatient commuters, pensive greens of calm café-dwellersIt was like seeing the world with new eyes—or seeing a new world altogether. Everything was charged with meaning and motion, pulsing just beneath the surface of the everyday.

A deep, innate knowing had settled in his chest: something major was about to happen for him. What could he be attracting into his life?

I'm gonna have it all . . . Clark thought. The idea was as certain to him as breathing.

Clark was a periwinkle orb gliding down the rainbow streets of a shimmering Manhattan, untouchable, uncontainable. It was beautiful. He never wanted it to stop.

By Friday morning, the coven had returned.

Lorena called him to her office first thing. She took a deep breath at the sight of him, fresh and relaxed, standing before her. Her empty green eyes gleamed like daggers beneath a haze of smoked shadow and vodka.

"Two things," she began. "First, we are going to set up your paperwork so that you can be on the payroll."

"Okay!" Clark said. His face broke into a smile. The day had finally arrived.

"And two . . . you are going on your first house call."

Clark blurted out, "I am?!" his voice practically rising an octave. "Cool!"

"Yes," Lorena said. "Fresh off a visit to Felicity's as her right-hand witch. Just don't tell this client that you're new."

"Oh my god! This is great! Thank you!" Clark exclaimed. "When is it? I'll start preparing now!" He was beaming so big he could practically hug her.

Lorena flatly replied, with a smug leer, the word, "Today." She smirked as she watched the smile come crashing down off Clark's face.

"*Today?* But—"

"Yes, *today.* Later, after work. You'll leave by 4. *Sharp.*"

Suddenly the air seemed to leave the room, and a minor panic set in. His first house call, at the end of the day? *But there's no time to prepare . . . !*

Lorena snipped, "Relax. You're the *great new assistant*, are you not? This one's not a regular client per se. She makes a living as a comedienne specializing in celebrity gossip . . . most celebrities being—rather annoyingly—Charisma's clients. Wouldn't want to get too close! Charisma never goes herself, of course, and the girls are reluctant to see her. A tarot reading here and there, a cleansing now and again . . . It seems she's in some sort of a *pickle* and wants some assistance or something or other, I dunno. The invoices fulfill and she pays her dues, so we have no reason to toss her out . . . for now." Lorena crinkled her nose as she said, "Plainly, the coven, including myself, finds her to be quite tacky. So, perfect for you!"

"I'll go!" Clark said.

"Of course you'll go," Lorena replied. She chuckled to herself when she said, "You have no say in the matter. But before you do, I need you to sign this Assistant NDA. I also have some . . . questions for you, to complete our . . . let's say our 'marketing.'"

Clark took the paperwork she handed him and began to flip through. The first set were bank wiring forms, which he could return to Morty the following day. As for the NDA, it appeared identical to how he remembered the original he signed last year except for some additional clauses:

Charisma Saintly Consulting Inc.
Charisma Saintly Inc.
Charisma Saintly Beauty Inc.

Non-Disclosure Agreement

This Non-Disclosure Agreement ("Agreement") is entered into as of [Date], by and between Charisma Saintly Consulting Inc., on behalf of itself and its affiliated entities Charisma Saintly Inc. and Charisma Saintly Beauty Inc. (collectively, the "Disclosing Party"), and [Receiving Party's Full Legal Name], in their capacity as Assistant Witch (the "Receiving Party," and together with the Disclosing Party, the "Parties").

1. Definition of Confidential Information
For purposes of this Agreement, "Confidential Information" includes all information or material that has or could have commercial value or other utility in the business in which Disclosing Party is engaged. Confidential Information includes, but is not limited to, spells, potions, rituals, strategic plans, personal affairs, proprietary knowledge, practices, documents, notes, recordings, and any other information disclosed to the Receiving Party by the Disclosing Party, either directly or indirectly, in writing, orally, or by inspection of tangible objects.

2. Obligations of Non-Disclosure and Non-Use
Receiving Party agrees to:

- Not disclose any Confidential Information to any third party without the prior written consent of Disclosing Party.
- Not use any Confidential Information for any purpose except to carry out their duties as an assistant to the Queen Witch.
- Take all necessary measures to protect the secrecy of and avoid disclosure or use of Confidential Information in order to prevent it from falling into the public domain or the possession of persons other than those persons authorized under this Agreement to have any such information.

3. Duration of Confidentiality

The obligations of Receiving Party herein shall continue for a period of one year from the date of disclosure of the Confidential Information, or until such time as the Confidential Information no longer qualifies as a trade secret or confidential information under applicable law, whichever occurs first.

4. Permitted Disclosures

- The obligations set forth in Section 2 shall not apply to Confidential Information that:
- Is now or subsequently becomes generally available to the public through no fault of the Receiving Party.
- Was rightfully in the possession of the Receiving Party before receipt from the Disclosing Party.
- Is independently developed by the Receiving Party without use of or reference to the Disclosing Party's Confidential Information.
- Is required to be disclosed by law, provided that the Receiving Party gives the Disclosing Party prompt written notice of such requirement prior to such disclosure and assists in obtaining an order protecting the information from public disclosure.

5. Return of Materials

Upon termination of this Agreement, or upon request by the Disclosing Party, the Receiving Party shall promptly return or destroy all documents and other tangible materials representing the Confidential Information and all copies thereof.

6. Non-Compete Clause

The Receiving Party agrees not to engage in any business or activity, including but not limited to establishing rival covens, collaborating with rival witches, or performing unauthorized spellwork for clients belonging to the Disclosing Party for a period of one year following the termination of their role as an assistant, unless with expressed consent—written, spoken, or otherwise—from Disclosing Party.

7. Non-Solicitation Clause

The Receiving Party agrees not to solicit or hire any other staff or followers of the Disclosing Party for their purposes or for other competing entities for a period of one year following the termination of their role as an assistant.

8. Intellectual Property Rights

The Receiving Party agrees that any and all intellectual property created, conceived, or developed during their tenure, including but not limited to magical creations developed such as spells, potions, rituals, incantations, enchantments, charms, or other forms of spell-work (herein collectively referred to as "the Work") shall be the exclusive property of the Disclosing Party.

The Receiving Party hereby irrevocably assigns any and all rights, titles, and interests in and to the Work, including any derivative works, to the Disclosing Party.

9. Consequences of Breach

The Receiving Party acknowledges that any breach or violation of this Agreement may cause irreparable harm to the Disclosing Party. In the event of a breach, the Disclosing Party shall be entitled to seek injunctive monetary relief through the *American Witches Tribunal* in Salem, MA, in addition to any other remedies available at law or in equity.

10. Governing Law and Jurisdiction

This Agreement will be interpreted and construed in accordance with the laws of the *American Witches Tribunal* in Salem, MA, without regard to its conflict of law principles. The parties consent to the exclusive jurisdiction of the *Tribunal* for any dispute arising out of this Agreement.

11. Entire Agreement

This Agreement constitutes the entire agreement between the parties with respect to the subject matter hereof and supersedes all prior or contemporaneous understandings, agreements, representations, and warranties, both written and oral, with respect to such subject matter.

IN WITNESS WHEREOF, the parties hereto have executed this Non-Disclosure Agreement as of the Effective Date written above. The Receiving Party irrevocably agrees to the terms set forth herein.

Disclosing Party:
Charisma Saintly Consulting Inc.
on behalf of itself and its affiliates, Charisma Saintly Inc. and Charisma Saintly Beauty Inc.

By: ____________________
Name: Lorena Henceley-Saintly
Title: Manager & Authorized Representative

Receiving Party:
By: ____________________
Name: [Receiving Party's Full Legal Name]
Title: Assistant Witch

At the end of the last page, pen poised, Clark hesitated: "It says to sign my legal name?"

"Yes," Lorena interjected with a cutting quickness, "your *real* name. Exactly as it was given to you by your parents, not the name you lied to us about."

Lorena leaned forward, her eyes narrowing as she said, "I'm sure you needn't be reminded that the only reason you landed an interview here was because Monica thought you were Ryan, *a woman*."

Clark chewed the inside of his cheek to keep from snickering. It was true: his email signature did sign him off as *R. C. Crane*, and in using his first name, Patricia had conveniently omitted any mention of his gender when making the referral.

Clark said to himself, *It's not my fault she assumed all candidates would be female . . .*

He could have sworn he felt a prickle—like a probing attempt to reach his mind—but this time, it didn't move past the barrier of his aura. Usually, the telltale tingle on his forehead gave it away. The best part about having his guard up was the certainty that Lorena wasn't eavesdropping on his thoughts. She gave him a side-eye.

Your given name as it appears on your government forms is the one that is binding," she snipped. *"Use it."*

Clark's pen hovered over the signature line. His hand betrayed the faintest tremble. He took a deep breath. Ink met paper, like a final nail in his coffin.

Lorena donned her reading glasses and, from above them, gave him a look as long as her nose. With a few clicks of her trackpad, she began:

"Did you graduate?" she implored, a mix of impatience and disinterest as she punctuated every syllable. "If so, from where?"

"I studied English at Hunter." Clark could feel the heat rise to his cheeks.

She lowered her readers and peered at him with a look that could make milk curdle. "I see . . ." Her fingers flew across the keyboard, the clatter of typing filling the room. Clark cleared his throat and shifted in his chair.

"Did you graduate with honors?"

"Um . . . no."

"Extracurriculars? Team sports?"

"No . . ."

"Tournaments? Social clubs?"

"No?"

"Other internships? Apprenticeships?" she pressed, her fingers poised over the keyboard, her expression tightening with each answer.

Clark took a deep breath. "No."

"Hmm." Lorena hurriedly typed away. The blood was pooling in his cheeks and ears.

"What languages do you speak?"

"Languages . . . ?" Clark repeated numbly, his mind scrambling for a better answer than what he knew was coming.

"Yes, languages," she repeated. "Take my sweet Alicia for example. Alicia has the Gift of Gab: she can learn any language." She ticked each off with a finger: "Alicia is fluent in French, Italian, Spanish, Portuguese, German, Russian, Arabic, Mandarin, Cantonese, and Japanese. She's even picked up some Hindi from her time in Mumbai. She picked up Swahili after a safari in Kenya. She can even speak to *some animals.*"

Clark sat very still.

"She is also an expert in Microsoft Suite, Google Suite, social media, Adobe Photoshop, and is proficient in Charisma's Big Three. Oh, and did I mention? She has *millions* of followers on her social media."

"Millions?" Clark echoed faintly, unsure if he was supposed to be impressed or absolutely terrified.

"Cor-rect," Lorena barked.

Clark lowered his chin, feeling the weight of her words dig in. "You mentioned . . . Charisma's Big Three?"

"Yes!" Lorena pulled off her readers with a deliberate snap. "Clienteling—the expertise in running a business, managing relationships, and understanding clients' needs before they do. Divination—tarot and astrology, the foundation of strategy. And finally, glamour—the art of image consultations and perception control. Without mastery of those three, you might as well not even call yourself a witch."

She straightened in her seat. "Or, how about our girl about town, Monica Chase-Whiteley. Monica is fluent in French, Spanish, Italian, and German. She's semi-fluent in Japanese and dabbling in Cantonese. She has the Gift of Vitalis. She works with life force—an energy vampire, so to speak . . . or just a bratty *twit.*"

A snicker escaped him.

"Let's not forget Emily Manitis, our Death Oracle. Emily is, of course, proficient in mediumship, divining death, and the Big Three. She studied Latin and speaks all its descendants: French, Spanish, Italian, Portuguese, Romanian, and of course Greek—all fluently."

"Melissa Silvestri, may she . . . rest in peace"—at this she cut a look at him through slitted eyes, making him almost choke on his saliva—". . . was fluent in Spanish, Italian, and surprisingly to us all, myself included . . . could drive stick."

"Oh, wow," Clark managed.

"Indeed," Lorena said flatly, donning her readers. "Now, what can you speak? Besides English and your apparent ability to, oh, I dunno, read a book to death." She snickered as she muttered, "English majors."

He sat in her chair wide-eyed. Clark straightened his posture—an attempt to regain his composure. "I, um . . . I was in Honors Spanish in high school and Spanish Honor Society in college so of course, I don't know Spanish, hahaha."

She blinked. "So you *don't* know how to speak the language?"

"Well," Clark said, "I can speak beginner's Spanish."

"So no, then." Her fingers typed away.

Lorena slid back from her desk and set her readers down once more. "Our clients expect the impossible, and the impossible is exactly. What. We. Deliver." Her tone grew colder as she said, "And you? Have you performed a spell? A ritual? Conjured the elements? Called down the moon? Stolen a secret? Summoned a spirit? Raised a demon? Do you have *any* idea of what you are doing? Hmm?! Besides running coffee orders and making your aura go *pretty colors*?"

Clark's eyes widened to the size of her marble ashtray.

"All magics you have not the faintest little inkling of how to do. You have no idea what you are playing at, boy. But I do."

Clark dared not utter a word; instead, he sat very, very still, as if any sudden movement might provoke her further. She lowered her gaze and bared her teeth in a growl when she said, "I was always suspicious about you, you know," she said in a hush, punctuating her every word. "I knew there was something to mistrust about you from the beginning. Your naive little *act*, your dangerous impulsivity, and now that aura that reeks of shadiness: you are a snake in our midst. I am onto you. *She* might not think anything of it, but believe me when I say, I do. To what end you are here, I will find out.

"THIS," she hissed, smacking her desk and startling Clark, "is not a game. The Art is witches' blood sport. To be a great witch takes craft. Cunning. *Charisma.* Until now, you've gotten by on sheer luck, grace, and that so-called *potential* of yours. You and I both know you are not qualified for this. That your Witch's Potential alone will not be enough. Do us all a favor and quit *now*—while you still can—and spare us from your mediocrity."

Mediocrity . . . Clark thought. *Is that what she thinks of me?* Every muscle in his body stiffened. All was motionless, save for the dust motes swirling in the cigarette smoke of her dark office. Lorena's face, dangerous and wild, softened into a wild smirk. She cleared her throat, smoothed her black dress, and said something else with a glint in her unblinking eyes: "No? Then it's time to show us what you're really made of."

For a moment, they locked eyes. Clark dared not back down and look away. He handed her the NDA in his lap. She snatched it without so much as a glance and popped it into a file in her cabinet.

"Complete this house call—*to excellence*—or don't even bother showing your face here again. Mess this up . . . *and you can kiss your life goodbye*," she said, her voice as cold as the air in the room. "You may go."

A knock sounded at her office door.

Loudly she barked, "Come in."

As Clark stood up, he watched as Lorena's lips curled into a sly smile. She said to Clark, "But before you do, meet the new juniors."

"Juniors" . . . ? Plural . . . ?! Clark turned.

In the pale sunlight of the sliding door appeared the silhouette of two girls. Into the dim office they stepped, their movement eerily synchronized: two pale, rail-thin, twin young women, dressed entirely in black. They couldn't have been much older than he was if they were even his age at all. Their sleek brunette hair bobbed in the wind, just past their narrow shoulders, as they strode toward Lorena.

"Darlings," she said in the most syrupy-sweet voice Clark had ever heard, embracing the twins with cheek kisses and hugs. The entire time, the twins kept their dark eyes on Clark with unnerving precision.

"Clark, this is Mandy and Milly Noble. They are the future of this coven."

Clark clasped his hands behind his back—and at Lorena's words, tightened his grip into fists.

"Girls," Lorena flatly continued with a languid wave of her hand, "this is Clark, the newest hire. He's shown a lot of . . . promise." At this, she curled her lips into a sneer, as if the words tasted sour.

"Hi," Clark said. He reached out to shake their hands, each as cold and lifeless as the last. Was that the semblance of a prickling on his forehead he could feel?

"How long have you been a junior?" Mandy asked, tilting her head in perfect synchrony with the other.

He replied, "I'm the new assistant."

"Ohhh," the two sang in unison. They turned to look at each other and broke out into a fit of giggles. Clark furrowed his brows.

"How long were you a junior?" Milly asked.

"About six months."

"Wasn't Monica hired without interning for anyone before?" Mandy remarked to Milly.

"Yeah, and I think everyone else on the coven."

"How old are you?" Mandy asked suddenly, her head tilted to the left.

Clark gave a terse look to Lorena, who was watching the exchange with wicked glee. His voice was tight as he answered, "Twenty-four."

Milly gasped. "You're so young!"

"Yeah, so young!"

"Yeah!"

"You must be really good," Mandy said. "It's the first Auntie Charisma's ever promoted someone."

"Aunt . . . Aunty Charisma?" Clark stammered. "She's your aunt?"

"Yeah!" Milly said cheerfully.

"Totally!" Mandy chimed, her grin identical to her sister's.

Clark thought to himself, *Nepotism hires . . .*

"Well, no, not by blood," Milly clarified.

"No, not blood," Mandy agreed. "We're more like . . . friends of the family. Really, really"—she punctuated her final word with a pat on his shoulder—"good friends. I think *we're* gonna be good friends, don't you, Clark?" Her voice dripped with honey, but the words felt far from friendly.

Milly added, "Really good friends." Their hollow, unblinking eyes locked onto his in perfect sync, and a chill crept down Clark's spine.

"Splendid," Lorena said. "Boy, why don't you introduce these two to the Closet? They can help you pack a kit. You'll find a spare luggage bag in the basement storage unit."

She tossed Clark a silver key. Clark caught it in mid-air. "I'm sure you will be well acquainted with where that is." A chuckle escaped the smile she wore, though it never reached those hollow eyes.

As the three left the office, Clark motioned for them to follow him one level down the utility stairs.

Milly's voice lifted with curiosity as she said, "We've never been this way."

"Or seen this room, for that matter," Mandy added as they passed through Hell's Entrance. It was a small, unremarkable room with a table and a window, the staff's coats and cubbies, and bins for incoming and outgoing mail.

Clark glanced over his shoulder. "You've . . . never been this way? This is where juniors come up."

"Oh, no," Milly said, shaking her head, "Aunty Charisma would never!"

"We'll stick to the front elevator, thanks!"

The three stepped into the freight elevator, and Clark immediately felt their eyes on him, their gaze heavy and invasive. He summoned the energy to keep his aura bright and steady.

"So," Clark began, "where are you both from?"

"The city."

"What part?"

The twins exchanged a glance, a silent exchange Clark couldn't read.

"The Upper East Side," Milly answered.

"Oh, cool," Clark said politely enough. "I'm from Astoria."

"Ew, you live in Queens?"

"That's so far."

"Yeah. Eek."

"It's right over the bridge," Clark said. "The train takes no time."

The twins froze for a moment, then exchanged another look before speaking in unison: "Wow."

"What?" Clark asked.

"Nothing."

"It's just that . . ."

"It's so brave."

"Yeah," Milly agreed. "So brave of you."

"What is . . . ?" Clark asked.

"To take the train," Mandy replied.

"It's not . . . Have you never . . . taken the train?"

"Oh, never."

"Yeah, never."

"Our parents would kill us."

"We wouldn't be caught dead."

They eyed him with their heads tilted like two curious birds in eerie unison. "Oooo-kay then . . ." Clark muttered. Their unmoving, porcelain faces, their unblinking eyes, left him so unsettled he was relieved to be walking ahead of them.

As they approached the storage unit, a knot in Clark's stomach tightened. Shelving obscured the tunnel in the wall from view. What bodies could be stashed in there now, unbeknownst to the world above, he wondered? He pulled a fresh black luggage bag off the shelf, the crinkle of its plastic wrapping breaking the silence and the hum of the replaced fluorescent above them. Its light cast a flickering, sickly pall over the twins, who stood and watched motionlessly.

Without words exchanged, they traveled up to the penthouse and into the private elevator, where Clark inevitably led the twins to Charisma's stockroom on the second floor.

Clark sang, "So this is the Closet," as if he were giving a house tour. He gestured broadly to the shelves and drawers that filled the space, but his eyes paused briefly on the terrarium staring back at him. "I'm the one who updated the system and reorganized everything. I'm actually a . . . little proud of myself."

The twins ignored him, slipping from shelf to shelf. Drawers were opened and closed without pause, the contents of each swiftly inspected.

"Oo, moldavite," Mandy said. "So rare." The two held up a small alien-green gemstone. Both were wide-eyed in turning it over.

"Careful," Clark said. "Some witches won't even *look* at that, let alone touch it. It's said to supercharge your spells, catapulting your life onto your highest timeline, but it'll burn everything down that isn't meant to come with you. Cute, right?"

The twins exchanged glances.

"Anyway," he added, clearing his throat, "I just track what comes in and out. It's all on a spreadsheet online." He held out his hand. Milly dropped the moldavite into his open palm without a word. Clark returned it to the cabinet, setting the stone inside with care. The drawer clicked gently as it slid shut.

"Umm," Clark interrupted, clearing his throat. "*My job* is to help the coven stock and monitor the comings and goings of everything in here. It's all on a spreadsheet online."

"How do you know what to stock the kits with?"

"Well, the girls usually give me a list of things they need. Otherwise, I track the assistants' restocks and set up auto-orders for their kit essentials based on predictive usage patterns. That way, replenishing their kits with their favorite things is easy."

"Smart," Mandy said, her lips curling into the faintest, most empty smile.

"Yeah! That will be *your job* soon enough," Clark said. They exchanged another unblinking glance. "Alright, let's get started."

With a flick of his phone, Clark duplicated a list and had the twins help him stock his kit. The shelves were pulled open with practiced ease. The scent of dried herbs filled the air. He knew instantly the basics in every kit, from having stocked and filled Monica's, Alicia's, Melissa's, and Emily's for so long: a satchel of tarot, bundles of salt and sage, tea leaves and crystals of every type he could manage. He knew the coven's favorites, the things that moved, the things that didn't. The twins followed silently, absorbing every word and item.

"These"—he pointed to the rows of tarot cards—"are Charisma's standard-issue backups. Everyone in the coven has their own deck preferences. Charisma likes a fresh deck every client, so the edges aren't dulled."

He moved to another compartment of vials, pulling a small vial of a glittering oil. "This," he said, holding it up, "is thieves blend. Cinnamon, clove, lemon, rosemary, and eucalyptus. Alicia swears by it. She leaves it for clients every job. You'll probably see it on every replenishment she requests.

"There's brass charms and talismans," Clark continued, opening a chest filled with heavy, polished symbols in various shapes. He plucked one out, an iron horseshoe, and handed it to Milly. "Good luck, apparently.

"Next up: crystals," Clark said, pulling out an acrylic tray filled with carefully categorized stones. "Amethyst for calming, rose quartz for love, citrine for abundance, obsidian for protection. These are essentials. Everyone's got their favorites. Usually they stay with the clients. Make sure these stay stocked, and keep an eye on the ones they replenish most often."

He handed Mandy a small cluster of clear quartz. "There are non-negotiables for every kit. Always start with these," he said, his voice taking on the authority of someone who had done this a hundred times.

Clark opened another cabinet, revealing a crate of candles—thick, tapering ones in every color, from black to white, and all in between. "Red for passion, white for cleansing, yellow for joy," he rattled off.

Alongside them sat candles of yellow tallow. He hesitated, catching sight of the label on one. "*Human* tallow," he said, shutting the lid on a group of candles and moving on. He muttered, "*Maybe not today* . . . Then, a little louder: "Some of these are pickled things you're better off not asking about," he nodded to a jar of what appeared to be pickled goat hearts, pale and tinged with green.

"The key," Clark finished, "is knowing the coven's favorites. What they burn through, what they never touch. Monica likes brand names, Alicia leans practical, Emily's all about the occult rarities, and Charisma demands perfection in every way." He paused, glancing at the moldavite the twins were still admiring. "And always keep a backup of everything. Every item here could make or break a spell. No mistakes."

"No mistakes," they echoed in unison, their voices perfectly synchronized.

Lorena called the twins to her office. The twins offered to take the keys to the storage unit and deliver them to Lorena, sparing Clark the need for another encounter with her, at least so soon. He dropped the keys in their hands without hesitation, grateful for the reprieve. The twins glided away like shadows, leaving Clark alone for the rest of the day. He exhaled, the tension in his chest loosening slightly. There was no sign of Emily or the others. Clark wondered if they were gone on business, or took the day off.

From the library, Clark grabbed a Gothic spellbook with an ornate leather cover embossed in silver runes. He figured it would cover every eventuality, though he couldn't shake the feeling that he'd need more than a kit full of witchcraft to handle what the evening had in store.

The hours ticked by until, at last, four o'clock arrived. Lorena had a car called.

"Do not embarrass us," she said as he closed the door to her smoky office.

Once he was on his way, Clark looked up the client. Leslie Parks was her name. His screen filled with a string of headlines and articles:

"Leslie Parks Cancelled for Hexing the President on Live TV." Clark raised an eyebrow, scrolling through the details.

"During a live televised comedy special, Leslie Parks performed what appeared to be a symbolic curse on the president. Widely viewed as a critique of the current administration's rollback of women's rights, her performance involved a poppet—an effigy made to resemble the target—which she stabbed, burned, and dismembered in increasingly graphic ways."

Clark clicked the video link. Onscreen, Leslie stood center stage, her silhouette engulfed in melodramatic lighting. She wore a gleaming Valkyrie costume, complete with an elaborate horned helmet and flowing cape. Opposite her on stage left was a poppet crudely adorned with a caricature of the president's face, his features exaggerated in colored marker, hung by its arm.

"Let's take men back to the Dark Ages with us, shall we?" she asked, laughing with bubbly innocence that starkly contrasted the spectacle.

Clark watched, his amusement growing, as she enacted every unspeakable thing upon the doll. Stabbing it, firing burning arrows at it, and eventually ripping it apart limb by limb.

"That feels kinda good!" she quipped. The audience responded with nervous chuckles, their discomfort palpable.

Clark couldn't help but laugh at the spectacle of it all. Was he in the wrong to admire her guts, to appreciate the sheer audacity of her performance?

The screen cut to a clip of the president, of course, publicly condemning Leslie. His face was flushed with indignation, lips pursed in a way that could only be described as petulant.

"This is terrible," he said, waving his small hands dismissively at his podium. "Absolutely terrible, folks. The worst. No one has ever seen hatred like this, believe me. It's disgusting, and it's coming from a failed comedian, a total nobody. Leslie Parks, if that's even her real name," he added with a scoff, "is a disgrace. And what she did? It's"—he shook his head—"it's un-American, okay? It's bad for the country, it's bad for the children, and it's bad for me personally!"

The article continued: "Within twenty-four hours, major sponsors severed contracts, and networks pulled Parks's content—spanning her career of over two decades—indefinitely. Parks's manager for most of this time, Joanne Feldman, reportedly dropped her as a client, citing 'irreconcilable professional differences.'

"Parks's career, for the foreseeable future, is over."

Clark winced at the accompanied comments below, where the vitriol was as over the top as the president's condemnation.

"How much hate can one woman have? Unbelievable!"

"She's gone too far this time! LOCK HER UP!"

"She's the one who should be burned!"

"This is why we need to bring back real America. Enough of this feminism nonsense! It's corrupting our children. No wonder this country is going downhill!"

"She's evil. Pure evil. Probably in league with Satan—just look at her eyes and how she laughs!"

Clark put down his phone with a sigh. The headline and comments churned in his thoughts. What could Leslie Parks, the infamous comedienne, possibly call on a witch to help her with? What kind of a fix would magic provide?

He peered out the window as the car crawled through the traffic of the Holland Tunnel, under the Hudson River, and out into New Jersey. It seemed that an accident ahead had caused significant delays. Traffic was at a standstill, horns blaring in frustration and brake lights casting an angry red glow over the road.

By the time the car pulled into Montclair, nearly twenty minutes late, Clark's nerves were frayed. His heart pounded as the car rolled up to a stately Victorian house perched on a quiet, tree-lined street. The house was grand, with a wraparound porch strung with fairy lights. He walked up to the door a frazzled, nervous wreck.

He thought, *My first house call . . . Here I go . . .* summoning the courage he didn't quite feel. What would become of him? His oversized coat felt suddenly too heavy, his backpack overstuffed, his luggage bag somehow *off* in his other hand. He rang the doorbell and fervently wiped his sweaty palms on his pants. The chill of the winter evening bit his skin as he stood waiting, feeling out of place. It took about five minutes to get his answer.

The door opened to a woman with long blonde hair in big, tousled waves over her shoulders, standing in a fuzzy pink baby doll robe and matching fuzzy heels. In one hand, she held a martini glass.

"Hhhhhiii," she said in a breathy voice. "I'm Leslie."

"Hi, I'm Clark."

Her hazel eyes gave him a slow, deliberate once-over, as he was so used to. She stepped back to let him inside. "Come in."

Clark loaded the kit first, then his backpack, before closing the door behind him. In the foyer, a tufted bench sat beneath a vintage burlesque poster, stacked high with unopened envelopes in angry script—some stamped "Return to Sender."

"Fan mail," Leslie said, tossing her martini back with a sigh.

The house was as eccentric as its owner, a mix of vintage glamour and kitsch: a taxidermy llama hung in the living room, peacock feathers, feathered fans, and vintage showgirl posters from the wallpapered walls, and a leopard-print chaise lounge was tucked next to a candlelight bay window. Velvet ruby curtains hung from the windows of stained glass in deep jewel tones—ruby, emerald, and sapphire—with tassels that swayed gently as Leslie strode into the living room to mute her TV.

Framed photos adorned the walls of Leslie in her prime, catching Clark's eye. In every one, Leslie was laughing and beaming for the cameras with awards in hand, posing at premieres for her comedy specials, and arm in arm with her celebrity friends. Even from behind the glossy veneer of her red-carpet smiles, Leslie seemed so sweet and so fun.

With care, he lowered his kit to the floor and unzipped it—and erupted in a cold sweat. Inside, there were no crystals. No tools. No spellbook. Just bundles and bundles of sage, a satchel of acid-green crystals he recognized as moldavite, and a case of human tallow candles, their labels mocking him in bold print.

The room began to tilt. His stomach flipped and he was going to be sick. He held on to the edge of the kit like a lifeline, trying to steady himself. *Stay calm, Clark. Breathe. Get a grip . . .* But the panic had already set in. *What am I going to do without a kit?!* The air felt thick, like he couldn't breathe, and his racing heart began to pound in his ears.

"That's Frank," Leslie said, making Clark flinch as she walked past and into the hall. "He's friendly." A fat tabby house cat waddled up on tiny legs to Clark for a sniff of his kit, which he quickly zipped. Clark gave him a quick pat before following after her.

Play it cool, Clark . . . he thought to himself. *Fake it 'til you make it . . .* He groaned internally.

"I love human names on cats, don't you?" He managed to say. He grimaced. *Clark "like Kent" saves the day again . . .*

"Oh, yeah? Me too!" she said, looking over her shoulder with a bright smile. "What's yours?"

"Jessica," Clark said, pulling up his phone for a picture.

"Aww, hahaha. That's funny." Leslie led them down the hall to a pink kitchen full of retro glam, copper appliances, and black-and-white checkered tiles. Frantically, Clark texted:

(5:55 p.m. Clark Crane): Emily! Quick! Help! I showed up to this house call and my kit's been sabotaged! There's nothing in it!! What do I do?!?!

"Care for a drink?" Leslie asked. Before he could respond, she held up a bottle of gin in one hand and a bottle of vodka in the other.

Clark thought about his maligned kit at the door. "I'll have a splash of whatever you're having, thank you."

"Suit yourself!"

She poured herself a refresh and for him a full glass before setting it in front of the seat across from her at the breakfast nook table and sitting down. Clark took her lead and eased into the chair.

"So," she said, fixing him with an amused smile, "you're Felicity's little helper, huh? You look like you couldn't charm your way out of a paper bag, but hey, I'm desperate, so here we are!"

Clark blinked, unsure how to respond. A smile crept across his face. "That's me!"

Leslie took a sip and smacked her glossed lips. She asked, "How long have you been working for Charisma?"

"Oh, a . . . little while," Clark said. "How long have you been working *with* Charisma?"

"A little while," she said coyly. "I don't get to see her often—only at parties and award shows . . . I know she and her girls don't like me very much."

Clark opened his mouth to speak, a polite protest already forming, but when her hazel eyes flicked toward him, he stopped himself and closed it again.

"It's okay, you don't have to lie. Women have always been so mean to me. Hollywood is just high school with better Botox and worse secrets. Trust me, kid, you've never seen a meaner lunchroom."

She punctuated her statement with a sip from her martini glass, her lips curling into a sly smirk as if she had just bestowed upon him some grand cosmetic truth. Clark wasn't sure whether to argue with her or to laugh along. The air between them was a tightrope, and he couldn't be sure which side he'd fall on. Clark peeked at his phone for a reply from Emily, but no go.

"Sure they like you!" he said. "Why wouldn't they like you?"

"Well, you're here—for one! And two, nobody likes a gossip, but . . . dammit, it sure does pay the bills . . . At least it used to." She motioned with her arms. "Well, I'm sure you know all about that."

"You have a beautiful home," Clark said in earnest.

Leslie's eyes lit up. "Thanks!" she said breathlessly. "I paid for it as soon as I saw it—in cash. From my first comedy special. My gift to myself. I had only met her once, but Charisma landed me the meeting and the rest is history . . . Say, have you gotten your hands on that cream of hers?"

"Cream?" Clark raised his eyebrows when he asked, "What cream?"

"Charisma's cream. Have you tried it?"

Clark shook his head and shrugged. "I'm not sure what you're talking about." Hadn't Felicity mentioned the same thing?

"Really? That's weird!" Leslie said. "Everybody's talking about it." She took a long sip, her hazel eyes watching him over the rim of her glass. The house was quiet save for the ticking of the cat-shaped clock with a wagging tail and rolling eyes on the wall above them, joined by the tapping of the grandfather clock in the hall.

Leslie's words drew to a slow. "So . . . how is she?" Clark watched as she carefully twirled the olives in her martini glass by their gold-plated cocktail pick. Its Art Deco flourished tip caught the kitchen light as it circled the rim, as if Leslie was spinning her thoughts into focus with it.

"How is who?"

"Felicity," Leslie said softly, her gaze steady on him.

"Oh, you know," he said. "She's fine!"

Leslie popped an olive in her mouth, chewing slowly. Her eyes narrowed as she spoke through a half-chewed bite. "What did you say your name was again?"

"Clark."

"You're cute, but you're a bad liar, Clark."

He gave her a sheepish smile.

"I haven't heard from her in ages. We met at a party in LA years ago—a big one, you know the type. We were very drawn to one another! It's crazy how this has all gone down. First, she had a baby with that asshole. Then her parents swooped in and took control of her life. And now she's standing up for herself. I say good for her, but also, I'd be lying if I didn't say I was worried about her."

Clark swallowed hard, unsure how to respond. He sensed her words weren't entirely for his benefit.

"Conservatorships," she said, "are for the incapacitated, not for people who are put right back to work. Especially not blockbusters and album tours. Gimme a break! Those damn parents of hers."

Clark nodded in agreement.

Her eyes narrowed as she leaned back in her chair. "Her parents are supposed to protect her, right? But instead, they're lining their pockets and driving her into the ground. It's disgusting. How can anyone justify that? How can anyone sleep at night knowing you've turned your own kid into a cash cow?"

"Well," Clark carefully replied, "I don't think it's solely her parents that are to blame."

Leslie froze, her martini glass poised halfway to her lips. "Ugh!" she said, setting the glass down with a clink. "Say no more. I know what you're about to say: it's 'complicated,' right? *Of course it isn't.* The media has been building up and tearing down women—especially young women—for a profit for centuries. And who's behind that? The people in power. And I bet you all of them"—she paused dramatically to take her sip before whispering—"they're all in Dortier's pocket."

"Oh, yeah, him," Clark said. "He's all over the news right now. Pretty dark stuff."

"I know, right?" She popped another olive in her mouth. "It

makes my scandal look like a fluff piece. You know the guy practically *owns* the media in this country, right? He controls the narratives, pushes the headlines, spins the stories. He's got his grubby hands all over this. The man's a puppet master."

Clark thought of Leslie's poppet effigy on fire. He crinkled his lips to one side. "I'm not saying you're wrong," Clark said carefully, "but . . . I don't think he's the one pulling the strings this time."

Leslie tilted her head, intrigued despite herself. "What do you mean? Then who is?"

Clark looked intently into her eyes. Slowly, he said, "You know who."

Leslie set down her glass with a clink. Her eyebrows arched in intrigue. "Charisma?"

Slowly, Clark nodded.

"No . . . You think Charisma is behind it all . . . ?"

"I don't think," Clark said, choosing his words carefully. "I know. Charisma is the mastermind behind the conservatorship. It's all her: the paparazzi, the media storm. Every move, every decision. She's got the lawyers, the judges, the entire system bending to her will. And it's . . ." He paused, letting the weight of the words settle. "It's not looking good for Felicity."

Everything was still. Outside the window, a light snow began to fall. Leslie asked quietly, "Is she in danger?"

"Whenever a witch like Charisma is involved, there's always danger . . . Right now, she was taken away a 5150, but no one's seen her since. She's got no voice. No rights. No one in her corner. I bet they'll have her back on set by now and . . ." He hesitated, trying to keep his voice from dropping with the weight of his words. "It's bad, Leslie. Real bad." He took a sip of his martini. The muddy brine swirled around in his glass like his runaway mind. "I'm afraid she won't make it . . . and Charisma is the one behind it all."

Breathlessly, Leslie said, "I *knew* it . . . " She popped the last olive in her mouth and after just two chomps, tossed the rest of her drink back. "That bitch! And here I am cavorting with the enemy! Stupid, Leslie, stupid stupid *stupid!* . . . You want more?"

"More?" He followed her finger to his glass, still half-full. Clark shrugged, and then surprised Leslie and himself both threw what was left back. "Yes, please."

Leslie grabbed the empty glass, shaking her head as she carried it away. Clark added, "You should speak nice about yourself."

"Oh, please."

"No, really. Don't beat yourself up. You couldn't have possibly known."

Leslie stopped at the counter, setting the glasses down with a clink. "Oh, but I should've!" She exhaled sharply as she reached for the vodka in the fridge. "You know, when I was younger, I thought I had it all figured out. Play the game, make the right connections, smile even when it feels impossible. That's all it would take to make it in this business." She let out a bitter laugh as she poured olive brine and vodka into a shaker. She turned to face Clark.

"Then you meet someone like Charisma and realize it's not about playing the game. It's about who's pulling the strings. And honey, it's *never* you."

Clark watched her stir the contents and pour their martinis, ice clinking on metal and glass punctuating the quiet.

"You know," she continued, "it's one thing when men try to tear women down. That's just . . . expected at this point, right? It's like, if a man says it, he's edgy. If I say it, I'm offensive and bitter. They say women like me are 'too much.' Too loud, too brash, too old. 'You're not young enough.' 'You're not willing to play by the rules.' 'It's a man's world.' And if you're a single, childless woman of a certain age? Forget it! They'd rather you disappear altogether. But women? Doing it to other women?" She shook her head, her hazel eyes clouding with something darker. "Mannn . . . If Charisma can do that to Felicity, what's stopping her from doing the same thing to someone like me? Or worse?"

"What if it is?" Clark began slowly. "What if . . . Charisma's the one doing this?"

"You think? Nooo . . . But then, why send you?"

"She's doing it to Felicity—why not you too? And I dunno, maybe they sent me so I'd fail? Get rid of us both, when you're supposed to . . . distract from her ex-husband's implosion, and I'm a disposable assistant?"

Clark tugged at his sweater collar, the heat rising to his cheeks. He shifted in his seat. "She's buried people in the headlines before. Controlled the narrative. Twisted public perception. What if she didn't just let this happen . . . what if she made it happen?"

Leslie leaned forward, stunned. "But I'm her client . . . !"

"And Felicity was her star."

Leslie shook her head and sighed. She walked back to the table, setting Clark's glass in front of him. "If I've learned anything in this business, it's that no one's coming to save you. Trust no one. Not your friends. Not your damn agent. Not even your witch. Everyone's turned their back on me, even friends in the business of twenty years."

Leslie tapped her nails on the table. "But maybe . . . I can save someone else. Maybe I can do something for her that no one ever did for me."

"That's brave, Leslie. What are you gonna do?"

"What am I gonna do? I'm gonna need a helluva lot more than bravery to pull it off . . . That's where you come in."

Clark blinked mid-sip of his martini, and promptly almost choked as the words registered.

"Look. I turn sixty in May. No husband, no kids. Just me and my fat cat Frank. I know this is a problem of my own making and, well—aren't they all?" She laughed to herself through squinted eyes and rosy cheeks. "I've made mistakes and, hell, I've made a career out of 'em. But this?" She gestured around her as if the walls were closing in. "This feels different. It's like they're trying to snuff out what's left of me. Right now, the whole country is against me and I've got no future."

She paused, her searching eyes wandering and finding his. What Leslie was about to say next, Clark could have sworn he could foresee, like an incoming train hurtling toward him.

"I'm not done yet. I have so much life to live," Leslie said firmly. "What I want is my career back—my peace. What I want is for *you* to make all of *this*," she said, waving her arms in big sweeping circles, "go away. And maybe if you can help me"—her lips curled into a smile and there was a twinkle in her eyes under her fake lashes and kitchen lights—"maybe I can help one more person. Can you do that? Can you help me?"

There it was, the answer that Clark had been dreading to hear. The real reason he had been called. Leslie wasn't just looking for card reading or a silly horoscope. No, Leslie needed a lifeline, and she wanted him to be it.

When he looked into her eyes, Clark didn't see a monster or a villain . . . he saw every woman—every person to ever live—yearning for the same thing: a voice, a place, a chance. He saw someone trying to carve out a place in a world where others seemed intent on reducing them to nothing.

Maybe he could relate. But was it right to help her? The gossip comic was being burned by her own fire for speaking her truth. Had her words gone too far this time? Was this just karma catching up? Would it be compassion or complicity? He couldn't be so sure.

"What do you say, Clark?" she asked. "Think you've got what it takes to help a washed-up comedienne like me?"

Clark opened his mouth, but the buzzing in his pocket caught his attention. He glanced down at his phone. An incoming call: "Lorena Saintly-Henceley," the screen read.

"Uhh, one sec!" Clark blurted, practically leaping to his feet. "Where can I find the bathroom?"

"Down the hall, on the left under the stairs!" Breathlessly, she said, "You witches are a *trip*. Gahhhd, I love ya!"

Clark darted out of the room so fast that he startled Frank the fat tabby waddling from his food bowl, whose little legs scuttled him in place on the hardwood floor before bolting past. Swiftly, Clark turned on the bathroom light, closed the door, and leaned against it, clutching his phone. He took a deep, bracing breath before picking up.

"Hello, Lorena, this is—"

"Yeah, yeah," she cut in. "Do we have the deliverables?"

"Um . . . the deliverables?"

Lorena clicked her tongue. "The deliver—*boy*!" she barked. Clark flinched. "What have you been doing this whole time? Whatever it is that she wants, *give it to her*. Those are the deliverables."

"Okay, well, she's sorta mentioned that she wants her scandal to go away." Clark laughed to himself as he said, "But Lorena, you won't believe me when I tell you that my kit must have been mixed up. There's no spellbook, there's nothing I packed, it's just a bunch of—"

"Rhetorical!" Lorena snapped. "I couldn't care less if she wanted to make a bloody disgraced clown *protégé* out of you! Whatever it is that she wants, just *give it to her.* I've been waiting at my bloody desk all night to write up this invoice."

"Wait, what?" Clark asked, his stomach tightening. "How can I possibly un-cancel her?"

A pause, and a dramatic sigh: "With a *spell!*"

"But without a spellbook?!"

"*Google it.* Make one up for all I care! You are to send me the spell you are proposing to solve her query. And then you are to perform it. This is the job you wanted, now you've got it!"

The small powder room seemed to tilt around him. "Make . . . one up . . . ? On the spot?"

"You claim to be an English major, do you not? Well?"

"Y-yes," Clark stammered. *Click.* "Hello?!"

Lorena had hung up the phone.

Clark sank onto the edge of the powder room toilet. With trembling hands, he called the next person—no, the only person he knew—who might possibly save him.

"This is Míjiàn."

"Hi, Míjiàn, it's Clark! Is Mother available? It's kinda important."

"Hold," she said. A pause. Then:

Three rings later, a familiar voice spoke through the line: "Lemme guess," Mother drawled. "They threw you in the deep end, sink or swim?"

"Yes!" Clark replied, trying to keep the hysteria out of his voice.

"Into your first house call without any preparation?"

"Nope, none whatsoever!"

Mother sighed. He could practically hear her shake her head. "Alright, listen up. This is how you work with a client. You follow CATS: Consultation, Appraisal, Terms, Spellwork. First, consult, which, you've already started. Good! Your job is to discover not just what the client *says* she wants, but what she truly needs. Uncover the hidden desires not even she is aware of. You're the witch, after all! So, what does your client want?"

Clark had hung onto her every word so intently that he practically stopped breathing. He came to. "She wants to make her scandal disappear." With rushed words, he explained how, in the week since her performance, the president had publicly condemned her, headlines had shamed her name across every tabloid, Leslie's peers had turned their backs on her, her contracts had been severed, and her career was teetering on the brink of collapse.

"Good," Mother replied, calm and measured. "See? It always pays to research your clients beforehand. Always gather your intel first. Know everything you can before stepping in."

Clark nodded to no one in particular, his phone pressed tightly to his ear.

"Okay, next: appraise the proper spellwork. Assess the situation, the obstacles, and the possible outcomes. Make sure your client's expectations are realistic. Never overpromise. Lead them to the answers themselves. Spellwork has a way of delivering us the solutions we need but often don't account for." She paused. Her voice sharpened. "*Never* overpromise, did you get that?"

"Yes," he said.

"When you're confident you can reach a desirable outcome, draft up the contract. This is your formal agreement before performing any service, binding both parties in an oath—a promise made being a magic in and of itself. Outline the terms, the conditions, the price of goods, compensation for your time—all of it. Don't even tell them what you're charging them for; you know what they need, not the other way around! Charge them your worth and no less. No freebies! *Still with me?*"

Clark was probably white-knuckling the phone. "Yes!"

"Breathe, baby."

"Breathing!"

"Good. Anyway . . . everything—and I mean *everything*, including magic—comes with a cost. Energy cannot be created nor destroyed; it can only be transformed in equal exchange. Nothing can be obtained, no change can occur, without an equivalent sacrifice or effort, whether through offering, energy, or intention. That's the law of conservation of energy, baby!"

"Understood," said Clark.

"But see this: do not overpromise. Better to perform a small feat first, earn their trust, and then get rebooked for the next. Get what I'm saying? Build your reputation, don't destroy it with big promises you can't deliver." She paused for a beat. "Also, never, under any circumstances, are you to perform death or resurrection without serious consequences for you and your client, ever."

Clark gulped. "Got it," he said.

"Love spells?" she continued. "*Uh uh.* Don't even think about trying to conjure love. Infatuation, obsession, good ol'-fashioned servitude, sure, if that's what they want. But true love? That can't be manufactured. Don't even try, don't ask me why. I don't make the rules."

Clark managed a faint laugh. "No overpromising. No love. Got it."

"Good. And finally, the easy part: perform the spell. Make your intentions pure; remove all doubt; speak in the present tense, as if your manifestation is already yours, as if it is already done. Watch as the universe bends to your will. Easy."

Easy, she says . . . Clark's head was reeling. "Easy, yeah. Got it!"

"Good. I'm sure Lorena can help you with the invoice since it's your first time. They probably have that shit on template . . . But pray tell, my little lamb, what exactly is it that you think your client needs, Clark? What do *you* think is the solution?""

"Me?" Clark said. "I'm not really sure, to be honest . . ."

"Think, honey," Mother said. "You have all the answers you need right inside you."

Clark buried his face in his hand. "Right . . ." *Think, you dummy, think . . .*

"Don't think too hard now!" Mother said. "And talk nice to yourself."

"Right. Sorry! I mean, right. Um . . . she said she wants . . . to make everyone forget this ever happened."

"Hmmm . . . forgetting isn't the easy answer. What she really wants, I think—whether she realizes it or not—is to be forgiven. By the public, by her peers, hell, maybe even by herself."

Clark hesitated. "Forgiven? You think so?"

"I know so. Forgiveness is the only thing that can neutralize this mess she's gotten herself into. And if she wants people to see her differently, that change starts with her. She's got to own her part in it and let the rest fall away. That's where you come in. Guide her to it, Clark. Give her a spell that helps her invite forgiveness—and extend it where it's needed. I'll text it to you."

Clark breathed a sigh of relief. "Thank you! You're a lifesaver."

Mother chuckled. "Don't mention it. Call me if you need anything else, okay? Good luck, pumpkin," she said. *Click.*

"Pumpkin" . . . that's what Maria calls me . . . he thought. He made a mental note to text his mother back . . . later.

Minutes passed before Clark emerged from the powder room. His phone was open to a series of pictures and messages: a thread of worn, yellowed pages with cramped texts, and scrawled with notes in the margins. He fired off a quick text message to Lorena: *Forgiveness Spell. Starting now.* Her response came almost instantly: a thumbs-up emoji. No further word.

Clark scanned the kitchen cupboards, grabbing what he could improvise: a tall tallow candle, a bundle of sage, and a large piece of moldavite from his kit; table salt and sugar from the kitchen. He filled the room with a faint smoky haze as he lit the sage bundle and smudged the air.

"I hope you don't set off the fire alarm," Leslie quipped, reclining in the breakfast nook with a glass of red wine in hand. Ignoring her comment, Clark slid a blank sheet of paper and a pen toward her. "Write down what you want to be forgiven for," he instructed. "Be honest. Be specific. Then fold it three times toward you."

Leslie paused, her pen hovering over the paper before she started writing. Clark busied himself at the table, lowering the lights and setting up his impromptu altar: the candle in the center and the ionized table salt beside it. When Leslie handed over the folded paper, he carefully placed it beneath the candle.

"What's this made of?" Leslie asked. She brought the candle to her scrunched nose. "It smells a little *off.*"

Clark gently took it from her hand and placed it back on the table while shaking his head. "You don't wanna know," he said. He lit the candle with a match.

Pouring the table salt in a circle around the candle, Clark recited the incantation.

"By this salt, I do thee cleanse,
Of grievous woe and dire offense.
Let now the past be cast away,
And hearts be pure as light of day."

He grabbed the honey bear container and with a squeeze, drizzled it over the candle and paper, saying:

"With this honey, sweet and fair,
I call forth grace beyond compare.
Let bitterness no longer stay,
And love doth bloom this very day."

Leslie muttered, "Well, if this doesn't work, at least we can eat something after."

"Shhh," Clark said. He extended his hand. She slipped her hand into his. The walls, dancing with the candle's flickers, were beginning to lean in, as if the room stood over the altar with them.

"Are you feeling the intention?" he asked. "Hold on to it and say this with me." Their voices, soft and deliberate, began to chant in unison, weaving together like a steady current:

"To those I've wronged, I humbly pray,
Let judgment fade, let hearts give way.

May wrath now wane, may wounds repair,
And forgiveness ride upon the air.

Through these words, I seek thy peace,
A chance to mend, a blessed release.
With love and light, I do entreat,
As this flame dims, let discord retreat.

May peace take root where pain once lay,
And compassion shine as break of day.
From the depths of my soul, to those betrayed,
From my heart, for the hurt I've made,
I do beseech thee with these words:
Wholeheartedly I say—"

On the final line, Leslie's inflection was unmistakable: "I'm . . . sorry?"

A sharp wind swept the room. The candle blew out. From the entryway, the grandfather clock let out a deep, resonant chime, marking the turning of another hour. Leslie looked to the candle, then back at Clark. "Is it supposed to do that?" she asked, blinking at the sudden darkness.

"I dunno," Clark said, squinting at her. "Are you not *actually* sorry?"

She hesitated, her awkward, breathy voice drawing out her syllables as she said, "Not . . . reaaaally."

"Leslieeeeuh!" Clark groaned.

"What? I'm not!"

"Why didn't you just say that?! What did you write?"

Clark bent over, yanked the note out from under the wax, and peeled it open. "'*I'm sorry I don't know how to keep my big mouth shut and that I'm always right.*' Leslie!"

She blinked. "What? I was being honest!"

"Forgiveness isn't for them. It only works when you want it for you."

"I thought that wh—oh, hang on. Shoot. Hold on, it's . . . it's my publicist. Probably calling to quit." She pulled out her buzzing phone and pressed it to her ear, giving Clark a sheepish shrug.

"Hello?" Leslie said. "Yes . . . *What?!*" In one swift motion, she snatched a remote control from the countertop and turned on her small kitchen television mounted in the corner of the ceiling.

The screen flickered to life. A stern-faced news anchor was mid-rant, her tone dripping with disdain. "—Disgraced American comedian Leslie Parks, where a growing crowd of protestors has gathered to voice their outrage following her controversial performance last week. Parks, once a household name, is now at the center of a heated national debate after her shocking actions during a televised comedy special . . ."

The camera cut to footage of Leslie's infamous act: the effigy on fire, the audience's uncomfortable laughter, and her girlish giggle as she declared, "That feels kinda good!" The clip froze on her smirking face, then faded back to the live shot of the house.

The anchor continued, her voice cutting through the chants. "Parks, who has remained silent since the incident, has been condemned by both political leaders and entertainment industry peers worldwide. Calls for boycotts have swept across the media, and major sponsors have severed ties. Protestors here are demanding an apology, but so far, the comedian has made no public statement."

"What the hhh—" But before Leslie could say anything more, a muffled sound reached their ears: chanting, faint but growing louder. Frank scampered out of the hallway and dove under the breakfast nook table, his tail puffed in alarm. Clark and Leslie exchanged nervous looks. Leslie darted out the kitchen and down the hall to the front door, with Clark shortly behind.

In the foyer, the tufted bench beside the door was no longer stacked with just a few hate-filled envelopes—it was buried. A mountain of mail with angry red script scribbled over, all screaming variations of "DIE BITCH" and "WITCH."

Leslie screamed and Clark jumped back.

At the base of the pile was a second crude effigy, this one unmistakably of Leslie: heavy-lidded eyes under false lashes, hazel-green eyes drawn with Xs over them, the whole thing scorched and stabbed through.

Leslie cried, "When did all of this show up?!" They flipped the Venetian blinds.

Outside, under the soft glow of a streetlamp and falling snow, a mob had gathered. They held picket signs reading "Cancel Leslie Parks," "Down with Hate!," and "Jail the Bitch!" Their voices rang in unison as they chanted, "Lock her up! Lock her up!" More news stations had arrived.

Clark's stomach turned. "Oh my god . . ."

"Ahhh, shit!" Leslie said with a click of her tongue. "On a Friday night! Don't these people have somewhere better to be?!" She put the phone up to her ear. "Carla, I gotta call you back."

Leslie turned to Clark. "Fix this!" she cried. Her hazel eyes poured into his. She began to groan, stomping her fuzzy pink slippers on the floor.

"I, uh . . . um," Clark stammered, backing away. *How are we gonna get out of this mess . . . Think, Clark, think . . .*

"Leslie Parks Cancelled for Hexing the President on Live TV" . . . The headline flashed across his mind's eye.

And she's on the verge of a full-blown tantrum, Clark thought, like a parent just handed a ticking time bomb.

Think, Clark . . .

Mob outside . . .

Hate mail . . .

Burnt effigy . . .

Charisma . . . Always Charisma at the center of things . . .

"Leslie . . ." Clark began. "What if . . . you didn't just hex the president on TV? What if you were hexed yourself? One second," he muttered. Clark focused inward, projecting his thoughts like a silent prayer on a mental image of Emily's face: her long blonde hair, her cotton candy perfume, her long eyelashes framing her sad smile. Clark spoke aloud, as if he had Emily on speakerphone, while he thought to her, *Hey Em? I really need you right now . . . What was the spell you used when the coven threw you off Charisma's yacht?*

Leslie tilted her head.

Hey babes, kinda busy right now . . .

Ha! It worked, Clark thought to himself.

You mean the return-to-sender spell?

Yeah! How did that go? How does it work?

It returns any energy or magic directed at you back to its source . . .

Can you tell me how you did it?

Clark blinked, his gaze snapping back on Leslie. A slow grin crept across his face.

"Hey Leslie," he said, his voice low and deliberate. "Screw apologizing. Do you wanna get even?"

She stood still and wide-eyed. She stomped her foot and said, "Fuck yes!"

"Good!" Clark said to Leslie. "I think we're gonna try something a little . . . unorthodox. It might be worth a shot, if you trust me. And it won't require you to sacrifice your dignity with an apology."

"Okay, just . . . hurry!"

Clark scrambled to his kit on the floor. He grabbed a piece of moldavite and rushed back to her. "Here, hold out your hand."

Leslie obeyed, her fingers trembling as he set the crystal squarely in her palm.

He glanced toward the entryway table near the front door—the one cluttered with unopened mail and a polished brass letter opener glinting in the dim light.

"We're gonna need one more thing," he said. "Just a drop."

Leslie followed his gaze. "What are you, nuts? You want me to cut myself?!"

"I want you to mean it," Clark said. "Blood seals the spell. It's the price of truth—yours, not mine."

She let out a shaky breath, stomped over to the table, and picked up the opener. "Oww!" she cried. A crimson bead welled up.

Clark held out her hand. "Let it fall on the moldavite."

She did. And the moment it hit the crystal's surface, the air in the room shifted. Heavy. Alive. The house held its breath and the universe leaned in as Clark began to chant.

"Energy sent with ill intent,
By this moment, be unspent.
Turn away, return to source,

Undo your path, reverse your course.
Let no harm linger, let no pain grow,
Back to its sender, let it now go.
Let falsehood fade, let hate relent,
Our hearts align in love ascent.

By the forces of truth and light,
I call this reckoning to ignite.
Let harm and wrong return their cost,
To find their source and balance what's lost.

By right, by force, by my command,
I cast your harm to meet its thrill.

Clark opened his eyes, locking them onto Leslie. He could swear there was a warmth vibrating from the moldavite in her palm, and traveling down their arms like a current. The air around them had grown heavy and charged, as if the house itself were holding its breath. It was as if the universe had shifted, the unseen gears of fate clicking into place like the grandfather clock in the entryway.

Leslie whispered, "Listen . . ."

They sprnag to the blinds at the door again. The scene outside had changed: the picket signs were gone, the chanting mob was disbanding, the news vans packing up their equipment, anchors climbing into their vehicles, the hum of engines filling the quiet air. A soft trickle of snow fell, muffling the sound of footsteps retreating into the night.

"It worked!" Leslie gasped, her face lighting up. "It actually worked!"

They both jumped for joy, holding each other's hands like giddy children.

She reached for her phone, scrolling furiously. Clark followed suit. The articles that had hounded her all week were buried by new stories, slipping further down trending lists to be buried at the bottom. Days later, they would eventually fitter out, to be forgotten.

On a victory lap, they returned to the kitchen, Leslie's arm over Clark's. The segment about Leslie had since ended. For a moment, relief washed over them.

But then—

"Breaking news," blared the TV.

They froze, their joy evaporating as the anchor's voice filled the room.

"Straight from Los Angeles, an unexpected death has occurred on the set of *The Cost of Magic*, starring American singer-songwriter and nine-time Grammy winner Felicity Tierres. Information is still developing. Stay tuned for updates as this story evolves."

The screen cut to an aerial view of Universal Studios, where the backlot was illuminated in a pulsating red glow of sirens and ambulances.

Leslie and Clark exchanged horrified glances, the color having quickly drained from their faces.

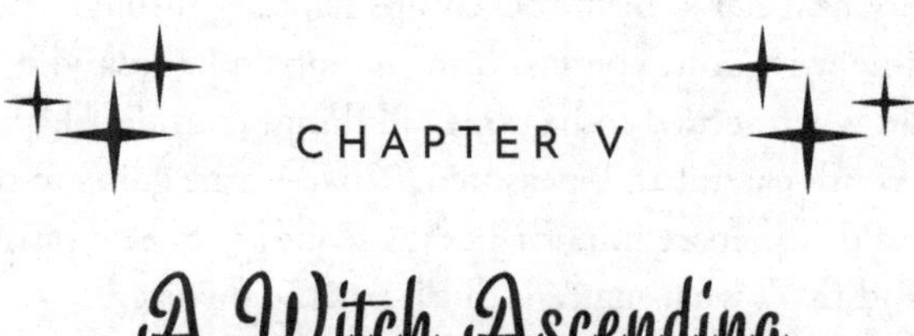

CHAPTER V

A Witch Ascending

"Well?" Lorena barked through the phone. "How did it go? What happened?"

It was nine o'clock when Clark rolled out from under the Holland Tunnel and back into Manhattan after Leslie's. She had insisted he stay for pizza—her version of a big New Jersey send-off. Neither of them was very chatty as they ate in front of television in the living room. The snow continued to glaze the tristate like powdered sugar, a blanket that softened the edges of everything it touched. The city, usually so restless, was still. A bittersweet homecoming, considering he had spent the commute refreshing the news on his phone every few seconds, for news of what might have become of Felicity.

"It went perfectly," Clark decided to tell Lorena.

"All on a Forgiveness Spell?"

"Well, first I smudged her kitchen, then I cleansed the circle with salt and honey—"

"You did all that?" she interrupted, erupting into a howling cackle that made Clark pull the phone away from his ear. "Darling, what are you, her housekeeper, or her personal ghostbuster?" He could practically hear her stiff, lipsticked lips flapping through the phone. "Next time, why don't you just bring a mop and a rosary?"

"I did what needed to be done, all things considered," he said at last, his words careful and measured. What was he going to do, argue that she didn't prepare him for Leslie's request? "She's a satisfied customer, and that's what matters. She'll pay the invoice."

"Ha! She'd better. This isn't charity work—it's witchcraft. Payment is due upon spellwork's completion." She drew a breath. "From now on, you are to send me a detailed recap of everything you do after every house call. Understood?"

"Yes."

"Good. Do it. *Now.*"

"Thank you, again, Lorena. Have a good"—*click!*—"night."

Lorena had already hung up the phone.

Clark caught his reflection in the rearview mirror, the streetlights etching weary shadows across his face. *I don't get it . . .* he thought, his head slumping back against the headrest. *I was just doing my job . . .*

As the car came to an idle stop at a red light, the evening replayed in one big, endless loop. He thought of the spell he'd so proudly concocted on the spot—what had felt like a triumph in the moment—and how it had backfired so spectacularly. And worse, it might have hurt Felicity in ways neither he nor anyone else could undo.

He wondered, *What have I done . . . ?* The regret sank into his chest like stones in his pockets. The light turned green. The car rolled forward, the snow continued to fall, and the world carried on, indifferent to his unraveling.

That weekend, Joey invited Clark to the bar at Northlight, if even just to sit and read while he worked. Clark politely declined. Instead, he chose to retreat into sleep, spilling from one endless dream into another, the cellophane sun slipping into winter night. All the world outside his windows had been blanketed in white and ash. Bedsheets and pillows floated away on sloping, snow-covered lawns. In his dreams, he was running—always running. Running toward something, running away from something . . . while a shadow, cold, dark, and hungry, lapped at his feet.

Every time, a greasy hollow laugh startled him awake. And every time, when his eyes opened, Jessica was there. Her big yellow-green eyes would look deeply into his, as if she saw the things in him he could not. Clark had thought the night terrors were over. He was thankful, at least, for the change, from the nightmares of the coven's witches riding his body into the early hours of morning.

In those moments of wakefulness, Clark's fingers stayed swiping on the news outlets, refreshing his phone again and again. The official word on who had passed had yet to be released.

There were rumors, of course. Clark read everything he could on the internet, scouring forums and threads, combing through comments and the murkiest corners of the web. Whispers from PAs and interns claimed that someone on that final scene had died by fire. Allegedly, they had caught it all on film. They said the final movie was going to be "epic." The body recovered, they said, was beyond recognition.

Please . . . Clark prayed. *Not again . . . Not another . . .*

His mind leapt to Melissa. It was enough to make his head spin, Linda Blair-style.

Then he saw it. A single headline: *"Two-Time Oscar Winner Cynthia Bernhardt Identified as Victim in Tragic On-Set Fire."*

Clark released a sigh so heavy, he swore it rattled the windows, startling Jessica with her tail puffed up and her ears pulled back.

He skimmed the article:

The entertainment world is in mourning after the tragic death of two-time Academy Award-winning actress Cynthia Bernhardt, who passed away in an on-set accident late last week. Sources confirm that Bernhardt, 65, died during the final stages of filming for the highly anticipated feature The Cost of Magic, *a psychological fantasy-thriller poised to be a major awards contender this season.*

While details surrounding the accident remain scarce, insiders close to the production describe the incident as "devastating" and "entirely unforeseen." The tragedy has cast a shadow over the film, which stars Bernhardt as the Queen Witch opposite actress and pop sensation Felicity Tierres in what many had speculated would be a career-defining role for both women.

Cynthia Bernhardt's illustrious career spans three decades, marked by unforgettable performances in films like The Shadows in the Park *and* A Quiet Rebellion. *Known for her unparalleled talent and commanding presence, she was widely regarded as one of the greatest actresses of her generation.*

Charisma Saintly, the film's executive producer and a close friend of Bernhardt, issued the following statement:

"We are heartbroken to learn of the passing of Cynthia Bernhardt. She was not only a dear friend but a luminous artist and a consummate professional, whose legacy will endure for generations. This tragic accident is a reminder of how fragile and fleeting life can be. Our thoughts are with her family and loved ones during this unimaginably difficult time."

Despite the tragedy, production is set to wrap on schedule, with the film still on course for its highly anticipated October 24th release.

In a statement issued by her representatives, Bernhardt's family announced that private funeral services will be held tomorrow, Monday, January the 18th. They have asked that the public respect their privacy during this difficult time.

Clark stared at the words, reading them over and over, searching for cracks in the veneer. The spin was as undeniable as it was chilling. *An accident*, he thought. *Charisma's behind this.*

But one thing mattered more than the headlines, the statements, or the suspicions curling in his gut:

Felicity was alive.

(Lorena Henceley 7:00 a.m.): Report to my office first thing.

Clark knocked lightly on the office door that early Monday morning.

"Come in," she barked, "come *in*."

God, Clark thought to himself, *she is so miserable . . .*

"Good morning, Lorena!" Clark greeted, his aura as bright as possible. "You wanted to see me?"

"Yes. Sit."

Clark closed the door behind him and did as told. But no sooner had he settled in the chair did a knock-knock sound at the door.

"Come in!" Lorena called. Clark looked at her. In the middle of their meeting?

The door swung open. Who entered but none other than Monica and the twins, all smiles that failed to reach their hollow eyes. Always the gentleman, Clark rose instinctively to his feet.

"Good morning, boss," Monica said.

"Good morning, Auntie Lorena," the twins chimed in sugary unison.

"We brought you your coffee," Milly said, presenting a cup.

"Just how you like it," Mandy said.

Lorena clutched her chest as if they'd brought her flowers instead of caffeine. She air-kissed each of them and cooed, "Thank you, my sweetnesses!" Her expression shifted as her sharp eyes flicked back to Clark, sizing him up with a sneer. "If only *some* people were more considerate around here. I was just beginning to review Friday's house call with our newest."

"Ha! With the clown from New Jersey? Do tell," Monica said, leaning on her desk. The twins stood and watched. Clark wondered if they ever blinked.

"Indeed. It turns out the comedienne completed her invoice . . ." Lorena began, her tone clipped, "in *cash*." She nodded toward a stack of printed papers on her desk. "She also sent Charisma and me an email . . . singing your praises and . . . even sent a tip."

Clark thought, *Why does she look so pained, like that's a bad thing . . . ?*

Clark raised the printouts. "Clark's expertise is so 'unparalleled,'" he read, "'he is like the Meryl Streep of witchcraft.'" He chuckled, glancing up to see Lorena's lip twitch. *Did Monica seriously just roll her eyes . . . ?*

He continued, grinning. "Clark is 'so sweet, he could easily have billed me for the therapy session. He changed my life for the better.'"

He skimmed to the bottom. "'Please accept my gratitude to you and your entire team. Clark is a gem and a treasure. Whatever you're paying him, double it.' *Awww!*" Clark gushed, clutching the printout to his chest. Lorena's lip was curled fully now, and Monica's hollow eyes were filled with loathing. He turned the page to the signed NDA and attached invoice.

At the sight of the number under *Total*, Clark did a double take. He was seeing stars. He practically launched out of his shoes: the rate was in the five figures. There were more zeros than he could ever have imagined—more than he thought possible for half a year's work, let alone a single day.

"This is . . ." he stammered, "all mine? Oh . . . my . . . g—"

"Absolutely not," Lorena said, reaching over her desk and snatching the papers from his hand. "There is a matter of the agency rate—which is to say, the coven rate—at forty percent. These are not your clients, after all, but Charisma's, as you might've well learned after Melissa."

"Ugh!" Monica interjected. "That stupid bitch had nothing on me. She was all hair, anyway."

The thought of Melissa's wild, wavy locks and untamed eyes, next to Monica's precision-perfect, pin-straight fringe and length, sent Clark over the edge. A laugh escaped before he could stop it—to dark looks shot at him by Monica and Lorena.

"*All hair*" . . . he thought, amused at her impressively creative hatefulness. *That's a first . . . Saving that one for later . . .*

"Right . . ." Lorena continued. "Anyways, there is also the matter of an agent rate, which is to say, *my cut*"—this she said with a theatrical hand pressed to her chest and a toss of her hair—"as booker. A twenty-percent add-on."

Clark came crashing back to the office, but this time planted a little more loosely in his worn-out high-tops than before. Something this time, however, had changed, had clicked into place.

"When is my next house call?" he asked.

Lorena's sharp green eyes practically bulged out of their sockets. It was as if he had just asked her to draw him a bubble bath and sponge his back.

"I don't think you get how this works, boy!" she barked. "*You* bring the clients to *us*, not the other way around! We don't work for you!"

Clark glanced at the twins, whose smiles dripped with smugness, and to Monica, who looked beside herself.

"You wanted to become one of the great Saintly assistants, well, now you are."

Where Clark might have once shrunk back ever so slowly into his chair, he chose instead to plant his feet firmly on the floor.

"Let me see that," Monica said, snatching the printouts out of Lorena's hand. "*Hmph!* My first Charisma Saintly house call was worth twice as much as this."

"Indeed," Lorena said. "Family name and experience will always win out, my dear."

"Bad breeding can't be helped, it seems."

Don't react, Clark . . . Don't react . . .

"Certainly not."

"Nope, most certainly not," Clark agreed. "Of course, while some of us get by on privilege, others prefer to let our work speak for itself. Didn't you see the news yesterday? Leslie booked a landmark TV interview."

Lorena and Monica paused, their stares cutting through the room like lasers. Clark met their glares with a smile. Lorena tossed him another printout. "Here," she huffed.

It was a chart, with graphs and numbers in neat, color-coded rows. "What is this?" Clark asked meekly.

"The breakdown of *your goal*," said Lorena.

"Per quarter," Monica smugly chimed, "then by month, and then by week."

Clark's own eyes bulged at the number that was his daily goal. He skimmed through the math and did a double take at the total. "It says my goal for a year is . . ."

"Correct," Lorena barked. "One million. *Chump change!* And if that seems daunting, just keep your eye on the commission . . . Now go make yourself useful," she spat, "and, oh I dunno, find something in the Closet to clean. Every second you breathe on our payroll is a penny wasted, as far as I'm concerned. Time is money, and I don't tolerate freeloaders."

Clark recalled with speed about Monica and all of her so-called *extracurriculars:* the mani-pedis, the hours-long lunches disguised as "client meetings," the untraceable gaps in her schedule.

Why does she get away with it . . . ? he wondered. *How come the assistants do all the work and take home a fraction of the profits . . . ? Did she save an icon from the brink of ruin like I did . . . ?*

"Ooo, Auntie Lorena," Milly chimed. He was finding it hard to keep track of which witch was which. "We wanted to tell you."

"We reorganized the Closet!" said Mandy.

"Yeah! We've put the Closet's stock list on auto-replenish. We took the old manual system and fully automated it," Milly said with pride.

"We've tracked the assistants' restocks and set up auto-orders for their kit essentials based on predictive usage patterns." The twins' eyes flickered to Clark, who stood motionless. They spoke this all with the biggest smile that failed to reach their hollow eyes.

Lorena clapped her hands together. "How marvelous!" Her face lit up. "Not even here for two days and already innovating. That's my girls!"

"Hey!" Clark could feel the blood rushing up to his face. "That was me! I automated the Closet's replenishments!"

"Trying to take credit for others' accomplishments?" barked Lorena. "Pathetic! I'll have Charisma hear of this at once."

"Out on his first job and already he thinks he can roll with the big dogs. Let me handle this, Lorena. Listen, you little twit—"

"Oh really?" Clark asked, his words smooth. The room fell into silence. He turned to the twins. "So can you tell me what specific brand of salt for cleansing Alicia prefers?"

The smirks fell right off the twins' faces.

"She also likes to update her tea blends for scrying every solstice and equinox," Clark continued, letting the words hang for a beat, "and replenish her moon water from seasonal sources: rainwater in spring, melted snow for winter. Can you tell us from where? Did you flag those, too?"

The twins exchanged glances. Their cheeks flushed pink.

"Right . . ." He looked at Monica and watched the faint smile tugging at her lips quickly falter. "Or how about how the system handles Monica's weekly replenishments of Chanel lipstick? Strange how those never seem to make it into her kits, too."

Lorena's sharp hawk eyes snapped onto Monica.

"What?" Monica said. "They're client gifts."

"I did not approve of that," Lorena said, her tone icy.

Clark gave a small, knowing shrug. "Guess some people innovate by stealing someone else's ideas and calling them their own. Kind of like switching my kit for Leslie's house call." He said this looking dead-on at the twins. "But hey," he added with a disarming smile, "if I were going to play the villain, at least I'd try not to look so constipated."

The twins stiffened. Monica shifted uncomfortably, smoothing her black dress.

"Now if you'll excuse me, I've got a coffee order to make—for me." Clark collected the printouts. "And work to do. Good day." There was a bounce in his step and a smile tugging at his lips as he turned on his heel and exited, leaving the room in stunned silence.

Clark's ears were burning and ringing the rest of the day. As he passed Monica on his way to the Library to return the spellbook he'd borrowed, she threw him a look so sharp it could cut a diamond. Or—at least shatter his security to pieces, if he hadn't been feeling so untouchable. But Clark didn't care. With his aura up bright and blue, he was untouchable. Nothing could faze him. He popped his handwritten thank-you note, in his Hogwarts-letter cursive, to Leslie in the mail with his chin held high.

With Charisma, Alicia, and Emily still in LA, Lorena and Monica were back to work in full swing, and so had kept the twins busy and away. On their way to the main elevator, he overheard them talking about being chauffeured in their own personal town cars for deliveries up and down the city. It was just like Joey had described to him last summer, when he had told Clark that was how the previous juniors had kept up with their miles of errands, whereas he been left to do them all on foot. For once, Clark was able to go home at a reasonable hour, not seven, eight, or nine o'clock as he was so used to.

He wished he could have at least run into Emily.

I heard the house call went well . . . she thought to him.

So well! I'll tell you about it when I see you next . . .

Can't wait, babes . . .

On the subway back to Astoria, and as he calculated his take-home, he couldn't help but marvel. It was more money than he had ever seen in his life.

That night, Clark broke the news. Joey gasped and screamed and burst into laughter with him. He picked Clark up and spun him around, as hard and as fast as he could in that tiny studio apartment. Then, they grabbed Jessica and smothered her in kisses, a cat sandwich. Laughter filled every corner of their space, of their beings.

To celebrate, Joey ordered them both a huge New York-Chinese takeout feast: there was hot and sour soup, General Tso's chicken, vegetable fried rice, pork fried dumplings, shrimp lo mein, beef with broccoli, boneless barbecue spareribs, fried wontons with pineapple-pink sauce, scallion pancakes, four orders of vegetable egg rolls, and two liters of soda.

Joey broke open his fortune cookie. He unraveled his fortune and read aloud, "'A light heart carries you through all the hard times.'" He grinned. "True!"

In Clark's fortune cookie, there was not one but two fortunes he unraveled. "Woah!" he said, holding them up. The first one read, "Beware the shadow that follows light. Every ascent faces its reckoning." He nervously laughed. "Whatever *that* means!"

He unraveled the second slip, his grin returning: "'A happy life is just in front of you. All your hard work will soon pay off.' Yay!"

The next night was McDonald's night: a delivery of Double Quarter Pounders with Cheese, McDoubles and large fries, apple pies, and Oreo McFlurries and Dr. Pepper.

"Joey!" Clark had protested.

"What?" he'd said. "You'll pay me back! It's on my credit card. Quit your worryin'!"

The third night, they had Joey's favorite, Italian: powdered cellulose turned to grated blocks of fresh Parmigiano-Reggiano, lasagna trays, chicken parmigiana, garlic knots, and for dessert, espresso with tiramisu.

The once-sparse, outdated white refrigerator was now piled up to the brim with leftovers—*for once . . . !* Clark thought, staring at the overstuffed shelves in awe.

Evenings turned into a continuous haze of cannabis and contentment, the two of them tucked in together after work, stuffed and sleepy, with Jessica at their feet.

Indulgence was their new norm.

"Get used to it, baby!" Joey had said.

When Clark received his first paycheck that Friday, he nearly dropped to his knees at the ATM. The numbers on the screen confirmed it: he had enough to pay Joey back and then some. Enough to pay his rent, his bills, and even a little extra. That, and Lorena had emailed him the open enrollment forms for their health insurance—for the first time since he could remember, Clark felt something he hadn't known in years: stability.

"Babe, look," Joey said during that third night's feast, dropping his fork and pointing across the room. It was as if they had blinked and Matilda, the weeping fig tree in the corner, with her braided trunk and vibrant leaves, had risen taller than either of them remembered. She had been a sapling at Christmas, barely more than a decoration. Now, she was practically a ceiling-height monument.

"She grew so fast," Clark said, running his fingers along her leaves. Matilda was a living reminder of how far they had come, a testament to their growth and hard work—one paycheck and one meal at a time.

Clark had received his goal that Monday. By Tuesday, it turned out that Leslie did have female friends—ones who liked her quite a bit. The referrals came in slow at first. A tarot reading here. A smudging there. Some just wanted to meet the great Clark Crane, Felicity's advisor and Leslie's not-so-private hero.

Each house call, Clark made sure to pack his kit correctly—his original bag, which just so happened to have miraculously shown up. He learned always to check before leaving Charisma's.

From that week on, things were moving. His work wasn't constant yet, but it was steady. Promising. The kind of steady that planted seeds in his mind—seeds of something bigger, something lasting. And for the first time in what felt like forever, he believed that maybe he wasn't lost anymore.

He wrote just three words in his diary: *I've made it.*

There was little time to stop and deliberate, little time to dwell in his diary or overthink his life away, no more time to stare at a bridge and wonder when he'd cross it. Money was beginning to flow, and Clark was flying up and down the island of Manhattan with his kit full of witchcraft in tow.

It was as though his aura itself was alive, reaching out to connect, to read, to understand. He wasn't just reacting—he was creating. Every book on his shelf, every witch story he had devoured, every fantasy movie or show he had absorbed seemed less like inspiration now and more like preparation, as if some part of him had always known he was destined for this. Witchcraft wasn't just something he had learned; it was something that had been waiting for him all along, calling him to step into his power.

Soon, he no longer needed to Google the properties of herbs or consult a guidebook to decipher what the tarot had in store. His instincts sharpened with every spell, every consultation. After Leslie, and with each client since, his intuition grew clearer. Their desires were becoming easier to sense from the first handshake, their thoughts open tapestries he was learning to better unfurl and explore. People, it seemed, were dying to be heard—and he was there to listen.

It was as if every book on his shelf, every witch story he'd ever read, every fantasy he'd ever watched—everything he'd ever gone through—had been preparing him for exactly this.

Word got around quickly: Clark wasn't just good at helping

people—he was great. By February, his name had begun circulating among clients eager for results, and though his schedule wasn't yet fully booked, it was steadily filling. Soon, he found himself venturing beyond Manhattan, into to the brownstone parlors of Boerum Hill, the sleek high-rises of Long Island City, and the new developments of Williamsburg. Clients of every shape and size reached out: by phone, by email, by text. Each consultation brought a new challenge, a new story, and a chance for Clark to test his growing power.

A struggling Broadway playwright called on him, writer's-blocked for months and teetering on the edge of giving up. Clark could feel it the moment he stepped into her space. Her energy was tangled, stagnant, like a thread caught in a knot. But as they spoke, her request took a darker turn. She asked Clark to perform a binding spell against a rival playwright, whose quick-founded success she deeply resented. She confessed her jealousy openly—this playwright hadn't worked nearly as hard as she had, hadn't sacrificed as much, hadn't spent years honing their craft the honest way. At least, she had done it honestly until . . . the very moment she called on Clark.

Clark hesitated. He felt her desperation like an ache, but beneath that he also sensed fear—fear of never living up to her own expectations. Instead of fulfilling her request, Clark gently guided her toward something more illuminating: a mirror spell, designed to reflect back the very core of her jealousy, allowing her to clearly see the insecurity beneath it.

After a thorough smudging, he swore the air even looked cleaner. He enchanted a bowl of water, whispering words of release and self-acceptance. He watched as fog lifted from her aura, absorbed into the quartz in his palm, which he then placed gently into the water. The crystal hissed faintly, like a hot coal meeting cool water. Then, he charmed a small, silver-framed mirror, whispering words of clarity, self-awareness, and gentle illumination. He instructed her to gaze into it, confronting directly the emotions she had been projecting outward. Her aura shivered, releasing its tension like a breath exhaled after holding it too long. She began to cry, and sank into Clark's shoulder for a hug.

A week later, she sent Clark an ecstatic email: "I don't know what you did, but after you left I stayed up all night finishing my play. It's good . . . really good. I think it's my life's work. You didn't just give me my creativity back—you gave me myself back. Thank you." The tip was generous.

A newly promoted, high-powered, five-foot-tall executive sought Clark's help after feeling her authority challenged in a boardroom full of men. Her title said she belonged, but their stares, interruptions, and dismissive tones said otherwise. Clark could feel it pulsing off her: the fury, the exhaustion, the refusal to shrink. He didn't need a tarot spread to see what she wanted. She wanted to be respected.

"I've worked twice as hard for half the credit," she told him, pacing. "And I know I deserve the room I walk into—but they don't."

"Not yet." Clark reached for a white box tucked away in one of the kits (two rolling luggage bags, by this point). Inside was a 3.4 oz bottle of Charisma Eau de Parfum. He handed it to her with a glint in his eye. "Wear this, but only when you mean business."

He tucked a tiger's eye charm into her hand. "This will amplify what's already there, which is . . . frankly, a lot. Just imagine your light filling up the room. You won't be ignored."

Two weeks later, she emailed to say she'd landed a massive investment, had three more deals on the table, and had started seeing someone new—two, actually. "I walk into a room and they listen," she wrote. "Men stand when I enter. I haven't felt this magnetic in years. Whatever that scent is, I need it for all the women on my team. And you? You're a genius."

One quick search later, Clark discovered one of those shiny new deals would displace an entire immigrant community in the South Bronx. He winced, then closed the tab. He wasn't the Department of Housing—he was a witch with commission to make. The check was excellent, and put him at the top of the coven for fragrance sales.

Even smaller, personal victories poured in. A young woman—Upper East Sider, Pilates-toned, married with two kids—called Clark in tears. "I think my husband's sleeping with the nanny," she whispered. "She's twenty-four, Swedish, and makes green juice before I'm even out of bed. I want her gone."

Clark, sensing her heartbreak beneath the rage, suggested a ritual not of banishment but redirection. A passion-drawing spell for her, paired with a blessing for the nanny's highest good. ("Trust me," he said).

Two weeks later, the nanny announced she was moving back to Malmö to marry her boyfriend. And the client? She booked a follow-up session, glowing. "We've been laughing like we just started dating again," she said of her husband. "Thank you, Clark."

Clark began to trust himself in a way he never had before. He wasn't just following rituals or memorizing techniques: he was creating, improvising, and letting his intuition guide him to results that felt were uniquely his clients' best interests. Clark's magic wasn't just about results—it was about empowerment. Clients left his sessions lighter, more confident, and ready to tackle their lives with renewed vigor—and so did Clark. It wasn't perfectionism driving him anymore; it was connection. Each success built on the next, and with every call, every email, every referral, Clark realized he wasn't just helping his clients, he was building something real, something lasting. The work was steady, exhilarating, and deeply consuming. Clark couldn't keep himself from smiling. Magic wasn't something he did: it was something he *was.*

One night, while home alone with Jessica purring in his lap, Clark's aura achieved new heights, even if for just a moment. Periwinkle-indigo blue transformed into pure, radiant gold. Its force spun around him, powerful, strong, and fortified. His blood was singing, his very soul on fire. He wasn't just a vessel: he was the light. It filled the entirety of his apartment and beamed out the windows.

Joey noticed the change, of course. "Move over, Astoria," he'd say. "Daddy's home!" On those easy nights, Joey would croon while cooking in the kitchenette wearing his red *Kiss the Chef* apron. Jazz would drift through the speakers, green would float out the tops of the windows, and in between stirring pots and plating dishes, Joey would steal a glance and a wink now and again at a calm Clark, sprawled in bed in front of the TV.

"What?" Clark asked, catching him mid-gaze.

"Nothing," Joey replied with a lopsided grin. "You're cute is all."

"You're staring!" Clark protested through hands covering his face, a smile, and a laugh.

"What? Is that a crime?!" Joey growled, tossing his apron aside.

"Get back in the kitchen!" Clark shrieked. "Don't you come any closer! I'm warning you! No! *No!*" Joey burst onto the bed in a running jump, pinning Clark beneath him with a triumphant laugh. That night, like so many others, they tumbled together in a flurry of neck kisses and tangled limbs, their breathless squeals and laughter flooding every corner of their little Astoria home.

Every night Joey and Clark spent at home was a chance to fall more and more in love.

By Super Bowl Sunday, Joey had inevitably traded his shift off. He batted away Clark's objections, saying spending time together on weekends was more important. "There'll be more work," Joey said. "But for today, we play."

At work the night before, Joey had served an Astoria couple who were new in town and not so far apart in age from them, newlyweds Ali and Cory. The pair had extended an invitation for Joey and Clark to join them at theirs that evening, up in the suburban enclave of Astoria-Ditmars, just two stops north on the train.

Ali and Cory were high school sweethearts, they learned, "by way of Asheville, North Carolina," as they put it. The couple proudly toured them around their Astoria townhouse, having just moved in, showing them pictures hung around their home of their large families back home, their farms, their schools, and their hometown church. Their two border collies, Justin and Beau, darted between their legs all the while. "We love human names on pets!" Ali had exclaimed. "Makes them feel even more like family."

The festivities were held in the back, under their heated, screened patio. Food and drink were laid out under heating lamps and around their coziest fire pit, with the game projected on a screen. A few friends and couples their age gathered on the cushions and blankets of a square wicker sectional, chatting intimately as the game unfolded, eager to meet Clark and Joey.

The two exchanged whispers. "Imagine having a house—a *home*—like this?"

Ali and Cory were "start-up yuppies", as they put it, and by the first commercial break, the dreaded question arose: "What do you do for work, Clark?"

"A lot of coffee runs," Clark said with a wry smile. Intern turned the latest assistant for Charisma Saintly, he confessed.

"And a big shot with clients of his own," Joey bragged. "The youngest they've ever had."

Mostly the girls squealed in excitement.

"How cool!" one said.

"What's it like working for her? What's she like?" another asked.

How could he begin to explain? The chaos, the labor, the horrors . . . and yet the undeniable allure of it all. Clark smiled to himself as he decided on one word: "Magical."

The halftime show was about to begin: the pop star who had burst from Charisma's birthday cake last year was set to perform, the one from the party he had so naively crashed.

After appetizers of cheeses and meats on charcuterie boards, dinner was served: first, a carrot and parsley-dill soup, followed by stuffed mushrooms and a hearty chili with plenty of sour cream to go around. ("This ain't no tailgate, y'all!" Cory announced, the proud cook. "You can have your chicken wings another day!"). By the end of the night, skillet brownies with vanilla-bean ice cream were served, and s'mores came out to roast over the fire. And of course, courtesy of Joey, there was a joint to go around and laughter for everyone.

"So," one of the girls teased, "who wears the pants?"

Clark and Joey exchanged a mischievous glance. Clark answered with a sly grin, "Well, you might be surprised to hear this, but Joey wears the apron in the kitchen—and nothing else. He loves to cook almost as much as I love to eat . . ."

"*Ohhhh*," the girls chorused, exchanging knowing glances and giggling. Joey's cheeks flushed as he turned to Clark with his mouth agape in mocked outrage.

Through the course of the night, whenever Clark felt like he was talking too much, or saying too little, or being too weird, all he had to do was turn—and like a magnet, Joey's eyes would find his. He would give Clark a subtle wink as if to say, *"I'm here. You're safe."*

As the conversation swirled and laughter filled the air, Cory raised a beer. "To new and old friends."

Clark and Joey clinked glasses with the others, but the night's most intimate toast was in the backseat of their taxi, where they shared kisses that tasted like infinity.

When Clark looked back on those days, he'd do so with great fondness: the delicate simplicity, and the brief lightheartedness. It was the last time he would remember things feeling that way, ever again.

New York Fashion Week turned the dial from zero to one thousand those next two weeks at Charisma's. She had returned to the city in a whirlwind of fittings, appearances, and interviews. Clients traveled into the city from around the world and filled the assistants' calendars, even Clark's.

"All but the best," Lorena had made sure to inform him. "Since you *still* don't know how to do a glamour."

She wasn't wrong. The magic he cast for Leslie had felt like a miracle. It was a manifestation so powerful and immediate compared to what he was called to perform in his current bookings. But for now, it was mostly simpler requests and feats, like candle magics, jar work, five-card tarot readings, and energy cleanses. The higher-level, transformative magic of glamours was still almost a total mystery to him.

Between packing his own kit for every inevitability and towing it around the city, on the train or in cabs, Clark had no time to stop at the penthouse library to look it up in hopes of teaching himself. Glamours, it seemed, would have to wait.

"I'll teach you," a familiar voice came from the entryway of the kitchen.

"Emily!" Clark exclaimed, jumping up and running for a hug. Lorena let out a sharp sigh, her disapproval palpable, but Clark promptly ignored her.

Whereas the rest of the coven looked gray and drawn from winter's work, Emily was as vibrant as the gold of her bright blonde hair. "I almost didn't come back," she admitted.

But work called. Charisma's fall/winter collection was set to debut in a runway show at New York Fashion Week the following day, and her fashion team was scrambling between her showroom, warehouse, and penthouse, while the coven darted in and out of luxury hotels and apartments near the park.

On Valentine's Day, Charisma's show ended the NYFW season at the Park Avenue Armory, an expansive venue, Clark was told, reserved for the most high-budget, extravagant productions. Emily, always in her element, whisked Clark backstage on a tour. The models were in the process of getting ready—hair teased, makeup brushed, nails polished, garments fitted—while photos flashed in rapid succession.

Most of the models knew Emily. Being with her made Clark feel like he had been granted a pass to the cool kids' table.

"Stay close," Emily said, settling into the makeup chair while Clark snacked on chocolate-chip cookies and champagne. *Keep your aura up and your thoughts to a volume only I can hear . . .* she added.

Clark nodded and couldn't help blushing and venting his gaze as some of the models changed wardrobe or were otherwise in various states of undress. There were some small children around, nannies even. Among the commotion, he noticed something peculiar:

No male models . . . ? Clark thought to Emily.

No menswear . . . she thought back. If he were being honest, Clark was a little relieved. Even in his newly purchased black button-down and skinny tie—appropriately sized for once—standing next to models, he still might've felt more cater-waiter than attendee. The absence of men meant there was no need to measure himself against chiseled jaws and gym physiques, no silent comparisons chipping away at his insides.

Come to think of it, there were no men whatsoever save for security, clad in imposing black suits, beards, and heavy leather combat boots. He realized he was the only one. And when his eyes did venture upward, they met many a hollow stare that quickly flickered away. The avoiding of his gaze was as if his presence was an unwelcome reminder of something unspoken. Something that didn't quite belong.

After catering—an expensive assortment from Eataly—the two made their way to the front of house. The runway was a massive ellipse, with the audience seated on elevated platforms surrounding it like an arena. A mist swirled around giant geodes of purple amethyst, soft pink rose quartz, and pale blue celestite. The walls were alive with projections of celestial imagery: astrological symbols, orbiting planets, and cosmic swirls. Light refracted through hanging crystal balls, casting dancing prisms across the room like stars. The air was perfumed in white flowers and tobacco, the unmistakable scent of *Charisma the Eau de Parfum* undoubtedly coming from the countless white candles weaving through the space. Around the audience, filled with celebrities and power players even he recognized, were lush floral installations, and trees bearing shiny red apples as though plucked from the pages of a fairytale.

It looks like . . . Clark began.

An altar . . . Emily finished, her thoughts brushing against his as they watched.

The lights dimmed, and the room plunged into a reverent hush. The music began. The voice was instantly recognizable.

"I've been lost in the shadows, searching for my light,
Carried dreams on my shoulders through the longest night.
But every tear that fell taught me how to shine,
And now the stars align, this moment is mine."

"Felicity!" Clark whispered.

Emily looked up from the show program. "They're debuting the extended version of the pop ballad from *The Cost of Magic,* called 'A Crown of My Own' . . ."

She wouldn't . . . would she . . . ? Their minds buzzed with curiosity.

"Oh, they tried to break me, silence my soul,
But I've found the pieces to make myself whole.
I'll rise from the ashes, I'll stand through the pain,
No more shadows, no more chains,
Watch me rise . . . oh, watch me reign."

The opening model emerged onto the catwalk. She wore a cascading gown of flowing white silk organza, its train rippling like water by hidden fans. The stage lit her every step. Fiber-optic veins pulsed through the bodice. A gilded, light-up halo crowned her head, reflecting oversized pearls that shimmered like stars. In her hand, she held a scepter sprouting delicate white flowers, topped with a glowing pearl orb.

Is she supposed to be . . . a goddess . . . ?

The Empress . . . Emily thought. *Look at the bed of wheat on red from the projectors . . . the Venus symbol . . . the twelve stars on her crown . . .*

The second model emerged barefoot. A little girl entered opposite. The two walked down the runway hand in hand. They wore sheer baby doll dresses of pearlescent pink, with puffy sleeves. The digital background projected a cascade of childlike doodles of flowers, moons, and stars.

That's her kid . . . thought Emily. *I get it now . . . It's a tarot spread . . . The Fool is the beginning of the journey,* Emily thought. *Childhood, new beginnings, and youthful* . . . Thin streaks of silver glitter traced downward from their lashes and clung to their cheeks like starlight frozen mid-fall. . . . *Innocence* . . . Emily finished. In her hand, a glittering apple purse encrusted in rubies dangled like forbidden fruit.

It's the Creation of Life and Eve . . . she thought.

A dealing of cards . . . Clark began, their eyes meeting.

—always has a message . . . Emily finished. What would Charisma's spread reveal?

The mood shifted dramatically with the third look: robes of deep crimson on two otherwise nude models reflecting gold in the light. Gasps rippled over the audience: black-green snakes coiled over their shoulders.

"This is my crown, I've earned my throne,
A love so deep, it's carved in stone.
I've climbed the mountains, I've touched the skies,
No chains can hold me, just watch me rise.
Oh, watch me reign, I'm breaking free,
This is my time, my destiny."

I'm not sure what card that is . . . Emily thought. *Two figures and a snake . . . I think it's the Lovers . . . Adam and Lilith . . .*

The runway darkened for the fourth look: the model appeared clad in a gown of deep indigo, silver, and blue. A dramatic high collar and flowing cape billowed behind her. Blue glitter shimmered off the model's cheeks, chest, and long legs, while a glowing crescent-moon crown sat atop her head. Around her, the four elements projected on the walls—fire, water, earth, and air.

The Magician . . . ? asked Clark.

Emily nodded. *It's the birth of witches . . .*

Next, a modern Joan of Arc walked the runway, resplendent in a broad-shouldered power suit of silvery chainmail and armor, down to a sharp, mod skirt, paired with black booties and a black choker.

"Through the storms I have wandered, felt the weight of fear,
But I've seen the sun breaking, and now I'm here.
Every trial, every fall, was leading me home,
And now I walk in gold, I've made it my own.

They tried to break me, silence my soul,

But I've found the pieces to make myself whole.
I'll rise from the ashes, I'll stand through the pain,
No more shadows, no more chains,
Oh, watch me rise . . . watch me reign."

Strength . . . they both thought in union.

The sixth was unmistakably the Devil, of skintight red lace and leather, black lips, black sunglasses, and two twisting horns extending from the suit's puffy shoulders of black bird feathers. She dragged a spiked collar behind her.

The seventh emerged like a specter. The model's floor-length gown was a shroud of transparent gray tulle that spilled over her shoulders and across her arms like the robe of Lady Liberty and cascaded onto the floor in a sweeping train. Her hair was teased up tall. Her gaunt cheeks mirrored the shadowy orbits of her eyes. Smoke curled ominously from the hem of her dress, drawing audible gasps. As she walked, the layers of tulle dissolved into smoke, layer by layer, until nothing remained but the nude bodysuit beneath. Lightning strikes were projected around her—even Charisma's tower made the cut.

This could only be the Tower card . . . Clark thought.

"This is my crown, I've earned my throne,
A love so deep, it's carved in stone.
I've climbed the mountains, I've touched the skies,
No chains can hold me, just watch me rise.
Oh, watch me reign, I'm breaking free,
This is my time, my destiny."

The crowd fell quiet as the Death card took the stage, a skeletal black corset with ribbed detailing, shoulders adorned in black-feathered angel wings. A single black rose was tucked behind her ear, and a black veil cascaded over her face, trailing to the floor.

The ninth look took them a moment. The model wore a stiff dress, bracelets, and anklets made of brass. Her brass heels with clear platforms gave her the appearance of flying down the runway . . .

That can't be comfortable . . . Clark mused.

Justice . . . ? Emily thought. *Or Judgment . . .*

"Ooooh, the stars shine brighter when you're unafraid,
And towers will crumble where truth is made.
I'm not who I was, I've grown so much stronger,
And every step I take, I'll fly higher and longer."

The lights softened. The Star emerged in a dazzling, weightless, iridescent gown that sparkled under the lights. Beadwork formed constellations across the fabric. The model was painted from head to toe in gold glitter. A light-up starburst crown hovered above her head.

Emily thought to him, *It's like they're all psychopomps or angels . . .*

If Emily the Death Oracle thinks so . . . Clark thought.

A model entered wearing a dress of cascading gold-copper chains that glinted under the light. Copper glitter reflected off her cheeks, eyes, and legs. A crown of sunrays sat atop her head, on fire, illuminating the runway around her.

The Sun card—obviously . . . Clark thought.

"A Crown of My Own" changed to a higher key for its final chorus. A heavenly choir joined.

"This is my crown, I've earned my throne,
A love so deep, it's carved in stone.
I've climbed the mountains, I've touched the skies,
No chains can hold me, just watch me rise!
Oh, watch me reign, I'm breaking free,
This is my time, my destiny."

The last look: a gown of exploding rainbow-iridescent ribbon burst from the center of the model's bodice like the union of all elements. Behind her, fairy wings arched high, and her glittering, teased hair billowed behind her. She wore bejeweled eyes and red lips, and stalked down the runway in gladiator heels.

The World . . . thought Emily. *All the looks together* . . . *Completion* . . .

First New York, Clark thought, *next, the world* . . .

They exchanged puzzled looks.

The outro to the song rang with runs and harmonies galore.

"Oh-oh-oh, watch me rise, yeah-eah,
No shadows, no chains . . . (No!)
I'll reign . . . (Oh, I'll reign!)
Watch me fly . . . (fly-y-y!)
This is my time, my destiny . . .
Oooh, watch me rise."

Finally, Charisma stepped into the light and commanded the runway, her copper hair unmistakable under the stage lights. She wore an all-black ensemble, of course—a little black dress made of glossy obsidian-like fabric, hugging her figure.

The audience rose to their feet, roaring with applause. A fury rose in Clark.

Did she really plan to off Felicity . . . *and use her song for her show* . . . ?

Looks like it . . . Emily thought, casting him a sidelong glance.

Lorena and Alicia walked out and joined her. Behind them were Charisma's two children he had only seen in pictures: Grace and Noble. Grace, about fourteen or fifteen, waved to the crowd, reveling in the attention, while Noble, who couldn't be much older than six or seven, stood stiff and uneasy. They were backed by a woman with silvery coiffed hair, stately posture, and a cold, commanding presence.

That's Charisma's mother, Iris . . . Emily thought.

I know . . . Clark thought. Clark recognized her instantly: last year in their first meeting, when Lorena, on vodka on ice, had let slip her memories: a young Charisma having beached dolphins and whales; a teenage Charisma torturing a classmate under an electric aura; and their mother coercing Lorena into the family business of building Charisma's empire.

Children of all ages dressed in tarot-couture wandered onto the runway, each walking up to their matching mothers. Charisma basked in the adoration, waving and blowing kisses at the crowd in thanks.

Twelve looks . . . Emily thought as the models returned and the show came to an end.

Thirteen if you count the queen . . .

He opened the program under his arm. The show's theme was spelled out clearly: *Âge de la Femme*. Clark flipped the page to a separate tarot card insert. Carefully, he slid it free.

His stomach tightened as he examined it in detail. "The Empress," the top of the card read. Pictured was a fair woman with fiery copper hair lying in cascading waves around her shoulders, complete with fringe, a backcombed bouffant, and a diamond crown, with rays like a halo and a crescent moon in its center that resembled an eye. In the scenic background of this queen's throne was a tall hill with a tree that bore the red, round apples lying at her feet.

The card weighed heavy in his hand, as if alive with an unspoken promise or warning. This wasn't just a souvenir. Charisma's kohl-rimmed gaze of yellow-green, feline-like eyes stared back, leering out from the card, giving him that telltale feeling that her eyes were watching him.

Emily dragged Clark to the after-party at Casa Cipriani's. Most of the models joined. The guest list was even more star-studded than the show.

Across the room, none other than Miss Monica Chase-Whiteley was drifting from one group to the next, her smile as thin as the champagne flute in her hand, not really finding her stride. He caught her eyeing Emily and him, having a blast. Her unease amongst strangers gave him a little satisfaction, for being so mean to him. That night, he made sure to miss her completely.

Even better than that though, he decided, was exchanging conversation no one else was privy to with Emily.

I think that guy is checking you out . . . Clark shared.

No, I think he's checking you *out* . . . she replied, her giggling smile sparkling in his mind like the champagne bubbles rising in her glass.

The night blurred into a carousel of handshakes, introductions, and clinking glasses. He even agreed to have his photo taken next to his best friend.

Eventually the clock caught up with him. Clark slipped out of the party as it was getting good to practically sprint to the express train, late for dinner with Joey.

"Hi, babe," Clark said when he finally arrived, slightly breathless. "I'm sorry!"

"It's okay," Joey said. "It's only been fift—"

"You won't *believe* the night I've had," Clark interrupted, falling over him. "Do you know how many celebrities I just met? Who already know my name?! All from working for Charisma?! *Crazy!*"

"Yeah, crazy . . ." Joey said. His eyes darted to the table and back up. "Were you drinking?"

"Yeah, just a little champagne and . . . Oh." Clark followed Joey's gaze, and that's when he saw it. A card, a box of chocolates, and a bouquet of roses. Clark had shown up empty-handed. His face flushed the same shade of red as his gifts.

"Oh, Joey . . . I'm sorry." He ran his hand through his hair.

"It's okay," Joey said with a gentle wave. "Really."

"How was your day?" Clark was eager to shift the focus.

The mood lightened considerably during their luxury Mexican dinner, just off Union Square. They were served fresh chips and guacamole on a massive rock mortar, designer tacos, gourmet tres leches, and all the spicy margaritas Clark could fit. Joey enjoyed his Mexican Coke.

"No more dollar store taquitos," Joey declared with a grin.

"No more!" replied Clark with a laugh. "Well—maybe sometimes!"

Clark paid, of course—despite Joey's protests. In the cab home to Astoria ("Keep your card away" Clark had playfully chided) they fed each other from the box of chocolates, and exchanged a few quiet, lingering kisses.

As they flew through the Queensboro Bridge, Clark looked over

Joey's shoulder. Manhattan glittered in the distance, a city alive with possibility. In that moment, Clark felt like he could kiss the sky.

By Emily's birthday on the twenty-first, New York City's snow had melted, taking with it its fleeting gentility, and leaving its churned streets slushed and dirty. Winter was gone, and Clark couldn't believe it was already late February.

(12:00 a.m. Clark Crane): HAPPY BIRTHDAY!!

One . . . two . . . three . . . and Clark's ears began to ring. Bingo. His telltale sign that she was thinking of him.

(12:00 a.m. Emily Manitis): Thank you!!!

It worked . . . ! He almost laughed to himself.

He closed his eyes and thought of Emily in the car on the way to the airport, her bright blue eyes flashing in the Holland Tunnel lights, and the feeling of her hand in his, the feeling of friendship.

Miss you . . . he thought to Emily.

Miss you too . . . she thought back. *Hope you're okay . . .*

I am . . . he thought. *Are you . . . ?*

I'm great . . . ! So great . . .

Emily texted him a selfie of her in a bikini on a Seychelles beach.

(12:12 a.m. Emily Manitis): Had to get away . . . Far away.

After Emily had confided in Clark last year that her mother had passed the year before, he couldn't blame her.

(12:12 a.m. Clark Crane): You deserve it. ♥

(12:13 a.m. Emily Manitis): ♥ ♥ ♥ ♥ ♥ ♥ ♥ ♥

When Clark woke up that Sunday morning, the last thing he wanted was to feel the stagnant air of another box, his tiny studio apartment. Clark threw on his clothes and dragged Joey out of bed and outside for, as Joey put it, a *cawfee* and a *tawk* and a *walk*.

It was an unusually warm day that day, a tease of spring left behind by a southern air mass. "But global warming is a hoax!" Joey quipped.

Their path meandered under the tower-eyes of the RFK Bridge, Manhattan looking like a distant fortress. They strolled down the South Hill lawn of Astoria Park, the same path Clark had seen in his dreams, retracing steps from a place that felt both familiar and strange.

"You know Jessica sleeps right up next to me most nights?" Clark asked.

"Yeah, I know, I've seen her! She's glued to you."

"I know, it's so cute. She's always in my face when I wake up . . . Did you know, cats are naturally light sleepers so they can fend off predators? It's partly why they wake you up so early, they're happy to see you're alive after being asleep for so long. Plus, dawn and dusk are their prime times to hunt . . ."

Clark confessed to Joey about his odd dreams: the shadow under the Hell Gate Bridge, and Jessica appearing in every one of them, as if protecting him.

They stopped at a plaque along the river, its weathered bronze retelling the tale of a steamboat disaster in June of 1904. The General Slocum had caught fire and in the course of twenty minutes, the East River had swallowed it whole, and with it an estimated 1,024 lives. It was the highest death toll of any disaster in New York City history until September 11th.

"Creepy," Joey murmured, shivering theatrically.

Farther north, past the main Great Lawn, they paused to look at the orange-and-blue Hell Gate Bridge mural, its name spray-painted in bold capitals. Clark cleared his throat as they filed on: "You know the Sydney Harbor Bridge was modeled after the Hell Gate?"

"I didn't know that."

"Yeah," Clark continued. "Supposedly, it was over-engineered to carry heavy rail traffic and instill confidence in its stability over the *tempestuous waters* of the East River."

At his choice in vocabulary, Joey chuckled.

"Like," Clark said, "they used more steel and concrete than necessary, more than other bridges in the city. According to *urban lore*"—Joey made a mock-spooky "ooo"—"it's said that, a thousand years after humans are gone, this will be the last New York bridge still standing. Cool, right?"

Joey nudged him. "Nerd alert!"

As if to interrupt the moment, a delivery guy on a motorbike zipped by, cutting across their path on the sidewalk. The way he smoothly glided through the air . . .

Clark froze. There it was again: *he* was gliding through the air, flying on broomstick through a dark Queensboro bridge tunnel, in that Other New York hellscape from his night terror last December. Had he lost them? All was unnervingly still and quiet save for the wind in his ears. Clark looked over his shoulder—when a gargoyle flung through the rungs, its death roar reverberating through him, its red eyes shaking him to his core.

A sudden flutter: a pigeon flew too close to his head. It startled Clark so badly, he let out a yell and shielded his head. Joey burst into laughter.

"Flying rats!" Clark shouted, managing a chuckle to himself. Joey put his arm around him.

"Be nice!" he said. "You know pigeons are domesticated, right? Humans trained them and then abandoned them. Now they're city-locked with nowhere to go."

Clark nodded thoughtfully. "I knew that . . ."

But the idea stayed with him. Trained, abandoned, stuck—Clark couldn't help but think about his own tiny, two-hundred-forty-square-foot, hand-me-down studio apartment. It had been enough when it was just him; growing up between his parents', it was the only place he ever really considered home. But now, with his hand-me-down dresser spilling over with his and Joey's clothes, Matilda the weeping fig tree growing ceiling tall overnight, Jessica and her toys scattered across the floor, their exposed subway-tiled bathroom offering them no privacy . . .

The two turned east and walked back down the park.

"Hey, Joey?" Clark said.

"Yeah?" he replied, looking over.

"I've been thinking . . ." Clark began.

"Oh?"

"Maybe you're right. It's time we spread our wings. I'm making real money now and well, maybe our little shoebox isn't big enough for the three of us after all."

Joey's face changed from an inquisitive curiosity into feigned menace. "Oh yeah? You've been thinking again, huh?" Teasingly, he pinched and poked Clark's sides, who laughed aloud in protest and tried to squirm away. "I told you to cut that out!"

Joey grabbed Clark by the waist and spun him around and around, until he pulled him close and planted a kiss on his lips. The warmth of his face pressed against his as their lips locked in the brisk park air. Clark wished that moment could last forever.

"You serious?" Joey asked.

"Yeah!"

"Alright, let's look into it. You wanna get a place closer to work for both of us?"

"Yeah," Clark after a thought. "That'd be nice."

"You and me," Joey said, one hand on Clark's shoulder, "we just make sense."

"I feel the same way," Clark replied with a smile. "It's just so easy."

"Yeah," Joey said, grinning. "You've got me under your spell, baby. I love you."

"I love you, too."

Joey leaned in for a hug. With a deep inhale, his lips brushed Clark's neck as he softly kissed him. "Mmm, you smell amazing." His eyes fluttered closed for just a second.

For a moment, Clark tensed up. Could love built this easily, this perfectly, actually be real? Joey's arms tightened around him, pulling him closer, but Clark didn't resist. For now, he let good things happen to him, and let the doubt melt away like the slushy, melted snowy streets of New York.

Then, Joey added, "Amazing as in like a grandma—but better!"

Clark burst into a giggle and slapped his butt. He pulled away just enough to meet Joey's big brown teddy bear eyes.

"Let's go home, yeah?" Clark reached for his hand. Joey took it in his.

Under the park's faux old-fashioned gas lamps flickering to life one by one, the two strolled out of the park hand in hand and back to their little home.

It was almost two weeks into March by the time Emily had returned. She invited Clark to her TriBeCa loft for a girls' night—"No boyfriends, just us. Queens only!" Her loft was everything Clark could have dreamed of if he were blonde, beautiful, single, and rich like Emily: exposed brick and white ceilings, enormous, soaring ceilings and an airy open floor plan, white pine floors and furniture with crochet lace comfort, blown-up photos of her family's seaside town of Sounion, Greece, and a sprawling collection of indoor plants far eclipsing Clark's on space alone. It was the lap of luxury. He almost couldn't believe she'd ever leave.

They talked over glasses of Vinho Verde about anything other than work—Clark and Joey planning to move, plans for the summer, the endless carousel of guys on Emily's roster who she had begging at her feet.

"You should definitely ask Lorena if you can rent out one of Charisma's apartments!"

Clark's eyes widened. "Really? I can do that?"

"Totally, babes! She's got tons of properties all over this city. Your jobs pay into the rent. Like, an apartment for agency models, but you know . . . witchier."

"Hmmm . . . Okay . . ."

"Just trust me. She won't say no." Then she added with a smile, "You're a star. You deserve it."

Clark grinned over his glass and took a sip. "That reminds me," he began. "I'm so curious, where do you go when you're out for so long? Like when I got back from LA or just now after your birthday?"

He expected her usual playful quip or teasing misdirect. But instead, Clark was surprised to see how, slowly, Emily's smile faltered, and that sad look in her eyes returned.

She set her glass down on the side table gently, her fingers brushing the stem. Her aura rose, encompassing the entire loft with its pearlescent pink glow. *I think it's best we talk like this . . .* she said mind-to-mind. *I think you're ready to hear it . . .*

He gently replied, *Okay . . . What's this about . . . ?*

Remember when you asked me about who the Order is . . . ?

Clark hesitated. Last year, he had intercepted a note about the Order from one of Charisma's clients. After taking it home, he discovered revealing its blank page wouldn't require anything nefarious like bloodletting or a witch's word, but simply flame to reveal its ink.

"I am the one all your beloved stories are about," he remembered Charisma telling him in their midnight meeting. Clark had thought, *Talk about anticlimactic . . . !*

Yeahhh . . . Clark replied uneasily. *I remember . . .* From an outsider's perspective, the two of them sitting silently across the couch, staring at one another, must have looked completely absurd. The thought would've made him burst into giggles had it not been for the gravity of Emily's expression.

And . . . Do you remember you asking me about the Powers That Be . . . ?

Clark shifted in his seat. Her serious tone was started to unnerve him. *Yeahhhhhh . . . You said the Order is a group of oligarchs that control "everything" . . . And that the Order answers to the Powers . . . who are beings not on this plane of existence . . .*

Right . . . thought Emily. *Well, sometimes the Powers . . . send me on side quests . . .*

Really? Cool!

Yeah . . . Well, no, not really . . . Sometimes it's really heavy stuff, these charges and their needs . . . Sometimes I'm called to help on some . . . really crazy shit, babes!

What do you mean . . .

Well, it's like, first . . . their calls don't come in via text, if you know what I mean . . . ! It's like . . . it'll come in visions, like when I touch a person's hand and know or see instantly how they'll die . . . But then there'll be more, like . . . These "downloads" I call them, this innate knowing, that'll come in whispers on the wind, or like . . . I'll keep hearing "Mullberry Street" on TV or in a song, and I'll keep seeing numbers 567 . . . Like my coffee order will be $5.67 and then I'll get a spam call from area code 567 . . . and then I'll get a name . . . all in the span of seconds . . .

Oh, shit . . . Clark said.

Yeah . . . ! So, this one charge in LA, I showed up and was like, "Hiii," to the guy at the desk. "Are you Steven?" Imagine . . . ?

And was it Steven . . . ?

Oh, it was Steven alright . . . I had seen his face in my mind's eye . . . Birthmark on his left cheek . . . No chin to speak of . . . Purple lunchbox on his desk . . . And I'm like, "I dunno how to tell you this but, if you leave this building for lunch like you do every day at exactly 1:45, you're going to get hit by a red Prius and die . . ."

Clark's jaw dropped. *You told him that . . . ?!*

Emily nodded. Her stone-cold, matter-of-fact, low-affect approach made Clark burst into giggles.

Yep . . . !

What did he say . . . ?!

He froze, obviously . . . I mean, what would you *say . . . ?!* Emily giggled too. *He thought I was a crazy off the street and almost called security . . . But then I stopped him . . . and I asked if his lunchbox was purple . . . and I told him I wasn't there to hurt him, I was there to help . . . and then he lifted his purple lunchbox and set it on the desk . . . and then he stayed behind his desk while I "explained myself" . . .*

Emily sighed. *And 1:45 rolls around, and guess what? We're chatting, and then, BAM!—we hear a crash outside . . . Someone else steps outside first—a patient or something—and a red Prius plows right into them . . . Right there in front of the building . . . Steven sees the entire thing . . .*

Oh my gosh . . . ! Clark thought.

Right . . . ! The kicker . . . ? I never know the full story—I never do . . . The Bosses Upstairs, they've got a sick, twisted sense of humor, I swear . . . I just knew he couldn't leave at that time . . . and that he was supposed to die in a multi-car pileup later that day.

Oh no . . .

Yes . . . ! You see, I still see how they're gonna go . . . Like with Steven—I saw he was going to die the moment I touched his hand, right as he was reaching for the phone to call security . . . Well, he leaves work after the cops come, he's all shaken up . . . I follow his route, just like in my vision . . . And sure enough, on the freeway, there's a collision . . . a multi-car pileup . . . Steven's car gets hit, and . . . as my car comes to slow, I see his soul on the side of the highway looking at the pileup . . .

No . . . !

Yep . . . Same day . . . just . . . different time.

Clark's eyes began to water. *Wow . . . So after all of that, you're saying you couldn't even save him . . . ?*

Emily shook her head. *The Powers just give me these nudges, like . . ." This person's death isn't supposed to happen here" . . . But they don't explain the ripple effects . . . It's like, maybe the other passenger in that car crash goes on to meet their next partner in the aftermath, and . . . maybe their child goes on to help people or save lives or . . . I dunno . . .* She threw her hands up. *I don't get the answers. I just . . . move the pieces . . .*

Clark thought to her, *That is heavy . . .*

It can be . . . Emily exhaled deeply, her aura pulsing faintly as she spoke in thought.

Like, I just met with a guy—finance exec, big name, top of the Forbes lists, huge penthouse overlooking the East River . . . He claimed to being haunted by something he called "the Shadow" . . . I wasn't sure what he meant at first . . . I thought it was stress, but then I could feel it, too . . . Whatever it was, it was feeding off him . . . His greed, his ambition, his insecurity . . . it opened something dark . . . His life was falling apart in a matter of weeks. Wife left . . . Kids gone . . . Company collapsed . . . It was like watching a soul being eaten from the inside out . . .

Clark gulped. What happened to him . . .

He took his own life, Emily thought.

A shiver prickled the back of Clark's neck.

You know, she continued, *sometimes I wish the Powers would give me a little more credit! Like, just a hint of why they're asking me to do this wild stuff would be nice . . .*

Clark tilted his head. *They don't explain . . . ? Like at all . . . ?*

Never, Emily replied. *But I've pieced it together over the years . . . It's not random . . . The Powers are trying to keep things . . . aligned . . .*

Aligned?

Emily nodded. *Every life, every choice, every ripple—it all fits into this web of energy . . . Everyone, including Steven and that finance guy, is part of something bigger . . . Our lives—or our deaths—can shift the whole web . . . Like . . . imagine a future political leader . . . Their existence could change the course of humanity, right . . . ? So the Powers . . . ? They nudge things to keep the web moving . . . They're trying to help humanity survive, thrive. But . . .* Her voice trailed off.

But what . . . ?

Her aura flickered. *There are also energies that try to keep it off balance . . . As above, so below . . . There's something else out there. Something born of the demiurge, the collective pain-body of Gaia that doesn't want humanity to thrive . . . Charisma and the coven, we call it, "Her" . . .* Emily's lips pressed into a thin line. *She's always meddling. Tying knots in the web. Ripping holes in it. Sending energy off-course so it collapses in on itself. The Powers call her the Great Saboteur, but you know her by another name: the Devil . . .*

Clark swallowed hard. *Of course . . . ! Of course, She's real . . . Like, actual evil messing with people's lives?*

Emily nodded grimly. *She's not just some cartoon villain with a pitchfork, babes . . . She's . . . subtle sometimes . . . She feeds on chaos, destruction, pain . . . The Powers work to align things for humanity's progress . . . She works to unravel them, to her own agenda . . . And it's not just the big stuff—wars, famines, dictatorships—it's the small, everyday moments . . . like a person relapsing, and getting into their Red Prius . . .*

Clark blinked. *You think She caused it?*

I don't think—I know . . . That crash wasn't supposed to happen . . . Steven's death . . . ? The passengers' survival . . . ? They were meant to lead somewhere . . . somewhere good . . . At least, I like to think so . . .

Clark's mind raced. *But he still died that same day . . .*

Because that's what was meant to happen . . . Emily's aura flickered, softening again. *I can't stop fate, Clark . . . but I can keep it from being corrupted . . . That's the job . . . I don't rewrite the web—I just help untangle it . . . And trust me, "She" keeps me busy . . .*

Clark shook his head, overwhelmed. *So witches like you . . . you're basically soldiers in some cosmic war?*

Emily chuckled dryly. *Something like that. Except this war isn't fought with swords or armies. It's fought in whispers and nudges and tiny ripples that no one notices . . . The stakes are huge, but the work? It's quiet. Unseen. You and me, Clark, we're Lightworkers . . .*

Her fair skin and blonde hair, perfect oval-shaped face, open, glassy blue eyes . . . Emily had an alien beauty about her, sitting there with her sad smile, sipping the last of her white wine.

Then, with a sudden brightness in her voice as if they had been talking about the weather, she held up the bottle of wine. "A splash more? And then we should get to bed."

"Okay!" Clark said aloud. "And then we should go to bed."

He took a sip and paused. He asked in thought, *Does Charisma know . . . ?*

Yeah, of course . . . she thought back with a shrug. *I just don't tell her the specifics—she doesn't really care, to be honest . . . But yeah, she knows . . . or at least, I tell her I'm away on business and that's that . . . So long as my numbers are in and my clients are happy, that's all she cares about . . .*

Clark scrunched his face. So there was some humanity in her yet . . . *I don't get her . . . !*

Yeah, you'll come to understand her . . . We're just here to do our jobs . . . Nothing more . . . Nothing less . . .

Clark let her words sink in, the weight of it settling somewhere in his chest. He wondered, would he ever be chosen to take a call like that, from a Higher Power? If he thought hard enough about it, would he really want that? Between Charisma's empire, Mother's agenda, and now Emily's unnerving revelation, every rung he climbed made the step below him feel more unstable.

Maybe having one boss was bad enough.

The next morning Clark rode up to the penthouse with Emily in her town car—but not before a spritz of her cotton candy fragrance.

"I still can't believe you wear Charisma's," she had commented. "It smells like cat piss on me."

Clark went straight to Lorena's first thing to ask about moving into one of Charisma's apartments. He didn't expect her to immediately call in Monica, who just so happened to be the former fourth assistant, Keyholder, and manager of Charisma's residences around the world.

"Which will be your problem soon, thank goddess!" Monica declared as she swept into the room. "I am drowning as it is since taking over Melissa's duties on top of mine."

"No one likes a complainer, Monica," said Lorena. She turned to Clark in front of her desk. "Since your numbers have been performing rather . . . well"—at this Monica glared at her, then at him—"this does seem to be in the realm of possibility."

"Anything's an improvement I bet, from whatever crumbling tenement he calls home currently," Monica said.

"Apartment," Clark corrected firmly. "Not that you'd know anything about Astoria. Only real New Yorkers allowed. Qualifications which"—Clark sized her up and down—"you don't seem to meet."

Monica threw him a mocking, miming sneer from over Lorena's shoulder.

"Enough from you," Lorena said, directed at Clark. "Let's see . . . How about . . ."

"There . . ." Monica said.

"Oh, tut-tut, not there," Lorena said.

"Then what about . . . ?" Monica

"You know, I was thinking the same thing," said Lorena. "But don't you think . . . ?"

"Oh, no, banish the thought. Not that . . . besides, that apartment is occupied," Monica said, looking intently at Lorena.

"It is?" Lorena replied. "Ohhh, right, it is. Then that means one thing."

"Yep." They both turned to Clark.

"It's done."

Monica said, "You're in luck, loser. Pack your bags."

4"This," Lorena said, swiveling her laptop around to him, "is the apartment."

Clark did a double take.

"And this"—rip went the paper she scribbled on and handed to Clark—"is how much you will need to bring in to the coven per month."

Clark took the sheet. He read it. His throat went dry. *Well,* this *is sobering . . .* he thought. It was almost double his current goal.

Lorena lowered her eyes. Her smirk deepened. She asked, "You *can* deliver that, can't you?"

"H-how can I bring in those numbers?"

"Well, that much is up to you!"

Clark looked at the paper in his hand—the daunting figure glaring back at him—and back up at the two smirking witch twits before him. Oh, how he so wanted to wipe the ugly smirks off their faces. *Am I going to back down now . . . ?*

He squared his shoulders, the fire rising in his chest, as he uttered the words, "Let's do it."

Moving day came fast, just that weekend. It was the spring equinox and a full moon, Saturday, March 20th, the first true day of spring. To Clark, packing what little he owned was still like a monumental undertaking.

When Clark returned from the car and pushed the door open, he found Joey fumbling over the last small box. By the way Joey's eyes widened, he almost seemed caught unawares. He asked Clark, "You ready, babe? Last box," slightly out of breath.

Clark sang, "Yes, sir!"

Jessica hopped in her carrier with a flick of her tail, as if she too were ready for the next adventure.

On his final moment in Astoria Blue, Clark lightly ran his fingers over the pencil markings Grandma Wanda had drawn on the door frame, marking little Clark's incremental height until he'd almost reached the age of five, when she passed.

His eyes fell to the bookshelf as he walked past, and, without a second thought, snatched Froggie up and tucked him on top of the carrier. Clark stood in the center of the space, taking it in: the inch-thick papier-mâché paint, the tall windows that bathed the space in northern light, the bridge steadfastly watching back from the west, the memories it all held and the memories it couldn't hold anymore. He pressed a kiss to his fingers, and tapped the doorframe before pulling the door closed behind him.

They drove over the RFK in Joey's compact Honda, with Matilda—wildly overgrown—sprawled across the backseat and trunk. The city spread before them, glittering in the first light of spring, as they drove toward their new chapter.

"How are we gonna afford it?" Joey had asked, after Clark told him how much they would owe in rent. "I can make it work with my bartending if I take up Fridays and Saturdays but you on your assistant salary . . . Can we do it? What's she paying you, anyways?"

"I'm gonna work even harder," Clark said. "Plus there's always commission."

"Commission on what?" Joey had asked. "What is it you do for her, really?"

Clark hesitated. Despite his growth in the craft and the conversation they had last December, when he came out as a witch, they still hadn't discussed the specifics of Clark's work—or revisited any of that conversation at all, for that matter. It remained a quiet tension between them, don't-ask-don't-tell and swept under the rug . . . for now.

"Beauty sales. Look, don't worry about it, okay? I've got it all under control."

Joey had not seemed so convinced. "You sure you don't just wanna find our own spot?"

"It's only a little more than what we would pay anywhere

else—plus the amenities! The square footage! It's a steep steal but a steal nonetheless!"

With Clark gone again on weekdays from house calls, often running going into the evening hours of eight, nine, sometimes ten, they had both agreed to keep Sundays sacred. But with the costs of their new space and continuing to cover his grandma's—modest and rent-controlled, but still considerable—rent, they both understood that sacrifices would have to be made.

As the car weaved its way through Upper Carnegie Hill, Clark hung his head slightly out the window, letting the cool air brush against his face. Clark couldn't help but wonder what Joey must have thought of him since his coming out. Did he seem unstable? Unwell? Did Joey secretly think he was completely psychotic? Still, he had the distinct feeling that this delicate topic, so carefully avoided, was bound to surface again . . . sooner rather than later.

Maybe Joey was thinking about it too, on their drive in. Clark glanced over. "You're so quiet," he said.

"Just tired," Joey replied, looking at the road.

Clark didn't want to press. He dare not read his mind and breach his trust. When had Joey ever hidden anything from him? If there was a problem, he'd come to Clark when he was ready. He wasn't going to dig. Instead, Clark rubbed the back of Joey's neck and leaned on his shoulder, and took a sip of his iced coffee.

Their new Upper East Side apartment—apparently one of Charisma's first properties in the city—came with steep rules and the oddest agreement, which Clark read over more than once.

Summonings, coincidences, and magical mishaps are at Renter's expense, it stated. *Renter agrees to hold Owner harmless and indemnify against all claims.*

"That's mad fucking odd, Clark," Joey had said, skimming the contract over his shoulder. "Lemme see . . . Yeah, totally strange. You don't think the place is haunted, do you?"

"Knowing my boss, one thousand percent," Clark had teased. "Would you believe it if I told you yes?" he had asked, with a wry smile.

"Maybe," Joey had replied. "Maybe not."

For all of Astoria Blue's hand-me-downs, the curbside furniture, and his grandma's dresser, Lorena had assured Clark that the new apartment would come fully furnished with its own vintage and antique pieces. According to the agreement, those items would have to remain and be maintained by him, unless explicitly agreed upon with written consent from Charisma herself.

"Just bring your clothes," Lorena had said with a wicked grin.

Monica chimed, "Better yet, don't! Burn 'em!" Their cackle rang in his memory for weeks.

On the elevator up from the prewar lobby, doorman included, the anticipation was making Clark and Joey's hearts race. The brass elevator doors creaked as it revealed the carpeted hallway. A short walk to the end of the hall and there it was: PH1.

Clark carefully turned the key in the lock. "Here we gooo," he said. He pushed it open and flipped on the light.

A thin layer of dust glimmered in the air as the light spilled across the space. They stepped in through the darkly painted foyer and front hallway into the main room, where they stopped in their tracks. Before them stretched the most magnificent apartment space they had ever known.

They had stepped into a grand, two-story tall living room parlor with fireplace, crowned by a loft that overlooked that and the adjoined kitchen. The furniture was an impeccable collection of vintage mid-century retro-futurism. Clean lines, bold curves, and pops of color on metal and grain filled the space, all coated in a film of dust. The apartment felt untouched, suspended in time—although Clark couldn't tell just how long it had actually been since the previous tenants had occupied the space. There was a lived-in stillness to it, as if someone had left in a hurry . . .

A sleek iron spiral staircase wound its way up to the loft, immediately reminding Clark of the Tower—the ceremonial workspace at the topmost floor of Charisma's penthouse. It felt like a deliberate echo of her world.

"Just like Northlight," Joey pointed out, marveling at the furniture. His voice was soft, almost reverent.

Clark set Jessica's crate down. The moment he unlatched it, she sprung out, her tail high in the air. She bobbed her head up and down as she explored, tasting the air with her mouth agape.

Joey grinned, his eyes darting to a small alcove in the kitchen. "The washer-dryer!" he exclaimed.

"The dishwasher," Clark added. "The balcony."

They looked at one another for a moment, their faces lighting up simultaneously as they shouted in gleeful unison: "No more white refrigerator!"

"Movin' on up," Joey sang, do-si-doing with Clark in his arms, spinning him around the room, "to the East Side."

"To a de-luxe apartment," Clark chimed in.

"In the sky-y-y," they finished. They made laps around the space, laughing and pointing out all the features.

"This place is huge!" Joey exclaimed.

"It's perfect," Clark said, his voice echoing in the grand living room. "I can stretch my arms without touching walls."

"And we have a spare room! We can have guests over!"

"Parties!"

"This is the life, babe," Joey said, putting his arms over Clark's shoulders.

Clark grabbed his waist. "It really is."

After unpacking just enough to feel settled and working up a sweat from all the moving, they ordered Chinese food. Compact oyster pails sprawled out across the sleek kitchen counter.

"Not as good as Astoria takeout," Clark said. "But almost."

They sat there in quiet contentment, sharing bites of food and clinking their cans of soda. This, Clark thought, was a fresh start. A new chapter. Their new life was already beginning.

After finishing the last of their takeout and tucking the now-exhausted Jessica into her bed near the radiator, Clark and Joey set about the last bits of settling in. The boxes had been unpacked (or shoved into corners for tomorrow's problem), and the apartment, though still dusty and foreign, already felt more like theirs. Like home.

They cleaned off the table and tossed the empty takeout containers into the recycling bin. Joey wiped his hands on his jeans, leaning back against the counter with a satisfied sigh.

By seven, the sun had set beyond the south-facing windows, leaving behind a soft twilight that melted into the glow of the city. By seven forty-five, Manhattan was fully alive, twinkling like a sea of stars caught on the thirteenth floor. The rooftops below puffed streams of smoke into the cool night air, and from the upstairs bedroom window, Clark could see Charisma's tower peeking through the skyline.

By the time they settled into bed, their lids were heavy and their bodies ached from the day's work. They lay wrapped in each other's arms on their new king-sized platform bed, the faint hum of the city outside their fortress of quiet.

"I always dreamed of this day," Joey said softly. "I just didn't think it'd come this soon."

"Yeah, me neither," Clark whispered. Slowly, he grazed the line of Joey's stubbled jaw with his thumb. "We're so young. We've got our whole lives ahead of us."

"Yeah . . ." Joey whispered back. "Of all the guys I've dated, you're somethin' else. You know," he began, "before my Nonna Margaret passed, she told me, 'Settle down with someone who prioritizes you, someone who treats you with respect. But above all else, settle down with someone who makes you laugh.'"

"I like your Nonna Margaret. A wise woman. Did she have any idea it would be with a catch as adorable, irresistible, and hilarious as me?"

"Something like that. Good thing I got all that and a smart-ass too!"

"Lucky you!" Then, Clark whispered, "Hey, you know what they say about Italian boys?"

"What do they say?"

"They taste like pizza and have pepperonis for nipples."

Joey roared one of his deep, low, belly laughs, which always had a way of making Clark laugh too. When their laughter finally subsided, they lay facing each other in the dark, the faint glow of the light of the full moon spilling through the crack in the curtains of the tall bedroom windows. In the dark, Clark could just make out Joey's big teddy bear eyes (his were surely twinkling too). They leaned in and the universe collided into infinity.

"We did it, baby," Joey said. "We made it."

"Yeah, we made it . . ." Clark said.

"I love you."

"I love you too," Clark said. "And your pizza kisses."

"Goodnight."

"Goodnight!"

In no time, Joey was sound asleep and snoring—and loud. In Astoria, Clark swore Joey could make the picture frames on the walls rattle. Here though, in the safety of their new apartment, the sound felt all the more secure. If he were honest, falling asleep had been difficult after the coven's ritual hazing. Next to Joey though, all was well.

Clark found himself lying awake for a while. He stared up at the ceiling just like he had those many years ago when, after his troubled coming out, he ran away from home to the solitude of his Grandma's apartment. He remembered the feeling of finding himself emancipated, free, and very much alone. A childhood left behind, and an adulthood come too soon. Just like in high school, the future that awaited was vast and terrifying, but, at the same time, looking up at the ceiling of his first Manhattan apartment, thinking about how far he had come, the career he was cultivating, the passion he was following, the love lying beside him, bestowed like a gift . . . Clark felt more alive than he ever had. Despite the unknown, there was sure to be adventure ahead.

Jessica hopped onto the bed and curled up in between them, purring softly and kneading the comforter. Clark reached out to smooth her fur.

After some time, he shut his eyes and tried to quiet his thoughts. His breathing slowed. He was drifting off into the in-between, that hazy liminal space between waking and sleep, when—

An ear-splitting scream ripped through the stillness.

Clark jolted up in bed, his heart pounding. But the room was dark. Still.

The sound was coming from the bedroom itself, but not *his* bedroom—at least, not as it was now.

"Who are you?!" an old man's voice screamed.

Glass shattered. A vase? Then—

"What are you doing? Don't come any closer! Stop! *Stop!*" The old man's voice was panicked, shrill, and full of terror.

Footsteps thundered toward the bed. A black figure—long legged and quick—jumped onto Clark's side of the bed. A loud thud followed a terrible scream.

Then, silence.

But Clark saw it clearly: the blood on the walls. Carnage left behind. And on the old man's forehead, marked in his own blood as he lay still on the floor: an upside-down pentacle, its points intersected by an infinity symbol stretching across the west and east wings.

Jessica hissed sharply, her fur puffing up as she darted into the shadows of the apartment.

Joey turned on the lamp and looked at Clark. "What's wrong?"

Before Clark could answer, the silence was broken by the slow, deliberate *clack . . . clack . . . clack* of heels retreating across the wooden floor.

CHAPTER VI

Spell(work)

As Clark lay still and awake, pretending to sleep, he knew Joey was awake too—worried about him.

What did I just see . . . he thought.

The scream . . . The dark figure . . . The body and the mark on his forehead . . .

At least now I know what happened to the previous occupant . . .

Eventually, the energy settled and all was quiet, save for the faint rustle of the sheets and sirens in the streets below.

Clark traced shapes in the ceiling with his eyes, trying to make sense of it all.

Then he lifted his head.

A woman dabbed powder over her olive-toned skin—the same tone as Clark's—with the puff in her black-and-gold compact. He studied how she did it: deliberate. Rhythmic. She replaced the puff and set it down, then reached for her eyeliner and applied it in the compact's tiny mirror. It was always the same order: Eyeliner, to frame the eyes. Blush, to highlight the smile. The ritual never changed. Lights, camera, news at eight.

Shoot, I really gotta text her back . . . Clark thought.

Maria reached for her lip pencil. *Brown . . .* he thought. *Always brown . . .* Then came the lipstick, the top of her black-and-gold tube coming off with a pop. She swiveled it up. *What color was it gonna be today . . . ?* Clark kicked his legs in the air, perched on her bed with his chin in his tiny hands, watching her in her vanity mirror.

Mauve . . . he thought. *Her favorite . . . Mine too . . .*

Every motion was a chance to admire. Now she was blow-drying her bangs. How he so loved the smell of cooked hairspray, talc, and coffee in the air.

"Shouldn't you be getting ready for school?" Maria asked, fingers curled around her mug of Folgers as she brought it to her lips. Through the rising steam, her eyes found his in the mirror

"I'll be quick," Clark replied. His voice was small. So small. Smaller than he wished it were.

"Good," Maria said, tight-lipped and stern, touching up her lip pencil. "Why do you watch me get ready, *loco*? It's weird."

"Because . . ." Clark murmured. He gripped Froggie a little harder. "I think you're pretty . . ."

"Aw, thank you, pumpkin," Maria said. She reached for her can of hairspray and locked it all into place.

She's almost ready now . . . he thought. *Just needs the . . .*

Maria misted herself with perfume, shoulder to power shoulder, and one on her neck. Then she did a double take at the clock.

"*Ay,* look at the time!" Her makeup was returned to the drawer two at a time. "We can't be late."

She always does this . . .

"It's time to go to work. Go get ready! *Go!*"

Clark rolled to the left—and woke up in bed with a start.

His chest heaved as he took a deep breath. He looked to his left, but his eyes only touched cool sheets. Joey was already up.

He checked his phone.

(6:59 a.m. Mother): Ready for another lesson?

(9:09 a.m. Clark Crane): Sure! When?

Clark scratched his head and yawned. His phone buzzed in his head.

(9:10 a.m. Mother): Today. Come whenever.

Clark padded out the bedroom door, down the spiral staircase, and into the kitchen. Joey sat on the couch with the television on low, a dishcloth in hand, wiping a faint stain on the coffee table.

"Good morning," Joey chimed.

"Good morning," Clark said, landing in the seat beside him and laying his head on Joey's shoulder. "Bugs Bunny for breakfast?"

"He keeps me sharp," Joey said with a wry grin.

"How'd you sleep?"

"I didn't."

"Kinda the same." Clark sat up. He hesitated before adding, "I got called for a job." It wasn't a total lie, but it was close enough that the way the words tumbled out felt unnatural.

"Today?"

Clark nodded.

"Babe," Joey whined. "We promised to take off Sundays so we could spend them together. And we just moved in," he said, gesturing toward the stack of boxes by the window and the cleaning products on the counter. "Do you have to?"

Clark could hardly look up to see the disappointment in his face.

"I have to go. I promise I'll be back as soon as I can." He kissed Joey on the lips, then on the forehead.

Joey let out a sigh. "Okay. I'll see you on your way out."

As Clark stood, he paused. "Hey, I don't think I've ever asked. Do you know any other languages?"

Joey raised an eyebrow, and a small smirk tugged at his lips. "*Sí, sí señor rico, tomé ocho años de español en la escuela y me encanta hablarlo. ¿Por qué?*"

Clark laughed nervously, rubbing the back of his neck. "Just wondering!"

"Your mom never taught you?"

His voice jumped an octave as he said quickly, "Not really!" He spun on his heels and hurried away.

A hot shower and a couple of stops on the subway later, and Clark found himself standing in front of Mother once again. This time, a divider in the living room sprang to life with the touch of a button. It hummed into place, cutting off the living room from the dining room and kitchen. Before it closed completely, Clark caught the eyes of the coven, fixed on him with unnerving intensity. Not one blinked as the divider sealed shut, leaving Clark alone with Mother.

"How are you?" she asked, her voice soft but probing.

Clark took a sip of his coffee, considering his answer. "Well, we moved! Keeping up with the bills is going to be a challenge, but the new place is a dream come true. I think we can do it . . ." He hesitated.

"Something on your mind, baby?" Her eyes locked onto his. *Mother sees all . . .*

Clark sighed as he admitted, "Well, we . . . had a rough first night."

Her voice whispered into his mind, *Tell me about it . . .*

Clark relayed everything he could. He could feel Mother press him—his forehead prickling—for what he saw when the old man startled him awake. He replayed the gruesome scene with a shudder, ending in the sigil.

"You're a quick learner," she said finally. The corners of her lips curled up.

Clark tried to muster a smile. *I learned from the best . . .*

"The infiltrated is doing the infiltrating," she said, tilting her head. "It's rather poetic."

Clark gave a nervous laugh. "I think I was doing that sorta unconsciously before. It used to just . . . happen." He recounted Lorena revealing her core memories of growing up with Charisma, the intense connection with Emily, and how everything seemed to heighten after his near-death experience.

"Her climb to the top is swift in every incarnation," Mother said darkly. "Leave it to death to enrich our lives, huh?"

"Haha, yeah . . ." Clark murmured. He pivoted, mentioning Charisma's fashion show.

"Âge de la Femme," Mother said slowly. *The Age of Woman . . . Interesting . . . What do you think that's about . . . ?*

I'm not so sure . . . First New York, next the world . . . Clark echoed. *She's planning something . . .*

What could a witch who claims to rule the world possibly want . . .

He shrugged.

"How's work going?"

At this, Clark's face brightened. He flashed her his aura, bright and blue. It sang up and out like a wave that spilled over the room, out the walls, and reached the trees in Central Park. Mother squealed in delight, clapping her hands together. Clark recounted his latest jobs.

No one's been really major like Leslie yet . . . Just simple things . . . Confidence spells . . . rekindling romance spells . . . jar spells . . . Candle magic is my favorite because I can leave it with the client and let the magic do its work . . .

Hmmm . . . Mother thought. *Ready to make some real money . . . ?*

"Yeah!" he exclaimed, leaning forward like a kid invited to pick out a new toy.

Let's teach you glamours . . . No doubt that is the bread and butter of her coven. They rose from the armchairs, and she led him to the gold floor-length mirror standing on a fluffy rug.

This is getting to be a pattern . . . Clark thought.

"Okay," Mother said, her voice steady, "the first rule of glamours is that it doesn't change what is, it changes what people perceive. And to do that, you have to convince them that what you want them to see is better than what they are actually seeing. You have to convince them that what you want them to see *feels better* than what they see. Get what I'm saying?"

His eyes darted between her and his in the mirror. "I think so," he said. "So what do I do?"

"First," she said, turning to him with a smile that could spark a revolution, "you start by changing how *you* feel about yourself. If you want the world to see something different, you have to believe it first. And I mean *really* believe it. Watch this."

She turned to face the mirror fully, her posture regal. Clark could see the outline of her sage green aura in the reflection against her white ceiling, humming like liquid silk. She closed her eyes, breathing in deeply, her chest rising and falling in a deliberate rhythm.

When she opened them again, her irises were no longer honey amber-brown—they were a vivid Charisma Saintly green. The shift was so seamless, and the effect so real, it sent a chill down Clark's spine.

Clark gasped. "Now me! Now me!"

"Magic is about intention, and intention is about focus and awareness. I didn't just think my eyes were green, I fully believed they always were, like there's no version of me where they aren't. I convinced reality that my will was better, and it bent. You understand?"

"Bend to my will. Got it! So I just . . . what? Close my eyes and wish for it?"

"Not a wish. You embody it. Feel it in your bones. You're not wishing your eyes were blue, or green . . . You're *simply deciding* that you're stepping into the version of yourself where they already are. And the world around you simply adjusts to fit the new you."

Clark hesitated, then took a deep breath. He squared his shoulders, trying to match Mother's confidence, and stared at his reflection. "Alright. Let's do this."

"Good," she said, stepping back. "Close your eyes. Picture it. Picture how it feels to have people look at you and see exactly what you want them to see. You're not changing yourself. You are simply deciding that your reality is the truth. You're letting them see the truth of who you are."

Clark inhaled deeply, feeling his breath and his heartbeat in his chest. He thought about his eyes—not just how they looked, but how they felt. Warm. Vibrant. "I am simply deciding . . ." he chanted.

"Exactly."

"I am simply deciding . . . I am simply deciding . . ." *I am simply deciding . . . I am simply deciding . . .* He felt the walls lean in, as if the universe had its ear pressed to the door of their conversation.

When he opened his eyes, he gasped.

In the mirror, his eyes weren't their usual dark brown. Now, they shimmered a rich golden amber like a tiger's eye.

"I did it! I did it!" Clark exclaimed, bouncing on his toes.

"Let me see!" Mother said, grabbing his shoulders and pulling him closer to inspect. Her eyes narrowed. "Aren't they . . . always that color?"

"No! They're darker, usually," Clark said, grinning as he leaned back into the mirror, still marveling. "But sometimes when they catch the light they turn gold and I just . . . I wanted them to look like, well, yours . . ." As he turned back to the mirror, the gold had flickered, and in the blink of an eye his vibrant-gold irises had disappeared entirely. The glamour had fallen as quickly as it had started, as if reality had snapped back into place.

"Oh . . . It's gone."

"That's okay," she said, squeezing his shoulder. "Glamours take practice. You have to embody the feeling, like an unwavering innate knowing. If your belief slips—even for a second—the illusion does, too. I'm so impressed you achieved this much!"

Clark frowned slightly, turning back to the mirror. "So it's not about just creating it. I have to . . . stay in it?"

"Exactly," Mother said. "You have to live in it, baby. Convince yourself, completely. The moment you start doubting, the magic goes *poof*."

Clark sighed, running a hand through his hair. "Well, at least I did it for a second. That counts, right?"

Mother smiled at him. "Are you kidding? Most witches take years to pull off even a minutia of change for a second's time."

Clark felt his pride swell again at her praise. He glanced at the mirror once more, wondering if he could make the golden glow return. This time, though, he wasn't just thinking about it. He was feeling it—what it felt like to shine, to bend the world with nothing but a thought.

"I'll get it," he said, his tone determined. "I know I will."

"I know you will, too, baby," Mother said.

* * *

That Sunday night was Leslie's interview.

After unpacking, with still more dusting and cleaning to do, Clark and Joey collapsed on the couch as they settled in to watch.

The show's intro played, dramatic music underscoring clips from Leslie's controversial skit. The footage cut to the host seated across from Leslie, seated in her Victorian home. Clips were aired from the original skit months ago. The camera cut to Leslie, with her hands in her lap, and a twinkle in her eyes under her heavy lashes and camera lights.

"She looks great," Clark said. Joey nodded.

"Leslie, thank you for being here. What made you decide to sit down with us tonight?"

"I wanted to set the record straight and show America that I'm just as much of an American as you are, to anyone watching."

The host listed the acts Leslie had inflicted upon the effigy. "Some critics feel you behaved inappropriately and crossed a line. That some of these acts were obscene."

"Look," Leslie said. "I'm a comedian. Crossed a line? Please. If he can say what he wants, then so can I. It's punching up if he's on top. I have the same rights as he does. If a man did it, people would call him bold or daring or funny. But when I do it, I get blacklisted? If my skit bothers you, then we've got bigger problems as a country. What are the repercussions for us if we can't even exercise our Freedom of Speech and dissent against a political figure—especially one as abhorrent as he is?"

"What is it about the president that makes you feel so charged, so strongly?"

"I'm from New Jersey, born and raised," Leslie said. "Growing up, he placed a huge order from a family friend's business. Marble sinks, countertops, you name it. They thought it was their big break. My friends and family, we didn't grow up with a lot of money, you see. They went into debt to buy the material, and when the job was done, he refused to pay them. They lost everything, including their house."

The host sat very still.

"Another friend in Atlantic City, he never paid more than the deposit for construction on the president's property. My friend's dad had to close."

"So you're saying this is . . . a pattern?"

"I'm saying, the truth is always more interesting. The tristate is littered with fragments of many, many businesses destroyed by that conman. I'm not about to let him take my career or our rights, too. That man has more in common with the Antichrist!"

Clark and Joey looked at one another. "I hope she doesn't catch hell for saying that, too," Joey said.

"She won't," Clark whispered. His chest swelled: of this he was certain.

The host asked, "Is this a personal vendetta?!"

Leslie leaned forward with a wry smile. "Vendetta? No," she was quick to say with a laugh. "But personal—isn't it for us all? Us girls especially? Look: I let them silence me. Swallowed my pride, played along to keep the peace. And where did it get me? Out in the cold. But not anymore. If they want me quiet, they'll have to burn me at the stake."

"You've riled up quite a following of supporters since the incident, fans rallying behind you. But, the cancellations, the No Fly List, the death threats . . . Do you regret it at all?"

"Regret it? If anything, I regret not sprinkling glitter on it." Leslie smiled and looked down. "I love glitter." She chuckled her girlish laugh. The camera panned down to her heels, a shimmering pink.

The host smiled. "So do you think your skit overshadowed your message?"

Joey clicked his tongue. "He's so awful."

"If by overshadowed, you mean went viral and made people pay attention, then yes, it went exactly as planned," Leslie said. "But the real tragedy? The real tragedy is that women and minorities in this country are having their rights stripped away every single day. And instead of talking about *that*, we're debating whether or not I went too far with a Halloween prop and some arrows.

"What worries me is that, if this can happen to someone like me—someone like me, with a platform, great hair, and a big mouth—it can happen to anyone. And it *is* happening. Take what's happening with Felicity, for example. She's been silenced for using her voice."

The host raised his eyebrows, leaning forward. "You think she's being silenced intentionally?"

"I don't think, I know. Completely. She's vanished from social media for months. No interviews, no appearances, nothing. And for what? For speaking her truth? For standing up for herself? It's like we're all just okay with powerful women being erased when they push back too hard."

"I heard you're good friends with Felicity, is that right?"

The camera panned to photos of the two, including smiling selfies, outings in Beverly Hills, paparazzi snaps out on the town, and front row at many of her shows.

"Oh, great friends," Leslie said, the twinkle in her eyes returning. "She's a great girl. A really great girl. She really loves her son. She's the best mother I know. Really."

"All of us here were shocked by the tragic passing of Cynthia Bernhardt while she and Felicity were filming."

"Gahhhd! Saaame!" Leslie exclaimed.

"Can you tell us: How is Felicity doing these days?"

"Ohhh gosh," Leslie said carefully. "I haven't heard from her in a while, either."

The camera panned to the host, listening.

Leslie went on. "Can I be honest for a sec? I'm really worried about the girl. She's been quiet on social media since February and it's so unlike her. The fans are wondering too. It's so unlike her to go even a day without posting. Someone should really check up on her!"

On that Monday morning commute to work, ten minutes door-to-door, Clark didn't have to search hard.

Clark opened Felicity's now-dark social media. The comments on her last post, a snapshot of her and Sebastian, were coming in by the thousands. Fans were rallying and the headlines were rolling in.

"Where are you??" they wrote.
"We love you, Felicity!"
"#FindFelicity"

That day, Clark was in the Closet, organizing his kit. It was one of those rare moments when Monica and the twins were there too. The terrarium sat unnervingly on its pedestal, its presence pressing on Clark like a pair of unseen eyes, watching his every move while he worked. What struck Clark as funny, despite the unease it stirred in him, was how the three ladies gave no indication of noticing anything unusual, oblivious as ever. They restocked in silence—or at least, Clark tried his best to work quickly and keep his nose down. His aura was up, steady, and at the ready.

Monica leaned against the counter, her manicured nails tapping a rhythm against a jar of bath salts. She whispered something to the twins, leaning in close, one to each ear. The twins whispered something back, then shot Clark a quick, synchronized look, their lips twitching into identical smirks. All three broke into quiet giggles, the sound crawling up Clark's spine like an itch he couldn't scratch.

Lorena waltzed into the room, looking a little too pleased to be there.

"Girls! Gather round." Then she turned on Clark, her finger wiggling like a hook, her tone brisk and gaze sharp. "You. Come."

Clark froze mid-motion, one hand wrapped around a jar of Venus Balm, an anointing salve for seduction spells. He set it down like it was suddenly hot to touch and walked towards her.

"I see on our calendar you're not booked this afternoon. Is that true?"

"Yes," Clark said. *Is she going to send me home early like Monica or the others . . . ?*

"We have a booking after work," she announced. "A group call. Charisma will be there, myself included. Look *sharp*." Her gaze flickered over him.

"Awesome!" Clark said, a bit too eagerly. The commission would be nice. It might even help cover the birthday party he was planning for Joey, and he'd been itching to prove himself further.

"Charisma is teasing her latest release, Charisma Cream, out this fall."

"Oh, I can't wait," Monica interjected. "I am obsessed. It's so good."

"Charisma Cream?" Clark repeated. This was the third time he'd heard of it.

"Yes," Monica goaded. "It's a glamour in a jar . . . and we've had months to harness its power on ourselves."

"You've had . . ."

"*Months*, yes," Monica said, her smirk growing wider.

"And now," Lorena cut in, "we are sharing Charisma Cream and the power of glamour with our clients."

"With . . . our clients?" Clark's heart skipped a beat. *Does that mean I have to glamour* someone else . . . ?!

"Why, yes!" Lorena said.

"B-But," Clark said, "nobody told me how to . . . I—I never got one."

Monica's face changed into exaggerated concern, with her lips curling into a pout. "Well, you never asked, did you? And now you'll be using it for the first time? Ha! *Good luck!*"

Lorena raised her hand to still Monica's mockery. "Now, now," she said, her sly grin growing darker and darker. "Don't count him out yet. Now he can show our fearless leader what he's really made of—our so-called little witch assistant. If . . . he can."

The room began to shrink around him. The shelves and jars leaned forward like spectators at trial, awaiting his verdict with accusing eyes. The injustice of it all burned hot in his chest—kept in the dark while they had months to master the product.

How he was going to get out of this one, Clark wasn't sure.

After work, at close to seven, the coven met at the address provided by Lorena: a glamorous Sutton Place apartment overlooking the East River. Clark had time to run home, change, and panic in private before heading out.

The apartment was like one of the many fabulous abodes he had been privy to visiting as a junior on the run, a ritzy floor-through. Its ornate, low-ceiling parlor was transformed into an intimate event space, complete with many small, round tables draped in expensive linen. Each was set with chairs for two.

Other assistants were helping to set up too, their many kits being unzipped and broken open. Clark recognized some of the new additions from the Blood Moon Ritual at Charisma's the night Melissa died. Only one approached him.

"You're the new assistant?" she asked.

"Yeah."

"How long have you been working for Charisma?" Clark found it odd that she didn't even bother to introduce herself.

"Since last August," Clark said.

"And how long were you freelancing for them?"

"Freelancing? I never freelanced. I was promoted to assistant at New Year."

"I've been freelancing for years. You *never* freelanced for her?"

"Nope!"

Her brows crinkled in abject dejection and disgust.

Emily entered then. Clark was quick to break away so as to shoot her a glance.

Emily . . . ! he thought to her. *Em Em Em . . . ! I just learned how to do a glamour on* myself*—yesterday! And it was me making my eyes go from brown to browner . . . ! How am I supposed to do a glamour on another person . . . ?!*

From the corner of her eye, she threw him a glance as she unpacked her kit, pulling a satchel of tarot and placing the stack on her table. *I dunno how to explain it . . .* she thought back. *The same way you do it on yourself . . .*

But . . . mine only lasted for a second . . . Are they supposed to wear them like, long term . . . ?!

Well, yeah, babes . . .

But how long can a glamour last . . . ? Like, realistically?!

Hmm, well . . . Usually they turn back into pumpkins at midnight . . .

Clark's eyes grew as wide as the circular table he sat at. Emily paused unpacking. Her lips pursed to stifle a laugh. *I'm sorta kidding, but also . . . not . . .*

In walked the twins and their hollow doll eyes, gliding creepily in perfect unison. Mandy rolled in two more luggage bags on the polished floor, while Milly wobbled in behind her on six-inch pumps, cradling a small cardboard box. All eyes in the room followed.

The assistants quickly gathered around it. Milly ceremoniously pulled back the flaps. Inside were a dozen handheld Saintly mirrors—and stacks of many small white boxes. Clark was quick to nab one.

Charisma Crème by Charisma Saintly, the box read in embossed gold letters. He swiveled it around to read the back:

DARLINGS, I have created a one-of-a-kind MAGIC YOUTH ELIXIR that harnesses the POWER OF GLAMOUR and ALLURE, and reveals the GODDESS WITHIN.

Featuring my PATENTED PLUMP + PULL MAGIC™ TECHNOLOGY with CELESTIAL WATER and POWER-ACTIVATING FLORAL EXTRACTS that REVERSE the SIGNS of AGING and ATTRACT hydration for 24-HOUR MOISTURE, revealing YOUNGER, HEALTHIER-LOOKING SKIN.

Its BEGUILING BLEND will BEWITCH the ONLOOKER, ENSNARE the SENSES, and help you UNLOCK the RADIANT LIFE of your DREAMS.

My innovative crème CONJURES CONFIDENCE, CHARM, and CHARISMA in the HEART and SOUL of every woman.

The ingredients list read like a potion, just like her perfume. After "Crystal-Infused Moon-Charged Spring

Water," Clark read through one floral extract after another:
Camelia, Jasmine, Geranium . . . Chamomile, White Tea Flower, Evening Primrose, Blue Lotus, and Tansy extract . . . Mallow Flower, Licorice Root . . . And finally, at the bottom, *"And a secret magic ingredient . . ."*
Beneath, in Charisma's unmistakable cursive, flowerier than Clark's, it read:

Always cruelty-free.

Made with love,
Charisma Saintly
xoxo

"Secret magic ingredient" . . . "Made with love" . . . Clark wondered, rereading the script. *Is the magic ingredient love . . . ?*

He pulled the box's two halves apart to reveal a lotus-flower box inside. Its petals unfolded to reveal the cream heart, a clear round jar with a gold lid. The box was set aside and he twisted the crystalline jar open. He lifted it to his nose: it smelled softly like sunscreen. He dipped a finger in and scooped a mound onto the back of his hand. Under the chandelier light, it was a pearlescent white molten gold. He rubbed the mound into his hand, working it in until its rich texture melted into his completely. He held his breath in anticipation when . . .

Nothing.

Nothing happened out of the ordinary. It left a moisturized sheen, sure, but no transformation, no spark, no shift had transpired. His skin was still his skin, if now a little softer.

How is it supposed to work . . . ? he asked Emily.

Don't worry about that . . . Just do what you do for yourself on your client and you'll be fine . . . But Clark . . . whatever you do . . .

It was gone almost as soon as it came: Clark's eyes were pulled to Emily's, whose face flashed him the gravest of looks. The sudden weight of dread that she dropped in Clark's stomach, he would remember the feeling for the rest of his days:

Don't use the cream . . .

The curtains were drawn, the candles lit. The assistants were called to stand in a line, directed by Alicia. The clients entered, marveling at the space. A gaggle of about ten or so girls walked in, one for each assistant he counted. Lorena walked in after them, holding what he could only grimly imagine was a stack of Saintly NDAs.

"Ladies," Lorena began, her voice cutting cleanly over the murmurs. "Welcome. Tonight, you will experience something few others in the world ever will: a night of beauty, feminosity, and magic. I now present to you . . . Charisma Saintly."

The room sprang into applause. That's the moment she strode in.

"Darlings!" Charisma cooed. She kissed the matron of the group cheek to cheek, then went down the line of girls. She swept in on a breeze of air kisses and a glimmering smile, the scent of her perfume trailing in her wake.

There she is . . . he thought. *Boobs and bling and all . . .* That presence, that power, that prestige: Charisma was without question the center of any room she entered. Her gravity demanded awe and admiration, pulling the attention of everyone in her orbit.

But in that moment, more than ever, Clark felt that same strange sensation bubbling up—the one he had always experienced when he stood this close to her.

And suddenly, he understood it.

He wanted that magic for himself. All of it.

"Thank you all so much for joining me and my team," Charisma said to the women now in their seats, and nodded to the line of assistants behind her with Clark at the far end. "It is truly an honor to be with you here tonight."

She paused, her eyes sweeping the room with practiced ease.

"Throughout my long career, twenty-something years of tastemaking, styling, and consulting, I have been sharing my own personal laboratory mix of moisturizer with my clients.

"Women," she continued, "even celebrities, are not immune to the effects of aging. I see it everywhere: society is stressing and aging women now more than ever. Between home, and marriage, and work, and children, I needed to find a way to do what I do and put the power of glamour directly into the hands of my beloved clients. I needed to bottle up my twenty years of expertise and give it to the world. Quite frankly, I needed to bottle *myself* up. I needed Charisma in a jar!"

She paused as the room broke out into polite laughter.

"I've worked with the best laboratory in the world, the very one that produces the top skincare in the industry. So good is this laboratory, in fact, there is actually a hunt for which lab it is." Her green eyes glinted; a smirk broke onto her lips.

"I've worked for twenty years to develop this youth potion, to bottle up the magic I give to my clients. It contains a youth-boosting mix of hydrators, emollients, peptides, and actives to make it the perfect anti-aging cream. But I took it a step further: I needed it to transcend mere cosmetic benefit. We added apple seed and angelica root, pomegranate extract, and camellia," she sang, "to give the wearer seduction, abundance, and sensuality.

"We imbued it with moonlight-infused quartz, citrine, moonstone, and rose quartz in spring water to amplify the wearer's natural charm. And then"—she paused for effect, her voice softened into a seductive lilt—"a final secret magic ingredient."

They sat in hushed silence, hanging on to her every word.

"Instantly, fine lines are visibly plumped. Instantly, skin appears brighter, firmer, and deeply hydrated. But more than that, a woman's vitality is instantly restored, turning back the clock, and returning to her the glory of her divine, Goddess-ordained beauty.

"The cream developed a sort of cult following amongst my celebrity friends—all the supermodels, the royalty, the stars I work with. 'I've got to get my hands on Charisma's secret Youth Cream,' they would say. *They* named it—not me!"

Charisma held her hand aloft, and Alicia, quick as ever, placed a fresh jar into her palm. Charisma held it up, letting the light glint off its golden lid.

"This cream," she said, her voice rich and commanding, "will elevate your love, your light, and your power. This cream will transform your inner and outer worlds into the beauty of your dreams. This cream will give you the power to create and achieve the life you have always imagined but dared not achieve—until now."

Charisma paused, lowering the jar slightly. "Empowering women has been my life's purpose. As a life coach to the stars, I have clients who come to me with 'nots'—not good enough, not powerful enough, not beautiful enough. And like a massage therapist, my job is to work the 'nots' out of their minds and hearts, and all of those limited self-beliefs out of their lives."

Her smile swept the room, and she gazed into the eyes of each of the women in front of her. "It is my deepest understanding that when you look good and feel good, you are unstoppable. Every woman wants to feel gorgeous, confident, and sexy, and cosmetic magic is one brilliant way to achieve this.

"First, I revolutionized the beauty world with my line of Charisma Lipsticks, so that women could speak into existence their love, their truth, and their beauty. Then, last year, I did so again with the release of *Charisma the Eau de Parfum,* which boosts a woman's aura and amplifies her Goddess within. And now, with my revolutionary face crème, I am forever changing not just the landscape of beauty but the world, and ushering in the dawn of the Âge de la Femme—an age where women step into their power and rise to take their rightful place at the head of the table. And you are here with me tonight to witness its birth.

"It's like I always say, darlings: *Give a woman a little Charisma, and she can conquer the world.* Thank you."

The room clapped enthusiastically, caught in the spell of her words.

"So tonight," Lorena said, "we will select one beautiful girl, and reveal the woman within by granting her beauty wish fulfilled. Then, you will break into individual sessions with our team of assistants who are eager to share their gifts so you too can experience the magic for yourselves. How does that sound?"

Again, the room broke into applause. The energy was electric.

Lorena said, "Hortencia. Please."

From her seat, Hortencia rose, walking carefully from her table to sit with Alicia at her table. Hortencia wasn't an unattractive girl, Clark thought, not by any stretch. On the contrary, she was, by his estimation, conventionally pretty in every way. Her skin was smooth, blemishless, and even. Her features were balanced. Her teeth were straight, a testament to her wealthy upbringing. Her hair was clean, her clothes pristine. In some ways, she was so pretty that to Clark she was almost uninteresting!

What could she possibly need from Charisma, Clark wondered. What would her transformation be?

Charisma reached out a hand, clasping Hortencia's hands with an intimacy that instantly drew the room closer. "What is your wish, darling?" Charisma asked. "What is the beauty of your dreams?"

Hortencia hesitated. Clark noticed her fingers twitching slightly in Charisma's grasp. She looked around the room as if the answer might be on the lips of her counterparts, somewhere outside of herself. The matron of the group gave her an encouraging nod. Finally, Hortencia turned back to Charisma. She had difficulty maintaining eye contact as she spoke.

"Um, well . . . I do wish my eyes were brighter," she admitted. "And that my eyebrows were fuller. My lips fuller. My cheeks higher. I wish I had that 'pop,' that certain something that other girls have. And . . ." She paused, her ears turning pink. She gave a sheepish smile. "And . . . if only this cream could make my butt bigger."

The room broke out into polite laughter, the amusement lightening the mood. Charisma chuckled along. "Very well, my darling."

Alicia twisted the jar and scooped a dollop of *Charisma Crème* onto the back of her hand. "Obviously, Hortencia already has her gorgeous makeup on, which we won't disturb. So, Hortencia, I want you to close your eyes and envision your most beautiful self, the one you just described to me. Think of her strongly. Give her all your love. Can you see her?"

Hortencia nodded, her brow furrowing slightly in concentration.

"Good. Now, Alicia is going to . . . press . . . the cream," Charisma said as she rubbed the dollop between her fingers, warming it up. Alicia gently patted the cream onto Hortencia's face slowly and deliberately. "Over her skin, like this."

The walls were leaning in. The universe sucked in its breath as if hanging on to her every word and motion. Charisma stood back in bemused satisfaction, as if admiring a masterpiece.

Clark blinked. The room collectively gasped.

Could it be?

Hortencia looked in her mirror and did a double take: her lips were fuller. Her blue eyes were bluer. Her cheekbones were higher. The her in the mirror looked subtly yet discernibly different and improved. She even looked down and grabbed her bottom.

"My ass!" she exclaimed, her voice bursting with disbelief and delight.

"Every time you apply the cream, I want you to envision your highest beauty, this woman you are tonight. Use this cream, and you will embody her for the rest of your days."

"Oh my GOD!" she squealed. "Thank you, thank you, thank you!" Hortencia jumped up out of her seat and hugged Charisma.

The assistants broke. The room swarmed into motion and murmuring. Assistant after assistant darted in front of Clark, making dashes for the tables. Like musical chairs, he was the last one standing.

"You can take *her*," Monica purred from the chair beside him. They both turned. The matron of the group, the mother, was seated quietly in the corner. Clark sized her up in ways he knew he was wrong for. She was a bigger woman, there was no doubt about that, and dressed impeccably well, from her jewelry down to her shoes. Her face was seemingly bare of makeup, especially compared to the girls in the room. Her two pale blue eyes staring back almost seemed to sink into the peaks and valleys of her cheeks.

She held herself with unshakable composure, her posture straight, her hands folded neatly in her lap. But Clark caught something beneath her stillness, a flicker of something lurking beneath those pale eyes. An unease.

Monica chuckled softly, low and mocking. He heard her mutter,

"Put lipstick on a pig, it's still a pig." How he so wanted to wipe that smirk right off her face.

Clark squared his shoulders and meandered toward the table with his head held high. As he approached, he noticed the way her eyes darted to the floor, then back up to him again. It wasn't hard to read. Clark knew what he was looking at: fear. He swallowed hard.

His hand extended with a smile, he said, "Hi. I'm Clark."

Her grip was firm, yet short. "Prudence," she said.

"It's nice to meet you," he replied, taking a seat diagonally from her.

"Listen," she said in a low voice, glancing over her shoulder. "You don't have to do all of that. I'm just here for my girls, my daughters and their friends." She gestured to the young women scattered across the room, poking and prodding their faces in their mirrors, chatting and laughing with the assistants.

"Oh," Clark said. "You mean . . . you don't want to try the cream?"

"It won't work," Prudence said flatly, her voice dropping even lower. "Trust me. This isn't . . . I'm not . . ."

Clark scrunched his eyebrows. He tilted his head as he said, "Wait, what do you mean? Of course it'll work."

Prudence quickly shook her head, and glanced at the room to make sure no one saw.

"Do you . . ." Clark pressed slowly, "not have a beauty wish?"

Prudence hesitated. "I'm not like them," she said finally, her gaze dropping. "This kind of thing isn't for me."

Clark gently asked, "Why not?"

Prudence gave a hollow laugh, shaking her head. "You wouldn't understand."

He puffed his chest. "I bet you I would."

"Beauty," she whispered even lower, "is for girls like them. Don't worry about me."

"Why do you think that?" Clark asked.

She looked at him then, really looked at him, her pale blue eyes filled with something Clark recognized immediately: resignation. "I've never been called pretty my whole life. *Ever.* My husband . . ." She searched to draw up the words. "My husband, he says I look like a pig in a wig." Her words landed like stones between them. "He doesn't love me," Prudence muttered resolutely. "No one does. But I love my girls. That's all that matters."

Clark reached out and placed his hand lightly over hers, which she held tightly in her lap. She flinched slightly at his touch, but he didn't pull away. His breath caught. His chest tightened. It all came to him at once.

It wasn't just the memories: it was the weight of them. The feelings that lingered in the corners of her soul. A hollowness where love should have filled her. A doubt planted by others and watered by her own quiet acceptance.

The ache he felt wasn't just hers. It echoed through him, resonating with a part of himself he'd tried so hard to grow beyond. He knew all too well what it meant to carry those feelings, the quiet, suffocating belief that you were not enough, that you would never amount to much at all. That you had little to offer the world. A world that had little in exchange for you but passing glances and half-hearted smiles. A world that passed you by.

In a way, Prudence was holding a mirror up to *him.*

But beneath it all, there was something else. Something faint but undeniable. A flicker of possibility—a tiny ember buried under the weight of it all, waiting for something, anything, to coax it into flame. *The world has not passed them by.* It had been waiting. Waiting for them to step forward, to stoke the ember into something brighter. Something unstoppable.

Clark leaned in. His voice hovered just above a murmur. "There's a smile in your heart, in the way that you love your girls, in how much you give. That smile is meant for you, too."

Her lips parted, and she blinked at him, as though she didn't quite believe him.

"And when you smile, the world smiles back at you. It's waiting for you. *Just give it a chance.*"

Around the room, table by table, the girls were bursting into squeals and giggles, their delight growing louder with each transformation. Prudence looked back at Clark, her pale eyes searching his.

"What do you say?" he asked. "Are you ready to meet her?"

A voice rang out from behind them. "How are things here, darlings?" It was Charisma. She did not wait for an answer. Clark and Prudence sucked in their breath and watched as she twisted the lid of the moisturizer, plucked a dollop with a finger, and lobbed it on the back of his hand.

"Rub it into your fingers," she said, grabbing his hand and directing him, "and over her skin." She whispered into his mind, sending chills down his spine, slipping right between the aura that he had left unattended. *You know what they need. Impose your will. Simply decide it. Convince the universe that your point of view . . . is simply better . . .*

I am simply deciding . . . he chanted in his head. *I am simply deciding . . . I am simply deciding, I am simply deciding, I am simply deciding . . .*

Up and across her cheeks he smoothed the cream on. I am simply deciding . . . he chanted in his head. I am simply deciding . . . I am simply deciding, I am simply deciding, I am simply deciding . . . The walls leaned in; the universe held its breath; and Charisma stepped back, a glint of satisfaction in her eyes.

"Wow!" she declared. "Now *that* is amazing. Look at you, Prue. Gorgeous."

Prudence's eyes fluttered open. She looked in the mirror and her mouth fell open. Her slack skin and hair, her downcast eyes, and the corners of her mouth and pale eyes that belied her poise: all transformed. All smoothed and blurred. Her cheeks were glowing, blushing high and bright, and bringing out her eyes, which sparkled piercingly blue under her soft fringe of lashes. Even her hair was as full of life as her grin, beaming out into a triumphant smile. It was as if she, this Prudence, had been sitting there all along. She was the most radiant woman in the room, bar none.

Clark turned to look at Emily. Her face, stunned, softened. She mouthed to him: *"Great job, babes!"*

"Watch out, girls," Charisma said to the room. "You have some catching up to do. Take note."

Charisma did something that caught Clark unawares: she patted him on the shoulder. It was a gesture so unexpected it left him momentarily stunned. Then, with her swift elegance, she strode off to the next table, leaving a hum of murmurs in her wake.

"Here, darlin'," Prudence said. She unclasped the purse hanging on her chair, and pulled out a roll of bills. They were in the hundreds. "Take this. Buy yourself something nice." Before Clark could say a thing, she placed the roll in his hand and closed his fingers. "*Thank you,*" Prudence whispered, inclined toward him. *"I've never felt so beautiful."*

He turned to look at the room again, his gaze sweeping across the sea of women to find, save for Emily, the fuming faces of Monica, Lorena, and the coven combined, burning into him.

Monica's lips twisted in disgust.

Lorena's eyes narrowed on him with irritated shock.

The rest of the witches, and even Prudence's girls, too, radiated the heat of envy and resentment. They bore into him like a spotlight.

Smugly, Clark smiled back at them all, turned around, and pocketed the money.

Clark Crane burst through the apartment door of PH1 and tore through the short hallway.

"Babe," he shouted, "just *wait* 'til I tell you about the gig tonight! I had the most ama—" He stopped short. "Joey, what's wrong?"

Joey was on the couch, TV on low, staring at the wall. Jessica purred softly in his lap. He was still in his pajama bottoms.

"Joey?" He dropped his bag in the hallway and stepped closer.

Joey didn't move. His voice came flat and hollow. "I got fired."

Clark's excitement evaporated in an instant. He crossed the room to plop on the couch next to him, wrapping an arm around Joey and resting his head on his shoulder.

"I'm sorry," he said. "What happened? Wanna talk about it?"

Joey only sighed.

"I'll understand no matter what. Promise."

Joey turned to him, his expression equal parts frustration and defeat. "My manager Louis, remember him? Well, Sundays off weren't gonna work for them anymore since *he* has Sundays off. They said picking up bartending shifts on weekends and lunch shifts on weekdays wasn't really gonna work for them after all, either.

"He said they need a more reliable assistant manager, someone with a more open availability on their schedule who can 'dedicate themselves fully.' I just . . . make more behind the bar, you know? He said my managerial duties were slipping, which is *not* true but . . . I dunno . . ."

Clark frowned. "That makes no sense. You work your ass off and you're so good. Everyone loves you!"

"Right. No one's as good as me. The regulars love me. It doesn't make any sense." Joey ran his hand through his hair. "I guess none of that matters to them." He shook his head. "They just want someone who can give up their whole life to the restaurant."

Clark squeezed him. Joey leaned into his embrace, the tension in his shoulders slowly easing.

Joey exhaled again, leaning back into the couch. "It's not even the job, really. It's the way they did it. Like I was disposable. Like all the work I put in meant nothing. I don't get it."

"You're not disposable, Joey. You're talented and hardworking and amazing at what you do. They'll realize they screwed up when they're left with some half-assed replacement who can't hold a candle to you."

Joey offered a small, grateful smile, but it didn't quite reach his eyes. "Thanks, babe. It's just . . . hard, you know? I didn't think it would hit me this bad."

"It's okay," Clark said. "We'll figure it out. Together."

Clark sat with him in silence for a while, his mind racing with thoughts of how to help Joey get back on his feet. For now, though, he knew what Joey needed most wasn't a plan—it was just knowing that he wasn't alone.

Joey spent the rest of the week sleeping in late. Clark would come home from work to find Joey on the couch, wrapped in a blanket. The TV would be on, but Joey's eyes would be glazed over, staring at nothing in particular.

By Saturday, an unruly beard had grown in. Clark came home to an apartment that was colder than usual. In the flicker of the television, Joey's aura wasn't its usual bright burnt orange. It had darkened at the edges, a candle struggling to stay lit.

Clark reached out, brushing Joey's shoulder. "Babe?"

Joey startled, turning toward him with glassy eyes. "Oh, hey. Didn't hear you come in."

Clark forced a smile. "You okay?"

"Yeah," Joey said slowly. "Just tired."

Jessica never left his side, perched on his lap or curled up by his stomach. She'd look up at Clark when he walked in, her yellow-green eyes seeming to say, *Don't worry, I'm looking after him.*

By the second week, Joey shaved his neck but left the beard, as if a full shave required more energy than he could muster, or remembering himself cleanly shaven, suspender-clad, and work-ready would be too much for him to face. He took to deep cleaning the apartment, scrubbing the floors, and wiping down every surface he could find.

One evening, Clark came home to find Joey in a bandana and sweats, surrounded by cleaning supplies and a bucket. "I feel like I'm constantly cleaning and it's never done," Joey muttered, not even pausing his furious scrubbing.

Clark wasn't sure what to say to that. He set his bag down and folded the pile of dishrags Joey had left in the kitchen.

By week three, Joey had gone back to working at his parents' pizza place. "I'm grateful to at least have this as a backup," he had said with a strained smile, though Clark could hear the ache beneath it.

"It's just for now," Clark had said.

Some days, Joey would drive his car down to Bay Ridge. More often than not, Joey would take the train, over an hour's commute each way, sometimes more, sometimes less. On the nights Joey came home around eleven at night, he'd bring a box of pizza for Clark, setting the box down on the coffee table with a tired grin. The smell of fried dough, marinara sauce, and sweat wafting off of him would fill the apartment as Joey collapsed on the couch, exhausted. Sometimes he'd be asleep before Clark even opened the box.

"You smell like pizza," Clark teased once, leaning over Joey's head in his lap. He brushed Joey's thick, dark hair back.

Joey chuckled faintly. "I *am* pizza," he replied, not even opening his eyes.

One Saturday, Joey texted Clark mid-afternoon: *Hey, I'm staying at my parents' tonight. I'll be back in the evening.*

Clark stared at the screen for a moment before replying with a simple, *Okay, love you, see you tomorrow*, and setting his phone aside. What was he to do alone on a Saturday night? Jessica hopped up onto the couch beside him and settled into his lap.

Emily had vanished again after the house call with Prudence and was now completely MIA. Clark sent her a faint, *Miss you* . . . but received no reply. He trusted she was on call and had her reasons for staying quiet, but the silence left a twinge he didn't care to name.

That was the first Saturday alone. By the second, Clark found himself agreeing to stay out for drinks with a client, hesitating for only a moment before texting Joey that he would be stepping out for the evening. And that was how every weekend went: Joey in Bay Ridge, Clark out in Manhattan. The hours stretched long and quiet between them, the rhythm of their lives starting to slip ever so slightly out of sync, one unspoken beat at a time.

At work, however, Clark was beginning to soar. Glamours had transformed his life.

Taking a cue from Charisma herself, Clark started writing personal thank-you notes to every client he worked with. The notes quickly became his secret weapon. He discovered how much work begets work, each referral leading to the next. Glamours had put him in high demand.

"I slept in it and woke up still gorgeous," clients would gush. "My husband can't keep his hands off me," they'd say.

The cream became a focal point of his services. As instructed by Lorena, Clark teased its release to his clients, quickly surpassing his presale goal to, again, lead the coven. With demand skyrocketing, he found himself swamped with preorders piling in by the boatload.

Reluctantly, Clark even enlisted the twins for help. Not foolish enough to trust them completely, he triple-checked their work at every step. For extra assurance, he handed off the mailing process to the post office, ensuring nothing slipped through the cracks.

The money rolled in faster than Clark could have ever imagined. In just four weeks, he managed to get ahead of his student loans, his phone bill, and rent, with plenty left over. For the first time, he had enough to start saving. As the distance at home widened, the gap between his dream income and his reality finally began to close.

Eventually, Joey's birthday arrived: Thursday, April 18th. Clark surprised him with two things: a shiny new bong (Joey having burned many a crescent moon into the bowl by the time evening came), and an intimate dinner at the Chelsea Hotel, its Art Deco refinery casting their table in a golden glow. Joey fit right in, in his button-down and slicked-back hair.

They began the evening with *croquette de chèvre*—honeyed goat cheese and caviar on crisp potato chips with chives—and *façon niçoise,* seared tuna nestled over butter beans and egg. Joey ordered the Chelsea burger with a soda, while Clark chose *steak frites* paired with the Tarot Garden: a blend of cognac, Grand Marnier, cherry, and lemon.

When dinner was over, Clark presented Joey with the largest size of a designer fragrance he loved—the one he wore daily and was running low on. Joey stared at the box, momentarily speechless, his face breaking into a grin so wide it gave Clark the butterflies. Joey was beside himself.

They ended the meal with a shared dessert: gold leaf hazelnut chocolate ice cream that felt as decadent as the evening itself. Under the low glow of the Chelsea's chandeliers, their booth became a world of its own. The other patrons watched curiously, but Clark didn't mind. They sat next to each other in the corner booth, ending the night in kisses.

I haven't seen Joey that happy in a while . . . Clark wrote in his diary. *It made every bit of it worth it. The page was bookmarked with a Polaroid taken of them that night.*

Joey's birthday dinner was a quiet triumph. But as Friday the 19th approached, Clark was determined to keep the celebrations going. Clark reached out to Joey's friends he gathered from his socials, as well as his own friends from his birthday back in October, the ones who had flaked out or couldn't, for whatever their reasons, make it. This time, everyone RSVP'd yes. Even Clark's auntie, his mom's best friend, Patricia.

"Hi, Clarky!" Patricia chirped as she bustled in, her unmistakable nasal Queens accent filling the room like a sitcom. He could practically hear a laugh track in his head. She set the cake she brought down on the counter and wrapped him in a bear hug so tight Clark thought his eyes might pop out of their sockets.

"Lookachu! It's been forevah!" she said, her voice going up half an octave as she pulled back to examine him.

"New clothes! New home!" Clark said, twirling around and gesturing to the apartment. "You like?"

"Like? Love!" Patricia squealed, clapping her hands together. "Oh my *gawd*, look at this place! And you, you're like a whole new person! You're so fancy now, huh?"

Clark mouthed "guffaw, guffaw."

Jessica trotted in from the guest room and froze mid-step. Her fur bristled. A low growl built in her throat, escalating into sharp hisses as she crept toward Patricia.

"Jessica!" Clark chided, horrified. "This is Patricia, she's family!"

Jessica grew more cantankerous by the second. Her hissing grew into cries, and she lunged forward at Patricia, swiping at her feet in a frenzy. Patricia yelped.

"I've *never* seen her do this!" Clark stammered. "She's so friendly usually! I'm so sorry!" He yanked her back. *"Jessica!"* She was flailing to break free.

"It's okay!" Patricia said, tucking her dark hair behind her ears with a laugh, though her eyes flicked down warily. "Jesus, she's feisty. Must've learned it from her *motha*—you."

Clark whisked Jessica out of sight and quickly launched into the tour: Patricia marveled at the decor Clark had set up after work while Joey was out. Silver and blue streamers and stars draped along the spiral staircase and the banister of the loft above. Jazz and R&B drifted from the speakers. He had laid out a spread of food that ranged from casual comfort to upscale indulgence—pigs in a blanket nestled alongside fine charcuterie, cheeses, and crackers. The bar cart was fully loaded, brimming with wine, liquor, and mixers ready to go. Clark had even been careful to stash away the fragile vintage glassware and any decor he worried might not survive a crowd. Their mid-century-modern abode was a Night Under the Stars, every detail executed with love and care.

By six o'clock, guests began arriving in lively clusters, their energy pouring into every corner. Patricia floated through the room, chatting with anyone and everyone, a glass of wine already in hand. Even Jessica trotted around the apartment, winding through and rubbing up on legs, cozying up to strangers on the couch, and sniffing curiously at plates of finger food. A quiet pride swelled in Clark's chest: he had never brought so many people together under one roof before.

And then Joey arrived. The door opened; the party erupted into a chorus of "Surprise!" Joey froze for only a second before breaking into a grin.

"Wow, baby!" he said when he caught up with Clark. He moved through the apartment, greeting friends and family with hugs, handshakes, and that big, booming, life-of-the-party laugh of his, the kind that carried through a room.

Joey's friends, Clark noticed, were as handsome as he was, paid little to no attention to him, and were in a league of their own that Clark couldn't quite ever imagine running in circles with: lean, built, and effortlessly fashionable, with straight smiles and classic haircuts.

Clark's friends made their entrances too. The first was Krystal Johnson, whom he had known since middle school, who swept in with her flavor of the week in tow. She wrapped Clark in a tight hug. "I've missed you! Oh my god, check out this place, boo! I'm so proud!"

"Thanks, babes!" Clark told her.

"What's work like? Tell me everything!"

He turned—then blinked.

Standing in the doorway like a glitch in time was Katie Bredford, his college best friend. The girl who once knew everything about him, and lately, almost nothing at all. She had declined the invite to his birthday dinner last year, and his many attempts to see her before and after.

"Miss me?"

"Katie!" Clark rushed over and wrapped her in a hug. She wore a leather jacket over a slip dress, her hair longer than he remembered, her smile, exactly the same. "You made it!"

"Of course," she said. "I owed you one. Plus, I had to see this glow-up for myself. Sweet digs, man! How's life been?"

Before he could answer, the door buzzed again. Clark turned just in time to see Alex Watkins and Justin Trinh walk in, arms wide and voices loud. The energy of the party had officially shifted.

Justin and Clark had met at a gay bar and would go out here and there, Clark's ventures out during and after college being infrequent. Alex, on the other hand, had started as a match on a dating app—until their first kiss revealed zero feelings, and Clark asked to be friends.

"Love your Aunt Patricia," Justin said. "Fabulous!"

"So that's your boyfriend?" Alex asked, eyeing Joey, who was entertaining his friends by the bar.

"Yeah!"

"How'd you meet," he asked, unable to hide the envy in his tone.

"At work. Why?"

Justin and Alex exchanged glances.

"What?" Clark asked.

"We knew him when he was a bartender at High Rise. You know, in Hell's Kitchen?"

"Yeah . . . So?"

Alex leaned in. "Rumor has it he was fired."

"Yeah, he's a hottie, alright, but one of the bartenders there told me he's crazy."

"I heard he got let go a year ago for drinking too much on the job."

"Really . . . ?" Clark's gaze flickered toward Joey. He was halfway up the spiral staircase, giggling, so high his eyes were barely open as he chatted with a friend up in the loft. Clark turned back to his friends, who nodded in reply.

"Huh . . ." Clark said. Clark had never really asked Joey about his sobriety. He had assumed it stemmed from growing up in a household where he had been exposed to alcohol at a young age. Joey had mentioned on their first date mixing his Nonna Margaret her amaretto sours, he thought he recalled. He'd said she liked to stay "zippy." But now . . . this was something different. Something to think about.

"Be right back," Clark muttered. He followed up the staircase, to see Joey's slick hair disappearing into the bedroom. Clark opened the door and sat on the bed. He swore he heard footsteps on the roof—until the flush of the toilet broke the silence and Joey stepped out, wiping his hands on his jeans.

"Oh, hey baby," Joey said in his smooth jazz singer way, flipping off the light. "Great party!"

"Can you believe it? Our lives are so cool," Clark said, wrapping his arms around his broad shoulders.

"Yeah . . ." Joey said, his eyes looking away.

"I'm glad you're having fun."

Joey hesitated. "Hey, how do you know those guys downstairs?"

"Who?"

"Your friends. The ones you were talking to."

"Justin and Alex?"

"Yeah."

"Oh. Out! I invited them to my birthday last year. How come?"

"Oh. Hmm . . . They used to come in to work when I worked in Hell's Kitchen, and . . . Never mind," Joey said. "I didn't know you were friends with guys like that."

"Okay. Is that a . . . bad thing?"

"I mean," Joey said, "I think you're better than them, is all."

Clark looked up in confusion. "What do you mean?"

"They didn't even show for your birthday, and now they're here, snooping around your life, counting your pennies? Doesn't that seem weird?" Joey sighed, running a hand through his hair. "Never mind. Forget I said anything."

Joey took a step closer, squinting slightly as he studied Clark's face. "Hey . . . are you wearing contacts?"

"What?"

"Your eyes. They look . . . different."

"Oh!" Clark let out a nervous laugh. "Yeah, I am! You like?" Clark batted his eyes at him with exaggerated playfulness, trying to lighten the mood.

"Yeah, very pretty, but Clark, they were fine without. You're already perfect the way you are."

"Aw, thanks." He looked away. "I'm just having a little fun . . ."

Clark stepped closer, pulling him in with a deep inhale and a sigh. But then, something gave him pause: cutting through the moment, the faint but unmistakable scent on Joey's breath lingered between them.

Clark pulled back slightly. He looked into Joey's eyes and carefully said, "Joey, have you been . . . drinking?"

Joey took a step back. He shrugged. "Yeah, so? It's my birthday."

"But I thought you were . . ."

At the look of incredulity on Clark's face, Joey furrowed his brows. His lips parted as if to say something, but he pressed them together instead. *"I'm just having a little fun,"* he replied. "Let me live a little, okay? I'm fine."

"Okay, babe," Clark said. Joey pulled away, brushing past him to walk out the bedroom door. Clark stared after him.

Beard and booze . . . Who is this Joey . . . ?

Clark turned to the mirror over the dresser to admire his eyes in the lamplight. His irises glinted gold-brown, the way they looked when the sun would hit them at just the right angle—just how he liked them best. And if he liked them this way, that should be enough for anyone else. Shouldn't it?

Clark darted to the bathroom cabinet and pulled out a jar of *Charisma Crème*. The walls leaned in as he swiped a dollop onto his fingertips and smoothed it onto his face. *I am simply deciding* . . . he chanted to himself. Back at the dresser, he pulled his bottle of *Charisma the Eau de Parfum*. A puff of its tasseled atomizer and—*pop*. A faint, subtle click fell into place. It was as if the universe had shifted on its axis and recalibrated reality just beyond the bedroom door.

The moment Clark reentered the party, every pair of eyes fell on him. He could feel the pull of his gravity as he moved through the crowd, drawing people closer like a magnet. Conversations paused. Guests stole glances. Their awareness sighed with every step he took, their attention hanging onto his movements, his every word.

Suddenly it wasn't Joey's party anymore.

Even Joey's friends, who had paid Clark no mind, now watched him with palpable interest. Their gazes lingered—curious and heated—their attention wrapped around him like a velvet rope. It made Clark blush.

Joey noticed, too. Clark saw something flicker across his boyfriend's face: confusion, and something else. Was it jealousy? *Good,* Clark thought. But he wasn't finished. He tried something else:

Clark reached out—not physically, but with his mind—and pulled, yanking in hard the energy of those around him. Like a quiet current of electricity. The guests drew into him, their focus tightening. They pined for his attention and a chance to speak to him, to be seen by him. He felt it surge through him—a new kind of power he hadn't known before. The room was his to command. Clark was the center of attention.

And just like that, something inside him clicked into place.

He didn't know if it was right.

He just knew it felt good.

CHAPTER VII

Limitless

The camera panned slowly across shimmering jars of *Charisma Crème,* stacked into a crystalline pyramid atop a glass pedestal. Beside the display, a sleek coffee table gleamed with Charisma Saintly Beauty's greatest hits: *Charisma the Eau de Parfum*, lipsticks, glosses, compacts, and glossy pamphlets proclaiming "Radiance, Redefined."

Lush applause swelled as the segment opened, the camera pulling back to reveal a dazzling talk show set: blush-toned lights, a live studio audience, and the soft sparkle of a branded backdrop reading *THE SPOTLIGHT* in gold cursive.

At center stage, Charisma Saintly herself reclined on a velvet armchair, copper hair cascading over one shoulder. Across from her, the show's host—a poised fashion journalist in a black satin pantsuit named Faye Monroë—sat perched with a gleam of admiration in her eyes, as if basking in the aura of cultural royalty.

"The word and name on everyone's lips," Faye began, turning to the camera. "Charisma Saintly. For more tha two decades, you've been the world's most influential tastemaker, shaping not just fashion, but working in film and television as an executive producer, standing at the forefront of New York lifestyle, and branding some of the most iconic figures of our time. You're a billionaire mogul, savant, and a mother. Your influence knows no bounds."

The audience burst into applause. Charisma offered a serene wave, crossing her legs with reverence as if she hadn't orchestrated every angle of lighting, laughter, and praise.

"*Tsssss*," Clark muttered, watching from his phone on the commute to work.

Faye leaned forward. "And now, with *Charisma Crème*, you're taking your magic from the beauty counter to the bathroom vanities of women everywhere. Tell us—what inspired this leap into skincare?"

Charisma's green eyes glittered under the studio lights as she launched into the same pitch as at the house call. Faye nodded enthusiastically.

"They say face cream," Faye continued, "is one of the most ancient and intimate beauty rituals for women."

"It's true!"

"How long have you been developing this?"

"Oh, for forever!" Charisma said with a coy laugh. "But I'd say I've been perfecting this moisturizer for the better part of twenty years."

Twenty years? Clark scoffed. *Or, if you're an ancient witch incarnate, literally forever . . .*

Charisma went down the same spiel: secret lab, celebrity following, finishing with her trademark promise: spending her whole life "empowering women," and how her cream developed a cult following.

"This cream will help you achieve the life of your dreams—it's certainly helped me achieve the life of mine!"

Applause swelled. Clark sat back in disbelief. *She's not even saying anything . . . he thought. It's fluff . . .*

Faye was beaming. "You've already conquered so many industries to much acclaim. Not just clothing and home goods, but you're an accomplished restauranteur. Your nightclub So Below has been hailed as reviving New York City nightlife to a year of yore. Besides the expert behind it, what makes *Charisma Crème* stand out in a market as oversaturated and competitive as beauty?"

"Oh, darling, everything!" Charisma's girlish voice, the emphatic uptick, how she spoke with her hands and made you feel like you were laughing with her and in on the joke, it was easy to follow and trust her every word. "Let me tell you, working with the most beautiful women in the world, I *know* the power of beauty. I wanted to capture what I do for my clients and bottle the power of when a glamorous woman walks into a room—how she walks, how she talks, how she commands attention. How she gets what she wants—*and bottles it.*

"I've sourced the world's finest ingredients and patented technology because women everywhere deserve nothing but the absolute best. *Charisma Crème* is clinically proven to reverse the signs of aging and give you plump, dewy, radiant skin for twenty-four hours, with a secret magic ingredient, so that you can ignite the goddess within. The woman you were always meant to be."

Faye eagerly leaned in. "Can you tell us what that secret ingredient is?"

Her smile to camera lingered, but to Clark, biting his nails as he watched, it somehow never reached her wild, cat-like eyes. "A magician never reveals her tricks, darling!" They shared a laugh. Clark blinked.

Was she for real . . . ? "Secret magic ingredient" . . . ? "Ignite the goddess within" . . . ? If you know what to look for, that witch isn't even hiding how fake and evil she actually is . . .

"It's love, darling, the secret ingredient is love! I put my heart, mind, body, and soul into every jar. It's like I always say, darling, everybody needs a little Charisma! Give a woman a little Charisma and she can conquer the world! When my clients wear this cream, they don't just say people tell them they *look* gorgeous. They say people tell them they *are* gorgeous. My cosmetics will change your life. You're not just glowing; you're unstoppable. *That's* the magic of *Charisma Crème*."

Faye nodded. "You're not just selling the promise of beauty, you're promising a new way of life."

"Ex-actly!"

"Your skin *is* amazing. I mean, look at you! Charisma, you're forty-two years old? You look not a day over twenty-four!""

"Forty-two years *young*, darling." She held for applause. Her laughter was like bells, bubbling over like Dom Pérignon. Clark wanted to hate her. "I am turning forty-three this August, and I am *very* proud of my age."

"Truly incredible. Speaking of glow, we have to talk about your hair. 'Charisma Copper' has become the number one most requested color in salons around the country. And it's so striking on you."

Charisma tossed her long, styled hair forward. "Ah yes, that's my redhead genes showing! Believe it or not, neither of my parents are redheads. But somewhere in the family tree was a fiery ancestor, and here they are, living on my head." She winked to camera.

"Everything you touch turns to gold—or copper, as the case may be. What, in your words, would you say, is your secret to your meteoric success?"

Oh, just blackmail, extortion, racketeering, a trust fund, and good ol' fashioned ritual sacrifice . . . Clark thought.

As if she could hear his thoughts, Charisma turned to camera. She leaned back with a grin. Clark nearly choked on his coffee. "My collection was the number-one-selling debut of any designer. My Charisma Lipsticks were the highest-selling debut of any cosmetic collection to date. My *Charisma Eau de Parfum* has a cult following. It's quickly becoming the best-selling celebrity fragrance of all time.

"I've continued to shatter records and glass ceilings everywhere because I pour myself wholeheartedly into every single thing I do: fashion, nightlife, parenting. I've worked very, very bloody hard for what I have, and darling, suffice to say, nothing was handed to me. I believe a woman can have it all, without sacrificing a thing, if she believes she can: ambition, beauty, love I believe in passion, dedication, and authenticity. There is nothing women cannot achieve. Think bigger. Think limitless. It's our birthright."

The audience erupted into cheers. It was magic—true witchcraft. Not the kind in books, but the real kind. Influence. Illusion. Adoration bought with charm.

"Charisma, if you could give our viewers three beauty secrets, what would they be?"

Charisma counted on perfectly manicured fingers. "First, be authentic. Authenticity is everything, darling, it's the cornerstone of beauty. When you're authentic, you're magnetic—and that's true beauty.

"Second, indulge yourself. Denial becomes etched on our faces.

"And third—above all else—be kind, darlings. Always be kind. Nothing ages you faster than cruelty, and nothing lights you up from the inside out like kindness."

"Your passion is so infectious, Charisma. You make us want to buy it all! America loves you!"

Clark was going to be sick.

Charisma laughed. "Of course, darling! And I love you, America! First New York, next the world, darling!"

The camera panned out. Her billion-dollar smile beamed at the camera. "Charisma's film, *The Cost of Magic,* starring megawatt pop-actress Felicity Tierres, is out in theaters this October twenty-fourth. You can preorder your *Charisma Crème* now on Charismasaintly.com."

The Tower's gargoyles spouting April rain gave way to fair May weather.

Wispy, low gray skies over New York City billowed back to blue, and from his perch, high up in the turret, Clark knew:

He was on top of the world.

By then, Clark's schedule was packed with consultations, divinations, and glamours. From readings to spells, the Big Three and everything in between. Every corner of the city seemed to call his name, he barely had time to breathe between appointments. Clark Crane was so good that witchcraft was becoming . . . automatic. Once a mystery, it had now become routine.

Making magic was his job, and spells would, of course, have to happen on the spot. But when it would come time to create, some mysterious power would pour over him from above, briskly and completely, always catching him in disbelief. The words were fairies skipping through his head all hours of the day and night, waking him up to jot down phrases or whispering in his ear to alter incantations he had read.

The work of witchcraft had become all Clark could think of.

Clark would fly through the homes of the affluent, his services more in demand than ever. Group calls were where he excelled, much to the resentment of the coven. Every time he would be relegated to the mother, he would create the most flawless glamour, or the most perfect solution to her problems—and every time, the mother would slip him an envelope so fat, the girls and their young clients would fume, their feathers thoroughly ruffled.

Clients would tell him their needs, and Clark would give them what they wanted. The coven would bristle. Clark would thrive.

Through it all, Mother had been oddly silent. Clark wondered when he would hear from her again.

Lorena, on the other hand, had plenty to say. In realizing how much money Clark could rake in for her, her tune had changed completely. She began raising his rates and booking Clark on major VIP clients of the coven: not just housewives but artists and diplomats. Some had belonged to Melissa. It seemed that Monica—to use Lorena's words—was "simply not fit" for them anymore. Clark, on the other hand, was "a studied craftsman." She billed him as "proficient in the Art and trusted advisor to Felicity, Leslie Parks, and New York's most elite." Clark had become a product, polished, packaged, and sold to the highest bidder—and he loved every second of it.

His checking account and Matilda the weeping fig were not the only things that had become overgrown.

"Joey, look," Clark had said one night. "My followers grew, like . . . overnight."

"How many?"

Clark told him. Joey's eyes grew big.

"Let me see." They huddled over his phone in disbelief. Clark's social media following had exploded—not just by the hundreds, but by the thousands, then the tens of thousands. Flocks of new followers descended on his account. *Wise-guy New Yorker. 4th Assistant to @charismasaintly, NYC,* his bio read.

"But, how?" Joey had asked. "Didn't you have, like, a couple hundred when we met?"

Clark shrugged. "People wanna know you when you work for Charisma."

Joey's face went pale.

Clark added to his diary that night, one entry of a few in those days.

I've found the thing I'm really good at being, he wrote: *Me. I'm not just good, I'm great.*

The feeling of safety, security, and success swelled in his chest like a balloon. His eyes sparkled with dollar signs. The bills were paid. There was love at home. And for the first time, Clark felt like he was truly flying. He could kiss the opal sky, so full of promise.

Sometimes in PH1, this apartment in the stars, I have pinch-me moments.

These views are mine.

These amenities.

This balcony.

This home we're building . . .

Even in the midst of his dizzying heights those three months, a small voice lingered in the back of his mind.

Where is Felicity?

At a small Upper East Side atelier, Clark's face lit up like the Fourth of July.

He turned from the mirrors and skipped down the platformed steps so hard he could have sworn he levitated. Clark threw his arms around Joey, planting a big kiss on his lips and almost knocking him back in surprise.

"You made it!" Clark cheered. "What do you think?" He stepped back for Joey to see.

Joey blinked, wide-eyed, and gave a wry smile. "Wow, baby, I . . . hardly recognize you."

"Isn't it great?" he squealed, sashaying in a mirror. Clark's custom black power suit and crisp white button-down were fit snugly to his every contour under the boutique lighting. He had never been this overjoyed to shop for clothes. The suit was his armor; dressing and looking the part was his newfound superpower.

"I had these recurring dreams last year," Clark began, "where I met the Ideal Me. He was so . . . everything I'm not. Confident. Composed. And—" He paused, and then through a laugh said, "You should have seen how he looked at me. I swear the suit he was wearing looked *just like this one*."

"Clark," Joey said softly. "You don't need a fancy suit to become someone you admire. You're admirable. *I* admire you!"

"You're sweet." Clark smoothed the lapel of his jacket, his eyes still locked on the mirror. "I'm getting you one, too."

"Wait," Joey said, "you're what?"

"I said, I'm getting you one," Clark repeated. "The neighbors talk, babes. Don't you hear them whispering when we walk through the lobby? Gotta give 'em something to stare at while I commit major plastic sabotage."

Joey glanced at himself in the mirror, standing next to Clark. His damp, slicked-back hair under his baseball cap that read *DiMuccio's Pizza,* his stained-white undershirt under his red windbreaker. Joey could almost see the smell of garlic and onion, frying oil, and sweat radiating off of him.

"Oh, babe," Joey said, shaking his head. "Please, you really don't have to do that."

"I do," Clark said in his ear, sidling up behind him and caressing his chest. *"I wanna."* Clark swung him around, grabbed Joey by the ears, and kissed him as hard as he could. "Because I can and I love you, I love you, I love you! And you deserve all the nice things." Clark playfully *booped* him on the nose. "And I'm renting us tuxes. We have Charisma's birthday party in August and we gotta look cute."

Joey let out a shaky laugh. "Claaaark . . . I really can't accept that."

"You can. And you will," Clark said. His hands traced down Joey's arms and held him at the waist. "I'm booking you an appointment here. Just accept it!" He gave Joey a shake and kissed Joey's cheek. Clark spoke low as he said, "And, listen, I've been thinking."

"Oh, boy, here we go," Joey muttered, glancing over his shoulder at the attendants, who were very obviously not *not* watching them.

Clark whispered, "If you wanna work part-time at the pizzeria, or go back to bartending while you finish your degree, or if you wanna break into acting like you really should, like you've always wanted, I'll support you."

Joey looked away, his jaw clenching. "Oh, babe . . . I dunno. I can't let you do that."

"Let me!" Clark urged, gently tugging his head back to face him. "You took care of me, now I take care of you. Besides: you have no choice. I'm Daddy now and what I say goes."

Joey shook his head and chuckled. Clark stuck his tongue out and beamed.

He spun on his heel and bounded back to the platform, a golden retriever off his leash. He skipped up the steps so buoyantly, he flew off the floor.

"Okay, I'm back!" he chirped to the staff. "Thank you for waiting!" Clark looked back at Joey, whose hands were stuffed deep into his jacket pockets. He smiled faintly, watching Clark as the tailor resumed pinning and adjusting.

Clark didn't notice the corners of Joey's mouth fall ever so slightly.

The fans were taking to the streets from social media.

Protests had erupted outside the Los Angeles Probate Court, their chants a rising storm demanding answers: Felicity had been found, her location exposed by whistleblowers and former employees of a so-called "wellness commune" hidden away in the Hills. The scandal had gained traction, with an increase of public awareness and media attention, thanks in part to Leslie's interview.

Like Persephone from Hades, Felicity was released, dragged back into the light by public outcry and relentless media attention. Felicity was finally home.

The financial backer of the commune? Traced to none other than "wealth management investment and consulting firm" Charisma Saintly Consulting.

Clark clicked through his new laptop, staring at Charisma's website like he had countless times before.

"CSC is a network of like-minded entrepreneurs, influencers, and trailblazers, all working together to grow, thrive, and succeed under the inspired guidance of their trusted leader, multi-media mogul, investor, and stylist to the stars, Charisma Saintly."

The next line always made his skin crawl.

"Our arms embrace every facet of our clients' lives," it read. Charisma Saintly Consulting provided a *"comprehensive suite of services including management, public relations, personal finance, asset management, life coaching, and more."*

Clark closed his new laptop and leaned back in his chair, the weight of realization pressing him like stones laid upon a witch's chest. He'd always known Charisma had power, but this? Wherever Charisma went, witches were bound to exist.

This commune wasn't just another retreat for troubled celebrities. No, this was a witches' stronghold. A web of control disguised as a sanctuary.

And whatever Felicity had endured, it wasn't over—not for her, not for the coven, and not for him.

Joey drove them out to Upper Montclair the evening of Friday, May 3rd, navigating the quiet, tree-lined streets until Leslie's home came into view. Her Victorian house stood like a whimsical centerpiece on the lush green lawn, its wraparound porch strung with twinkling fairy lights. Bright streamers swayed in the soft spring breeze, and the pulse of music spilled into the night air, mingling with bursts of laughter from inside.

When they pulled up, a young valet politely took the keys to Joey's Honda and sped away to park among a line of luxury sedans, SUVs, and convertibles.

Clark glanced at Joey, smoothing the collar of his button-down. "Ready?"

Joey ran a hand through his slicked-back hair, his usual casual demeanor now slightly self-conscious. "Ready!"

The two stepped into a lively scene. Inside, a famous DJ spun classic disco near the main staircase. In the dining room to the left, a long table was laid out with an impressive spread: delicate hors d'oeuvres, steaming platters of lamb chops and salmon, and a decadent birthday cake shaped like a Janice-the-Muppet-resembling Leslie, with squinted eyes, over-the-top lashes, blonde hair, and a frozen smile that teetered somewhere between sultry and totally spaced out.

The scent of vanilla-amber candles mingled with the rich aroma of the food. Servers in black-and-white uniforms weaved through the crowd, offering champagne flutes and trays of bite-sized canapés. Laughter rang from every crook and cranny of the home. Even Leslie's taxidermy llama was part of the festivities, decorated in a party hat and party horn dangling from its mouth.

Clark's eyes wandered over the guests. Some celebrity faces stood out, some that Joey pointed out to him—an actor here, a talk show host there. The rest were an eclectic mix of producers, writers, and comedians who'd undoubtedly worked with or come to know Leslie over the years, and of course, a few friends of Leslie's that Clark had come to know well as clients. To his and Joey's amusement, the party was mostly full of gay men of all ages. "Hhhhey!" Leslie's unmistakable voice rang out in her breathy way, eyes a-squint under her heavy false lashes. "You made it!"

"Happy birthday!" Clark said as they approached Leslie, with champagne in hand, wearing a bold sequined pink dress and pink glitter eyeshadow.

"So handsome!" Leslie exclaimed.

Clark started to smile, his hand smoothing his button-down. "Oh, this? Thanks. Well, you look fab—" But then Clark realized she wasn't talking to him. Her eyes were fixed on Joey, who flushed under her attention.

After exchanging rather giggly pleasantries, Leslie grabbed Clark's hand. "There's someone I want you to meet!"

Leslie meandered around the party and introduced him to her showbiz friends, gushing, "You've *got* to work with this guy! He is the real deal." At the mention of his assisting Charisma Saintly, reactions varied. Some nodded enthusiastically, visibly impressed. Others regarded him with wide-eyed curiosity, their expressions bordering on awe. And there were a couple who excused themselves—polite, yes, but fervent enough to understand the weight of Charisma's social cachet *(more like stigma* . . . he thought, his smile never wavering).

Through it all, Leslie never let go of his hand. Clark looked over his shoulder at Joey, who smiled back encouragingly.

Eventually, Leslie turned to him and lowered her voice as if she were about to reveal a secret. "Hhhey, come with me for a second," she said. She dragged him toward the stairs, bubbles locking in her glass, not waiting for an answer.

Joey looked around. "I'll just . . . entertain myself," he muttered after them. Clark shot one last look at Joey before disappearing with Leslie.

She pulled him into her bedroom, a large, lavish space full of mismatched charm—an antique chaise here, a modern vanity there, and a crystal chandelier casting soft, golden light. Clark barely had time to take it in before Leslie clapped her hands.

"Out!" she barked to the couple tangled up and Frenching on her bed. They broke apart with sheepish laughter and stumbled toward the door.

"Not you, Frank!" Leslie exclaimed with a throaty, girly laugh as he tore out from under the bed and scampered away. She sauntered to her jewelry box and pulled out a small organza bag tucked into one of its velvet-lined drawers. Leslie turned back to Clark, her expression softer, more serious.

"I put my nice stuff away in my safe but . . . here." From the bag she pulled something small and shiny, and placed it in Clark's open palm.

It was the evil eye ring that Emily had given him.

"How did you . . . ?"

"A friend of a friend made sure I got it—to give to you," she said. Leslie's eyes were swimming. "It comes with a verbal note: *Thank you.*"

"Babe," Joey asked one day at the end of May, "shouldn't you slow down on the spending?"

"Huh?" Clark was distracted by two doves on the balcony, one following the other.

"It's fine! I'll make more," Clark replied with a wave of his hand. Boxes and boxes of deliveries had piled up. Clark had taken to shopping with his new credit card, having never had credit before or the money to put toward one. It was a door to another life, and he was walking right through it, arms full.

When he wasn't at work, Clark had spent his money upgrading his wardrobe, his electronics, new shoes, tailored clothes, high-end appliances, the latest tech. Anything and everything he had once denied himself or that had been neglected.

Gone even was his out-of-date phone—the one he had begrudgingly kept for years, a relic of his parents' frugality, no doubt gifted to him for his birthday when he started college out of guilt. Now, he had the newest model, sleek and gleaming. His wardrobe had transformed, his electronics upgraded, his apartment curated with the kind of effortless luxury he had only ever seen in magazines.

Paychecks came and paychecks went, vanishing into shopping bags and merlot-filled nights.

Clark yawned and shuffled into the kitchen the next morning, bleary-eyed. He moved toward the coffee pot but paused, nose crinkling.

Why does it smell like . . . rotten eggs? He opened the fridge and admired its contents: full and bountifully stocked, a sight he never tired of. Clark clamored around, rummaging amongst the produce, checking the milk carton, and opening and closing the tray of eggs, but to no avail. He shut the door with a sigh.

It was the start of June. Clark had just returned home from work when—

"What is it, Jessica?" he asked. "There's food in your bowl."

She meowed incessantly, pivoting to the staircase.

"I'm not sure what you're trying to show me. What?"

Jessica darted up the stairs, pausing every few rungs to meow. Clark followed her up apprehensively.

"What is it, girl . . . ?"

Jessica stopped and meowed at the bedroom door for him to see before disappearing inside. Clark flipped on the hallway light. Was the apartment colder than usual?

He came to the door, slowly pushed it open, and flipped on the light to—nothing. Nothing in the room was out of place: the room was exactly how he had left it that morning before work. Jessica was on the bed, looking up at the corner of the ceiling, meowing.

Clark let out a breath. "Silly girl!" He ran a hand along her back, smoothing her fur from head to her tail. "For a moment, you scared me there."

Clark did notice one thing, however . . .

That night, when Joey got in and kicked his shoes off, Clark welcomed him on the couch, arms open. Their usual routine.

"I'm exhausted," Joey muttered. He dropped his head on Clark's lap, where after some time watching their shows and Clark running his fingers through his thick dark hair, he was bound to start snoring. "I gotta get back to bartending. I love my parents but they drive me crazy. The money is way, way better."

"You'll figure it out, babe."

"Yeah, I've got an open call tomorrow. Follow-up interview Friday."

"Oh, yeah, that's right! Proud of you! You're gonna land somewhere great, just give it time . . . Hey, speaking of, have you seen my diary? I can't find it anywhere."

Joey shifted slightly but didn't lift his head. "No, haven't seen it."

Clark frowned and crinkled his brows. It was so unlike him to misplace it. Usually it lived on the bedside table. He hadn't taken it to work in weeks. He actually hadn't written in it much at all lately. Was there a risk in anyone reading it, he wondered? Clark hadn't written any incriminating, hadn't written much about the specifics of the coven, had he . . . ?

Joey turned to look up as if remembering something. He asked, "Clark, did you see the news? Northlight is being raided by the feds."

Clark gasped and brought his hands to his mouth. "Oh my god, no way! When?"

"Before opening. They took Louis in for questioning. Drug and money laundering claims tied to Dortier."

"Holy shit. How did I not hear about this at work? That's huge."

"Yeah." Joey nodded. "I told you something was up."

Clark remembered Joey's story of coming in to work one day to find unlabeled pills spilled outside the building, just like some that he'd run errands for at Charisma's.

"Come to think of it," Joey continued, "there was always some numbers that didn't make sense. Deliveries that never ended up in the stockroom, private dinners that would cost crazy amounts of money. Louis would brush me off when I'd ask." He exhaled sharply. "Yeah. I wonder."

"Yeah, I wonder, too," said Clark. "See, babe, you got out of Northlight just in time."

Joey stiffened. He looked up. "Just in time? Is there a good time to get fired?"

Clark blinked. "Joey, c'mon, that's not what I meant."

Slowly, Joey sat up. "What about you?"

"What about me?"

"You're not one to talk when you're still working for Mafia Queen Charisma."

The lofted room felt somehow smaller. Clark's jaw tightened.

"Yeah, for now. It's just a means to an end. A year there and I can go anywhere.

Joey snorted. "Yeah. Sure, Clark . . ."

"What's that supposed to mean?"

"A year? C'mon."

Clark crossed his arms. "What? I'll leave soon!"

"You're never gonna leave, Clark." His voice was so matter-of-fact, like he wasn't even trying to argue. "The money's too good."

"Of course I will," Clark said. But as he sounded out the words, not even he believed them.

"I dunno," Joey said. "You wanna talk about what it is you do at Charisma's again? What you do with her clients specifically?"

This time Clark was quick to answer. "I'm a consultant."

Joey scoffed. "A consultant for what?"

"Lots of things—image, style . . . I'm a life coach."

"Oh, that's such bullshit, Clark. Life coach? You're twenty-four."

"So?"

"So! You told me last year she's a witch who sells potions and spells or whatever, and you're one, too. What happened to that? What was *that* supposed to mean?"

Clark's throat went dry. He stammered, "Y-yeah, well, when I said that I didn't mean . . . What I meant to say is that she's—"

"I found your goodbye note, you know." Joey pursed his lips. He knew he had gone too far.

"You read my diary?!"

"It slipped out, okay?"

"When were you going to tell me?"

"When were you going to tell *me*?! You think she's an actual witch queen who killed her assistant—and you think you're a witch, too? What's going on, Clark?"

"So you're the one that took it," Clark said flatly. "I knew it!"

"Clark! I didn't take your freaking diary, okay? I have no clue where it is."

"I can't believe you would do that," Clark said. "I feel so . . . violated!"

Joey bristled. "Yeah, well, I didn't read it, okay? I only read your note."

"Oh really? That's all?"

"Yes, really!" Joey's fingers curled into his palms. The two sat in silence.

Joey said, "So that's it, huh?" His voice was quiet now. Too quiet. "You were in some kinda trouble and you weren't going to tell me?"

Clark's breath caught. "What?"

Joey's jaw tightened. "That's what you wrote, Clark. You literally wrote, 'If I don't survive, tell Joey I love him.' Like you—like you really thought you weren't gonna come back."

Clark felt something lurch inside him. Panic crept up his throat. The blood was rushing up to his ears, and his heart was beginning to pound out of his chest. "Joey, listen, I was confused when I wrote that, paranoid from all the weed. "I didn't mean—"

"Nooo." Joey's voice cracked. "Don't do that. Don't you blame it on my love for smoking and insult my intelligence at the same time. You meant every fucking word."

Clark exhaled hard, running a hand over his face. "Joey, it was—it was a worst-case scenario thing, okay?"

Joey laughed, sharp and humorless. "Worst-case scenario? Clark, it sounds like a fucking death note."

Clark flinched.

"You think I wouldn't have wanted to know?" Joey's voice had an edge to it now, his hands shaking. "You think I wouldn't have wanted a chance to stop you? A chance to—" He cut himself off, inhaling sharply. "I thought we were in this together."

Clark swallowed hard. "We are."

"No, we're not. Because if we were, you would've told me. If we were, you wouldn't be keeping secrets. Where is all this money coming from, Clark? What are you actually doing? *Magic?* C'mon, Clark . . . ! You know, no matter how hard you try, you're not gonna be a superhero."

The walls were leaning in—in a bad way. The apartment was suffocating him, too many things unsaid pressing in on him.

"You don't trust me," Joey said finally. "Whatever. Keep your secrets."

"Babe," Clark said, "of course I do. Don't say that." What was he to say? That some things Joey didn't have to know—for his safety? Was that so true after all?

Clark opened his mouth again, but nothing came out.

And Joey saw it.

He nodded to himself, sitting back like he'd just had a revelation he didn't want. "Yeah," he murmured, mostly to himself. "That's what I thought. You make me feel like a real fucking idiot for even trying to get close to you."

Joey got up off the couch, donned the spiral staircase, and turned toward the bedroom.

Clark should have stopped him. Should have said something, anything.

But he didn't.

What just happened . . . ? Clark thought.

"Mrs. Rosenthal gave me a B- on my essay. Ugh."

"Really?" Clark said. "She gave me a hundred."

Rosa shoved him—harder than usual. "Nerd."

"Stahp it!" Clark adjusted the straps of his backpack. Lockers clanged shut around them. A group of students darted past, sneakers squeaking against the waxed tile floor. The halls of their high school stretched endlessly ahead of them, teal lockers blurring past.

"You're a total teacher's pet."

"Just in English."

"Come talk to me in Spanish class."

"Hey, I'm doing *muy bueno en la clase de español,* thank you very much!"

"Double nerd."

"Yeah, maybe," Clark said. "Ryan and Maria only notice me when I bring home an A . . ."

"School doesn't matter for me anyway," Rosa said. "My dad says I'm gonna be a *star* New Jersey car dealer like him."

"That's cool," Clark said automatically. Something about the hallway stretched too long. "Is that why you speak Spanish at home but are in Beginner's with me?"

Rosa boomed a boisterous cackle. "Bitch. You know you can't come back to my house, right?" Rosa's tone shifted, like she was reminding him of something he should've already known. "Your dad's a total asshole. My parents still talk about him."

"Yeah, I know . . . But your father *is* sorta a chronic liar."

"Yeah, he is!" She cackled. "What's yours's issue with immigrants if he married a Puerto Rican? And *when he's one himself?*"

"No clue, to be totally honest."

Rosa snickered. "Men are so stupid."

"Totally."

They pushed through the double doors into the roaring cafeteria of foldable tables. It smelled of milk carton cardboard, cleaning agent, and locker room sweat. A group of sophomores at a long table turned their heads to Rosa and Clark. Others followed. Clark raised a brow, wiggling his ear with a finger to make the ringing go away.

Clark sighed. "I'm *still* waiting for my Hogwarts letter that must've gotten lost in the post."

"Get over it, nerd! Magic isn't real."

Clark wondered, if they hadn't been neighbors at his father's growing up, if they would even be friends at all.

"What is everyone staring at?" Clark muttered.

A junior stood up ahead of them. Clark clocked him from the corner of his eyes. As he walked by them, Clark swerved, but it made no difference: the junior shoulder-butted him hard. Too hard.

"Heard you got kicked out for being a queer. Way to go, faggot!" He jeered and laughed.

His lunch table broke out in laughter. Clark's ears grew red.

He spun around. "What the fuck, Rosa! You told?!" Clark cried. She was the only person at school who had known he had left home that summer. That was the day everyone in school found out, even the faculty.

Rosa looked at him wide-eyed, mouth agape, at a loss for words. She shrugged.

Clark turned right around and walked back out through the double doors—

—and stepped into his grandmother's studio apartment. Only now it was moving day. When he pushed the door open, he found Joey fumbling over the last small box, containing the contents of his bedside table. By the way his eyes widened when he turned around, slightly out of breath—as if he almost seemed caught unawares—Clark thought, *He's probably just read my diary . . .*

"You ready to go, babe?" Joey asked him.

Jessica sat on the bed, inquisitively flicking her tail, watching.

Clark's throat was dry. "Not yet."

"You're never gonna leave, Clark," he replied with a slow shake of his head.

Instead of heading out the door, Clark turned the other way. He lifted the window and climbed onto the fire escape, just like he always did when the weather allowed, up onto the roof a floor above.

He looked out at the glittering skyline over Astoria and the East River at sunset.

A firefly buzzed onto the roof, just like it had last August, before his eyelash wish and all the moments that had led up to May. Clark held his hand aloft, and it landed gently on his palm.

He blinked.

The firefly was gone.

In its place sat a large brown cockroach, twitching its wings and rubbing its feelers up at him.

Clark jolted awake in bed with a scream and a start.

Beside him, Joey sighed and rolled over, turning away.

Clark swallowed hard, rubbing his face.

Jessica lay curled at the edge of the bed, watching. One paw rested lightly on his arm.

"THE TRUTH BEHIND FELICITY'S CONSERVATORSHIP"

For more than a year, the world believed pop star Felicity's conservatorship was for her protection. But her father, Michael, is finally speaking out—exposing the real force behind it.

"Before the conservatorship, Felicity's mother was drowning in debt. That's when Charisma Saintly entered the picture, posing as a mentor but preying on her desperation." Michael Tierres, 55, who never sought his daughter's fortune, saw the warning signs.

Speaking with us last year, he recalled the battle over his daughter's autonomy. "With Hope—who can't manage her own finances—and Charisma—who had only been in Felicity's life for a few years—trying to take control, I had two choices: fight it outright or push for conservators who actually care about Felicity as a person, not just as a source of income. That's what I'm working toward now.

"And no, I have no interest in being her conservator or her money, but I'll be damned if someone who barely knows her or someone who can't even manage their own affairs is put in charge. Felicity deserves people in her corner who are invested in her well-being, not just her bank account.

"All I wanted was for Felicity to be surrounded by people who truly love and care about her, not those who only see dollar signs," says Tierres. "But they didn't have her best interests at heart. They only cared about the money."

Pictured was Felicity's mother. She was just as stunning. Something about the way she leaned in and clung to Felicity too tightly, smiled too brightly in a way that didn't reach her eyes, gave Clark pause. Stage mom, Clark thought. Living through her daughter maybe . . . ?

But Michael Tierres knows exactly who was behind it all.

"There is one woman responsible for putting my daughter in that conservatorship, and that woman's name is Charisma Saintly."

By July, things were different at home.

Clark had worked most weekends that start of summer. If he wasn't at a client's home, he was working toward being at one: restocking his kit at the Tower, submitting his invoices, shmoozing over drinks and dinner. Anything to stay in business.

So did Joey, picking up extra shifts at his new bartending gig—weeknights and Sundays included, whenever he was needed.

It was easier that way.

It turned out burying oneself in work was the best way to avoid the things one preferred were swept under the mid-century modern rug. Clark didn't know if that made things better or worse.

Then came Fourth of July weekend. The Sunday before festivities. A rare moment when neither of them were working, the good shifts having gone to the senior bartenders, and the Fourth being one of the witches' quietest holidays.

Clark felt Joey's eyes on him. He looked up.

Then came the look.

Clark was in the armchair by the window, sitting with his legs tucked under him while on the phone, filing his nails. With one hand, he flipped a tarot card face up onto the side table.

"Oo yeah, girl," he said with dark melodrama, admiring his fingertips. "Call the doctor. You're definitely allergic to gluten." He giggled.

There was a pause, Clark put his nail file down . . . and then he erupted into a fit of giggles. "Staaahp! You're too much."

Joey cut him another look.

Clark giggled again: "Oh, yes, I am well aware . . . You think? No . . . ! It can't be *that* big. Ha!"

Joey hissed, *"Clark!"*

Clark mouthed "What?" while covering the phone with one hand. "I'm on the phone with my client, Janelle!"

Joey crinkled his brows and rolled his eyes. He raised the volume on the remote.

"What was that, babes?" Clark asked into his cell while plugging the other ear with a finger. "Ugh, tell me about it. My upstairs neighbor keeps hosting parties on Saturday nights. Joey's so lucky he's out; I can barely get any sleep. Oh yeah, no, that's okay, I gotta go, too . . . Okay . . . It was lovely talking to you as always . . . ! No, you! Stahhhhp! Okay, okay, we'll talk soon . . . Okay . . . Okay, bye for now." Clark put his phone down and smoothed his clothes. Joey took a look at him, up and down.

"New shorts?" Joey asked.

"Yeah! You like?"

"They're . . . awfully short," he said. And short they were: they must have been no longer than three or four inches at the inseam. "I hardly recognize you."

"Oh, please," Clark said to Joey. "They'd be cuter if I weren't gaining weight. Last year when I was an intern on foot running all over Manhattan, I could've used some extra pounds. Now that you're keeping me fat and happy at home . . ."

"Me? Keeping you fat? I dunno what you're talking about," Joey said, half joking, half eyebrow raised, popping a chocolate in his mouth. These days, even Joey was looking soft around the edges.

"Prove me wrong," Clark said, hopping out of his seat. "Let's go out for a walk!"

"A walk?" Joey asked. He washed his chocolate down with a swig of soda. "In those? Lemme ax you a question: your motha let you outta the house looking like that?"

Clark threw a belly laugh. He couldn't tell if Joey was joking or being serious.

"Joeyyyy," Clark moaned while coming up behind him. "C'mon! Let's get off the couch. It's beautiful out."

"Off the couch?"

"Yeah!"

"I dunno . . ."

"Joey, let's go do things. Get some air. Meet people . . ."

"Meet people?" Joey asked.

"Yeah."

"Who you meeting?"

"I dunno . . . people!"

"Which people?"

"Witch people? Oh!" He nervously laughed. Joey raised an eyebrow. "I meant 'new people.'" He put one hand on his hip. "Joey, what's this about?"

"We have all anyone could ever want right here," he said, smoothing the couch and giving it two pats. "At home."

"But Joey, I don't wanna be home. I wanna be out!"

He turned back to the TV. Clark walked around the couch,

grabbed the remote, and turned the volume down. Joey's eyes remained fixed on the screen, refusing to meet his.

"All we do is sit here and smoke weed and drink wine and eat in our boxers. Look at us." Clark shrugged toward the coffee table. Joey followed: on it were scraps of candy wrappers and food, crumbs of marijuana, and his empty soda cans. Then he followed Clark's line of sight, which looked down at Joey's robe he had lived in on their off weekend, then down to his checkered boxers, and on to their tiny food stains. Joey's beard, usually neatly trimmed, was so scraggly and unkempt that his neck was obscured in overgrowth. Hastily, he folded his robe over and looked away in a huff.

"Joey," Clark said, "look at me."

Joey remained unmoved.

"Please?"

Joey shook his head.

"Joey, please!"

After a moment, Joey turned.

"Joey, you don't understand: I finally have money!" he cried out. "I wanna go out! I wanna make friends! I wanna go out on weekends and dance! I wanna *live*, Joey! I can finally do the things I've always wanted to do."

"You're living right now," he said. "With me!"

Jessica jumped off the windowsill, eyeing the ceiling as she sometimes did. She stalked off and away.

"Joey," Clark said. "For once, there's something in my life that I'm really good at. I'm not just good: I'm great. I am really great at this. I have a job I love. I wish you could be happy for me."

"I am happy for you!" Joey sighed and shook his head. "You know, of all the boys, you're different. Everything's so easy between us, but now?" Joey scoffed. I would trade it all for you," he said. "Why can't you for me?"

"We're only twenty-four! We're so young!" Clark said. "There's so much I want to do—with you! Out *there*!"

"I don't know why you can't be happy with just being here with me. What are you running from?

"Running from? I could ask you the same thing." Clark pointed to the empty wine bottles stacked on the counter, ready for the recycling. Then to the glass on the table.

They stared at one another.

"You know what I think, Clark?" His voice lowered, but the edge in it sharpened.

Clark braced himself.

"You won't tell me what you really do for work. You work insane hours for a woman who's probably being watched by the FBI."

"Joey, I'm s—"

"No, let me finish." Joey's voice wasn't loud, but it cut through the room like a blade.

"You told me your boss is a witch and so are you. You said she killed her last assistant. Then you shut me out completely. Do you know how *insane* that sounds? One minute you're confessing this huge thing to me, and the next, I can't get a straight answer out of you about anything. God knows what even happened to you in LA. Am I going crazy?"

Clark stayed silent, his stomach clenched.

Joey shook his head. "And then I find your death note and you totally deny it. As if you could make me forget about it all."

Joey kept going. "Suddenly, you're promoted. Suddenly, you're making all this money. Buying new toys, new clothes, like some Real fucking Housewife of Waverly Place."

Clark's mouth fell open.

Joey scoffed. "Suddenly you walk different. You talk different." His voice dropped to almost a whisper. "I don't even know who you are anymore." His eyes flickered over Clark, like he was staring at a stranger. "I don't even know who this Clark is."

Joey watched him for a second longer—waiting for him to say something, anything.

But Clark had nothing.

Without another word, Joey grabbed the remote and turned the volume back up.

* * *

"Late again, Maria. As usual."

"I can't help it that I work," Maria said, adjusting her purse strap as they came bursting out the classroom door. Her slight accent curled around the syllables as she said, "The segment ran long. You know how traffic is this time of day."

"He deserves a mother who is on time. Not some *hoochie* news anchor chasing the spotlight," Ryan shot back, his voice rising. The fluorescent light above them flickered and twitched.

Maria's head snapped toward him, her eyes narrowing into slits. *"Excuse me?"*

Clark turned, suddenly aware of the entire hallway stretching long and dark behind him. The other parents and his classmates held their gazes, quietly watching.

Ryan exhaled sharply. With his hand, he dragged his face down from his eyes to his salt-and-pepper beard. "You know what I mean, Maria. Running around in your high heels and little dr—"

"My little *what*?" Maria cut in. "My little career? My little paycheck? That thing that put food on your table? *Hmm?*"

She turned to Clark, her expression softening, just a little. He was fidgeting with the straps of his backpack. "You don't mind that Mommy works, do you, pumpkin?"

Clark shook his head. Of course he didn't.

"Oh, c'mon, don't put words in his mouth, Maria!"

"Don't you dare try to say I'm not doing my best for him as a mother!"

"Maria." Ryan's voice was cold and low. "Didn't you hear her? His teacher said he's been falling asleep in class, staying up late watching TV. Some parent you are!"

The fluorescent light above them flickered again, longer this time.

"*Ay,* Ryan, cut the bullshit!" Maria's voice was a roar now too. "Those nights, he was at yours! Should I have told the judge that, too? Along with why I'm always on the phone begging for your child support? Huh?! Answer me that!"

Ryan scoffed. He muttered something under his breath about

Latinas and their fiery pride. Before she could clap back, his teacher stepped into the hall. "Parents, please, let's take this outside," she said, tight-lipped. The three voices overlapped, sharp and rising.

The fluorescent light above them buzzed . . . and went out.

Clark blinked, and then opened his eyes. He was lying in his bed, staring at his ceiling only . . . he wasn't really awake.

Something was crawling in the walls. Scratching.

Like it was dying to get inside.

He turned over, reaching for Joey, but the bed beside him was empty.

And then—he woke up for real.

From the idea that his life had ever been anything close to normal, Clark wrote in his new diary, Wednesday, July 31st, 11:11 p.m.

Joey says I laugh in my sleep sometimes . . .

He's working late nights again. Sometimes I go days without seeing him. He's so lucky he's out of the apartment on Saturdays.

Jessica is always sitting on the bed, watching the corner of the ceiling.

Batting her tail.

No purr.

Jessica lay sprawled across Clark's stomach. He scratched behind her ears, scrolling through his unread texts. Five from clients. None from Joey.

Monica tried to sabotage yet another house call for me by giving me the wrong time and *address. Classy. Too bad I triple-check every booking and record them myself instead of relying on the coven's shared calendar. She and the twins have been so quiet otherwise . . .*

I wonder why.

I hate her . . .

She'll get hers soon . . .

Felicity once said when all of this disappears, you only have yourself to face.

"What did I have to gain actually?" she asked.

"Was it worth it?"

I got the job a million girls would kill for. Melissa was offed on a technicality, the fine print of the job.

Does that make me a villain too?

Clark paused.

I have more money now than I ever had in my life. And yet, here I am, lying in the dark, counting the hours between work, listening to Jessica's tail thump against the bed, waiting for something that isn't here.

I miss him.

It was almost midnight when his head met the pillow. A quarter to three when Joey's finally met his.

Clark scooted closer, over and onto Joey's pillow. Their faces were inches apart.

Joey's big brown eyes were soft in the dark.

He whispered, "Why do you love me?"

"Because," Clark whispered back, "you're the city and the stars and everything in between, and I am forever reaching for you." Gently, hands met cheeks in a slow caress.

A quiet beat.

"I'm not proud of everything I've said and done," Clark admitted. "Or haven't said or haven't done."

A moment's pause. Softly, Joey said, "Me neither."

Clark whispered, "I'm sorry."

Joey pressed their foreheads together. "I'm sorry, too."

Their touch sparked, stirring something deep in Clark. He whispered to Joey, mind to mind: *Let me show you how much I love you . . .*

For a moment, Joey held his gaze, quiet and searching. Then, finally, a thought sounded from across the pillow.

Fly me to the moon, baby . . .

Clark drew in a slow breath. He closed his eyes, and Joey followed.

Their deepest kiss pulled them into infinity—and time exhaled.

The same universe, which had always leaned in to listen, folded inward and, at the same time, expanded, stiff and soft all at once.

From where the butterflies stirred, they launched into the heavens, two streaks of fire leaping skyward. The bed, the walls, the city below, all fell away—their blue home behind them, fading to nothing but stories forgotten.

The dust of the moon's surface stirred, roused by their passing.

The planets swelled in their wake, turning to watch, drawing close and then drifting past in quiet awe. Even the stars surrendered to their gravity, orbiting them instead. Now it was the sky that was looking up at them. They were light, they were fire: two celestial bodies streaking through an ocean of eternity.

Every gasp was an expansion.

Every kiss, the universe reborn.

They pressed closer. The sky opened wider, deeper.

Clark reached for Joey's hand, and in that spark, the laws of existence ceased to matter. Joey heard the song of his soul in Clark's heart, and for a moment, there was no boundary between thought and body, between flesh and the infinite.

They were not bound by time.

Nor fate.

Nor the ache of their human bodies.

There was no skin, no breath, no self. Only the unraveling of light. They were the question and the answer, the echo and the sound, the current in the river and the river itself. They rode on the melody of their sighs, an endless cadence as old as the universe itself.

The taste of forever clung between them, stretched thin like spun silk between their lips, dissolving only to reform—the thread of consciousness pulling them closer again and again.

In every inhale, the shimmer of stardust, sugar-sweet and searing.

Every exhale, the voice of a billion suns counting all the milky ways—until nothing remained but the knowing of their infinite embrace.

They were the heartbeat of the infinite, fireflies dancing to the thump of the hush between constellations, rising, rising, rising.

From the pull of their union, a cosmic love ignited; from the heartplace of their souls, a symphony bloomed into spiraling galaxies. Their fire birthed the night itself. They were nothing, and they were everything.

Together, they were freedom itself.

Together, they were one with All.

As they drifted, Joey thought, *Is this really happening . . . ?*

I think so . . . thought Clark, the calm certainty of his answer sending a shiver through the ether.

Are you doing this . . . ?

Yes . . . thought Clark.

The stars in Clark's eyes, that limitless twinkle, rang like bells of childhood joy and laughter. They burst upwards, comets gamboling into the cosmos, bursting into a magnificence of fireworks that showered them in a starfall. They swished and swirled in the orbit of their convergence, bathing them in their light. Clark wrote Joey's name in their trail. A meteoric magic meant just for him.

Clark looked into Joey's eyes and saw wonder there, marvel and awe reflected back at him.

But then, something shifted. In the stillness of their celestial gaze, Clark saw it: the flicker, the fracture, the shadow curling at the edge of his face. Joey's breath hitched. His pupils dilated. His thought came back to Clark, clear and sharp:

Make it stop . . .

Clark felt the words strike like meteorites to his heart.

In an instant, and to Clark's horror, Joey imploded and collapsed. His spirit had buckled, the radiance eclipsed, their once-vast grandeur reduced to a dim flicker in the void.

And then, they fell.

Together, they plummeted, two satellites tumbling through nebulous sheets of dust, trailing smoke and silence, and careening through the skies.

Galaxies and their despondent faces scattered.

Planets weeping their nitrogen tears blurred past.

And the rocky, dull face of Earth rused up to meet them.

They came crashing back down, back to their bed in a heap of fading embers, breathless and still.

For a moment Clark lay there, feeling the ache of distance that no word could bridge. He turned his head. Joey lay curled away from him, back hunched, as small as Clark had ever seen him.

Gently, Clark reached for him. His hand rested on his shoulder, feeling the subtle quiver of fear beneath his touch.

"Joey?" he whispered, his voice thick with longing and apprehension. "Did you feel it too? Did you feel the . . . ?"

The question hung unanswered as Joey curled further into himself. The memory of the stars still lingered in Clark's his mind, yet here they were, grounded and worlds apart again. The comforter was stretched over him as Clark rubbed his shoulders.

"I'm sorry," he whispered with every caress.

Clark didn't need to be an Intuitive to know that Joey lay there awake that night, a cold, dense fragment of himself.

What had made Clark feel so mighty and powerful had made Joey feel so insignificant and overwhelmed, the vulnerability, the creature fear too big to bear . . . Clark had reached for infinity. Joey had been swallowed up by it. And now Clark couldn't help but wonder if his magic could fix what was fractured between them after all, and if Joey was scared to death of sleeping next to him.

The silence between them stretched, long and endless.

Clark raised his lips to Joey's ear and, with a whisper, erased it. "Forget," he breathed, *And this will all be just a dream . . . A bad, bad dream . . .*

The memory was scooped up in his hands, fading like a footprint in the sand as the tide rolled in, and drifted away like a dandelion on the wind. Clark kissed his forehead. Joey's scrunched brows softened, the tension in his limbs unspooled, and eventually, he surrendered to the safe, deep slumber of forgetting.

Jessica, who had been watching all the while, jumped onto the bed and pawed at him. Without a sound, she darted to the doorway, pausing long enough to flick her tail at him before disappearing down the hall.

Clark hesitated. But something pulled at him—a whisper in the dark, a weightless thread tugging at him from his heart. He slipped out of the sheets and followed.

The hallway stretched endlessly now, twisting into darkness, the walls dissolving into shadow. Jessica's footsteps were soundless ahead of him, her ears twitching—dialing like a radio, scanning for something unseen. They walked farther, and farther still, for what felt like forever.

Where are we going . . . ?

She twitched her ears and meowed. *To finish what you started . . .* she thought to him, not in words but in feelings. *Listen . . .*

Their footsteps began to soften underfoot. Wet grass glistened through a pulsing mist. Was it the sloping lawns of Astoria Park again?

Sure enough, the feeling of being watched and followed carried on the wind from behind, lapping up the air around them. Jessica's ears pinned back. Then, she ran.

Clark bolted after her, lungs tight, feet slick on the grass. This time, he dared to glance over his shoulder.

Could it be? Lurching out from behind a park bench in the shadows, low to the ground, something quickly moved toward them. Crawling. *Scuttling*. Laughing a sickly, greasy laugh on the wind that bubbled up from deep underground, and slithered up and down Clark's spine.

He turned around. The danger disappeared. Jessica came to a stop, and so did Clark. He followed her gaze up.

This time, a massive tree towered over the moonlit field they stood on, making Clark shudder.

Massive. Breathing. A titan.

Its roots writhed like serpents and its bark pulsed like flesh. The air around it trembled. A low hum vibrated through Clark's bones. The closer Clark got, the more he heard whispers—his own name spoken in countless voices.

And then, suddenly—fire.

The branches erupted, flames licking the sky in eerie blue tongues, their shapes twisting into screaming faces. The whispers turned to pleas, voices begging him to finish what he'd started. At the base of the tree, Jessica sat, waiting. Tail flicking. Eyes knowing.

A soft thud landed at his feet, making him step back. Clark looked down.

At his feet lay a single blackened apple. Clark picked it up by the stem. There was something terribly wrong with it: its split skin was rotten, cankered, and squirming with maggots from the inside out.

In its rot, putrid eyes and mouth stretched into a piercing shriek that filled the air.

And Clark awoke with a gasp.

To celebrate her birthday, Charisma's fashion house flooded social media with memes: her head pasted over history's most iconic moments.

The Signing of the Declaration of Independence. The Birth of Venus. The Library of Alexandria, right before it burned.

In *The Creation of Adam,* her perfectly manicured hand extended toward God's. "A timeless presence," the caption read.

Under *Raising the Flag on Iwo Jima*: "Life, Liberty, and the Pursuit of the LBD."

Under *The Last Supper*: "Breaking bread since 33 B.C."

It all led to a final scene: a re-enactment of *The Examination of a Witch.*

"Because looking this good is simply sorcery," Charisma's voice cooed.

Then, an onlooker cloaked in black turned around and lowered her hood, uncovering a flash of copper hair and glittering green eyes. With a wink, she brought a finger to her glossed lips.

Shh.

Charisma looked down. In her hand was a crystalline jar with a gold lid.

"A witch never reveals her secrets . . . but darlings," she said, "I have something magical to share. Coming this October."

Sunday, August 11th, 10:10 a.m.

Summer smells like burning asphalt and garbage.
Sometimes I'll crack the window just to get some texture outside the central air . . .
Sometimes I realize, with a pang, how I miss the sound of the crickets of Astoria . . . though my dreams are always sure to take me back to the park . . .

Clients are starting to ask for me by name now. Not Charisma.
Not her lackeys. Me.
The delegates. The thought-leaders. Melissa's high-profile clients
Monica couldn't take: all mine.
Sucks to suck!
And I can feel it happening: the shift.
Their grip is loosening and I'm here to get what's mine.
I just don't know what they're going to do about it.

Thwack!

Joey smacked the counter with a paperback—Clark's worn copy of *The Handmaid's Tale*—making both Jessica and Clark jump and look.

"Ugh. Nothing's stopping these damn roaches," Joey grumbled. "Food spoils fast. I feel like I'm constantly cleaning," Joey said, "and everything just gets dirtier. Your plants are dying and it's summer . . . This place gives me the creeps, babe!"

He was right: Clark turned to Monstera, Rita, Drita, Fern, and Matilda the weeping fig tree. The leaves, once lush and thriving, were now wilted and graying, crisping at the edges.

The clients, the power, the growing name: it meant nothing if home was falling apart.

"I'll get us a maid!" Clark blurted out.

"Clark, we're gonna be late!"

He sang from the powder room mirror, "Almost ready!"

Joey groaned from the kitchen.

Clark emerged, adjusting the cufflinks on his tailored silk black tuxedo—a rental, sure, but flawless. The fabric was crisp, the silk lapels catching the light just right. So did his golden eyes and gleaming skin.

His shiny black loafers barely made a squeak against the hardwood floor as he stepped forward with a practiced air. Every movement was effortless, every detail sharpened by the glamour he had cast.

"Okay, ready," Clark said. "How do I look?"

Joey didn't answer right away. His gaze lingered, slow and studying. Clark could feel it, the way Joey's eyes traced over him. He imagined what Joey saw: the crisp tux, the gleam of his skin, the light catching in his eyes like liquid gold.

He gave a low whistle. "Is that my boyfriend or a Bond villain?"

Clark grinned. "They say villains have more fun."

"I'm sure," Joey said dryly. "It's really awful she's hosting a black-tie party in August."

"Or," Clark challenged, "it's really wonderful and we're lucky to be invited. The jackets will come off, as will the bowties. We'll be fine! Let's go."

Joey swiveled off the stool and the kitchen island.

They hopped into a taxi, the AC blasting as they pulled onto the West Side Highway. The city blurred past in a haze of neon, the humid air thick with summer's final stretch.

The driver pulled up to the dock at Pier 92 on 52nd and 12th, a short way from Charisma's penthouse. There it was: a black-hulled superyacht, sleek as onyx and gleaming under the harbor lights. Nearly three hundred feet of unapologetic excess, towering decks stacked high above the water. It might as well have been a cruise ship.

L'IMPÉRIUM was emblazoned in 24-karat gold script lettering along the stern, the name glowing in the floodlights like a coronation. *The supreme power*. It was a floating palace on the Hudson: an empire on the water, untouchable, commanding, and utterly ostentatious.

A red carpet with velvet ropes lined the gangway. At its base, two security guards in tailored suits stood stone-faced and bearded, scanning guests one by one as they stepped up to board. Photographers snapped pictures, catching glimpses of Manhattan's elite in gowns and tuxedos.

Clark stepped out of the car first, smoothing his lapels.

Joey followed, smoothing his fingers through his hair. He glanced at the yacht, then at Clark.

His gaze lingered again. The golden glow. The sharpened edges.

Clark caught him staring. "You look so handsome."

Joey loudly exhaled. "Thanks, babe." A beat. He glanced past Clark, eyes unfocused. "You too," he added, like a reflex.

They approached the gangway, their shoes clicking against the polished wood. Crew members in black gloves greeted them with silent nods, their postures stiff with practiced formality. Joey cast a glance around at the fleet of black SUVs pulling up, at the names on the guest list being checked twice, and at the effortless way Clark strode forward as though he belonged here. He turned and gave Joey a wink.

The main deck hosted an infinity pool lined with black volcanic stone. A row of marble columns lined the edge of the upper deck, flanking a grand staircase that led into a marble-clad atrium.

Waitstaff in tailored black uniforms circulated with crystal flutes of Dom Pérignon. Each step was rehearsed, each smile practiced.

Inside was a nightclub disguised as a luxury lounge—onyx floors, mirrored ceilings, and an LED constellation map that pulsed to the music. The DJ booth was built into an actual throne, gilded and tufted, positioned just below a twenty-foot portrait of Charisma herself: a Renaissance-style painting—but make it couture.

Clark and Joey weaved through the party of celebrities and socialites, all dressed to kill, sipping gold-flecked champagne and murmuring between bites of caviar. At the center of it all: Charisma. A queen among courtiers, floating through her kingdom in a custom couture gown that draped like liquid light.

After the yacht pushed away from the pier, and a series of pleasantries and judgmental once-overs, Joey whispered to Clark, "Some of these people are so fake, they're *yeesh*."

Clark hid a smirk behind his champagne flute. "Oh, totally."

"How do you deal?"

"I smile," Clark mumbled through a gritted grin, "and I forget on my way to the bank."

"Ha! Yeah right. You actually like this kinda scene. There's something . . .off about these people."

They looked around. Women with unsmiling, hollow eyes flashed them looks.

Clark leaned into Joey. "Babes, you're the one who wants to be an actor. Here they are—Hollywood producers, Charisma's industry friends. Go act! Maybe you'll be discovered."

"Yeah, yeah . . ." Joey said. "Like that'll happen. The guys here are checking me out but I dunno if it's a movie they wanna cast me in. Maybe as their dog walker or because they think I park their cars."

"Oh, they're definitely not checking you out," Clark said.

"Oh no?"

"Nay. Verily, their gaze doth linger upon *me*, my raven-haired prince." Clark stuck his tongue out at Joey and Joey rolled his eyes.

"I'm done."

"I'm just teasing, babe. C'mere!" Clark leaned in, puckering dramatically. Joey feigned dodging him with mock distaste.

"Ugh, get away from me," he teased, but Clark planted him where his dimples deepened, sending Clark into a fit of giddy laughter. Joey pulled away faster than usual.

Some stiff-necked attendees watched with wide eyes, raised brows, and whispers behind champagne flutes. Clark didn't care. He looped an arm around Joey's waist and pulled him in closer. "Let them stare." The ship cut through the harbor in that moment, gliding past Ellis Island and Lady Liberty herself, standing tall in her glowing crown—a beacon of promise. "We're free to be who we are."

"So you came," a voice interrupted from behind. Clark turned. Lorena Henceley stood in floor-length black gown, no doubt a Charisma Saintly piece. Seeing them pull away, she said, "Please, by all means, don't let me stop you . . ."

Joey excused himself to grab another flute of champagne at the bar. Clark offered, "You look great!"

"Thank you," she said. She sized him up and down, rolling her shoulders as if unable to decide, holding back jab after jab. What would she say next? He braced himself.

"You, too," she said tight-lipped.

Clark blinked in shock. "Thanks, Lorena!"

And just like that, she turned on her heel and stalked away, her nose held high, as if the pleasantry was too much for her to bear. Clark laughed to himself. An almost-compliment? From *her*?

He barely had time to process it before the night pressed on. The food was exquisite: caviar-stuffed blinis, lobster ravioli, wagyu tartare, plated and passed with effortless elegance. The ship erupted into applause as the grand, towering birthday cake was wheeled out, each tier adorned in sugar flowers and edible gold leaf.

At the center of it all, Charisma Saintly stood dazzling in a sculpted birthday crown, lifting a crystal flute of champagne in a toast to herself, something about pride in the upcoming launch of her cream, her beauty, her age, her monumental success and looking practically . . . closer in age to Clark than her counterparts. "To timelessness," she declared with a wink, as if she had discovered the secret to immortality. Maybe she had. Laughter rippled through the crowd. Glasses clinked. Cameras flashed.

Joey, meanwhile, did what he did best: charm. They had instinctively divided and conquered, drifting through the crowd like seasoned socialites. Joey networked, toasted, and exchanged numbers with producers and talent agents, effortlessly slipping into conversations that could—if luck struck—lead to something bigger.

Clark kept his composure, his best *I belong here* smile in place, though the weight of the evening pressed at his edges. He let the champagne fizz against his tongue, let the bass from the DJ's set thrum beneath his skin.

As if the crowd had parted just for him, he saw them.

Alicia and her boyfriend.

Clark realized, with a start, that he hadn't ever seen the two of them together before. Not like this. Not with *that* look in her eyes. She looked . . . happy. Truly, effortlessly happy in a way Clark had never known of her. He always thought of her as Charisma's right-hand, always on call. No life of her own to speak of, no existence outside of Charisma's world. Like a machine you shut down at the end of the workday, to be rebooted the next.

It struck him then, that moment of intimacy: Alicia, who was always composed, always "on," always standing in Charisma's shadow, had her boyfriend's head cupped in her hands. Clark watched how he gently held her like she was the only person in the room that mattered. How their foreheads pressed together as they murmured in hushed, wistful words. A tenderness passed between them so fluid, so attuned, that for a moment, Clark couldn't tell where one of them ended and the other began. They moved in perfect synchrony, intuiting each other's every breath, every glance. Together, they seemed . . . whole in a way that didn't make sense. That's when Charisma billowed through, a hurricane of copper hair and diamond brilliance, the air around her shifting like the pressure drop before a downpour. Partygoers instinctively parted to accommodate her, their conversations pausing mid-sentence, eyes flickering to her presence.

She leaned into Alicia's ear, murmuring something only meant for her. Clark didn't hear the words, but he saw the reaction, which struck Clark as odd knowing how much of a skilled telepath she was. A power move. A reminder. Clark watched as Alicia's face changed, her spine stiffened. Resolute. Back to work. How the light in her eyes dimmed just a fraction. Just as quickly, Charisma swept past, her touch like the fleeting sting of cold wind before the sky broke open.

Hand in hand, Alicia and her boyfriend pulled away. She walked to the side of the ship toward the railing. She hurriedly typed on her phone, her fingers trembling slightly. Was she writing an email? Something in his gut told him this was the moment.

With a glance at Charisma, now holding court near the head of the deck, Clark slipped away from the crowd, weaving through glittering guests and trays of caviar. If he was going to make a move, it had to be now.

"He's cute," he told Alicia, watching her boyfriend from the corner of his eye. Her coppery hair like her aunt's, bobbing in the wind, floated away like her gaze.

"Yeah, he's great," she said.

"How long have you been together?"

"Eight years this January," she said. "He's the love of my life."

"That's so sweet," Clark said. "How did you know?"

"Know what?"

"That he's the one," said Clark.

Alicia gave him a studying look, as if weighing whether to answer honestly. She put her phone down. Then, slowly, she placed a hand on her stomach. "It wasn't butterflies," she said. "It was stronger than that." Her hand traveled up to just beneath her clavicle, as her eyes went somewhere else entirely.

"According to *The Symposium*," she said, "humans were originally made with two faces, four arms, and four legs. But because our power threatened the gods, our souls were split into two. Each half spends its life searching for the other, and that longing—that recognition—is what we call love." A wistful smile flickered at her lips. "I knew he was the one the first moment we met. Our chemistry was . . . insane. So different. We mirror each other in every way. Like meeting myself in another body. I've experienced big love before but nothing like this. This one made all the previous look like child's play—like preparation. It was intense. He ran—of course! I chased." Alicia uttered a small, breathy laugh. "I was devastated. But eventually we were magnetized together like on a string, and he could finally admit that we were meant to be together. I love him so much and . . . God, I dunno why I'm telling you all this!"

"Oh." Clark's eyes widened.

"How about yours?" Alicia asked.

"How about mine what?"

"Is yours the one?"

Clark looked to Joey, regaling a couple by the piano with a story about his grandma. Loudly. Waving his glass as he spoke.

Clark exhaled. "I hope so." Turning to her, he asked, "Is yours a witch too?"

"God, no. Is yours? Well . . ." She caught Joey from the corner of her eye. "Never mind."

Clark chuckled. "Aren't you getting married?"

She looked back at him. "Eventually.

Clark leaned in slightly. "So then what's keeping you?"

"I'm not sure . . ." Alicia said. "It's not that simple."

"Why not? Maybe it is?"

"Maybe. Will you?"

"Maybe . . ." Clark hesitated. "I dunno, we're so young. There's so much I want to do, so much of myself I want to explore and discover."

"So what's keeping you?"

"It's not that simple," he said resolutely.

"Maybe it is." She flashed her wild green eyes at him.

Carefully, he asked, "So then, what's your end goal here? Where do you see yourself?"

The look she shot him was dubious. "No one's ever asked me that," she admitted. "Not even Charisma."

"What do you mean?"

"Everyone just assumes I want to follow in the family business, like my aunt. Getting what I want means taking time away. I can't just step away from my duties, from my family. Not yet."

"Hmm," Clark said, nodding. "We don't get to be Charisma by working under her. Plus . . . wouldn't they understand?"

Alicia turned toward the window, gazing out at the black sea rolling beneath them. The sun was beginning to set.

"What do you have to gain by putting your life on pause?" Clark asked quietly. "Don't you want more for yourself than to live under her shadow?" Clark tilted his head toward her boyfriend. "Don't you want to write your own story instead of living in someone else's?" His voice was quieter now, more insistent. "Don't you want what matters? Don't you want to write your own story instead of one they made up for you?" Like on that group house call with Prudence, Clark leaned into her ear and whispered, "*Don't you want what matters?*"

Alicia hesitated. And then, as if drawn by some invisible force, she turned back to her boyfriend, chatting with one of the husbands.

Clark watched their eyes connect instantly. A small, private smile passed between them. Their magnetism was palpable, undeniable. To Clark, the yearning in her eyes screamed.

Alicia exhaled again, longer this time, as if she'd been holding her breath for years. "She'll kill me," she muttered.

"She won't," Clark assured her.

She scoffed. "You just want to get rid of me."

Clark frowned. "Not at all. I don't even know you."

"You're doing so well, you know," Alicia murmured. "Better than any of us thought you ever could." She looked Clark in the eyes. "You're nicer than any of us put together. I thought it was a weakness, but now . . ."

"Oh, c'mon," he whispered. "We're not so different."

A beat.

Alicia studied him, searching for the lie.

And then, finally—something shifted.

She looked at her reflection in the glass, then back at Clark.

Alicia straightened up, glancing at the phone in her hand. Back to business again. "Where do *you* see yourself here?"

Clark smirked a wry smile. "Nobody's asked me. I dunno . . . I've got a good thing going right now."

"Maybe you can be her first assistant someday, working side by side with her," Alicia said. "You'd learn a lot."

Clark's eyes widened again. "Really? Think I could?"

"Maybe."

Clark turned to look over the railing. "I want to be a great witch someday. One of the best."

She almost laughed. "It's cute you're so ambitious. Stay a while. A year here and you can go anywhere. You should see what happens to those who quit."

"Quit? What do you mean? What happens to them?"

Alicia didn't even lower her voice for passersby. "Last year, one of the juniors got fed up with Monica pushing her around." She was suppressing a laugh as she said, "A box turned up on our doorstep with her head in it. Some obsessive stalker *psycho* of Charisma's who calls herself Mother."

Clark choked on his saliva. His pulse quickened, pressing against his ribs. He turned to the dance floor: Joey had disappeared, out of sight. Clark sputtered, swallowing hard before excusing herself. "I—I should find my boyfriend. 'Scuse me."

Quickly, he wove through the party, scanning the dance floor, then slipping downstairs as the sun dipped lower, the ship carving its way around Long Beach and into the North Atlantic. Floor by floor, he searched—guests laughing, drinking, some even floating in the heated pool, oblivious to anything beyond their own indulgence, until . . .

Joey was at the grand piano, crooning to a circle of guests, his drink sloshing over its rim as he swayed. He sang, "Fly Me to the Moon." His voice was rich, evocative—it reminded Clark of their meteoric dream. His stomach clenched.

The song ended with soft applause. Before Joey could stand, Clark was beside him. "Hey, babe, can I talk to you?"

Joey exhaled sharply. "Don't start now, Clark."

"Please? It's important."

"What, now you wanna talk?" His voice was low, but the edge in it was sharp. He took a long sip of his drink. "You always do this. You always try to bring me down."

"Wait, what? It's not about you. I just need to t—"

"Yeah, *because it's always about you*," he said, yanking his arm free. Joey stalked away from the piano.

Clark reached for him. "Joey—"

"I let you live *your* fantasy," he snipped, "the least you could do is let me live mine."

"Joey, what?" Clark said, chasing after him. Were they really fighting? In public? He spoke low to avoid any eavesdropping ears as he said, "This isn't like you. You're drunk."

Clark followed him through a shaded sitting room on the eastern side of the boat, where twilight was breaking on the horizon. The air thinned to cool. Joey spun around.

"Leave me alone, Clark! *I'm not a drunk! I mean—drunk!*" He wobbled over, stumbling on his feet and catching himself on a chaise lounge.

A few more guests glanced over, eyes flickering with intrigue.

"You don't know me. Hell, I don't even know you. Do you even know yourself?" Joey jabbed a finger in Clark's chest. "Who fed you while you were a starving intern?"

"Yeah? Well, who supported us when you lost your job?"

"Us? There is no us. There's just you. You and your goddamn witch and your dirty money."

A hush fell over the surrounding guests. Their hollow eyes found his, darting around despite their owners standing frozen in place. Somewhere, a champagne flute clinked softly, an eerie contrast to the stillness pressing down on Clark's chest. Clark did the only thing he knew to do: he enveloped Joey in his aura, and the world went silent, so the words might stay between them.

"You're just like her, aren't you?" Joey scoffed. "You're a witch, too, alright. You're her little bitch."

He threw his arms out, looking around at the opulent deck, the circling guests. "All of this—your clothes, your rent, your rise—is fake. Dirty. None of this means shit if you have no dignity. You let all of this change you. And you've got no one to blame but yourself."

Clark's face went hot. "Joey, *please*, lower your voice. This is a work par—"

"Stop telling me what to do, Clark! A *work* party? Let me tell you about *work*, Clark. I chose to work mornings and take off Sundays. You forgot all about them. I chose to be there for you, and you forgot all about me. You left me behind—when I needed you."

Clark's throat tightened.

I chose to make this work. You're choosing your work! You're choosing this circus, this *cult* over me. Over us. Choose us, Clark! Choose me. I'm right here!"

They stared at each other. The ship rocked gently beneath them. Clark could feel the weight of the moment pressing down on him.

"Joey, please. That's not fair," he murmured. "You think I wanted this? I had no choice."

Joey's lips parted. He let out a breath, almost a laugh, but there was no humor left in him. "You wanted this, alright, and you always have a choice, Clark. You just keep choosing you."

He turned, walking away—no, stumbling away. Clark dropped their soundproof bubble. The music from the dance floor spilled into his ears. Joey barely made it to the bar before nearly tripping over a chair. A few guests exchanged looks, then turned to Clark, watching, waiting. He looked away, his gaze falling to his polished shoes. His pulse pounded in his ears. It was true: Joey was very much in need of him, and he wasn't helping anyone but himself. Clark followed after him.

Clark found Joey outside, at the back of the boat slumped into a chair. The sun had finally set.

"Joey, please . . ." Clark approached carefully.

Joey didn't look up at him. Instead, he reached into his jacket and pulled out a folded, stapled packet of papers. He tossed it at Clark.

"Here," he said flatly. "I got you something."

Clark frowned, hesitating before bending down and picking it up. Joey was already staring out at the water, eyes unfocused, lost. Carefully, Clark unfolded the pages.

A lump rose in his throat and his eyes widened.

It was a hotel booking. A trip. A gift.

For his birthday.

CHAPTER VIII

Salem

The morning after Charisma's birthday, Alicia didn't show up for work. No call, no text, no email. At first, everyone assumed it was a sick day.

Well, that was easy, Clark thought.

But by mid-week, with her phone unanswered and job post neglected, rumors spread fast through the witching world:

Alicia had eloped.

A quiet courthouse ceremony early in the week, passports stamped, and she and her new husband were already overseas on honeymoon.

Clark overheard Big Red the next day, as indifferent as ever. "Leave them be," she said.

Lorena was, of course, besides herself. A nervous wreck who would break down into tears any time she was left alone too long to her thoughts.

Monica didn't mind, though With Emily out on call and Alicia gone, she was more than happy to assume the title of first assistant—and with it, absorb Alicia's duties, Emily's as second, and Melissa's as third—leaving Clark in charge of keeping the keys to her estates and properties.

She looks frazzled and overworked as all hell . . . Clark laughed to himself. *I would've told Alicia to spread her wings sooner . .*

All the keys and passcodes were handed over to Clark. On top of managing clients, he was now responsible for making sure all her properties ran smoothly. Clark, now on a first-name basis with the staff, the delivery guys, and the stylists, wasn't worried whatsoever. In fact, he was quietly thrilled for the added responsibility. It must've meant that Charisma trusted him.

As for Charisma's birthday that August the 13th, what, Clark wondered, was he to get for a woman who already had everything? More importantly, what did she actually need?

He presented her with a sleek, engraved silver cigarette case—a nod to her Old Hollywood aesthetic and her infamous chimney-like smoking habit. Inside, a simple note:

To the boss of limitless inspiration—
xoxo Clark

That September, as New York Fashion Week took over the city, Clark was in high demand, bouncing from client to client—five in one day. The paychecks were major, his reputation growing, and so were the dark circles beneath his eyes, hidden under layers of concealer and glamour.

Fashion Week bled into October like it did the previous year—no time to stop when work was to be done, clients to cast, money to make. Things at home were . . . strange. He and Joey had fallen back into their old rhythm, the tension of Charisma's birthday swept under the rug like every fight before it. But this time, something had shifted.

"I'm going out," Clark said one night, catching a car. "Don't wait up."

"Alright," Joey muttered.

His apathy stung more than any fight could have. Clark hesitated, but what was there to say? Joey refused to come out with him, to mingle with clients or friends.

"Not all of them are bad people," Clark had reasoned once.

Joey had scoffed. "Listen to yourself."

Clark didn't push the issue again.

The week before his birthday arrived, and with it, Felicity's long-awaited movie premiere, set for Friday, October 18th. The last the tabloids reported, Felicity had fled the country—and really, who could blame her? The media hounded her as if she'd disappeared for no reason, but Clark understood. A tragedy on set. A stint in a "clinic." If anyone walked a mile in her heels, they'd have done the same.

A Brooklyn designer had reached out to Clark—a lovely, bespectacled fairy of a person. And so, on the night of the premiere, Clark stepped out into the autumn air, the red carpet rolling out before him, Joey at his side. Clark wore a glittering black suit, a statement in its own right, while Joey kept it classic—the suit Clark had gifted him. He looked the part, poised, polished.

Clark was in his prime.

"Clark! Clark! Over here!" The cameras flashed in a frenzy. "You're a star!" one photographer shouted.

Joey stepped aside, his expression shifting—just a flicker, a fall of his face—as he let Clark have his moment.

He beamed, tilting his head just right, basking in the moment. But even as the shutters snapped, that flicker on Joey's face gnawed at him. *Thank Goddess for the glamour cream that could hide the shame . . .*

The film opens on a quaint Los Angeles diner in 1949, where a young waitress, Tessa Delacroix, dreams of escaping her dead-end life. She serves coffee to men who never look her in the eye. Just another pretty girl among Formica countertops and linoleum floors—places where pretty girls like Tessa fade to dust.

Then, Tessa is invited to an elite actor's party. Like Cinderella, she's the belle of the ball—until an impossibly elegant woman in black appears, Madame Cordelia Devine, played by the late Cynthia Bernhardt. Clark saw the telltale signs at once—the hollow eyes, the predator's smirk: Bernhardt was one of Charisma's, no doubt. A witch in reality.

She offers Tessa a Faustian deal for her heart's desires: fame, fortune, and adoration. Tessa laughs it off, but Devine says slowly, "All it takes is a signature . . ." Treating it as a party trick, Tessa signs without hesitation.

As the ink dries, Devine slides a delicate gold ring onto Tessa's finger—an evil eye ring, rimmed with fine, lash-like ridges. "When you listen to your heart, all the answers are easy to see," Devine purrs with that hollow smirk. "And when you don't . . . a little protection. My eye will watch over you—always."

Her transformation is immediate. With a new name, Thérèse Starleigh, she skyrockets to stardom: flashbulbs, award podiums, studio heads whispering she's "the future of cinema." The American Dream personified.

But soon, shadows creep into the gilded life. At first, they're just whispers—an unnerving dream, a flickering light, a shadow in her periphery following her every move. She brushes them off. After all, she has everything: a glamorous career, a swooning public, and a perfect little family. A golden-haired son, played by Sebastian.

Inevitably, the witch returns to collect. "We had an agreement, my star. Why, you didn't think all of your success was by your own merit, did you?" Thérèse is shocked.

She begs: take the wealth, the fame—anything but her son. Madame Devine is unmoved. She has no use for trinkets; the real payment is in suffering. A life for a life.

From there, Thérèse's world splinters. The press turns on her. Friends abandon her. Directors stop calling. Headlines howl: unstable, addict, unfit mother. She searches for an escape, but every door closes—and at every turn, Devine finds her.

On screen, a Judy Garland look-alike delivers the dagger line: "Hollywood is a strange place if you're in trouble. Everybody thinks it's contagious." Clark went rigid in his seat when a famous singer in the film even echoed the same chilling warning Felicity had once confided in him: "Retire early, kids. You're worth more to them dead."

By the film's climax, she has no choice but to face Madame Devine.

Thérèse stands tall, defiant, declaring in a monologue, "I would never sacrifice my child. I love him with all my heart."

But the witch only smirks wider. "That's all that was ever required: a single proclamation of love to seal the sacrifice. Speak it, and you will belong to me . . . and so will he.""

The audience barely breathes as Devine reveals the true cost of magic. The deal was never just about a ritual sacrifice. It was about love itself—the raw, unconditional devotion of a mother. Thérèse, so desperate to escape her fate, had tried to outmaneuver the witch, invoking magic she barely understood. But she was never meant to win: only to fail beautifully.

It was never about her rise to fame. It was about crafting the perfect tragedy.

A woman too loved to be forgotten. A legend immortalized through suffering.

Or . . . would she?

The theatre held its breath. Clark bit his nails to the nub.

As the final scene unfolds, Thérèse is led to a towering funeral pyre, hands bound behind her back, her fate seemingly sealed. Flames roar in the pit below, that burn all the way down . . . A flashback flickers onto the screen: Devine sliding the ring on. "When you listen to your heart, all the answers are easy to see."

In Thérèse's present, the ring's serrated lashes have been sawing the ropes for minutes. In one swift motion, she breaks free.

Thérèse tears away the bindings and rushes to Sebastian. Behind her, Devine lunges—too quickly. Her leather bootie catches on the discarded rope.

She teeters on the edge. "No! No! *Nooo!!!*"

She plummets.

The gasps in the theater were deafening. This was Bernhardt's final moment, on or off the screen.

The camera pulls back, revealing Thérèse and Sebastian in each other's arms. The nightmare is over. The film's final shot lingers on the star—at peace, but never untouched. She has escaped the fire, yet the embers remain. Fate, like the American Dream, is a game that demands a far greater cost than anyone could ever imagine.

The credits rolled.

The audience erupted into applause, rising to their feet in a standing ovation. Murmurs of "Oscar win" flitted from mouth to ear, weaving through the theater like an unspoken prophecy. As far as

Clark read, blogs claimed the final insert—Devine's hand sliding the ring into place—was finished with a hand double and digital touch-ups after Bernhardt's death, but the magic felt seamless on screen.

Felicity's voice filled the space, the opening notes of "A Crown of My Own" swelling through the speakers, her final word, her victory.

Joey leaned over, eyeing Clark, slouched low in his seat, shoulders drawn up to his ears.

"You good?"

Both glanced down at Clark's hand, his thumb absently running over the gold evil eye ring on his pinky.

For the first time in a long while, a Wednesday at seven a.m. sharp did not find Clark at Charisma's tower or behind the counter of a coffee shop. Instead, he and Joey were on the road to Salem, a birthday trip Joey had planned months ago and Clark had so been looking forward to ever since.

The five-hour trip meandered up the Northeastern highway, a scenic stretch of autumn fire, trees dressed in their richest reds, golds, and burnt oranges. They made a quick stop for *cawfee*—Clark teasing Joey about his accent—before pressing on toward the cobbled streets of Salem, Mass.

All the while, Clark had a sense of Joey's unspoken feelings about his don't ask, don't tell witch at home. *It's not mind reading if it's just his feelings . . .* Clark reasoned. *Not if they're written all over his face . . .*

He turned to Joey behind the wheel, catching a hesitation of something whirring under the hood. A reservation. One day, he'd have to look at it head-on. But not today. Not with the risk of poking the wound and bleeding all over their trip.

Joey met his gaze, offering a small, pained smile with a pained signature—a silent resolve. At some point, he had made his decision. Joey had come this far; he wasn't about to turn back now . . .

Even if Clark suspected, he still wasn't so sure just how far gone Clark was. How lost he was to Charisma and her glamorous web.

Still, the road carried them forward. And by that time, Salem was fully dressed for Halloween.

Pumpkins sat on stoops, dried cornstalks lined doorways, and every home seemed to be in on the magic. Ghosts, witches, and skeletons perched on front lawns, welcoming spirits or warding them off, depending on how you looked at it.

It was this Halloween baby's dream come true, Clark mused.

Clark could swear there was something about the air here. Thick with history, of course, but something else, too—an old-world memory, a lingering presence that rustled between the buildings.

They checked into the Hawthorne Hotel, dropped off their bags, and stepped out onto Salem's historic streets. Clark felt eyes on him almost immediately. He caught a hollow stare here, an averted gaze there. *So much for blending in . . .*

The House of the Seven Gables was their first stop after they *pahked the cah*, spoken like true Bostonians. The black wooden mansion stood like something out of a Hawthorne novel come to life. Inside, the scent of timeworn banisters, timber, and history clung to the air as they explored narrow hallways, hidden doors, and the famous secret staircase that Clark insisted on climbing twice.

A woman dressed all in black and a gauzy scarf did a double take. This time, Clark caught the glance: not curiosity. Recognition. Hesitation. Was it just him, or did she bolt the other way?

He looked to Joey, but Joey hadn't noticed. Or maybe he had, and chose not to say anything.

From there, they made their way to Ye Olde Pepper Candy Companie, where they stocked up on old-fashioned brittles, taffies, caramel corn, and saltwater taffy—an assortment of sweets in quaint, old-timey boxes that looked like relics from another century. Clark eyed the sticks of molasses warily before trying one and immediately regretting it, while Joey had already made a dent in their stash of fudge before they'd even made it a block.

By lunchtime, they landed at Mercy Tavern, settling into a cozy booth over burgers and bourbon-rum cocktails.

Afterward, they wandered past the historic Derby Wharf, the salty breeze rolling in off the water as they took in the scenic harbor views. Ships rocked gently at their moorings, and for a brief moment, the world felt untouched by time.

They strolled through Salem Common, where Clark turned in a slow circle, arms outstretched like a kid at recess.

"So much open space," he marveled, taking in the rolling green, the towering trees, and the historic gazebos.

At the line for the Salem Witch Museum, a guide in a dark cape lingered a beat too long when stamping Clark's ticket. She said shakily, almost dropping them, "Enjoy your time." Joey and Clark breezed through, pausing just long enough to take in the eerie tableau before moving on. At the Jonathan Corwin House—better known as the Witch House—they didn't stay long. Something about the place felt off, and neither of them cared to find out why.

"It's got a funny feeling," Clark relayed as they stepped back outside.

Joey shrugged. "What'd you expect? The guy sentenced people to die."

At the town center, they paused by the iconic statue of Elizabeth Montgomery, forever caught mid-bewitching grin. A drag queen—too friendly to function—insisted on taking their photo, fussing over their poses until the result was Halloween-card perfect. Clark and Joey thanked her before slipping back into the bustling streets.

The famous Ropes Mansion was just as gorgeous as in the movies—and strangely, they managed to snap a photo in front all by themselves, unobstructed by the usual crowds. *Too unobstructed*, Clark thought. *Where is everybody?* But it was the storybook garden in the back, however, that made Clark never want to leave. Trellised pergolas wove through beds of vibrant flowers, butterflies flitting between them.

They wandered into the street market on Essex Street. Clark picked up an organic hand sanitizer and lemongrass lip balm.

The vendor, an older woman with a knowing smile and an unmistakable New England frankness, said to a radiant Clark, "You two are such a handsome couple."

Clark grinned. "Thank you," he said. Then, stealing a glance at Joey, he added, "Isn't he beautiful?"

He is . . . Clark thought. *He so is.* Joey rolled his eyes, but the glint in them gave him away—a shadow of a shy tugging at his lips, like he was trying not to let it show.

At Old Town Hall, tourists paraded by in their best witch garb, capes swirling, brimmed hats tilted. Salem in October felt like a movie set brought to life.

As they strolled, another same-sex couple, with their two children in tow, passed by them hand in hand, maybe in their forties. Comfortable. Easy. They nodded in quiet acknowledgment. As Clark watched them go, a thought unfolded softly: *Could that be us?* He squeezed Joey's hand a little tighter.

"Having fun?" Joey asked, nudging him.

"I'm in heaven."

As evening settled in, they arrived for an early dinner reservation at Ledger, the old bank turned dining hall, where candlelight flickered against brick walls and pressed tin ceilings.

They started with oysters and chicory salad, followed by roast duck for Joey and a white fish that tasted of beach bonfire for Clark. They shared each other's plates, swapping bites of squash bisque. For dessert: orange liqueur-soaked pistachio cake for Joey and sticky toffee pudding for Clark.

"How English of you, me lord," Joey teased. Both he and Clark smiled so much, the dimly lit restaurant twinkled through the blur of red wine eyes.

At the table beside them, an elderly couple whispered, "They look alike."

"Must be brothers."

Clark and Joey met eyes before dissolving into quiet, giddy laughter.

After dinner, they ducked into a narrow backstreet called Higginson Square, the kind of place you'd miss if you weren't looking. Joey grabbed Clark's arm, spinning him around beneath a turning tree, crisp leaves raining down around them.

"You know what's right up my alley?" Joey murmured before pulling him into a kiss.

A surprise cookie shop appeared just steps away, as if conjured from nowhere, the scent of warm sugar curling into the cold night. Like a magician pulling a rabbit from a hat, Joey produced a fresh post-dinner roll from his leather jacket. They smoked until a woman leaned from her third-floor window, screaming for them to get lost.

"Wench!" Joey cried, to their hysterical laughter.

They popped into a witch supply store, the scent of clove, patchouli, and something faintly metallic curling around them like unseen hands.

Clark's mind ran abuzz as he scanned the shelves. Jars of dried herbs lined the walls—mugwort, damiana, vervain—the same ingredients stocked in the Closet back home. There were polished crystals in every size and beeswax spell candles in every shade, intricately labeled oils, and small bundles of graveyard dirt tied with twine.

Clark noticed a Rider-Waite tarot deck—a classic he'd been meaning to replace. He took it to the register, where Joey met him and dropped a novelty witch's broom keychain on the counter.

"Visiting?" the cashier asked.

"Yeah, from New York," Joey answered, his Brooklyn accent unmistakable.

"That's nice," she said offhandedly.

"Yeah," Clark added. "I'm an assistant for Charisma Saintly."

The cashier froze, dropping the tarot. "Sorry," she mumbled, before quickly excusing herself.

After a moment, an employee appeared from the back and said to Clark, "Please come with me. Miriam would like to see you now."

Clark exchanged a glance with Joey, who simply shrugged.

He followed them through the store until they reached a small back room, where a tiny, bespectacled woman with tortoise frames and wild, burgundy hair sat at a cluttered table, idly shuffling a deck of tarot cards. She clicked her tongue, shaking her head.

"So many jealous women. *Tut tut tut.*" She took a sip from her tumbler and set it down. "Come. Sit." Clark sat opposite her.

"I'm addicted," she added, raising it in the air like a chalice, coffee on her breath. He smiled.

"Me too," he said. He gave her his name.

"I know who you are." She fixed him with a knowing stare that broke into a small smile. "When one of us rises from the ground up, the rest of us witches take notice. I'm Miriam, High Priestess of this little corner of Salem."

She placed a card on the table between them: The Fool. "Last year was about finding trust and acceptance in yourself," she began. The Nine of Pentacles, the Chariot, and the Eight of Pentacles reversed. "This year, it's all about expanding."

She drew her next card. The Moon. "Your familiar is a reflection of your intuition. Cats are the Keepers of the Realms, you know. Conveyors of the liminal spaces. She is your tether through the astral realm. You need to listen to her more. Let her guide you."

"Okay, I will," Clark said quietly. Clark felt the restless energy in his body—his hands twisting together, his leg bouncing beneath the table. Why was he so nervous? He sat on his hands to still them.

"And what a name," Miriam said with a wink. "Mine's a Walter." Clark giggled.

She set The Lovers down. Miriam closed her eyes for a moment, tilting her head to the side as if listening to something unseen. She scrunched up her face, nodding faintly, then opened one eye to study Clark with a glint.

"He moves fast, huh?"

Clark blinked. "Who?"

"The bartender."

Clark's eyes widened. "Oh! Haha . . . yeah. Yeah, he does."

"What's his name?"

"Joey."

A rough shuffle, and card after card came to rest: the Knight of Cups, the Four of Wands, the Eight of Wands, the Ten of Cups reversed, the Hierophant, and the Four of Pentacles. She tapped the spread, then looked up at him, matter-of-fact. "You know Joey wants to marry you, right? And quick."

Clark's eyebrows shot up. "He does?"

"Oh yeah," she said. Clark found her Boston-area accent to be charming, almost like the women he knew growing up.

"You're it for him," she said. "He's done with the partying and wants to settle down. He wants the kids, the dog, the white picket fence: the whole nine yards."

Clark's pulse kicked up. *How did she know . . . ?*

She asked, "Do you?"

"Do I what?"

"Want to marry him?"

"Oh . . ." Clark hesitated. "I think so."

"What gives you pause?"

"Well . . ." Clark searched for the words: "I feel like my soul sings when I'm with him, but . . ." And he winced when he said, "It feels so fast." Hearing it aloud felt corny, clumsy. But it was the truth. "We're so young. There's so much more I want to do!"

Miriam nodded. As she shuffled again, two cards flung forward: the Two of Cups, and the Lovers card, both upside down. "Enmeshment's a bitch, isn't it?"

"Tell me about it," Clark said.

"I think you should listen to yourself more."

Listen to myself more . . . Clark said. *How novel . . .*

She pulled a card from the bottom of the deck. Temperance in reverse. Miriam clicked her tongue. "Your attempt to connect with him was . . . misplaced. Try again. Your intuition is never wrong. His heart moves faster than his mind. That's where things can get tricky. The way he was raised, there's something unhealthy about how he copes with stress. Sometimes, the loudest one in the room screams the loudest on the inside . . ." She tapped the card. "Fast love burns hot. If you don't tend to it carefully, it burns out. Move slower." She shuffled her deck again.

"I do have a question," Clark began. "It's kind of about . . . Did I . . . witch Joey into loving me?"

"You mean, which came first: the perfume or the guy?"

"Yeah."

"One can quicken the passion, but one cannot manufacture love. Not the pure kind, the real, lasting stuff. No spell or witch in the world can do that . . ." She leaned in. "Not even *her.* See, love is what powers a spell. Love is the energy that drives the universe. The universe, god, whatever you want to call it: it's consciousness. It's pure, unconditional love. Magic is love, love is magic. See what I mean?"

"I think so . . ." Clark said.

"When is your birthday?"

Clark told her.

"Happy birthday!" she said. Then, without missing a beat, "Birth time and place?"

He gave her the details, and she nodded, shuffling her deck.

"Love is a major thread running through your life. Love from family, love at home." Her eyes flicked up, sharp. "But what kind of love do you want? That's for you to decide and create. Life doesn't happen to you. *You* happen to life. You are the creator of your story."

Clark looked back at her, wide-eyed. "I think I got what I wished for. He's like a gift hand-delivered by the universe, a fairytale come true, but . . . I don't know . . ."

Miriam nodded. "You asked for love and now you've got it. The question is, what are you going to do about it? I can't answer that for you. The choice is yours. Let all the rest—all that is illusory—fall away."

She put another card down: Four of Wands reversed. Her mouth twisted.

"Huh. There's something funny about your home. It belongs to her?"

Clark nodded. "Yeah."

"Something feels off, but I'm not able to . . . I can't see what it is. Hm."

Miriam flipped a card, tapping her nail against it. Justice.

"You know you scare them, right?" she said, leveling her gaze at Clark.

He blinked. "Who?"

Miriam gave him a look. "Your coworkers. *Your light irritates their demons.*"

She drew another card. The Star.

"These witches, they take. They control. They devour. That's not how you work though. You listen. You empower. You love. That's your superpower."

She sat back, watching him carefully. "Wherever a heart like that goes, light is sure to follow. Whatever you did to the one with wild eyes, Silvestri? Sweetie, you have them shaking. You are a damn good witch, you know that?"

Clark hesitated again. "Wait a minute, I didn't . . ."

"It's okay. Word travels fast. She was one of ours. A descendant of the illegitimate daughter of beggar and witch Sarah Good. They were part of the exodus to New York. She came from nothing and acquired their wealth through cunning and cheating . . . We've got another one, too. A descendant of Tituba . . . But when we heard about Silvestri, we had a celebration."

Melissa Good, Clark thought. A smile crept up onto his face as he relished in the irony . . . until it faded as quickly as it had come.

"I dunno if I'm that great," he said finally.

"Are you kidding me?!" she retorted. "You're a damn good witch, and that's that." She sat back and sipped from her tumbler, nodding. "That empathy: doesn't it tell you things? Paint pictures of people? Show you who they really are? Don't shut that down. Open yourself up to it. You care about what people think, and that's not always good, but most importantly you care about what people *feel.* And that's what makes you different."

"I dunno . . ." he began. "Everything gets to be so confusing lately. What's right, what's wrong. How to be an adult. If I'm a good person, or just as bad as they are . . ."

"Clark," she said. "We all do bad things. We're all light and dark. You just have to listen to yourself—to that voice inside. It'll never steer you wrong." She shuffled her deck and smirked. "And when those bitches try it, *there's grave dirt for that.*" She winked.

To Clark, it was as if there was no hiding from her—like Miriam knew everything about him, including his deepest, darkest secrets. She was like Charisma in that way, like nothing got past her, yet where Charisma saw through him, Miriam gave him the grace of an elder.

She pulled another card. The Six of Cups. "How was your upbringing?"

"Weird," Clark said.

Miriam's eyes bore into his, and Clark almost looked away. She shook her head. "You didn't always get the unconditional love you needed growing up. Children who go unseen and unheard grow into adults. Still, it's your actions that define you, and only you can decide for you who it is that you want to be. You have the chance now to give yourself that unconditional love . . . but it doesn't come from the money," she said, waving her hands around as she spoke, "or the clothes"—this, eyeing his new apple-red bomber—"or the jobs."

Miriam's face softened, and so did Clark's, as she said, "It comes from inside of you, here." She placed a hand on her heart.

Miriam closed her eyes and scrunched up her face: "Now, hold on a minute . . . Someone related to you wants to talk, and they are coming in strong."

Clark's heartbeat started to quicken.

"A woman. She's speaking in . . . some English and some . . . Spanish? A Cunning Woman. Witchcraft runs in your blood."

Clark said quietly, "Grandma Wanda."

"She wants me to tell you that she's so *proud* of you." The edge slipped from her voice. "That she's watching over you. Protecting you. She visits you in the form of mourning doves. Did you know?" She paused and blinked. "She's showing me a toy. Is it a . . . turtle?"

"A frog."

"Right, right," she said. She scrunched up her face and leaned to the side as if someone was whispering into her ear.

Clark liked to imagine that she was.

"She's saying *she will always be with you when you have your Froggie.* And that she loves you . . . always and forever." Miriam smiled, her voice rounding with warmth. "And that you'll always be her little pumpkin."

Clark's eyes were swimming.

She pulled another. The High Priestess upside down, facing Clark. "You know what she is, don't you? An ancient witch reincarnate."

"Miriam . . . Do you know how she was stopped in her previous lives?"

"Her weaknesses were always exploited. In every fairy tale, in every story, the witch always has a weakness. The hero always finds the witch's Achilles' heel hiding in plain sight."

"The blind witch is tricked into the oven by Gretel."

"Rumpelstiltskin gloatingly—"

"Reveals his name," they both finished.

"Her hubris is key. I'm afraid, however, as long as that tree exists, she will remain untouchable—timeless. See, when we die, we reincarnate backward in time, or forward, wherever our soul's journey takes us. Time is a non-linear construct. But with her? Her soul resides within that tree. *Bound to it.* That's why she always comes back. That tree is hidden in a pocket dimension—anchored to this place, to this timeline. The Tree of Life. Avalon, they've called it."

Clark inhaled sharply. "So it's not just . . . 'connected.' You're saying it's . . ."

"Holding her soul. Yes."

"So if the tree dies, she dies?"

"Not quite. I'm saying, if the tree dies, she becomes mortal, bound to the natural laws of the universe again," Miriam confirmed with a nod, voice grave. "No more resurrections. No more rebirths. No more cheating fate. Without a phylactery, her soul has nowhere else to go but to rush back into its original vessel, forced to rejoin the natural flow of the universe. She will no longer be a witch reborn—just a woman who must succumb—"

Smack went her hand on the table, making Clark jump.

"—succumb to the natural order of life, the same as the rest of us."

Clark said, "So she'll be vulnerable in ways she hasn't been before . . ."

She let the moment settle. The last of the cards practically flew from the deck onto the table, upside down.

The Tower, lightning-struck and in flames: "The question is, do you have the stomach to do what needs to be done? When the time comes, be strong."

Another: Death, an armored skeleton on a white horse with a black flag. "You've got a mountain to climb, but . . ."

A horned ram on a throne, staring back at him: The Devil. Miriam's eyes grew large.

"Well, that's our time!" The cards were snapped together in one clean fluid motion. She grabbed her coffee tumbler and stood up briskly. "Cash or charge at the front. *Good luck, sweetie!*"

And in a second, she was gone, leaving Clark to scratch his head.

Joey was waiting outside, arms crossed, pacing. When he saw Clark, his expression smoothed—but not all the way.

"You okay?" Clark asked.

"Yeah. Just ready to go," Joey said, too quickly.

Clark glanced at him sideways, unsure whether to press. He didn't.

On the way home, and even days after, Clark would find himself running over the encounter in his mind, and finding different meanings of her words—the words that more so seemed to run over Clark.

"*When those bitches try it . . .*" she had said.

Clark had an idea.

A damn good one.

In it, the spell called for grave dirt.

And Clark knew *exactly* whose grave dirt he would use.

CHAPTER IX

Reckoning

Last night, I dreamt of Miss Honey.

The wayward maid with honey eyes from last year. The one who got too close to Charisma and went up in flames for it.

I haven't seen her in ages. Not since then.

Not since our midnight meeting.

Not since my promotion.

We were back in Hell's Entrance, where I met her for the first time. She was saying it again,

"You've got a heart of gold and a light—a big, big light out of that gold heart—and a soul that's worth more than all of these bitches combined. Don't you let 'em have it, you hear me? Don't you let them! You just keep your wits about you, just keep to yourself."

I looked up.

At the leak in the ceiling.

A slow, steady drip from the light fixture. The dim glow of the bulb flickered erratically, struggling to stay on.

Something about the way the water collected at the fixture, how the bulb kept trembling like it was about to go out.

I don't know why, but the sight of it made my skin crawl.

"Don't show fear, but don't be too sweet either," she warned, "or these witches will eat you."

A noise behind me.

From the elevator of Hell's Entrance, there was running, pounding footsteps from the shadows.

Heavy. Fast.

They rushed toward me.

I heard it laughing, that oily, greasy, maniacal laugh.

And then it said my name.

Then I woke up.

My heart slamming against my ribs.

But nothing.

No one was there.

The air felt thick, wrong. I stared into the dark, straining to see or hear anything—breath, movement, the shift of fabric—anything that might explain it.

But there was only silence. Except for the sound of my own pulse drumming in my ears.

I don't know how long I stayed like that, frozen in place, waiting.

Waiting for something else to happen.

Eventually, I forced myself to shake off the dream—or whatever it was. To go back to sleep.

But I don't think it was just a dream.

"Happy birthday, sweetie," Mother said. She handed him a slim, elegantly wrapped box.

Clark peeled back its layers.

"Oh my god . . . Aw, Mother! A watch? Thank you! You shouldn't have."

"Don't be silly," she said, waving away his protest. "Put it on."

Clark did as he was told.

It was a luxury gold watch. "How much . . ." he started, his voice trailing away as he lifted it to the light. Heavy. Real. Expensive. The numbers were engraved with almost imperceptible detail.

He brought his wrist down, swallowing. "It's . . . beautiful. I can't accept."

"Shh! None of that. I don't wanna hear it," she said. Her tone was light, but her eyes held firm. "A man of your caliber deserves only the best."

Clark gave a slow, appreciative nod. "Wow." He set the box aside. "I'm in awe. Seriously—thank you. That's so kind." He ran his fingers over the band, getting used to the feel.

A slow smile broke onto Mother's face as she said, "I have one more present for you."

"Mother . . . ! I couldn't accept, really," Clark said, his eyes lit up as he pressed his hands to his cheeks.

This was a box of similar size, and almost as heavy. He unwrapped it, and yanked off the lid to find . . .

"A pet rock!" Clark announced.

Calmly, Mother asked, "Do you know what that is? What it does?"

Clark lifted the acidic, alien-green gemstone to the light. "Yeah, I'm just kidding. It's moldavite." The moment it touched his fingers, something buzzed—light and electric—up his wrist. He set it down gently. "Mother! This is really *rare*—and expensive. You really shouldn't have! Thank you!" He got up to hug her.

Mother let him go, brushing his shoulders as she settled back into her seat.

"So," she said carefully, "how was your birthday?"

Clark told her about the surprise day trip to Salem was. Joey hadn't been able to request off that weekend, deciding the money would be too good to pass up, and Clark had work too gearing up for Halloween.

"That's lovely."

"Yeah, it was great . . ." Clark scratched his nose absentmindedly, gaze flickering up at her. "Did you see the news? Felicity is free!"

"I know. I saw."

"Yeah, I'm so happy. The movie was . . . wild," he said, twirling his evil eye ring. "You would not believe."

"I'm sure . . ."

A pause hung in the air.

"I wanted to talk to you today before your next lesson. I've seen what you've done for Felicity. The question now is . . . what have you done to free yourself?"

Clark gulped. "Free myself?"

"You have had all this time," Mother said, very still. "What is taking you so long?"

"Just to be sure," Clark asked carefully, "to do what, specifically?"

Mother leaned forward, barely blinking. "You know what I am talking about."

"Ah . . ." Clark sighed. He looked at his wrist again, at the watch—his new gift. Gleaming. Perfect. "The coven."

Slowly, she nodded.

"Oh, that. Well, I convinced Alicia to elope! That was easy."

Mother sat back in her chair, studying him. It seems she was unmoved by his flippant attitude.

"Clark," she began, "don't you want your payback?"

"Yes. Of course."

Her gaze sharpened. Unhurriedly, she said, "I thought we had a deal."

"I know," he started slowly, cautiously. "It's just that—"

"'It's just that' what?" Her head tilted inquisitively, but her honey eyes gleamed with something sharper. "Mmm? A deal's a deal, darling." A pause. A stillness. Then, cool and clipped: "Are you going back on your word now?"

Clark squeaked, "No!" He cleared his throat. "It's just that things are really good right now. I have money. I have a beautiful home. I have a career—"

"None of those things," Mother cut in, her voice like steel, "matter. You will never benefit, you will never be free—*none* of us will—so long as you uphold her throne. Didn't I tell you? Didn't you listen? She will never let you rest so long as you keep playing her game."

Clark's lip twitched. "Yeah, but—"

"I said, NONE OF THESE THINGS," Mother bellowed, rising up in her chair and throwing Clark backward, "ARE YOURS!" She leaned over him then. "Don't you get it? These things she gives you: when has she ever let one of her little witches keep what she's given? The answer is NEVER."

Clark froze.

"Look at you. Look. At. You," said Mother, very slowly, very quietly. "You act like you're in control. Like you've got it alllll figured out . . . But you're not. And you don't. Never have. Never will. You are just her pet. Still wagging your tail, hoping she gives you a pat on the head. Convincing yourself that your gilded leash is freedom.

"I thought you were meant for more," Mother leered. "Or was I wrong?"

Wordlessly, Clark shook his head.

"ANSWER ME!"

"No, Mother."

Mother pulled away, and that silence was worse. Clark watched her carefully, but the fear wasn't from the moment that had just passed.

It was from not knowing what she would do next.

She turned and began to pace.

When she finally spoke, her voice was like ice.

"Don't forget: I made you."

She rounded back on him, eyes flashing. "Everything you are, you owe TO ME! Leave it to a white man to step on the shoulders of a Black woman and think it was all his doing. Hmph! Who taught you all you know?"

Clark sat very quiet. "You did, Mother."

She peered down at his watch, and then back up at Clark. "You had one job," she said darkly. "Cut the coven down from the inside out. Perhaps you allowed yourself to get a little distracted, mm? Carried away."

"I—I—"

Her eyes grew large. "Yes?"

Clark took a breath. He responded, "I found out about the terrarium. It's the Tree of Life—*a* Tree of Life—that isn't just connected to her. It's merged with her soul. A soul tie. And when it's destroyed, her soul will return to its original vessel and leave her mortal."

"Yes," she said. "Of that I'm sure. She made a deal with fate. One can only wonder what the cost of that magic was, the sacrifice. Her firstborn, perhaps. Severing the cycle of motherhood was the ultimate act of defiance. The ultimate sacrifice."

Then, she inhaled, rolling her shoulders, as if the very thought filled her lungs with something intoxicating.

"And yet," she continued, "what a waste it would be to destroy something so . . . magnificent."

Clark stiffened.

"Imagine the power of that tree in the *right* hands . . ."

Clark could hardly move.

"In the right hands . . . ?"

Clark stiffened. A chill ran through him.

"Stand up."

He exhaled, steadying himself. Clark's fingers curled around the armrests, and he pushed to his feet.

"I said STAND UP NOW!" Her voice cracked through the air like a whip, a force so powerful it slammed into his chest—and just as he'd found his footing, it sent him stumbling backward, flipping his armchair over with him.

The walls shuddered, the air vibrated, the windows rattled with her command. Clark scrambled upright, his pulse hammering.

"Stand," she barked. "There." She pointed across the living room rug. Clark rose again and did as he was told. Then, with slow, deliberate steps, she paced to the opposite side, positioning herself like an adversary preparing for a duel.

She locked eyes on his.

Then, she spoke.

"A witch," she began, "can wield great power without the use of silly little incantations and spellwork—regardless of what you might have come to believe. She is old school, that Saintly. It all comes down to the power of intention."

She took a step closer.

"It starts in the heart and moves through the mind. The heart is the source and the mind is the wielder. Understand?"

Clark's eye twitched.

"Erase memory? Mind control? Influence . . . perception?" Her eyebrow came up in a smirk. "Mental witchcraft is easy."

Another step.

"But bending spacetime? Wielding energy? Manipulating the very fabric of reality? A will so strong, the universe bends to meet it, a witch's will manifested before her . . . that is the ultimate power."

She stopped, her eyes dark and fixed.

"You are going to show me what practical magics you can wield."

The vase on the coffee table began to tremble.

At first, it was just a soft vibration, a subtle shudder against the glass surface. Then—harder. Faster. The shaking turned violent—until the vase launched into the air like a missile, aimed straight for Clark.

He barely dodged it.

The vase exploded against the floor behind him, shards skidding across the hardwood, scattering toward the windows like tiny, glinting knives.

Clark turned to Mother, heart hammering.

The books on the tall, floor-to-ceiling shelves opposite began to rattle. One fell. Then another. Then another.

Then—one zoomed toward him.

He ducked.

Another flew, a heavy one this time—missing his head by inches.

"FIGHT!" she screamed. Mother's aura crackled, pulsing red and black, raw energy spilling from her like a storm.

Clark stumbled back. He tried to summon his courage, but—to levitate a book? To throw something back? How?

How am I supposed to fight against this . . . ?!

The air thickened. Energy swelled. Her aura crackled. Then, a blast like a gunshot. A violent force slammed into his chest, sending him flying backward. He hit the floor—hard. The sting barely registered over the sheer force of the impact. He groaned, and propping himself up on his elbows.

Mother stepped over him. Slowly. Deliberately. She loomed—utterly still—locking eyes with him and letting the moment stretch.

"I am going to take that tree when she leaves it unattended on the Witch's New Year, when the veil is at its thinnest."

Halloween . . . Clark thought.

"And you are going to hand it over to me."

Clark's throat went dry.

"The code to her home. Give it to me. Now."

What was Clark to do? If he lied, she would surely find out. He could warn Charisma, have her change the codes . . . but then she would know he was consorting with the enemy.

Clark did as he was told.

Mother entered it into her phone, securing access to Hell's Entrance.

"Good," she said.

His hands wouldn't stop trembling.

"Now scram."

It was one in the morning. The night before Halloween.

Clark stepped out of a yellow cab. His route had taken him not back home to PH1 on the Upper East Side, but northwest to just above 155th and an avenue over. He shut the door gently, slipping a glance over his shoulder.

"Keep the change," he said, though the driver barely grunted in response before pulling away.

The streets in this part of town were quiet. Still. Even for a full hunter's moon hovering above. Clark adjusted his backpack, feeling the familiar weight of its contents as he moved.

As he approached Broadway, he instinctively walked to the

opposite side of the street, avoiding a smoking stranger on her stoop. She exhaled a long, lazy drag, watching him with mild curiosity as he unzipped his bag and rummaged inside.

From its rattling depths, he pulled a black beanie first, tugging it over his hair—then paused, swapping it for the ski mask instead. The clean-cut holes for his twinkly eyes stared back at him in the reflection of a parked car.

A burglar. A robber. A lunatic.

Clark giggled to himself.

I can't believe I'm doing this. Look at me . . . ! Clark thought as he adjusted the mask. *The spell calls for this one thing,* he reasoned. *I'm just making sure it's extra potent . . .*

He darted across Broadway with his head down and hood on low, quickening his pace and jaywalking to avoid both traffic cameras and unnecessary attention.

Since leaving Mother's that Sunday, shaken and rattled, he'd been practicing cloaking himself with his aura, allowing it to bend light and shift perception, just as he had done a year before in the Tower during the Taking Down of the Blood Moon.

If anyone reviewed the footage, they'd see only a shadow, a figure blurring fast.

Finally, he arrived.

Trinity Church graveyard.

Clark wasn't naive enough to jump the iron fence at the main entrance, spiked at the top and tricky to scale, and knowing full well the risk of trespassing and getting caught. "Violators will be prosecuted," the signs would say, or something to that effect.

No shit . . .

On the opposite side of the graveyard, the northeastern walls shifted from iron to stone—over six feet tall and dark. For this, Clark had come prepared.

Past the corner, outside the light of the streetlamp, he drew a rope and anchor from his bag. Clark aimed for the nearest tree branch over the wall and, hard as he could, swung.

He missed.

The anchor came down with a loud clang, bouncing off the stone and landing in a pile of autumn leaves with a heavy crunch. Sweat erupted all over his body.

A car approached. Headlights swept past. Clark ducked his head before trying again.

Swing . . . Throw, he thought with a heaving breath. Up and up it went until . . . *Clink!*

Yay!

He scaled the wall as quickly as he could, an ungainly black shadow and backpack with a nervous rattle. The rope was left for his return. Clark trekked up and over the hill, his high-tops crunching softly over the cold, damp ground. Eyes adjusting to the dark, as he descended into a cemetery shrouded in shadow.

He took only a few short paces before there was a rustle and the crunching of leaves ahead of him, and that telltale tingling between his eyebrows, stopping him cold where he stood.

On Halloween's Eve, when the veil was at its thinnest, the boundary between the living and the dead, between flesh and spirit, past and present, was paper-thin. Even then, he could hardly believe what he saw. If he hadn't known any better, if he hadn't been paying attention, he might have even missed it entirely:

Sitting ahead of him was the silhouette of an unmistakably large, shaggy black dog. It sat perfectly still on its haunches, several feet in front of the graveyard road ahead of him. Watching. Waiting.

A graveyard grim . . . he thought. *A guardian protecting graves from malintent, just like the ones from legend . . . Cool!*

Carefully, he lowered himself onto one knee, bowing his head in quiet deference. He avoided direct eye contact, his movements slow, measured. From the bottom of his black backpack, he produced a small, shiny blue ball—a simple offering, but one he hoped would be accepted.

He extended it forward, presenting it to the grim. Clark held his breath. The night had gone completely silent. Still. Even the crickets, Clark noticed, had stopped chirping. What would happen if it didn't accept the offering?

Clark tossed the ball in the air and peeked up ever so slightly. The grim stood up too. Clark tensed. But then, to his delight, it began to wag its tail and pant, a dog through and through. It let out a small huff, its tongue lolling as it panted in the light of the moon.

"Who's a good boy?" Clark called out, his voice light with relief. With a flick of his wrist, he hurled the ball down the graveyard road and out of sight. The grim galloped along after it. One, two, three times he heard the ball's long bounce and the raking of claws on cement before the sound and sight of the two disappeared into the shadows. A breeze whispering at his back bade him admittance.

The steps he retraced by his phone's lowest light felt like an eternity, unforgotten. Almost a year to the day, he could still smell the earth, electric with coming rain, the odor of a tree branch scorched by lightning, could hear the gasps and screams of a dead body tumbling from its coffin . . .

Clark's ears were abuzz, red and burning as he stepped closer and closer. His forehead had not stopped prickling. His aura was up. He choked down the feeling that he was being curiously watched.

By his phone's dim light, the words carved in shadowed relief came into view. Clark stood in front of none other than the charred remains of his dead manager put to rest:

In Loving Memory of Melissa Silvestri
Beloved Daughter, Mother, Sister, and Friend
Loved and Missed by All.

Clark snorted at that last part.

He set his phone up on her tombstone, the dim glow casting long, eerie shadows over the grass. By its light, he laid down his bag and dropped to his knees about six feet in front of the tombstone, where the sod was still the freshest. He could have sworn he caught a whiff of singed skin and hair, the same gut-churning stench that had lingered in the Tower after Monica had Melissa's body removed and Lorena made him clean it up. The thought of it still made his stomach curdle.

Hesitantly, he smoothed and patted his hands on the grass over her grave as if it were a blanket that had simply tucked her in for sleep.

"H-h-hey, Melissa!" His voice cracked. "How you been, baby girl? It's me . . . Clark. Long time no . . . speak, huh?"

Silence. All was quiet in that dark graveyard. The crickets had not returned, but the feeling of being watched hadn't left either. The trees themselves were asleep with one eye open.

Clark cleared his throat. "Um, listen, I, uh . . . I need your help with something."

From his bag, he pulled a silver garden trowel borrowed from the Closet, its handle etched in runes and sigils. He raised it above his head, and drove it into the earth. It barely sank an inch. The ground was unyielding and unbreakable.

It was then that the buzzing in his ears spiked.

It came to a shrill, deafening fever pitch.

Uh oh . . .

As if in frenzied protest, the cemetery air whipped around him, a maelstrom of leaves and dirt spiraling skyward. The trees shook at him, furious and angry. The wind was awake with a hundred howling, wailing, shrieking screams—and through them all, one voice cut through shrill and unmistakable. Melissa.

In the chaos, Clark could have sworn he saw her pallid face and wild eyes on the wind as his mind was flooded with an image straight from his nightmares: Melissa's hairless, burnt body crawling on the Tower room floor, catching sight of him behind the iron banister, one arm extending out, reaching. Her lips moved, mouthing a single gasping word.

"YOU!" the wind screamed. Melissa was dead, and it was all his fault.

Clark yanked the trowel from the dirt and toppled backward.

As quick as it had started, the wind and the howling ceased. Gravestones and trees stood motionless once more. As he clamored back up, he drew a deep sigh of relief. *Cool . . . Now what, genius . . . ?*

"Okay, okay, I'm sorry. I know—who am I to ask you for help, right? But hear me out: I need your grave dirt for a spell. It's to end Monica and the coven."

At the very mention of that name, the noise of the city air seemed to chill to icy silence. No distant honking, no rustling leaves. Not a sound could be heard. *Now I've done it . . .* Clark licked his lips and pressed on.

"What did you call her? A 'little British bitch house sitter'?" Clark snorted. "C'mon, don't you want to put her in her place? I know you do!"

Nothing.

Melissa answered with silence.

Clark shifted. "You know, you're a way better witch than Monica ever could be. Yeah, I said it!" Clark caressed the sod at his knees. "I mean it. Way prettier, too. Everyone knows it."

Still, there was silence.

He leaned in, voice lower now, coaxing. "You know what they say, don't you?"

The world around him seemed to hold its breath.

"You had the better hair."

Could he be imagining it? Had the air gone down in temperature, a sleeping spirit roused? Clark grinned.

He spoke in a singsong voice when he said, "I brought you a surprise." He rummaged through his backpack, pulling out an item he had too often raided from the penthouse's pantry and delivered to her himself. Something he knew she couldn't resist: Famous Amos cookies. Melissa's compulsive vice.

"Your favorites. I remembered."

He placed them gently on the grave, an offering. Would she answer?

The wind picked up, a sudden whispering howl in his ears. The temperature plunged so low, he could have sworn he saw his breath.

Bingo.

Clark checked his watch. "I think I'm running out of time here." He rubbed his lips together. "Help me give her a taste of her own medicine. You know you want to. What do you say, Melissa? Please? Help a gayby out?"

For a moment, nothing.

Clark dipped the trowel into the sod—and was pleased to find it slid in without protest. Not even in the slightest. "Thank you!" he said aloud. He worked fast.

What had felt cold and dry before, he unearthed in a minute flat: the grass revealed dark, cold earth. From the seemingly never-ending contents of his backpack, Clark produced a small, lidded mason jar, and with the trowel, filled the jar with grave dirt.

"'Dirt of thine enemy,'" Clark recited with glee.

There were other contents in his bag he unearthed too. "Hyssop, bay leaves, garlic, and wormwood . . ." he murmured as he poured the ziplocked contents into the jar.

"Dried sage ash and rose thorns. Rusty nails of a dead man's coffin," he said, giving the jar a shake, the nails clanking against the glass. "Chili powder, black pepper and salt, and dried sage ash for spice and nothing nice . . ."

But the final touch—the thing that made him most pleased—was at the bottom of his bag.

A ziplocked bundle of Monica's hair he had fished out of the bathroom sink after following her for a week. He dropped it into the jar with a satisfied, sprinkling flick of his fingers.

The jar seemed to hum in excitement with him. It was almost ready. Almost.

Clark inhaled. "And for a wicked magic, the strong and powerful kind . . ." He pulled out a small athame, its blade gleaming in the dim phone's light.

"A drop of thine own blood." With a sharp prick of the tip of his raised middle finger and a small yelp, he let a single red drop fall onto the jar of dirt. It didn't bead up and roll—it sank and disappeared into the dark soil of the jar.

Quickly, he sucked his breath and slapped on a princess Band-Aid. The jar was complete.

Now for the real fun . . . he thought. Clark pulled a black candle and a black-clothed, drawstring bag from the front of his backpack. Delicately he pried it open and retrieved the final prize: Monica's gold lacquered powder compact, which he had pocketed just days before from her open makeup bag left out in the kitchen.

Ladies, her text on the team thread had said, *if anyone finds my compact please let me know!*

Fat chance, Clark thought, just as he had then, opening the compact. The mirror inside caught his reflection, his own eyes staring back at him. He summoned every memory, visualized every abuse, every spiteful word, every villainous act she had committed. The mirror bore witness; the spell of justice, long overdue.

It was one minute until three o'clock a.m.: the same time as his early morning night terrors that had started over a year ago.

He lit the candle standing in the sod. The jar was warm in his palm, as if it knew. Clark reached into his bag and held the moldavite Mother gifted him. The trees seemed to lean in to listen as he spoke the words committed to memory:

"By voice, by will, by rightful claim,
I break the ties upon my name.
The harm you cast, the spite you spun,
Returns to where it first begun.

Let harm and shade, slander and slight,
Find its sender, swift as night.
No more power, no more claim,
Your curse returns, your work now tame.

With mirrors strong, my enemy's own,
Reflect their harm, return it home.
This grave a witness, their truth made clear,
Malice reflected, your fate sealed here.

The energy cast is bound, turned round,
To break the cords where I was bound.
No hurt, no hold, no chain on me,
Your wrath dissolves, my soul walks free.

By burning wick and salted land,
No spell of yours shall withstand.
The veil is shut, the door is sealed,
Your will revoked, your fate revealed.

No harm I send, no vengeance sown,
But what you gave is now your own.
And by the breath of night and sea,
As I will it, so mote it be."

A singed face and blackened eye flickered in the mirror, sending a jolt through him so powerful, he almost dropped the compact and gemstone.

Then, it hit.

His head snapped back, his eyes rolling behind fluttering lids as a surge of energy rushed through him. His aura flashed hot and bright, shifting from indigo blue to solid gold.

It lifted—an invisible weight lifted.

In his mind's eye, he saw her. A terrible, high-pitched screech ripped from her throat as she jolted upright in bed—then shot into the air. She crawled up the walls and onto the ceiling.

All the night terrors.

All the fear.

Monica was living in the terror she inflicted, trapped in the nightmares she'd made real.

She crashed down and darted from wall to wall in pure, manic frenzy.

I am rubber and you are glue, trash . . . Clark thought. *Whatever you do bounces off me and sticks to you . . .*

His lips curled as he snapped the compact shut.

"Happy anniversary, Melissa, you beautiful witch bitch!" he said to the night, laughing, throwing his arms out wide.

Clark strolled out of the cemetery the way he had come, lighter and looser. The grim wagged its tail as he waved bye. He walked west, on the pathway to the Hudson.

He held the jar to his lips, kissed it once, slow and deliberate.

And gave it a hard chuck over the railing.

The glass arced into the night and splashed into the water, vanishing from sight.

Clark smiled to himself the entire cab ride home.

CHAPTER X

The Great Awakening

"Charisma," the red carpet host asked at the Los Angeles premiere of *The Cost of Magic*, microphone angled toward her, "what do you say to the rumors about you being a witch?"

Charisma was a vision of power and beauty—and dressed an awful lot like Madame Cordelia Devine. Her lips curled into a knowing smirk, and for a moment, she paused, letting the anticipation build as if she had all the time in the world.

"All powerful, successful women are witches in the patriarchy's eyes. History has shown that. A woman who doesn't shrink herself? A woman who bends the world to her will? That terrifies people."

She tilted her head, letting the weight of her words settle.

"And honestly? What would be so bad about that?"

Clark blinked. *Did she just—was that a confession . . . ?*

His mind scrambled for a reaction, anything to say, but Charisma was already dismissing the question with a flick of her wrist and a knowing glance.

She smiled, her straight, perfect teeth gleaming, lips curving up to the apples of her cheeks. Yet the smile never reached her hollow green eyes.

She wasn't there to convince anyone otherwise.

She was here to be worshipped.

The next morning at Charisma's, Halloween day, as Clark found Lorena in a full-blown tizzy in the kitchen.

As it turned out, Monica wasn't coming back to work. "Not for the foreseeable future."

"What happened?" Clark asked with feigned curiosity. He tapped his under-eyes in the mirror of her compact, making sure his glamour and the extra bit of concealer were in place.

"She had some kinda episode in the middle of the night—so disturbed, she was inconsolable. She bolted from bed screaming and wouldn't stop. She clawed at her husband, she locked herself in the bathroom, I—I . . ." Lorena placed a palm to her forehead.

"Woah," Clark said, distracted. "Crazy."

She stopped short. Slowly, her gaze dropped.

"Crazy, indeed," she murmured, voice thin as paper. "Wait 'til I tell you how I'm putting the twins forward."

Clark's concealer wand froze mid-stroke. "Forward for what?"

"To be promoted to assistants," she said, as if it were the most natural thing in the world. She smirked. Clark's jaw went slack.

The twins . . . ?

Assistants?

The machine, he realized, never stopped. It simply swapped fresh bodies for broken ones . . . and he knew he couldn't let that happen.

They climbed into the backseat of Charisma's Escalade.

"Hi, Oksana!" Clark chirped, buckling in as she pulled away.

From behind her black sunglasses, Oksana met his eyes in the rearview mirror, her expression unreadable. Then, without a word, she turned back to the road.

Their destination: a grand meeting at Saintly Church.

Clark glanced over. "Where is it?"

"You know where So Below is?"

Clark raised an eyebrow. "Yeah . . . ?"

She shot him a look—one he didn't have to be a witch to decipher.

His eyes widened. "No way."

Lorena nodded.

As it turned out, So Below—Charisma's infamous nightclub—had another face. By night, a playground for the rich and the unholy; by day, a temple, called As Above.

By the time they arrived, Halloween had draped the building in full spectacle for the biggest party of the year. Attendants were still at work, hanging cobwebs, adjusting floating candle fixtures, ensuring every eerie touch was perfectly placed. But what struck Clark more was the transformation inside.

The sprawling dance floor, usually packed with bodies under pulsing lights and music as he remembered from last year, was unrecognizable. The plush tables and velvet couches were gone, replaced with neat rows of pews that stretched toward a raised altar. It looked less like a club and more like a cathedral. The sun beamed through the round window in the rafters—a perfect, unblinking eye—casting its golden light scross the front stage. Clark squinted against the glow, a strange sense of being watched settling over him.

"What is the meeting about?" Clark had asked Lorena.

"You'll see," Lorena had said, smiling out the car window.

Clark didn't like that answer very much.

Inside, he took his seat at the very front of the audience. The seats to his right remained conspicuously empty—spaces where Lorena, Alicia, Emily, Melissa, and Monica might have sat. He turned, casting a glance over his shoulder, scanning the crowd. For what, he wasn't sure.

He found so many hollow eyes staring back. The who's who of the witching world—powerful, renowned, ruthless coven leaders. Not just from New York, but from covens across the globe. Their eyes flashed in the dim light, hollow and ravenous. And they were watching *him*.

Or rather, the empty seats beside him, and flicking up to him with distaste, suspicion, and envy.

Everyone wants to be me . . . he reminded himself. *Everyone would kill to be in my place . . .* Clark exhaled sharply and turned back around.

A hush fell over the room as Lorena appeared on stage. She stepped up to the podium in the center.

"Are the doors locked?" she asked, her voice carrying across the hall.

Somewhere in the back, the chained door rattled and shook.

"Good. Let's begin."

The light of the single circular window blinked shut. The outside noise of New York City faded to mute. The air in the room stiffened. Clark could practically feel the women sit up straighter at attention.

"Please welcome our Greatness," Lorena said, "my sister, our queen: Charisma Saintly."

As she stepped onto the stage from the side, the room exhaled. The audience rose to their feet in a thunderous ovation: a blending of reverence, dread, and something Clark could only describe as devotion.

"Divine feminines! High priestesses! My coven leaders of the world!"

Charisma lifted a single hand, and the witches roared in response, the sound swelling like a wave crashing against the walls of As Above. Lorena stepped down and claimed the chair to Clark's right.

Charisma let the moment stretch, surveying the sea of witches before her, each showcasing power in clothes, jewels, or cold, immaculate beauty. A congregation of the world's most influential women, and yet, here, they were merely her audience. Clark couldn't help a fleeting, absurd thought: was Charisma about to make them peel off their wigs and shoes like in his beloved witch story?

Then, with nothing more than a slight flick of her wrist, she commanded silence. No words were needed. And so she began.

She smiled.

"I have gathered you all here today, on this, our Grand New Year, to share with you something I am most deeply excited to *give* to you."

A murmur of anticipation rippled through the room. Clark felt it too—that pull, the weight of her presence, her promise.

"When they burned us for our power, we fled the Old World for the New. When they hanged us, we fled to the greatest city in the world.

"New York."

The walls themselves seemed to lean in. An invocation. The witches clapped.

"This city was our escape during the Trials, and still remains the heart of our empire. To this day, we hold the largest population of witches in the entire world."

"But we did not come here out of choice." Her voice darkened. "We were forced to flee. Forced to *survive*."

The clapping stilled.

"They have hunted us and hanged us. They have suppressed us and erased our names from history. They have co-opted our ways, stolen our symbols, repackaged our wisdom as their own."

A soft hiss carried through the air from her audience.

"All the while they have destroyed our palaces of worship and poisoned the world with their religions, their dogmas, and their *stigmas*—all in the name of man . . ."

Then she smiled.

"Until now."

A ripple of anticipation spread through the room.

"We live on in the shadows . . . no more! No more will we live in persecution. No more will we live in fear. No more will we hide!

A storm of cheers surged through the chamber, the energy tangible. Charisma lifted a hand, commanding silence once more.

"For too long, *they* have dictated our place in the world. But now, we take theirs. And what better place to start . . . than at the very top?"

The applause was beyond polite: it was pure reverence. She let her words hang, making them *ache* for her every utterance.

"First, we launched our debut ready-to-wear collection—my ten little black dresses. Then came shoes. Then lingerie. So that women could embody power."

A murmur of satisfaction spread through the crowd. Clark turned to see the women nodding. Some adjusted their clothing—a shifting of shoulders, a straightening of the spine. Perhaps they were decked hat to heel in Charisma Saintly fashion. Her eyes swept across the crowd with pride.

"For our foray into beauty, we launched Charisma Lipsticks," she continued, "so that women can speak power. Lipsticks named after myself, of course, and some of my good friends and family, Charisma, Grace, Noble, Iris, Queenie, Darling, Angelina, Celeste, Verity, Devine . . . and even my good friend, Felicity."

At this the witches broke out in a fit of enthusiastic, sycophantic giggles. Clark's stomach turned and the blood rose up to his face. He swore he could vomit.

"Then," Charisma continued, her voice lilting as she lifted her chin, "we launched *Charisma Eau de Parfum*." She took a slow step forward. "So that women could heighten their auras, and command confidence, power, and prestige in every court they rule."

At this, she gave a pointed look toward Clark, sending a shock through him. He shifted in his chair. She must have known he wore it himself.

"It is no lie that I have been empowering women my whole life. I have continued to shatter records and glass ceilings everywhere, so that women can live the limitless lives that we deserve. So that we can live as the women that we were always meant to be.

"I am in the homes and closets of women around the world. In their handbags. On their lips. And now with my latest concoction . . . in their medicine cabinets and on their vanities."

A smile broke out across her face.

"We have already begun reshaping the world of man, haven't we? You have redirected their focus. You have redirected their worship. You have infiltrated and dominated their every space. With our combined power, this election, it is my hope that we put one of our own in the White House as the first female president of the United States of America."

The room erupted into applause. The room hummed with power. A charge crackled through the air. Clark could feel it in his bones. She silenced them once more, a conductor halting her chorus.

"They might push back, true, but we push back harder. Lift your sisters up. And use . . . my cream."

The lights in the room shifted, shadows pooling at the room's edges. The projection clicked. A crystalline glass jar appeared on the screen, its sleek white packaging and black-and-gold label catching the light. The witches were fixated.

"So many of you have asked what my clients *beg* for," Charisma continued, her voice lowering to a near whisper. *"Guidance on glamour."*

Clark glanced at Lorena, who sat rigid in her seat, eyes forward, and throat tight as she swallowed. Charisma let the silence stretch, allowing their hunger—their need—to build, before pressing her hands together.

"I have always wondered how I could bottle up my essence and give it to you. And now . . . I have. You see, for the better part of twenty years, I have been perfecting my own personal mix of moisturizer. 'Charisma's Secret Youth Cream,' my clients would call it. With *Charisma Crème*, I have harnessed witches' coveted Gift of Glamour so that women everywhere—not just witches—can regain their beauty, and with it, their goddess-ordained power. With *Charisma Crème*, I have sourced the world's finest ingredients and patented technology to create a potion that gives you plump, dewy, radiant skin—and in an instant, reverses the signs of aging, stopping it almost dead in its tracks!"

The witches cheered.

"This, in part, thanks to my friend Dr. Blair Leache-Courtland. Dr. Blair, would you please stand?"

A woman rose from the audience. She was dressed in a black doctor's robe, sleek and ceremonial, the only hint of color a blood-red eye brooch at her collar.

"It's like I always say: give a woman a little Charisma, and she can conquer the world. It's not just skincare; it's not just self-care; it's *empowerment*. I want every woman to feel like the best version of herself, so he can achieve the life of their dreams. This cream will help you achieve the life of your dreams, the same way it helped me achieve mine. That, I can promise! Bringing *Charisma Crème* to market has been the greatest achievement for not just womankind, but humanity to date!"

Applause erupted.

"For the world's most powerful youth potion," she continued, "I am the first to bottle glory, beauty . . . and a secret ingredient."

The room fell still.

"A witch never reveals her secrets . . . until now."

Charisma paced the stage with slow, deliberate gravity, microphone in hand, then turned back toward the audience, her smile growing. The slide clicked again. Footage played: promotional imagery, campaign visuals, commercials. Each clip featured their queen bee and her brands, at the head of her boardrooms, dazzling on her red carpets, at the top of her tower—always with the same lisping, honeyed poise. The room watched, rapt. Enthralled.

The slides changed to something . . . different. The footage was still Charisma, polished, gleaming. But this time, she wasn't on red carpets. She wasn't in boardrooms. She was in As Above. And around her—orphans. She walked among the children with ease, with affection, like a benevolent queen surveying her kingdom. They clamored around her, smiling up at the camera. Her voice echoed over the footage.

"Always the children first."

"For this elixir—this youth potion, this créme—I have harnessed the power, the very essence . . . of children."

A collective shudder rippled through the room.

Another slide: images flashed rapidly. Faded photos and reports of missing children. Grainy security tapes, blurred CCTV footage, their small figures slipping through the cracks. Faces pixelated, barely captured before they were last seen. Stories of runaways, untraceable orphans, vanishing acts with no trails left behind.

Clark had stopped breathing.

The slide changed once more. Darkened rooms. Doctors in black like Leache-Courtland. Rows of small, still bodies on silver tables.

"No longer will ritual blood baths be required. From their blood, the seat of their love, innocence, and youth, we have harnessed their essence, sacrificed, it, bottled it up, and given it back to the world. It is the perfect youth potion."

A glowing crescent moon C for Charisma appeared, her logo. It flickered through its phases, waxing to full. At its peak, it opened: an eye. The All-Seeing Eye from his nightmares. The eye that had always been watching. It blinked once, twice, three times, then faded to black.

The audience fell silent. Clark turned to Lorena, whose face was blank.

"Yes, sacrifices have had to be made . . . but for the greater good of all. The Great Culling isn't *coming*." She paused, letting the words settle. Then, she smiled. "It's already here. So choose the right side of history, if we are to do more than simply survive."

She crossed the stage to the podium.

"You have been completing your preorders with reverence. We are currently on track to become the best-selling face cream launch of all time. But I need more from you: continue to be the great witches I know you to be, the ones our ancestors burned for."

A murmur of agreement rippled across the hall.

"Continue to influence their orbits. Continue to round up their strays. Continue to infiltrate their governments, their cabinets, their very homes."

Clark's mouth hung open in total, abject horror. Charisma wasn't just harvesting something—she was culling stray children.

It all made sense now.

The whispers, the disappearances, the allegations against her husband—all of it snapped into focus.

"They are still trying to burn us," she said. "Not with fire, but with boardrooms and bedrooms. They never stopped and they never will. Because it is *our* power they fear. It is our magic they covet. It is a woman's light that they need."

Charisma's blazing eyes swept her audience. She lifted her chin, voice rising, swelling. "Let us remind them," she said, "why they feared us so much they had to burn us. We alone know the truth. We witches are here to elevate humanity. To lead us into the dawn of a new Earth. This is our moment. Our revolution has come. I welcome you to the Great Awakening."

She swept her arms open. The witches rose to their feet, a deafening roar filling the chamber.

"First, New York. Next, the world. There are empires to conquer, and this world is yours to claim. Do you hear that, ladies? It's the sound of the dawning of an Âge de la Femme. My darling, divine feminines, are you with me? Our time . . . is now!"

A single roar became a standing ovation.

A storm of cheers and laughter.

Some witches pounded their fists against the pews, the deep thuds reverberating like a drumbeat of war. Others wept, throats raw with emotion. Some shrieked, the sound sharp, ecstatic—a kind of rapturous glee that bordered on something inhuman.

Through the steady rhythm of his clapping hands, without stopping so as to raise suspicion, Clark whispered low into her thoughts. *Is this what you want, Lorena . . . ? You stand behind this . . . ?*

Lorena's lips were pursed and thin. For a long, suspended moment, she said nothing.

I've seen your heart's not in this before . . . but children . . . ? His voice curled through her thoughts, relentless, gentle. *Lorena, they're* children *. . . ! Is this the life you imagined for yourself . . . ?*

Still, nothing.

Clark said, *Where do you draw the line . . . ? Where does she . . . ? If we're all expendable . . . doesn't that make you, too . . . ?*

Then, finally, her voice slipped into his mind, the thought a threadbare a whisper:

I have no choice . . .

Clark looked at her from the corner of his eye.

She did the same. A heartbeat.

Clark replied, *We always have a choice . . .*

The sun was setting as Clark made a dash for it. He barely felt his legs, New York City a blur as he willed himself forward. One moment he was in that church of madness. The next, he was flying through crowds, shoving onto an uptown train, and running past Miranda the front desk woman (who threw him a look like she knew he was in trouble). He could hardly catch his breath while in the private elevator up to Charisma's tower, 131 stories high.

His steps pounded against the marble as he ran past the looming portrait of Charisma in her standing room, eyes tracking him up the stairs to the Closet.

All he could think of was, *The Great Culling, she called it . . . She's culling children . . . for her witchcraft . . .* The words wouldn't leave his head, circling like a curse.

As Clark caught himself in the mirrored wall of the Closet, he paused. Blazer and button-down, hair tapered high and tight; the Ideal Self he had always wanted to become. He dressed the part, but was that really him staring back?

The tree was happy to see him. It had been waiting for him. He could feel it through the soles of his shoes, a slow hum thick in the air. Clark put his hand to the glass.

"I understand now," he said to it. "If I try to enter, if I desire to harm, it'll trip her defenses . . ." A gargoyle's kill roar flew through his mind. A flash at the corner of his eyes. And then—

Clark ducked, but something heavy and dull caught the side of his head.

His vision burst into stars and he was on the floor. Pain detonated, white-hot and sudden. The world reeled, warped, spinning too fast for him to anchor himself to anything but the sharp, splitting pain behind his eyes.

When he opened his eyes, it was none other than Monica Chase-Whiteley hovering over him.

She straddled his chest, knees digging painfully into his shoulders, pressing him to the cold marble. She peered over him, looking disheveled. Her raven-colored hair was plastered to sweat-damp skin. The strands clung to her sweat-dampened skin. Her wild blue-gray eyes leered into him, unblinking. Hollow. Angry. Slowly, she lowered herself toward his face until her ragged breath fanned across his cheek.

For a moment, Clark actually thought she would sink her teeth into his neck and rip out his throat. But she didn't.

Instead, she spoke, low and venomous as she said, "Somehow I knew our ugly little duckling would wander back home." She giggled, and her fingers found his clavicle as if testing where best to snap him in half. "A Reckoning Spell, huh? I knew I never liked you from the start. You're gonna get it." She laughed maniacally now, a wicked, greasy laugh. "Oh, you're so gonna get it."

Clark turned to look past her curtains of hair: a heavy amethyst geode lay by his hip.

"I know you ratted me out to Melissa," she continued. "I know you've been plucking us off one by one . . ." Her fingers trailed up his throat, resting just over the hollow beneath his jaw. "And still, she picked you. You of all fucking people. You to be the next assistant."

Her pupils swallowed up what little color lived in her irises.

"You'll never be one of us," she spat, her words one long growl. "You're a grubby little rube—no, a roach—*standing at the feet of gods.* You don't deserve to be here and you never will."

Her breath was shallow, erratic.

That's when the giggling started. Thin, shrill, unraveling at the edges. It poured from her mouth like sour wine.

"Anoint the space in blood," she whispered. "Let it know your scent. Let it know there's something of value. Then let the hate rot and fester."

Her eyes were wide with deranged delight. "You don't even know what you've summoned, do you? You haven't even realized what the hell is coming for you. And now that it's tasted you, it won't stop."

She leaned closer, her smile twitching at the corners, until Clark could smell the heat of her breath. "You should do yourself the favor and kill yourself now before it does. Or better yet—"

She lifted the geode high above her head, the whites of her wild eyes were bulging.

"I'll just kill you myself." The whites of her wild eyes were bulging. Clark braced for impact. He turned his head, held his breath—and what he saw stole the air from his lungs.

His reflection moved first. His aura flared violet-gold in the mirror, linking with Monica's and the amethyst geode. His Other Self met his eyes, gave Clark a wink and in a flash, unleashed a burst of aura light that blasted Monica backward. The force knocked the wind out of her as she fslid across the floor into the pedestal table and chairs.

Quickly, she scrambled upright, barefoot on marble, gasping for air, while Clark got to his feet and steadied himself.

"I'll kill you, you little faggot," Monica snarled. Her voice cracked with rage. "I'LL KILL YOU! I'LL KILL YOU! I'LL KILL YOU!"

"Hey, Monica," Clark said, picking up the amethyst, "you can't fucking call me that."

Monica ran toward him.

Clark's aura went off like a bomb: from indigo to gold, pushing the air between them in a pulse so violent it knocked her clear off the ground.

Monica didn't even have time to scream before she flew over the cabinets and into the opposite mirror. Glass spider-webbed from the impact before she fell to the floor in a slump.

The room was still. Clark straightened his sleeves.

"Now, where were we," he said, returning to the terrarium. He laid a hand on it one more time. "I know if I try I'll come up short, but if *you* let me in . . . I know you want to . . ."

"Let me in."

With one hand on the terrarium, Clark slipped out of this world.

It was that primordial realm of his dreams, and the sun was a pillar between realms. A golden sunlight filtered through the massive branches, thick and heavy like sun through stained glass. The ancient tree towered overhead, its trunk trailing skyward. This was the source. This was where it all started. The seat of her power. The place where her soul lived. Where souls were sacrificed. Where blood had seeped into the roots, and magic was leeched and repurposed. Where children's lives came to an end.

This is where it all ends . . . thought Clark.

End me . . . it said.

"Tell me how to do it," Clark said. "Tell me how to finish this. I'm listening."

A single word followed:

"No."

Clark was yanked back, back to the reality that came rushing past. He was standing in the Closet again—and he wasn't alone.

"I can't let you do that," said Mother.

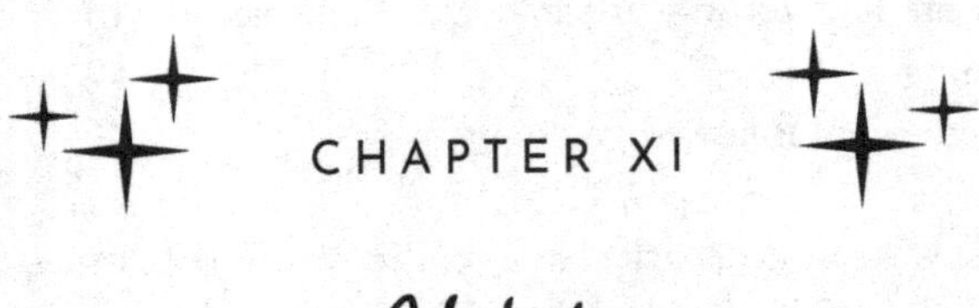

CHAPTER XI

Hubris

"You don't know what you're doing."

Mother's voice was ice. "No, Clark. *You* don't know what *you're* doing."

She seized him by the back of his neck. He grimaced, muscles tensed as her nails dug in.

"Take me to her altar." Her grip tightened. "It's time you learned your place."

Clark led them to the hidden door in the mirror. In his reflection he saw a small trickle of blood forming on the side of his head. His pulse quickened. Could he try that same mirror magic?

"Don't even think about it," Mother said to him. Clark did as he was told.

His raised his left hand toward himself, fingers trembling. In a deliberate motion, he flipped it out toward his reflection, and then pushed his palm up into the air.

Click.

The mirror swung open to reveal its iron staircase within.

"Nifty!" she mused—before shoving him hard. Clark stumbled into the landing.

"Ew." She nudged Monica's arm aside with her heeled boot. "Well. One less mess for me to clean up."

Together they ascended into the dark, round ceremonial space of his nightmares. The lights came up automatically from the edges of the ceiling. Beneath them, New York City stretched out like a constellation of lights. The glass floor extended, seamless and infinite, as if they were walking on air.

But something marred the surface. A chalk diagram he recognized instantly.

An upside-down pentacle, its points intersected by an infinity symbol, stretched wide across its west and east wings. The one he saw drawn in blood the night he moved in.

The air stank of sulfur.

Crumbled in the circle lay to torn halves of a Polaroid—the one of Clark and Joey at Joey's birthday dinner, torn right down the center.

And next to it—his missing diary.

He exhaled sharply. As soon as he placed his hand on the diary, something strange happened—

"We need something of value."

It was Monica.

"It'll be easy."

Patricia.

He was heartbroken all over again.

Clark watched as she snuck into his bedroom during Joey's birthday party. Patricia's silhouette—a hand sliding his diary off the nightstand. Joey's laughter, muffled in another room.

He gasped, wrenching himself out of the vision.

"*What the FUCK is going on here . . . ?*"

"So this is it, huh?" Mother muttered, walking forward, stepping around.

She stepped to the center of the room, peering down where the floor beneath the glass sloped gently into the oculus—a perfect, yawning aperture that revealing the Tower's inner eye: the terrarium below. She tilted her head.

"How odd. And they say New York is a nexus of power. All these lives, all this desire. The tower is her conduit. Now it finally makes sense."

"This is what you've been after all along, isn't it?" Clark asked.

"Oh, sweetie. You have no idea." The way she said it—too pleased, too knowing—sent blood rushing to his head, and gave him an instant, pounding headache. "And you made it so easy."

Clark rubbed his temple. "What do you mean?"

"'You got a heart of gold and a light—a big, big light,'" Mother mocked. Her laugh echoed in that ceremonial room.

Clark's stomach dropped. "Miss Honey was—"

"Me, you idiot! Miss Honey was me all along," she said. "Well, a projection, that is. My Auntie Joan was a real woman, penetrating Charisma's system for intel, and, well, you know how that ended."

Clark's hands curled into fists. He was angry, but not shocked. "That's why I stopped seeing her? Because—"

"You stopped letting me," Mother finished. "I taught you well."

Clark shook his head in revulsion.

Mother shook her head. "It was all *too* easy, if you ask me. Scope you out at the *cawfee shop* on weekends, follow you around town on your errands. Peer into your open windows . . ."

At this, the warmth came up to his cheeks.

"You think I'd come looking for *you*, to join *my* team? Please. You're pathetic. You have no real power. People like you will always do exactly what they're told *not* to do."

Clark stood very still.

"So . . . a new life for a new life? How's that going for you, huh?" She chuckled. "You're about to lose it all. Shame you won't get to see me take this tree—this power—for myself."

Clark's simply stared at her. "Go ahead. Kill me if you want to. You'll never be like her."

"Oh but I will, and there's nothing you can do to stop this," Mother said. "You're the lightbulb and we're about to play whack-a-mole. The universe is always listening for when a soul goes pop! A powerful sacrifice indeed."

A voice cut through the room.

"*Darlings.*"

Both Mother and Clark whipped around, shocked. Charisma stood before them, effortless and regal. She hadn't come up the stairs. Clark wasn't sure how she had appeared, but he had an idea.

"Well, well, well," Charisma said. "At last we meet."

"We've met before! Many times," Mother said.

"Oh, we have? Doesn't ring a bell!" Charisma's expression was pure amusement.

Mother's jaw clenched.

"Honestly? It's rather pathetic how obsessed with me the both of you are."

Clark furrowed his brows. "Are not!"

"Are, too!"

"Are not!" Mother and Clark snapped simultaneously.

Mother shot him a dirty look. "*Quiet, you.* The adults are talking." Clark's jaw snapped shut, locked in a clench that he couldn't break. Pain shot through his head, right to where Monica had struck him.

"Oh, please, there's nothing more to say! Our time here is done. And I'd say see you in Hell but then, we're already there. Are you? Not even cool enough to be invited."

Mother's face contorted with rage. "Listen here, you cunt! I'll—"

"No, thanks! *Not listening!*"

The way Charisma and Clark locked eyes was instinctive. It would've been almost beautiful if Clark didn't hate her guts. While Mother fumed, Clark lunged for the window and yanked the latch. The pane burst open, slamming hard against its twin.

Before Mother even had time to react, Charisma flicked her wrist. A gust of wind ripped through the Tower. Mother staggered back. Then farther. And farther. Her expression twisting from fury to shock.

For the rest of his life, Clark would remember this moment—the frozen second before she fell, her wide-eyed disbelief, the way her outstretched fingers grasped at nothing but air before she fell out the Tower window. It had taken all of ten seconds for Mother's magic to come to a crashing end, and for Clark's jaw to unlock.

"I swear, I was at my clit's end. Now," Charisma said, "where were we?"

"You were gonna tell me why you're so fucking evil."

"Oh, don't get your knickers in a twist. That's all relative."

Clark's blood boiled. "Relative? You set Leslie up. You tried to kill Felicity!"

Charisma waved her arms. "Oh, *pish posh*, darling. America loves a martyr!"

"You are killing children. *You are evil!*"

"Is it evil if it's for the greater good?! Besides," she said coldly, "if only you could see the purchase agreements their parents sign."

"That's why you're being watched by the FBI, then? Because you're doing us all 'a favor'?"

"Watched by the FBI? Sweetie darling, the government has been using my women for decades. In this lifetime, the FBI knows who and what I am . . . and they work for me."

Clark's pulse thundered in his ears. "Greater good? This isn't about the world. It's about you." His lip curled. "Your vanity. Your hunger. And for what? You'll always be ugly—inside and out."

"Ouch," Charisma mocked, "that stung. No, the truth is, darling, I could've killed Felicity at any time I wanted to. A goddess of love reincarnate? Worshipped by millions? That sacrifice is *poetry* in and of itself. No, she's free-range for now—but even the most pampered show pony ends up in the glue factory."

Her voice slithered through the air. Clark scowled. Charisma inhaled deeply, savoring the moment.

"As for the comic, well . . . Why on earth would I do that? For my ex-husband? Friends of the President's, owner of the West's news outlets? No, darling. I did no such thing.

"No, only men like *you*, Clark—men who want to consume women because of their own unrealized self-hatred—pit women against each other. You think I'd burn another woman to protect a man?" She scoffed.

"Sweetheart, that's what men like *you* do. You've made me out to be the villain in your story, when the whole time . . . It was you. I just held up a mirror."

Clark was stunned. He tried to speak, but no sound came.

"Time to WAKE. THE FUCK. UP, sweetie." Three times, she clapped her hands to punctuate her every word. "As for the children, well . . . those in the know understand."

"Understand what?"

"Understand the bigger picture."

"And what is that exactly?"

"Oh, naive, arrogant little one . . .

"We in the know understand that the Order is leading humanity to enslavement, and, on the other hand, the Powers to humanity's untimely end."

Clark's voice dropped. "The end of humanity?"

"Yes, that's what I said. Look sharp!" Charisma's gaze flickered to the open city below. "And while *She*, *Her*, the Devil, the Demiurge—*whatever* you want to call her—leads us all to Hell on Earth . . . the Powers That Be sit back and do nothing but let humanity play out, run its course, and disappear forever."

"You're wrong."

Charisma's smirk disappeared. Both she and Clark turned sharply.

Emily walked up the tower stairs, followed by none other than Lorena.

Emily's voice was resolute. "The Powers want to help us."

"Oh, goody, the White Witch has come to rescue our petulant little prince." She spat the words like venom. "But you?" She narrowed her eyes at her sister. "I thought better of you."

"The children," Lorena said. "Sissy, please. This has gone too far."

Emily and Lorena strode across the Tower, stopping at Clark's side. The wind outside whistled through the open window, pushing the loose glass against its hinge with deep, rhythmic raps.

"I am afraid you are sadly misinformed, darling. The Powers That Be," Charisma said, "have already written humanity off."

Emily, Clark, and Lorena exchanged a look.

The room crackled with unspoken tension.

"I, on the other hand, want to see us thrive. I want to take humanity to the New Earth. The Great Awakening. One where witches assume our rightful place and reign. And I am doing that very thing."

"I still don't understand," Clark said, voice raw. "How can you murder children and call that help?"

"I am giving their lives purpose! A small price to pay for the security of humankind . . . You, of all people, will understand very shortly."

Lorena shook her head in dismay. Clark clenched his fists.

"I'm not gonna let you," Clark said. Emily took one hand, Lorena the other. Were they stopping him? Joining him? Could they really do anything to stop Charisma? His face was so boiling hot with rage that he was about to cry. A slow, devilish smile unfurled cross Charisma's alabaster face.

"You already have."

"That's not true!"

"Oh please. You, the Eternal Victim? Living in the perdition of your own making? My foolish boy, you played right into my hand."

"What are you talking about?" Emily snapped.

Charisma chuckled softly to herself. "I kept everyone in the dark and told no one, not even my sister. If they knew to hire a Lightworker for sacrifice, well, he wouldn't last very long now would he. Our good sister Patricia, however, was all too willing to contribute the cause!"

Clark's mouth hung open. The sting of betrayal made the world come crashing down around him.

"It turns out," she continued, "you knew the cost of staying would far outweigh the cost of leaving. That you had nothing else to live for. So you stayed, one small violation at a time, thanks in part to our insolent Monica."

Clark thought his knees could give out at any moment.

"I knew she couldn't survive you. I knew you would be the end of Melissa. I knew Emily would save you from the girls' insipid initiation. That you'd climb the ranks. That you would snuff out my coven of stars one by one. I knew you would draw that *twit* in and eat us alive from the inside out, you little shit. And I let you."

Lorena asked, "But, sissy, why?"

"Consider it killer acquisition. I am closing this chapter. Tying up all the loose ends. On this story, on this world. Because tonight . . ."

Charisma lifted her arms. As if answering her call, clouds surged over New York, rolling in from the east.

"You both are here to bear witness . . . and lend your sacrifices to . . . my ascension. Tonight, I am to ascend to the Powers That Be."

"They don't want you," Emily said, breathless. Her eyes were welling up.

"You can't deny my ordained birthright, and neither can they. I am so tired of this existence. I am fucking due my promotion," she said. "For mastering this world and leading witchkind to greatness despite even their best efforts."

"You were . . ." Clark began. "You hired me f-for—"

"For a sacrifice. Yes, you knobhead!" Charisma cackled. "Empathy. Unconditional love. These are the highest of magics. Lightworkers wield the Light of the All, the same current the Powers themselves draw from. Who knew a betrayed, bleeding heart empath would make such a bloody delicious sacrifice. Just as delicious as, say, a certain lucky singer-actress!"

"And you," Charisma spat at Emily, "you traitorous bitch. You are the betrayer you foresaw, come to finish me. If you can. I've seen your power, your apathy. Absolutely *lazy*! Pathetic. You will be the first to go."

Charisma turned to Lorena, who flinched. "You, *Lorraine*, I will deal with later."

Thunder cracked high above the tower like a war drum.

"You, my furry little friend, my slippery little snake," she said to Clark, "are *fired*."

Clark didn't flinch. He squared his shoulders. "You can't fire me."

A pause.

"I'm not even your employee."

Charisma's already lecherously arched brows disappeared into her bangs. "Oh, I can't?" she said, dripping with mockery. "And why is that?"

Clark exhaled, steady and sharp. "I never signed your Employee Contract. Your NDA. It asked for my given name. And Clark Crane isn't my given name."

For half a second, Charisma didn't move. Lorena clasped her hands to her mouth.

"As far as I'm concerned? I'm just a freelancer."

Her jaw clenched. "No matter." Charisma's eyes flashed from yellow-green to blood red. The sky had an answer. It tore open above them.

A bolt of lightning ripped through the open skylight ceiling and into Charisma's crackling black aura—rising around her like a living shadow, electric with power.

Clark moved first. He lunged, running full force at Charisma.

"Stop!" shouted Lorena.

"*Clark!*" Emily screamed.

Thunder shook the Tower. Lightning cracked from Charisma's aura, striking Clark down with the force of a bomb of fire and light.

His name was still echoing through the room when it hit. Emily and Lorena were hurled to the edge.

Charisma's blood-curdling scream split the air.

The tower windows burst in unison, raining glass onto the smoldering wreckage of her empire. The sound wasn't just rage—it was a death knell.

Their pulses roared in their ears as the vision took hold, burning behind their eyelids, branded into their minds: Charisma's tree, set ablaze. The infernal roots curled away. The ancient tether to her soul, severed—a hellish inferno. A crackling inferno. A prophecy fulfilled, white-hot and blue.

And yet, it sent no pain.

No defeat.

Just relief. Just sweet surrender to the afterlife it had been denied all those years.

That's when Charisma threw herself from the window—and flew into the night, a streak of copper silk and shadow, vanished.

Gone.

And Clark lay fallen on the floor.

Motionless and still.

CHAPTER XII

The Cost of Magic

Smoke curled through the air, tinged with the scent of burnt ozone.

Emily and Lorena hurried to Clark, who sat up, his breath heaving, his pinky still sizzling with a red-hot burn mark. On the marble floor beside him lay the two blackened halves of the evil eye ring Emily had given him in January. He let out a breathless laugh.

"Ha!" It worked. The eye had protected him.

"Clark!" Emily said. "Why did you do that? Are you out of your mind?!"

Clark let out a shaky, breathless laugh. "Someone once told me the ring would work if someone cared." He looked up at her. "I had a feeling."

In the center of the floor was a crater where the lightning had struck him, straight down to the terrarium. It was as if the Tower itself had exhaled—finally free of the weight that had bound it.

As the three descended the stairs, Clark said, "I don't think that was our girl, Charisma. I mean, not the physical, real her."

Lorena said, her face pale, "It wasn't."

Emily asked, "How do you figure?"

Lorena replied, "Charisma is a skilled astral projector. She can be in two places at once. That was just one of her manifestations."

Emily pulled out her phone, fingers flying.

Sure enough, there was Charisma on the red carpet of her Halloween party at So Below. She was painted head to toe, heels and all, in molten copper glitter, the same as her hair, as Circe the witch. A trail of male models, dressed as pigs and leashed, crawled the carpet on all fours behind her.

A smirk curled on her lips—sharp, knowing, almost taunting. Her eyes, lined with smoky kohl, seemed to cut through the screen, as if she were looking right at them.

Emily said, "This was all my fault. I'm sorry."

Clark shook his head. "You can't blame yourself."

"Yes, I can. I told Monica to interview the new security guard. I knew that slut was a glutton for fun. I knew she'd get caught."

Clark stared at her. "You told . . . ?"

"I gave Melissa the idea about venturing out on her own. 'Your clients love you, they'll follow you anywhere!' I knew she'd try to take them with her. I planted the seeds."

"Oh . . ." Clark blinked, the pieces clicking into place.

"The Powers told me I'd have to leave until I knew it was time to come back. I'm glad I did but—maybe you didn't need me after all!"

"That's when I found her," Lorena jumped in. "At the bottom of the tower. We arrived at the same time. We both just looked at each other and *knew*."

Clark asked, "Why didn't you tell me what you were up to?"

"I couldn't risk it. This was your fight to face. I had to let you fight your own battles, or you'd never learn. You'd never step into your potential," said Emily. *"Except the whole coffin thing."* Clark and Emily looked at Lorena, who threw her hands up.

"Oh, c'mon!" she remarked. "It was just a bit of fun!"

They rounded the corner into the Closet. The terrarium had cracked, a ring of melted glass around it. Shards like shrapnel littered the floor. Inside, the tree, once a bonsai of ancient proportions, was burnt to a black crisp, its trunk split straight down the middle. The smell of smoked wood filled the room.

But Monica's body was nowhere to be found.

"Now what?" Clark asked. Emily shrugged.

As they descended the stairs into the foyer, Clark glanced over his shoulder—and paused.

Charisma's portrait in her western landing room had withered. The once-vibrant image of her glowing in couture now stood as a rotted corpse. Her skeletal grin stretched ear to ear.

A chill ran down Clark's spine.

And just as soon as it had come, he blinked and it was gone. The portrait had returned to how he remembered it: flawless, composed, eternal.

Clark had a hunch that her ascension had truly been foiled.

But something told him . . . she wasn't finished yet.

After that night, there was no place Clark would have rather been than home. His Superman costume would have to wait another year.

Right now, there was only one person he wanted to be with.

But when Clark opened the door to PH1, it was as if he had stepped into an icebox. The air was sharp and still. It wasn't even that cold outside for it to be this way indoors.

When Clark walked in, Joey was at the top of the spiral staircase, descending. Luggage bag in hand.

Clark froze. "Wh—where are you going?"

Joey didn't hesitate. "Home."

"But—" Clark stepped forward. "This is your home."

Joey wouldn't look at him. "Not right now . . . Not anymore."

"Joey. Babe, what are you saying?"

Joey shook his head.

"Joey," Clark pleaded. He reached out, but Joey's grip only tightened around the handle of his suitcase. "Babe, please. Look up. Look me in the eyes . . . We can work on this. Give me a chance. Give us a chance . . . Please."

Joey exhaled, slow and unsteady. His eyes were glassy, barely holding back the weight behind them.

"I need to go home for a second," he murmured. "I need to get out of . . . here."

His gaze lifted—not to Clark, but to the gray high-rise walls, to the cold, sterile expanse of their apartment. "I need to figure things out."

"Wait," he urged, "let's talk about it. Stay with me."

Joey's jaw tensed. He shook his head. "There's no talking about it. I don't trust Charisma. You won't talk to me about it, and I dunno what to believe. If you're in danger, or in trouble, or . . . Why are you home, anyway?" His eyes darted at Clark, looking him up and down. "And what happened to your head? Are you bleeding?"

Clark opened his mouth and closed it. "I can explain."

"I dunno if I'd believe you, Clark," Joey said.

Clark flinched.

Joey spoke again. "I'm just secondary to everything in your life."

"That's not true."

"Yeah, it is." His voice wavered, but his conviction didn't. "I miss the old Clark. Where's he? Where's the guy who was perfectly happy just staying in and watching TV with me?"

"Joey that's . . . That's not fair."

"You're right. It isn't."

Clark tried to reach for him again, but Joey took a step back.

"You're rubbing shoulders with big people. Big money. And I don't know who I am to you anymore." He blinked fast, looking away. "You don't need me."

Clark's chest tightened. "Of course I need you. C'mon, what are you talking about? Don't go! W-where is this coming from?"

Joey's lips parted like he wanted to say something—but instead, he laughed under his breath.

Not a happy laugh. A hollow one. It was the kind you let out when you've already admitted defeat. That you've lost.

"Clark," he said finally, voice raw. "I was pulled into the wake of your orbit the first moment we met. I knew right then and there that you were the one for me. That there was going to be love here, but . . ."

He inhaled sharply, voice barely a whisper.

"I'm drowning now. And I don't have you with me."

Clark felt it—the final blow.

"You have your career, and your social life, and more adventures to have, but me . . . ?" A tear broke free, trailing hot down Joey's cheek. Quickly, he rubbed it away quickly, as if ashamed of it. "I feel so alone."

Clark reached for him again. "Joey . . ." he croaked.

Joey closed his eyes.

"Maybe you need to go out there and explore," he said. "And maybe it's not with me."

Clark's breath caught in his throat. "Don't say that."

"Maybe you have more frogs to kiss. Maybe you need to get the poison out or somethin'. But not with me, Clark."

Clark shook his head, panic creeping in. "That's not—"

"I'm the real deal," Joey cut him off. "And we're looking for different things. And I can't wait for you to see that anymore." His voice broke.

The suitcase rolled softly over the floor as Joey pulled it toward the door.

Clark grabbed his wrist—one last desperate plea. "Joey, please—"

Joey hesitated for half a second.

Then, he pulled away.

He didn't turn around. The door clicked open. And then it closed.

Footsteps faded down the hall.

All that was left was silence.

Silence too big for the walls of that Manhattan apartment.

Clark staggered back, numb, lost, until his knees finally buckled under him. And then he fell to the floor. And then he broke.

His chest heaved as the first sob tore through him, then another. He pressed his palms against the cold wood floor, his body shaking, unable to contain it, unable to hold it in any longer.

For the first time in a long time—

He felt small.

And for the first time in a long time—

He was alone.

* * *

Something soft nudged Clark's cheek.

At first, it was gentle. Then, a little more insistent. His heavy, salted eyes, swollen and wet, quivered open.

A paw.

Jessica stood over him and meowed.

For a moment, his mind was blank. Just . . . empty. Numb. How long had he been lying there?

He lifted his head, realizing he had been curled in a ball on the living room floor. Some of the apartment lights had been left on. With only him there, the apartment had never seemed so big.

So empty.

Clark pressed one palm to the hardwood and tried to sit up—when a sound cut through the silence.

Scratching.

Somewhere down the apartment.

Jessica's ears tensed back. She turned toward the noise, then back to him.

They stared at each other.

Another scrape.

The sound was coming from the bedroom.

Carefully, Clark forced himself upright, his limbs trembling. First to his knees. Then on his two feet. The air was colder. Had they left a window open?

Another noise. Further ahead. Clark stopped short.

It wasn't just scratching anymore.

It was whispers. Murmuring voices.

His stomach twisted.

His bare feet against the hardwood floors were the only sound as he moved toward the hallway. Jessica stayed by his side, silent now. Tense.

The temperature kept dropping. There was light spilling through the crack of the guest room door. That light hadn't been on before.

Clark exhaled, steadying himself, and pushed the door open.

There, standing before him, were his parents, his grandmother, and himself at three years old.

They stood around his grandmother's full-size bed in their tiny

Astoria walk-up. The air smelled different. Warm, familiar. A little like arroz con gandules, her gardenia perfume, and cigarettes.

"What is that?" Clark's father asked, stopping short. Clark had his toys laid out on the bedspread.

"Ay, Clark," his mother sighed. "Boys don't play with Barbies."

"Clark," his father said, voice already heavy with disappointment. "C'mon, you know better."

From the doorway, Clark stood frozen, watching as his first memory played out before his eyes.

Am I dreaming . . . ? he thought to himself. *I almost forgot about this . . . or try not to remember . . .*

"Oh please," exclaimed a white-haired, proud Grandma Wanda in her thick Puerto Rican accent. "Let the kid have a Barbie for Christ's sake. Eet's just a doll!"

Clark had forgotten how she used to defend him. His protector.

"You gave him this?" Ryan asked, his tone clipped. "Wanda, the boy has plenty of toys. Toys appropriate for boys." He pointed to the toy firetruck and Superman on the bed. "He's not a girl."

Wanda huffed. "And? It's a damn doll, Ryan! He likes it!"

"¡Mamá!" a younger Maria hissed. *"¡No empieces!"*

Clark, standing outside his own past, whispered the words before she even finished:

"This is our child . . ."

"This" Clark echoed to himself. The memory felt so real, the air so thick with tension, Clark could feel it pressing into his skin. And then—

Back and forth, the three adults started yelling. They hurled words like bricks that couldn't be taken back.

"Don't you talk to my mother that way!" Maria shouted.

"He's my son, too!" Ryan shot back.

Clark could feel it as if it were happening all over again.

"What was I going to do, tell him 'no'?! *¡Es solo un niño, es solo una muñeca¡ Let him be a child!"*

"Exactly!" Ryan snapped. "Look at the garbage you let him watch on TV. What is this shit, *Bewitched*? You want him to grow up to be a man or a woman? Jesus fucking Christ . . ."

Little Clark froze. His tiny frame locked in place, barely breathing, afraid that even the smallest movement might make him a target. From the doorway, Present Clark watched him carefully, remembering that feeling all too well. How he wished he could make it all disappear and go away.

Be careful what you wish for . . . Clark thought to himself.

"Clark," Ryan barked, voice cold. "Bring your doll here. Now." He was standing next to the trash can.

Maria's tone softened, but the words still stung just as deeply. "If you want to make Mommy and Daddy proud, do as Daddy says. You want to be a good boy, don't you, pumpkin?"

Little Clark looked up at the adults, then back down to the doll in his hands. Barbie seemed so innocuous, so pretty, so benign. Why did loving her feel like such a crime?

At the crossroads he found in his hands, he froze.

His father opened the kitchenette cabinent and yanked out the silver trash can.

His mother said, "Good boys do what their parents say."

Little Clark walked forward, his legs stiff, mechanical. His fingers hesitated. Just for a second.

Then he placed her in the trash. His father slammed the drawer shut.

"Good boy!" his parents said in unison, patting his head like a pet.

Little Clark returned to the bed, quiet, having learned the cost of loving was a conditional love returned. Present Clark wanted to grab his parents, shake them, scream at them, "Pick her back up!" He wanted to tell Little Clark, "It doesn't matter what they think! You don't have to throw her away!"

But he didn't.

He couldn't.

"I don't know how you let your mother live like this," Ryan sneered. "Especially with our child."

Wanda huffed, waving a dismissive hand. *"Ay, no le hagas caso."*

Maria said, "Mama, speak English to him, or he's not going to know how to be American."

"¿Para qué sirve hablar otro idioma si no podemos rajar?"

And then, the arguing started again.

Back and forth. Louder, sharper, crueler.

Wanda rolled her eyes and walked to her purse.

Both Little Clark and Present Clark watched her carefully, their heart pounding, as she pulled something from her purse, the details coming back to him like flickers of an old film reel. She pulled something out, tucking it behind her back before returning to the bed.

Steadily, she came to sit down on the bed beside him. She leaned into him so that he could smell her gardenia perfume. "*Mírame, mi amor*. Look at me." And suddenly—

As he looked into her bright brown eyes, the arguing faded to mute like someone had turned a dial, lowering the volume on reality itself, until the world around them disappeared. Her smile was like a secret kept just between them.

"Froggie," she said, holding up Clark's lifelong stuffed animal friend, "has more fun than Barbie."

Little Clark reached up his tiny hands, flipping him over, inspecting him. Green and plush all over. Big twinkly dark-marble eyes like his own. Clark—both Little and Present—stared at her, curious.

"Whenever you feel alone or lost, and life feels too hard," she whispered, softly raking her polished nails through his hair, brushing away an unseen tear. "Froggie is going to remind you that I am with you always."

She tucked the toy into his arms, pressing a warm kiss to his forehead.

"*Feliz cumpleaños, mi amor*," Wanda murmured. "*Te quiero mucho*. I love you."

Little Clark squeezed Froggie tightly and buried his face in her embrace. "I love you, Abuela."

Like the air pressure popping in his ears, the past fell away. The city returned, screaming back into the present with the force of a lifetime of setting and rising suns.

The room shifted, the light slanting in a blur—

The sun diving into the horizon and springing back up.

Again.

And again.

The northern light streaming in on a weekday morning.

And then—

Darkness.

The warmth ripped away like a pulled thread.

A scream pierced the air, shocking and raw.

Jessica hissed, her fur standing on end. Clark spun around, chest seizing with panic. He wasn't in Astoria anymore.

His breath clouded the air, the cold wrapping around his throat like fingers. The air reeked of sulfur.

Pungent. Rotten.

He walked through with Jessica in tow. Clutched in his right hand, he realized, was Froggie.

The temperature had plummeted. Clark could see his breath.

Then, a sound.

From the bedroom above. Clark and Jessica flinched.

Clark whipped around, heart hammering, just as Jessica leaped into his arms.

They climbed the spiral staircase.

Another noise sounded from inside. This time, Clark could make out for certain it was the sound of a giggle. It made the hairs on his arms stand on end. Jessica jumped down, her back arched, fur bristling. The same cold stench was here, clinging to the walls—rotten eggs, decayed garbage.

Clark's fingers trembled as he slowly pushed the door open.

The light switch snapped on—then immediately blew out.

A single, blinding flash of light filled the room.

And in that second—

Clark saw it.

Hanging from the corner of the ceiling, opposite him.

It opened its eyes and stared back.

Piercing yellow slits.

Clark froze.

They were the eyes from his nightmares. The same slitted, hell-yellow stare.

Its gaze locked onto him with an unnatural, torturous hunger. Like it had been waiting for this exact moment.

And then—

It grinned.

Jagged. Oily. Mocking.

The grin spread too wide, splitting its face apart to reveal rows of pointed teeth, each one razor-sharp.

A gurgling laugh rumbled from its throat, its clawed hands ringing and rubbing together like a roach.

Jessica hissed, back arched in full alarm. Her mind wailed like the sound of an alarm: *The Shadow Who Eats . . . ! The Shadow Who Eats . . . !*

Clark's mouth opened to scream, but no scream came.

He tried to summon his aura—but without joy or light to recall, the energy flickered and died like the lightbulb above him.

The demon's grin widened further. It laughed its greasy laugh. It delighted in the fear it knew it inspired. And behind its gaze, embers of rage burned—fixed on the bounty Clark knew it had come to collect.

Clinging to the wall sconce and on the curtain rod, it sprang. Chitinous limbs snapped across the room, scuttling faster than anything should move.

Clark staggered back into the wall.

A clawed hand ripped through the dark and seized his arm.

Clark screamed like he had never screamed before.

The demon roared back in his face, its breath so hot and foul that Clark gasped through tears.

"LET ME GO! STOP!"

Its grip was scorching, unrelenting—a vise of fire-red flesh, scabbed and decaying.

Clark struggled, thrashed—

And then—

A glow.

A hum.

It wasn't coming from him.

It was coming from—

Froggie?!

Clark's eyes widened as the stuffed animal in his grip began to vibrate, a soft, golden-white glow emanating from its seams.

The air around them pulsed—

And then—

"Mi amor.

One voice—Wanda's—then a chorus of a thousand voices. Every ancestor who had walked before him.

The sound rippled through Clark's body, rising from his heart, through his throat, down his right arm—and straight into the demon's grasp.

Its claws began to smoke where the golden light touched. Its grin vanished. A shrieking wail tore from its throat as its hand burned and blistered white-hot. It ripped itself away from Clark, clutching its wrist.

In that moment, Jessica sprang—a whirlwind of fur and claws. She tore into its face, her claws sinking into its eyes.

The demon howled, swiping wildly, missing. . . But Jessica was too fast.

She attacked again.

And again.

Scratching. Biting. Hissing.

The demon let out a final, wretched screech. Clark thrust Froggie's light toward the creature, and it staggered backward—

Back into the blackness of the room and out the window, dissolving into shadow and smoke.

Clark gasped for air, his arm throbbing where it had gripped him. A welt had already formed, shaped exactly like its claws.

Clark wasted no time.

He held Froggie tight. He grabbed his diary. He scooped Jessica into his arms—and ran.

Down the stairs.

Down the hall.

Out the door and never looking back.

ABOUT THE AUTHOR

A. T. Napoli went from starving artist to celebrity makeup artist before writing his B*tchcraft novels. Having studied English literature and women & gender studies at Marymount Manhattan and Hunter College, he now boasts over a decade of experience in fashion and beauty. Napoli has worked with world-renowned entertainers such as Halsey and Lizzo as well as the editors of *Allure*, in which he is frequently mentioned. Like Clark in B*tchcraft, he often tries to save the day. Napoli is a first-generation American who resides in his native Astoria, New York.